• Praise for *Tower Down* •

"Kirk McGarvey is original, vibrant, and intelligent. Once again, Hagberg will have you firmly in his hands, each page a tasty treat, all leading to an ending that packs a wallop."
—Steve Berry,
New York Times bestselling author of
The Lost Order

"Hagberg keeps the suspense high through the thrilling climax as McGarvey and crew race against time to find out Kamal's next objective and who's paying him and why."
—*Publishers Weekly*

• Praise for David Hagberg •

"Hagberg edges out Tom Clancy for commander of our uniquely American military-based thrillers and espionage novels."
—James Grady,
New York Times bestselling author

"Hagberg writes the most realistic, prophetic thrillers I have ever read. His books should be required reading in Washington."
—Stephen Coonts,
New York Times bestselling author of
The Art of War

"Hagberg is the grand master of the contemporary espionage thriller."
—Douglas Preston,
New York Times bestselling author of
The Kraken Project

"Hagberg runs in the same fast, high-tech track as Clancy."
—New York *Daily News*

"Hagberg is a master."
—Larry Bond,
New York Times bestselling author of
Fatal Thunder

This is a work of fiction. All of the characters, organizations, and events portrayed in this novel are either products of the author's imagination or are used fictitiously.

TOWER DOWN

A Forge Book
Published by Tom Doherty Associates
175 Fifth Avenue
New York, NY 10010

www.tor-forge.com

Forge® is a registered trademark of Macmillan Publishing Group, LLC.

ISBN 978-0-7653-7872-9

Our books may be purchased in bulk for promotional, educational, or business use. Please contact your local bookseller or the Macmillan Corporate and Premium Sales Department at 1-800-221-7945, extension 5442, or by email at MacmillanSpecialMarkets@macmillan.com.

First Edition: May 2017
First Mass Market Edition: March 2018

Printed in the United States of America

0 9 8 7 6 5 4 3 2 1

TOWER DOWN

DAVID HAGBERG

A TOM DOHERTY ASSOCIATES BOOK
NEW YORK

FOR LORREL, AS ALWAYS

PART
ONE

New York City
Spring Art Auctions

ONE

A tall man wearing a dark business suit stood at the open rear door of the Cadillac Escalade waiting for his clients. He was a Saudi intelligence special operations subcontractor whose code name was Nassr, "the Eagle." And he was very good at killing people because he was well trained and he had absolutely no conscience.

He had done other jobs around the world, for other intel agencies, but for this specific op he was working directly for a Saudi intelligence officer, whom he suspected was in turn a paid operative of ISIS. It was the only thing that made sense to him.

But he didn't care. The money was good, and the thrill of the hunt and the kill were even better.

The Alouette III helicopter coming from JFK appeared low over the East River as it made its way to Atlantic Aviation's East Thirty-fourth Street Heliport, shortly before eight-thirty in the evening, thirty minutes past the facility's closing time. No one had given the slightest thought of denying the incoming flight. The passenger, Khalid Seif who owned PSP, Dubai's main offshore bank, had an estimated net personal worth in excess of thirty billion dollars. People in his category were never denied anything.

Eagle, whose real name was Kamal Al-Daran, had come to kill the man, along with his mistress Alimah, and as many as three or four dozen other billionaires in the AtEighth penthouse on Eighth Avenue and West Fifty-seventh, and one thousand or more on the ground at Carnegie Hall.

The blame would go to ISIS, of course, as would the downing of a second pencil tower here in Manhattan with even more devastating results than this evening's act of terrorism. Bringing down the two towers would be a copy of al-Qaeda's destruction of the Twin Towers, only this time airplanes wouldn't be needed.

It was thought by his control officer that the attacks would be even more devastating to New Yorkers and to the entire nation than the ISIS attacks in Paris and Brussels and elsewhere. The U.S. military would be ordered to take out the entire ISIS war machine as Operation One, saving Saudi Arabia the bother.

Kamal was a handsome man, with a skin tone light enough, and facial features Western-looking enough, so that he could pass for just about anyone from Europe, but especially England because of his cultured British accent. With hazel contacts in his naturally black eyes, makeup, a five-hundred-dollar haircut, and a mustache, he was a close enough match to Khalid to fool anyone at the penthouse party this evening. He'd done his research. None of the other multibillionaires had ever met the banker, though just about all of them had done business with him.

The helicopter flared neatly, the pilot rotating it ninety degrees to the left so that its passenger hatch would open toward the terminal building.

Two line crewmen in white coveralls came across in a run as the chopper set down, one of them chocking the wheels while the other opened the luggage compartment and took out three matched suitcases.

The supervisor came out of the terminal as Khalid and the young woman, who was an Egyptian movie star, were helped out of the machine by the pilot.

They were too far away for Kamal to hear what they were saying, but their body language seemed cordial.

He opened the Caddy's hatch as one of the crewmen hustled over with the luggage and put the bags inside.

The manager brought Khalid and the woman, who Kamal guessed was in her early twenties and stunning-looking, over to the car. The mid-May weather was cool, and she was dressed appropriately in an attractive white pantsuit, a cashmere sweater over her shoulders. The banker was dressed in a white linen suit and a black T-shirt. But he had shaved his mustache.

"This gentleman will take you to your condo, Mr. Seif," the manager said.

"Who sent you?" Khalid asked, not harshly, but demanding.

"Mr. Callahan, sir," Kamal said.

George Callahan was the developer of the Tower, as well as one of the leading private equity creators in the U.S. His worth was estimated above twenty billion dollars. He was one of the players.

Khalid chuckled. "One hundred fifty million for my penthouse, sight unseen, he could have sent me a Maybach."

"I can arrange that, sir," Kamal said.

Khalid waved it off. He handed Alimah into the back seat of the Cadillac, and as she got in, he stared at Kamal for just a beat. "Eton?" he asked.

"Yes, sir. Interesting school."

Khalid laughed, but without humor, and got in the car.

Kamal closed the door. "Thanks for holding your people for Mr. Seif," he told the manager.

"Orders."

Kamal went around to the driver's side and got behind the wheel. He'd rented the Cadillac because it was roomy, and because its windows were so deeply tinted that no one from outside could see the rear-seat passengers.

Rush hour was finished and traffic was relatively light even on the FDR Drive, which they had to cross under to reach East Thirty-third, which was a one-way west.

As they entered the tunnel, Kamal took out a Glock 29Gen4 subcompact pistol, which fired 10mm rounds, half turned in his seat and shot Khalid and the woman in the forehead.

He glanced at the road, and turned again. They had slumped over in the seat, only a small amount of blood oozing from their wounds. He fired insurance rounds into their heads.

Turning back to his driving he holstered the pistol, as he came out onto Thirty-third Street. At Fifth Avenue instead of taking a right up to Fifty-seventh, he waited for the light to change and went left.

His only regret to this point was the girl. He would have loved to fuck her before he killed her, but that would have added an unnecessary complication.

"No need to tell you, my friend, that you are merely a tool," his control officer had told him six months ago.

The briefing was conducted at a private compound outside of Riyadh that Saudi intelligence used from time to time as a safe house for interrogations of politically sensitive people. The CIA officer Landon Jones had been questioned here, before he was taken to the vicinity of the border with Iraq and set free. Within the hour ISIS fighters had captured him, and had videotaped his beheading two days later.

Kamal was not impressed. In his estimation most of the upper-level Saudi princes were crazy. One of them even had a series of strokes recently that had all but crippled the man's ability to think rationally. But he was at a high enough level within the family so that his word was practically law.

And yet he couldn't bring himself to believe that the Saudi royals were so insane that they would risk the destruction of their country if the U.S. ever got wind of the fact that they had ordered the attacks on the two pencil towers in New York.

He'd had the definite feeling at that meeting that something else was going on. ISIS was his best bet, but at that point he couldn't fathom the reason behind the over-the-top dangerous plan.

He was a contractor, nothing more, and totally deniable. For each success he'd been paid handsomely enough to maintain an elegant lifestyle in a seaside house in Monaco, and travel as a wealthy man—not a billionaire, but with more money than he could use in an ordinary lifetime.

But his was not an ordinary life, and in a large measure he was an assassin for hire because killing was one of the few acts that meant anything to him. Eating gourmet meals at the Jules Verne on the first level of the Eiffel Tower, attending operas at La Scala, gambling in Las Vegas, and spending weekends with geisha whores at exclusive Ryokans outside of Kyoto were nothing by comparison.

They had met in a small room that was used as a torture chamber. A steel table with leather restraining straps was the only furnishing. The control officer spread a dozen eight-by-ten photographs on the table. Half showed an area south of what was obviously Central Park and the others near the United Nations complex on the East River. In each of the shots extremely slender skyscrapers towered over every other building.

"The New Yorkers call them pencil towers, with names like 111Fifty-seventh, or One57. Elegant but arrogant. One hundred million dollars or more for the penthouse condominiums. One of our princes owns one of them.

Playgrounds for men of talent when it comes to making money," said Sa'ad al-Sakar, his control officer.

Kamal knew of the towers, as well as the name of the Saudi royal family prince who had bought one of the condos. He'd learned very early on, during his training at Sandhurst, to be very careful not only with his skills and his tradecraft, but especially with his homework. He'd graduated near the top of his class ten years ago, received his commission, and three months later faked his own death, apparently falling or jumping overboard from the *QM2* in the middle of the Atlantic. No body had ever been found, and he finished the crossing as an unimportant passenger on the ship in its cheapest inside cabin.

He'd known from the beginning what he wanted to do with his life. At the age of eight he'd been taken to London, along with his sister and mother, where his father, a Jordanian banker, had been transferred.

They lived in a Knightsbridge tony neighborhood near a park, the name of which he couldn't remember, except there were a lot of trees and a pond. One late afternoon he saw one of the boys from school urinating behind some bushes.

No one else was nearby, and on an impulse he came up behind the younger, slighter boy and strangled him. It seemed like it had taken forever before the boy collapsed, and Kamal went down with him, not releasing his grip for a long time.

Two things had left deep impressions on him that day. The first was how hard it was to actually kill someone, and second was how much he had enjoyed it. He'd gotten an erection, and that night in bed he'd relived the killing as he masturbated.

Within the week his father had moved them to another part of the city, because of the murder. The neighborhood was no longer safe.

TWO

Through the fourteen-foot-tall windows on the 101st and 102nd floors of the AtEighth penthouse condo, 1950 feet above the street, the sun had set much later than on any other residence anywhere in the northern hemisphere except at the pencil tower known simply as the Tower. That nearly completed two-floor penthouse rose nearly two thousand feet above the street. The edge of its narrow shadow sliced the UN's General Assembly Building in two.

Both buildings were the financial creations of George Callahan, and he had in mind the development of at least three taller buildings.

Special Agent Dr. Daniel Endicott came from the elevator entry vestibule, a scowl on his jowly bulldog face. He worked for the FBI's counterterrorism group, and his voice had been the leading opponent of buildings like these. AtEighth's floor print was just fifty feet on a side, and except for a special computer-controlled counter-weight near the top it would sway so much in the wind that people would actually get seasick.

"It's like Wall Street sticking its middle finger up into the sky, for anyone in the world to see," he was fond of saying. "Up yours."

"Not just the Wall Street barons," Callahan had countered eighteen months ago when ground had been broken here. "I sold the penthouse to a UAE billionaire for a hundred fifty million, without showing him even a blueprint. For a five-thousand-square-foot condo that's thirty thousand bucks a square foot."

"Yeah, Khalid Seif, Treasury's keeping a close eye on him. But what about the other tower over by the UN? How are sales going for it?"

"More than ninety percent were sold preconstruction," Callahan said. "We'll have the grand opening soon."

"Insanity."

"My buyers don't think so."

The caterers had finished setting up tables throughout the condo laden with everything from caviar to paté de foie gras, dozens of different varieties of oysters, Iranian and Russian caviars, cheeses and meats from around the world. Pretty young women servers were waiting for the guests, who were due to arrive in a half hour.

Bartenders were standing by at their stations, where they could mix and serve just about any cocktail from every country in the world. Cristal and Krug champagnes, vintage wines, fine vodkas and cognacs and tequilas. Plus a variety of beers for the few whom Seif had invited to the housewarming who drank beer.

Nearly one hundred thousand dollars had been spent on food and drink for the seventy or eighty guests, and most of it would either be thrown out or taken home by the staff.

Callahan, a tall, very slender man who looked much older than fifty-seven because of his startlingly white hair, stood at one of the tall windows facing north across Central Park. Dressed in a dove-gray Armani suit, open-collar silk shirt, and handmade Brazilian loafers, he knew exactly the image he projected, that of a successful entrepreneur who'd been a billionaire by the time he was twenty-three.

He was a happy man. Happy with his businesses. Happy with his friends, all of them members of the international billionaires club. Happy with his wealth. Happy with his beautiful wife, ten years younger than him. Happy with his son and daughter. Happy with his mistress, Elizabeth Kennedy, currently the highest-paid Hollywood actor of either sex, and the richest because she trusted Callahan to manage her money.

At the moment she was in Berlin shooting the principal scenes of her new movie. Which for Callahan was no real hardship. His executive assistant Melissa Saunders, who was also one of the partners of the prestigious law firm of Wolff, Stearns, Rosen and Williams, had agreed to be his co-host for the evening. She was beautiful, and possibly the smartest woman he'd ever met, and one of the few who wouldn't sleep with him. Yet. And he smiled thinking about her.

"I'm glad that you have something to smile about," Endicott said. He held his PhD in structural engineering, and he'd acted as an unpaid consultant on this building and the Tower over on the East River.

Callahan turned. "As I told you, every unit in this building is sold, and the UN Tower isn't far behind."

Endicott nodded. "And there'll be more."

"Why not?"

"Because you know damned well that every building has its flaw. The taller the structure the more dangerous the fault."

"Two airplanes took down the World Trade Towers; we didn't make the same design mistake."

"No, but you made these damned buildings too narrow. Without the counterweight they'd be in serious trouble in a one-hundred-mile-per-hour wind—not an unknown event in Manhattan, and especially not at this height. They wouldn't go down, but there'd be some serious structural damage. You'd be closed down."

"You're wrong and you know it. In any event the counterweight system is foolproof."

Endicott snorted. "No such thing as foolproof. Not to mention a terrorist strike."

Callahan's blood suddenly ran cold. "When you have a specific threat on your boards, act on it, do your job. If it's credible we'll close this place down in a nanosecond. In the meantime security is tight, and the computer codes running the counterweights are practically hackproof."

He turned and looked across Central Park again. This building and the Tower on the east side near the United Nations would not collapse like the World Trade Towers had done. A strike by an airliner to one of the upper stories would take out a couple of floors above, and burning fuel would severely damage a half dozen floors below, but the building would stand.

The real threat was the underpinning—columns of steel beams—encased in special concrete that anchored the building to the bedrock. If several of them, all on one side, were to be taken out, the building would tip over and fall to the ground, the collateral damage almost impossible to imagine.

His engineers assured him that only a military-grade demolition device could do the job. It'd have to be the type that was used to take out dams.

"Like a suitcase nuke?" he'd asked.

"We're assured that such a thing doesn't exist, but yes, something like that would do the trick."

"But they leak radiation, don't they?"

"Small amounts. They're meant to be man-carried."

"But they leak."

"Yes."

"Install radiation detectors at every column. Mate them with an alarm system that ties directly to the NYPD, the fire department, and the FBI. Problem solved."

The devices had been installed and had been tested against a tiny amount of radioactive material of the size and potency of the chip in a smoke detector, and they'd worked so well their sensitivity had to be dialed down so that the actual smoke detectors in the sub-basement wouldn't set off the alarm.

But still a worry nagged at the back of Callahan's head.

The problems they had not thought of. Unks-unks—"unknown unknowns"—that cropped up in just about any sophisticated system from space shuttles to tall buildings.

"Nice view," Endicott said.

"Yes, it is."

"I wouldn't pay a hundred fifty mil for it. But then, I'm not worth thirty billion."

Callahan had to smile again. "There's a waiting list, did you know that?"

"I'm not surprised," Endicott said. "I'd like to take another look at the guest list."

Callahan brought the list, which included each guest's background, up on his iPhone and handed it to the counterterrorism agent. "No one's worth less than ten billion, and most of them show up for just about everything on the circuit."

The circuit started at Norman Abramovich's New Year's party in St. Bart, then to the World Economic Forum at Davos near the end of the month. The players were here for the spring art auctions, before they'd catch the tail end of the film festival at Cannes, which was also happening right now. The Grand Prix at Monaco on the twenty-fourth, then the art fair in Basel; the Ideas Festival in Aspen; the mega-yacht milk run from St. Tropez to Capri. Pebble Beach for the Concours d'Elegance in August, back here, then to London in October, Miami in December, and the Cote d'Azur for New Year's Eve, where it would begin again.

Endicott scrolled down the list. "Venture capitalists, private equity and hedge fund managers, real estate developers, bankers, wine merchants, a few Russians including Gennadi Mashnin, who's pals with Putin and just about owns Gazprom. And one Eyptian movie star whose net worth is something around eighteen billion, according to this."

"Nenet Akila," Callahan said. "But she's more than just a movie star; she owns five studios, including two in India and one in Brazil."

"You're part of the circuit."

"When I can get free. It's the only time I can talk to people to whom I don't have to explain myself. They understand."

"I'm sure they do," Endicott said, handing back the iPhone. "I'm going to take another look around, then get out of your hair. Good luck tonight."

THREE

Kamal stood at the Caddy's rear door looking at Seif and the woman. He was parked in a private garage he'd purchased a few months ago on Jane Street in the Meatpacking District. It was coming up on nine, and the housewarming party—his party—would be starting soon, but in this set it was fashionable to be late.

His research had taken him to a brick wall at first. Almost everyone at these sorts of gatherings knew one another. They'd met face-to-face many times. Except for Khalid Seif, the reclusive offshore bank mogul whose photograph was posted nowhere so far as Kamal had been able to find. He dealt with all of his clients only by computer and by text messaging. Even his voice was unknown; he never spoke on the phone or on Skype or on any other media.

"To protect the integrity of my bank," he would say, "my clients wish to remain anonymous as I do."

Careful to get no blood on himself he went though the banker's pockets finding the man's cell phone, passport, wallet with not much more in it than a few business cards and a platinum Amex credit card, which he probably never used. His business card was enough to get him anything he wanted just about anywhere in the world, even North Korea, a few of its citizens owning bank accounts with PSP.

He had a handkerchief, and a few hundred American dollars, and in a jacket pocket a small vial containing three blue pills—unmistakably Viagra.

Kamal lifted the girl's head by the hair so that he could get a better look at her face. She was pretty in an artificial way, like the highly made up girls who sold cosmetics at department stores, but Seif cared enough for his and her happiness that he'd carried Viagra in his pocket.

Too bad, he thought, lowering her head to where it had lain on Seif's shoulder.

He pocketed Seif's cell phone, plus the man's passport and wallet, and recharged the pistol with a fresh magazine of ammunition.

He tossed his own wallet, containing a driver's license under the name Roger Attenborough, on the front seat. He wouldn't need it. By eleven-thirty at the latest he would be back in his suite at the Grand Hyatt, under the name Thomas Bland, blue eyes, no mustache, a businessman in a businessman's hotel, here from London for a few days.

Taking off the tie, he undid the top button of his shirt, and closed the Caddy's front and back doors. There was no need to wipe down the handles and steering wheel; his prints were on no files, not even in Riyadh, nor were his blood type, retinal scans, dental work, and especially not his DNA.

All of which broke two ways: He could disappear, while by the same token Sa'ad could deny they'd ever met.

Letting himself out by the service door, he walked to the end of the block and went down to West Twelfth. The area was not as busy as it was during the day, but no one paid the slightest attention to him. He was just another man going somewhere.

He caught a cab almost immediately and gave the driver the address of AtEighth.

"If you ask me, all those towers have just about screwed the city," the driver, an older man who spoke with a Middle Eastern accent, said.

"I agree," Kamal said, flattening his British accent so that it sounded more American Midwest.

The driver glanced at him in the rearview mirror. "You work there?"

"Not me, I'm taking a friend to dinner in the Village. She's meeting me in front."

"I get it. I can take you both wherever you want to go."

"Thanks, but she's always late, and I'm always early; it's better that way," Kamal said.

"Safer," the driver said.

The cab pulled up at the corner of Eighth and West Fifty-seventh. The pencil tower rose so high that it was impossible to see the top of the building from inside the cab.

"Looks like a strong wind would blow the thing over," the driver said.

"You're right," Kamal said. As he paid the driver, including a good, but not extravagant tip, he glanced at the man's name and cab number. If it came to it he would find out where the cabby lived and kill him. No loose end could ever be tolerated.

The impossibly thin building dominated everything in all directions, even One57 a block and a half to the east. A lot of people were out and about, traffic still heavy. A light breeze, a little cool, funneled up the avenue from the Hudson, and it smelled faintly of the waterfront mixed with exhausts. For just a moment it reminded him of London.

When the cab was gone, he walked down to the entrance of AtEighth, where a uniformed man opened the wide glass door. The glass and stainless steel lobby soared five stories to a ceiling that appeared to be a series of mountaintops, some of which were nearly lost to the distance. From straight overhead, a narrow waterfall dramatically dropped eighty feet to a pool, with low, irregular sides made of rock, that flowed away in both directions in what were designed to look like narrow mountain creeks, complete with live trout and a futuristic-looking bridge on each side.

An attractive woman dressed in a business suit, an iPad in hand, came across one of the bridges. Her expression was completely neutral. "Good evening, sir. May I know your name?"

"Khalid Seif, I've come finally to have a look at my penthouse."

Her demeanor changed immediately. She straightened up as if she were coming to attention and smiled, but she seemed a little flustered. "Sir, since we have no photograph of you on file, may I be permitted to see your passport?"

"Of course," Kamal said and he handed her Seif's passport.

She glanced at the photograph, and immediately handed it back. "Thank you, sir, and welcome to AtEighth. I'll inform Mr. Callahan that you have arrived, and take you up immediately. Your package of passwords and entry cards have been delivered." She looked beyond him. "We were expecting Ms. Samaha."

"We had a slight disagreement, she'll not be joining me this evening."

"Yes, sir," the woman said. "If you'll follow me we'll go up in your private elevator."

Callahan was waiting in the vestibule as they arrived. Kamal recognized him from photographs. Two billion dollars of the man's fortune were secretly deposited with PSP, which made him not only very rich, but also made him a criminal under U.S. law.

"We meet at last," the developer said, shaking hands. "Welcome home."

Music played from somewhere inside, and Kamal could hear the low murmur of voices. "Have all my guests arrived?"

"A few are late, but most of the people you asked to be invited are here, and anxious to meet you."

Everyone Seif had invited were customers of his bank. Kamal decided that this evening would be more interesting than most of his previous operations, and he found that he was actually anticipating the next hour or so. He smiled.

"Nothing serious with Miss Samaha, I hope? Miss Akila has produced a number of her films, and was looking forward to meeting her in the flesh."

"A slight disagreement, she's a temperamental girl."

"As are all actresses."

"Personal experience?"

Callahan was taken aback for just a moment, but then he laughed. "You've done your homework, Mr. Seif."

"I do with all my clients," Kamal said. "But now that you have some of my money, instead of the other way round, you may call me Khalid."

"With pleasure, sir."

"I would like to have a glass of champagne and meet my guests, especially Miss Akila."

FOUR

Endicott had poked around the elevator room on the fiftieth floor, and the security center on the fortieth, where four uniformed employees monitored all of the building's systems, especially fire suppression, which was absolutely vital to a structure this tall. In fact the fire department admitted that it could not effectively battle a blaze in any building much above the seventh floor.

Video monitors were connected by cameras to nearly every conceivable space anywhere in the building, from the roof all the way down to the sub-basements. Except for inside the condos without special owner-only codes.

A flat table monitor in the middle of the room was capable of manipulating everything in the system. A wave of the hand could bring up an outside view of the building, ground floor to the top, and pair it with weather conditions and the building's actual movement.

Using his red pass card that allowed him entrance to every space inside the building, with no exceptions, not even for the private residences, Endicott took the service elevator to the top floor, where he let himself into the cavernous two-story equipment room on the 112th and 113th floors. Many of the building's systems machinery, including electrical, environmental, plumbing and the massive counterweight, technically named a tuned mass damper, were located here.

Nine hundred tons of steel beams and plates welded together, about the same weight as a half dozen fully loaded Boeing 787–8s, dominated the center of the room. Sitting on a pool of oil, and rising twenty feet from the floor to near the ceiling, the computer-controlled weight was driven by eight huge pistons—two on a side—that in combination could move the entire mass in any direction in increments of four degrees to counteract the effects of the wind. Dampers and springs on each of the piston rods, as well as safety locks in the computer program, limited the range of motion to just a couple of feet and the speed at which it moved to just a crawl.

The engineers were insistent that the system had nothing to do with the building's integrity, only about comfort. People who paid $80 million–plus for a condo did not expect to get seasick in their own home.

Staring at the thing, lit dimly by overhead LEDs, Endicott was even more skeptical now than he had been at the beginning when he'd first been handed the blueprints and the assignment of making the place as safe from attack as was humanly possible. Skeptical not only of this system, but of the columns in the basement that anchored the structure to the bedrock.

He'd met with Thomas Held, who was the head of the FBI's counterterrorism division, and with Cameron Flynn, Endicott's boss, who headed the analytical section of the division, two years ago after he'd had a chance to study the engineering specs.

Years ago when he was in his late twenties, and a freshly minted PhD, one of his first jobs with the Bureau was analyzing how 9/11 happened. Not so much how the terrorists managed to get control of the airplanes but how the buildings had come down, and how al-Qaeda knew it before everyone else. Now in his forties he was the old man of the unit, and one of its most experienced and knowledgeable.

"So what do you think, Dan?" Held had asked. The counterterroism chief, who reported directly to the executive assistant director, of the FBI's National Security Branch was a sharp-eyed man with large ears who seemed to hear everything, even whispers at the end of the hall.

He was a career man who'd worked his way up in the Bureau starting as an ordinary field agent in Minneapolis. Only two years younger than Endicott he was more of a cop's cop than a director. But he did his job very well because he listened to his people—all of his people.

"I wouldn't live in the place, or any of the other pencil towers," Endicott said. "Money no object," he added.

"Why?"

"They won't collapse on themselves like the World Trade Center buildings did. At least I don't think so. But there're a dozen other possibilities. Fire, for one."

"The suppression systems look robust," Flynn said. "But Dan has a point."

"Propane cylinders packed in the central elevator shaft at or near the top could be made to suddenly release their gas. Since it's heavier than air it would flow down the shaft and at the right moment a spark could set it off."

"How would they get it inside the building in the first place?" Held asked.

"How'd they take control of a pair of 747s?"

"What else?"

"Blow a few of the support columns in the basement. Military-grade shaped charges might do it. Or tunnel under the building and set charges lower in the columns. The method has been used by bank robbers who built a boring machine."

"Continue."

"The tuned mass damper system worries me. If it were somehow to get out of sync it's conceivable it could do some serious damage."

"Come on, Dan, that's stretching it. The engineers I spoke to said the systems are so well limited that they could never get into the range of harmonic oscillation that could cause any real damage."

"I don't like the word 'never'," Endicott said. "But aside from those possibilities, I worry about the stuff we haven't dreamt up."

"It's your project, no one else in the branch knows this engineering like you do. Assemble your team and get to work; you have two years before the building opens for business, make it safe."

Staring at the weight he no longer knew what the concept "safe" really meant, only that he didn't feel safe here.

He took the elevator down to the security center again. Bob Wheeler, the shift supervisor, looked up from the master console. "I don't know what else I can tell you that you don't already know," he said. He was a tall black man with a serious demeanor.

"Have there been any glitches in the system?"

"Hell yes, Doc. But nothing we didn't suspect would come our way."

Endicott was vexed. "You didn't mention it earlier."

"You didn't ask."

"I'm asking now."

"It's mostly in our video feeds. Rolling blackouts that so far haven't lasted more than ten or fifteen seconds at a time. And never has the entire building gone out, only cameras here and there."

"Any pattern to it?"

"No, and we think we've narrowed it down to a couple of lines of code. Charlie Bell is working on it. He says we'll be at one hundred percent shortly." Bell had been a hacker working out of a commune in Amsterdam, and for whatever reason he decided to move back to the States and go straight.

"How soon?"

"Twenty-four hours."

The news was more bothersome to Endicott than he thought it should have been. He was having a severe case of the willies. "I'll have a word with Charlie, but in the meantime does he think it's just a mistake in the program, or has the system been hacked?"

Wheeler came around from his console. "He thinks that a hack is an outside possibility, but he's put a temporary patch on the firewall."

"Goddamnit, why wasn't I told?"

"Because it's nothing serious, and it's in the process of being fixed."

Endicott glanced up at the ceiling.

"What do you want to do? Tell a bunch of multibillionaires and their girlfriends they have to evacuate the building in the middle of their party?"

"That's exactly what I want to do."

"Lots of luck."

Endicott was torn. Wheeler was right, but he couldn't get the bad feeling out of his gut. The entire building reeked of something.

"It's just the video feeds," Wheeler said. "Go home, Doc, the building is secure, but I'll have Charlie call you as soon as he finishes debugging the system."

"My people will be on it tonight. We'll want to know who the hackers are."

Wheeler nodded. "It's late, go home."

Out on the street Endicott crossed Fifty-seventh, so that he could look up all the way to the top of the tower. Tonight's party was just a private gathering for Seif and his multibillionaire clients from the circuit. The grand opening wasn't until next week when the outside of the entire building would be lit up by cascading lights in every color.

"Like Fourth of July fireworks," Callahan had said.

For now it was nighttime business as usual. Traffic busy, restaurants full, people coming and going.

The lull before the storm? Endicott wondered, as he stepped off the curb and raised his hand for a taxi.

FIVE

By ten-thirty the penthouse party was in full swing. A quartet from the New York Philharmonic on the open upper level played chamber music. Servers with trays of hors d'oeuvres, others with trays of champagne, mingled with the guests, while the three bartenders put on a show of their own. The game among the guests was to stop them with a request for something unusual. The bet was for ten thousand dollars. They'd not been stumped yet.

Callahan had taken his time introducing Seif around. This was his party, and he had done business for the past five years or so in the equivalent amounts of several billion dollars with each of the principals here. And in all that time no one had ever met or spoken with him. Everyone was more than curious.

The only American other than Callahan was Alex Barkin, a short, fat venture capitalist who in Kamal's estimation was a complete idiot. The man knew how to make money, but it was the only thing he could talk about. He wasn't interested in fine art or jewelry, vintage wines or rare cognacs, and especially not mega-yachts or mansions. He'd never had a chauffeur-driven limousine, and it was widely known that he preferred driving his old Ford F-150 pickup back and forth to his office in Austin. But he was worth in excess of $30 billion and he showed up at most places on the circuit, which made him a player.

"The elusive Mr. Seif," he said when Callahan introduced them. "I thought these sorts of things weren't your cup of tea."

"My condo, my party, I thought I'd have a look at my investment."

Barkin's left eyebrow rose. "Investment?"

"Prices are going up."

"I can think of better uses for my money. In fact when you have the time I'd like to discuss a couple of points with you."

"Tonight?"

"Sure."

"Stick around and after everyone is gone we'll talk," Kamal said.

"I'm looking forward to it."

"With pleasure."

"He's an asshole," Callahan said when they were out of earshot.

"I rather think most of them are, caught up in their own little fantasies."

"That include me?"

Kamal laughed. "I wouldn't have put my money here if I'd thought so. And I do intend on making a profit, perhaps even tonight."

"Puts you in competition with me."

"Your new building won't be ready for occupancy for several weeks."

"But it's already more than ninety percent bought out."

"Then I'd best be quick," Kamal said.

Madi Farhad, the Iranian oil billionaire and his wife, Zahara—one of the few wives here—stood at one of the tall windows looking south toward the Empire State Building and beyond, to the new World Trade Center. They turned as Callahan and Kamal approached.

"Quite a view," Farhad said.

"Yes, it is," Kamal agreed. "It's a pleasure to finally

meet you, and your lovely wife." He took the woman's left hand and kissed it. Not exactly the Muslim way of things, and the gesture, an insult, did not go unnoticed.

Farhad stiffened, but his wife smiled. "We've all heard so much about you," she said.

"And I, you," Kamal said. It was another small insult, and he didn't really know why he was doing it, except that all of a sudden he felt irascible in the middle of all these hedonistic, shallow people whose only interest was more money. In his research he'd learned that Farhad had a fierce Persian ownership of his wife. And for a man to say that he'd heard about her was a slap in the face. It implied an intimate knowledge.

She blushed slightly, and turned to her husband. "I'd like another glass of champagne, please."

"Of course," Farhad said. He gave Callahan and Kamal a slight nod, and he and his wife walked off.

"That was interesting," Callahan said.

"I've done business with him that was totally unsatisfactory."

"May I ask why you invited him?"

"To let him know exactly what I thought about him," Kamal said. But another reason was that like a cat, he wanted to play with at least one of the mice simply for the pleasure of it, before killing them all.

A stunning bronze-skinned woman, with very wide, dark eyes, a thick beautiful mouth, impossibly white teeth, and a long Nefertiti neck came across the room, a glass of champagne in hand. She wore a white silk evening dress so deeply cut her small breasts were almost completely exposed. Backless and slit to the thigh the gown was nothing short of a tease, and everyone in the room knew it.

"Miss Akila, a pleasure to finally meet you," Kamal said.

"Call me Nenet," she said. Her voice was rich, the slight Egyptian accent almost royal.

"It means 'goddess of depth.' Call me Khalid."

She laughed lightly. "I haven't seen Alimah tonight."

"We had a slight disagreement. I sent her to a hotel."

"All actors can be difficult at times."

"Does that include you?"

"Especially me," Nenet said. She handed her glass to Callahan. "Show me around your new home," she said, taking Kamal's arm. "From what I've already seen its stunning."

Callahan had given him a blue key card, which would get him inside the building, up in his private elevator, and open the door to his condo, and operate all of the computer-driven systems in the unit.

"Will my card allow me access to the rest of the building, if I wanted to show Miss Akila around?"

"No, but mine will," Callahan said. He gave Kamal a red card.

"I'll give it back later."

"Not necessary. The code will change at midnight. The Bureau insisted."

"The Bureau?"

"The FBI's counterterrorism branch. Just as a precaution."

"That's comforting to know," Kamal said.

Callahan smiled. "Enjoy," he said and walked off.

"Are you game for a little adventure?" Kamal asked.

"More than game, as you say," Nenet replied, her voice husky.

"Then come on, I want to show you something interesting."

They headed down five floors to where they could get the service elevator. Before they arrived Kamal made a brief call on his cell phone and entered a short code.

"No one home?" Nenet asked.

"I left a message."

The code had shut down the closed-circuit cameras and they would stay dark for fifteen minutes. On the way up in the service elevator she came into his arms and they kissed deeply. He brushed his fingertips across her breasts, lingering for a moment at the nipples, while she pressed herself against his growing erection.

When they parted she looked into his eyes. "Who are you really?" she asked.

"Khalid Seif."

"No. Alimah told me all about him. You're not him."

The elevator doors opened, and taking her arm they walked out into the machinery room. "This is what I wanted you to see," he said.

She looked up at the building's massive counterweight. "It almost looks like a miniature Kaaba. People could come here for the hajj. But if we're going to make love, I'd rather it be someplace else."

Kamal pulled out his pistol as she turned. He shot her once in the forehead, and she crumpled to the concrete floor. Too bad, actually, he thought. He put an insurance round in the side of her pretty head, then holstered his pistol and took out his cell phone again.

SIX

The wind had picked up from the east, and as the number Kamal phoned answered with a low tone, the massive counterweight slowly moved a few inches to negate its effect on the building.

It was ponderous, and the low sound it made was completely drowned by the noises of the other machinery. A

monitor displaying readings from inclinometers a few stories higher showed that the building remained on an even
keel.

He entered a sixteen-digit alphanumeric code, and three
beeps indicated that he was in. Hashtag "53," would activate the program that a friend of Sa'ad's in China's Ministry of State Security had sold him. The man was part of
the old boys' network that operated unofficially among
every intel agency in the world. Often among agencies
from enemy states.

"Am I to be told who this man is?" he'd asked his control officer at the interrogation house.

"You will not learn who he is."

"But why not just hack into the systems from a safe
distance?"

"I'm told that they're hardened now. Electronically
shielded. The code has to be entered from inside."

"You've covered your tracks."

"And yours. It's the least we could do. Once you begin,
you'll have a window of less than ten minutes to get away."

"Won't security detect what's going on and try to stop
it? Or at least sound the alarm and evacuate the building?"

"You're a professional, how you handle them is up to
you."

Kamal entered all but the comma for the activation code
before locking the keypad and pocketing the phone.

He stared for a long moment at the counterweight, which
had shifted ever so slightly again to counteract the wind.
A comma and then "enter" would erase the computer code
that would limit the weight's speed and movement, sending it in the opposite direction of the wind, greatly mag-
nifying its force.

Callahan and his engineers were wrong when they told
prospective buyers that the tuned damper could never
reach the point of harmonic oscillation; like a bridge upon

which a brigade of soldiers marched in step, it could be brought down.

The building's girders, which connected with the concrete-encased beams driven into the bedrock, would be stressed to their limits and would fail somewhere between the second and fifth stories. The building would topple toward the southeast, directly onto Carnegie Hall.

It would happen so slowly at first that very few people on the street below would notice anything until it was too late for them to get out of the damage path. The collateral destruction and deaths would be nothing short of awesome. Still, tonight's act of ISIS terrorism would be nothing compared to the next one.

Kamal took a long last look at Nenet's body. The thigh-high slit in her dress had parted, revealing that she was naked underneath. It was too bad about Seif's mistress, Al-imah; it would have been a pleasure fucking her. But this one would have been even better, especially if he could have killed her just at the point of his orgasm.

He turned and headed back to the service elevator, never once considering just how insane he actually was. He knew that he was brilliant and it was enough for him.

On the fortieth floor Kamal pulled out his pistol as he walked across to the security center. Using Callahan's red key card he opened the door and stepped inside.

A large black man stood at the table display. He started to look up as Kamal shot him twice in the chest.

The other three at their consoles turned, their faces animated with confusion. One of them reached for a red phone, when Kamal shot him once in the side of the head, and then he walked around the table and shot the other two men, one of them crumpling forward, the other sliding to the floor.

He went to them and fired one insurance shot into their heads, and then turned and fired a shot into the back of the black man's head.

Reloading the pistol with his last magazine, he pocketed the nearly empty one and holstered the gun.

He went to the center console and, careful not to get any blood on his shoes or hands, reached over the body and brought up the screen to the elevators and shut them all down except for the service one.

Presumably the only red key cards that would gain access to the one remaining means of escape were held by Callahan, who'd given his to Kamal, and by the four security officers, all dead.

The front doors on the street level were locked, and he'd spotted the pretty receptionist coming to Seif's condo presumably to help Callahan with making sales pitches to the other players. The doorman was gone. No one was downstairs.

None of the other condos was occupied yet, though it was possible there were still workmen here around the clock making last-minute tweaks. He didn't anticipate any of them causing trouble.

He was leaving the security office just as the service elevator arrived and the doors opened. The receptionist stood there. She had a red key card.

"Mr. Seif," she said, then spotted something through the half-open door behind Kamal. She reached to the left and pressed one of the elevator keys.

The doors started to close, but Kamal was in time to jam his hand between them, and they reopened.

"I didn't expect you," he said, getting in.

"What's happening?" she cried. "Who are you?"

The elevator started back up to the penthouse, but Kamal pressed the cancel button, and then the button for the ground floor.

All of a sudden she bulled him aside with her shoulder and grabbed for the emergency phone compartment.

He grabbed her arm and pulled her back, but she came at him, screeching, trying to rake his face with her nails.

Shoving her back against the wall, he stepped aside as she tried to knee him in the groin, and backhanded her with enough force that her eyes fluttered. She slid down the wall to the floor, ending up on her knees, her breath coming in blubbering gasps.

Her red card was still in the slot.

Just above the fifth floor he stopped the elevator as she was coming around.

He had a mind to let her ride back up to the penthouse. Without a red card none of them could escape. But most of them had cell phones so they could call for help.

In the end it wouldn't matter. Nothing could be done to stop what was going to happen.

She looked up at Kamal. "Did you kill those men?" she asked, her voice a whisper now. She was frightened, but determined.

He found that he admired her. She deserved the truth. "Yes."

"My God, why?"

"You'll see."

She struggled painfully to her feet. "What about Miss Akila?"

"Unfortunately she's dead as well," Kamal said. "She was a loose end, just as you are."

The receptionist came at him again.

He spun her around and grabbed her head with both hands, then twisted it down and sharply to the left, her neck breaking with a crunch.

As she slumped to the floor on her back, she looked up at him in horror, not able to move or breathe. She was dying and she knew it.

The assignment was just in its opening moves and already Kamal was enjoying himself more than ever in his life.

He turned the elevator back on, and as the light began to fade from the young woman's eyes he took out his cell phone, unlocked the keys, and hit the comma button.

She was unconscious by the time the elevator reached the ground floor. He punched the button for the twentieth floor and stepped out before the doors could close.

Time to watch the show.

SEVEN

Callahan had sent Melissa down to security to find out what had happened to Seif and Nenet, rather than call them on a house phone. There were too many ears listening to everything he said. He didn't want to worry anyone, but she had taken too long and now he was concerned.

He went upstairs to the study. Two of the women were deep in discussion about something and he shooed them away. They went out giggling. The players had chosen them for their looks, not their brains.

When they were gone, he called Wheeler, at the same time someone downstairs shouted something, and the quartet stopped playing.

On the second ring, his stomach did a slow roll, almost as if he were getting seasick.

He let the phone ring twice more without answer. A pencil lying on the desk rolled a couple of inches to the left, then stopped and rolled several inches the other way.

Crashing down the phone he rushed out to the loft, where the musicians were on their feet, looking confused.

Downstairs people were gathering around the big

windows facing south down Eighth Avenue, toward One World Trade Center.

Even from the head of the stairs Callahan could see that all the buildings to the south were rocking slowly at an angle to the right and then to the left. All of Manhattan was moving.

"What's happening?" one of the musicians asked. "Are we having an earthquake?"

Manhattan wasn't moving, the building was. "It's windy outside, we're swaying a little. But it'll straighten out in just a minute."

"Bullshit," another of the musicians said, and he started to pack his violin. "I'm getting the hell out of here."

Callahan raced downstairs. Most of the guests were getting excited.

Someone shouted something in Arabic while another said something in German.

"Make it stop!" a woman screamed.

Callahan held up both hands. "People, stay calm. You're perfectly safe here. It's just a little windy outside."

The building lurched even farther to the left, nearly knocking a couple of people off their feet, and sending several bumping into the window. It hung in place for a seeming eternity, before it started back to the right. Manhattan stopped moving for a moment, but then the building began to sway again.

Callahan hurried to Seif's private elevator. The car had returned to the ground floor for some reason, and it did not respond to the call button.

For the first time in his life he was frightened. All he could think of was the World Trade Center towers coming down. He'd seen the television news flash of the airplane slamming into the first tower, on the Jumbotron in Times Square, while he was on the way to a meeting in the South Tower.

He had the cabby let him out on West Broadway just after it crossed the Avenue of the Americas and stood watching as the second airplane came in. People were transfixed. No one, including Callahan, could believe what they were seeing.

And then the South Tower collapsed in on itself, and he thought that the United States was at war, and this attack was going to be a million times worse than Pearl Harbor.

Kamal stopped at the corner of Ninth Avenue and Fifty-seventh, unable not to look back. He tried to imagine what it was like for the people in the penthouse. By now all of them had to realize that they were in serious trouble. Callahan would understand it more than the others. He would not have been able to raise security, his red card was gone so he couldn't reach the service elevator, and the penthouse's private elevator was locked out, as were all the other elevators in the building.

Soon the people in AtEighth would realize that they were going to die and no power on earth could save them. He wished that he could be there to see the fear in their eyes. The panic. The bargaining with their God for a miracle, for salvation.

He decided that it would almost be worth dying with them to experience how the last moments felt.

Almost.

Already some people on the street were taking notice that something was wrong. Tall buildings were expected to move several inches in a strong wind, no more than that. The pencil towers were especially prone to swaying, but engineers had supposedly fixed the problem with the tuned mass damper systems.

A number of people were on their cell phones, at least some of them surely calling 911. But it was far too late.

In a way, Kamal figured he was taking a chance with his life standing here less than one thousand feet from the building. If the program controlling the mass damper was off, if the engineers who figured to topple the building to the east were wrong, and instead it came down to the west, he would get his wish and die with the players in the penthouse.

The hell of it was, he didn't think he gave much of a damn one way or the other.

Callahan was pressed up against the elevator door, people frantic to get out completely packing the vestibule behind him. But then the building swayed back to the east, and just about everyone lost their balance and skidded away.

The building had to be displacing off the vertical by seven or eight feet each way now, and it would only be a matter of seconds before the structure somewhere below failed.

They'd welded thick steel plates across the riveted joints that held the building's girders to the support columns. The engineers had learned that method from the near-disaster at the Citicorp Center in the late seventies. In that building the girders had only been riveted to the support columns, and an engineering student had suggested that in a strong wind those joints could fail. The student was right, and without causing a panic, patches were welded in place.

But with a nine-hundred-ton counterweight somehow out of control—and Callahan was almost certain that was the problem—no building could withstand the stress.

A large twanging boom suddenly rang through the steel skeleton of the entire structure, like someone had plucked the bass string of an impossibly large musical instrument.

The tower shifted back to the west, slamming Callahan

into a tangle of bodies. At least two of the men were shouting into their cell phones, while women screamed.

Something crashed upstairs, and Callahan thought the building would surely have to topple now.

But it held, and for just a brief few moments, he wanted to shake the hand of every son-of-a-bitch engineer who'd had a hand in designing the place. They were geniuses.

Then the tower started back toward the east.

An even louder boom shook the building.

This time the tower didn't stop its long fall toward the street.

Kamal stared, with a feeling almost the same as sexual arousal, as something on the fourth floor of the tower suddenly blew outward, sending glass straight out as if there'd been an explosion, and the building started down, to the east, slowly at first, but accelerating with a horrible speed as it toppled.

People on the street began scattering. many of them in the wrong direction.

Traffic came to a standstill. No one seemed to know what to do, where to go.

Kamal turned and headed up Ninth Avenue, figuring that he would take a subway far enough from the disaster but where it would be close enough to walk the rest of the way to the Grand Hyatt.

He would have a couple of drinks at the bar and watch the news reports on television. It was all he could do not to sing one of the tunes he'd learned at Eton and then Sandhurst.

The best part for him was that this was just the beginning.

PART
TWO

Cannes Film Festival

EIGHT

Kirk McGarvey, a fresh bottle of Valpolicella in hand, stood at the open slider to the pool deck, but Pete was gone. It was nearly eleven o'clock and they had been sitting outside since just after dinner, talking about everything, except their relationship.

McGarvey, Mac to his friends, at fifty was a tall man, built somewhat like a rugby player, with thick brown hair, an honest square face, and expressive eyes that sometime were gray and at other times almost green. He was in superb shape because he exercised just about every day, and when the need arose he could move with the grace of a powerful ballet dancer. He was an outstanding marksman with a wide range of weapons, including his old and trusted standby, the Walther PPK in the 9mm version.

Pete Boylan, on the other hand, was a voluptuous woman in her midthirties who had the looks and style of a movie star. She too was in outstanding physical condition because of her Central Intelligence Agency–designed exercise program. And although she had started out with the Company as an interrogator she had shifted over to operations to be closer to McGarvey, a man she had loved for a couple of years now.

Mac stepped outside and tried to spot her down by the dock on the Intracoastal waterway, where his forty-two-foot Whitby ketch was tied. His large house on Casey Key, a Gulf Coast island about sixty miles south of Tampa, had 150 feet of waterway at the rear, and just across the street the white sand beach that stretched the entire nine miles of the narrow barrier island.

He walked around the pool and stepped down onto the paved path, away from the lights, and he saw her leaning against the rail of the small gazebo just up the lawn from the dock. His heart skipped a beat and he almost dropped the bottle as a million thoughts raced through his head at what felt like the speed of light.

The gazebo had been his wife, Katy's, refuge. After assassins—bent on killing him—had murdered her, their daughter, and son-in-law, he had promised himself to tear it down. But in the end he couldn't do it.

Pete turned and spotted him standing on the path and she waved.

He went the rest of the way to her. "I didn't know where you had gone."

"I had to come down here to take a look," she said. "It's really nice." But then her mouth turned down. "What?"

McGarvey forced a smile. "Nothing," he said. "More wine?"

She got their glasses and they sat at the small table, the view up and down the waterway, with the lights on the houses and the swing bridge not far away, wonderful.

"Katy used to sit here at night," McGarvey said. "But she liked it better during the day, just at dawn when she could see the birds, especially the pelicans."

Pete didn't say a thing for several long moments, leaving McGarvey with his thoughts about the women in his life—every one of them murdered because of who he was, what he did.

He had joined the CIA more years ago than he cared to remember, and trained for black operations—what the Russians at the time called *mokrie dela,* "wet work"— another term for assassinations.

Almost immediately his past—even before he had much

of a past—caught up with him, and Kathleen had given him an ultimatum: it was to be her and their two-year-old daughter, Elizabeth, or the CIA.

He'd just come off an assignment in Chile in which he was ordered to kill a general who was known as a butcher because of his torture and murder of more than one thousand Chileans. But it had gone horribly wrong and when he got back to their home in Chevy Chase, he was rubbed so raw that he had quit both and had run off to lick his wounds in Switzerland.

A woman who worked for the Swiss federal police had been assigned to watch him. Ex-CIA operators made most cops nervous. In the course of the thing she'd fallen in love with him, and shortly after he'd been called to another assignment, she had been killed. The same thing happened to a Frenchwoman whom he'd tried to push away. But she had followed him back to Washington and had been killed in a terrorist explosion meant for him.

Then his wife and daughter, and his daughter's husband, had been assassinated because of him, because of who he was, because of the assignments he had accepted and successfully completed.

He had only ever taken down bad people, but in his thoughts and especially in his dreams, his hands would never be clean because of what had happened to the women in his life.

And now there was Pete.

"I shouldn't be here," Pete said softly, almost timidly.

"It's okay. I wanted you to see Casey Key, how I live."

"Here I am. Do you want to talk about it? About Katy?"

"One step at a time. Tomorrow I'll take you up to Sarasota, to my office at New College. Maybe we'll have lunch on St. Armands Circle—the Crab and Fin is a good restaurant."

"Yours and Katy's favorite?"

McGarvey looked toward the bridge as a boat beeped twice for it to open.

For a time after Kathleen's death, and his return to Langely he'd been taken out of the field and put in charge of the National Clandestine Service—also known as the Directorate of Operations. He'd hated the job, being confined behind a desk, and his next job as the temporary director of the entire agency was even worse.

He quit the service again for a while and had taken a job as adjunct professor of philosophy at the small liberal arts college. His specialty was the eighteenth-century French philosopher Voltaire because there was no bullshit with the man. No doublespeak, no preaching, only real-deal straight talk.

Common sense isn't so common.

It's better to risk saving a guilty person than to condemn an innocent one.

And McGarvey's favorite, but for a lot of reasons he usually did not want to think about: *It is forbidden to kill; therefore all murderers are punished unless they kill in large numbers and to the sound of trumpets.*

His young students loved that one and the debates that followed, never suspecting that their instructor was an assassin.

"We used to go there mostly in the winter when it wasn't so warm," he answered her.

"You don't have to do this, you know," Pete said. "I love you, and I'll never be ashamed to say it, but the next step is up to you. Either forward or backward."

"I want to try," McGarvey said, after a long bit of silence.

"Try what?"

"To find how to tell you that I think I'm in love with you."

A huge bittersweet smile lit up her face.

"But," he said.

"But what?"

"You scare the shit out of me."

Pete threw her head back and laughed from the bottom of her toes, the sweetest thing Mac had heard in a very long time. "Well, it's a damned good start, Kirk, and I'll help you work on it. Promise."

The house phone up at the pool rang, and McGarvey debated for a moment not answering it, but the only person who knew that he was here was his friend Otto Rencke, the director of the CIA's Special Operations Division, and the resident computer odd-duck expert. They had a long history together and there was no one on the planet, for the moment, whom he trusted more.

"It's probably Otto," he said and Pete followed him up to the pool.

He put the call on speakerphone and answered on the fourth ring.

"Wow, turn on your TV, right now," Otto said. He sounded out of breath, as he usually was when he ran into something big.

Inside, Mac turned on the TV in the kitchen.

"Any of the major networks, it doesn't matter," Otto said.

McGarvey brought up NBC just as AtEighth coming down replayed. The anchor was saying that the images were from a cell phone camera, as were others which came up on screen, all of them at different angles, but all of them showing the same thing.

"Looks like the building's structure failed at the fourth floor and the entire thing landed down Fifty-seventh, a big piece falling directly on Carnegie Hall," Otto said.

"It wasn't an accident," Pete replied. "And a lot of

people in New York are not going to be overly sad about the thing coming down. Payback time for billionaires sticking it to the little guy. Tower of Babel and all that."

"ISIS has already claimed responsibility," Otto said.

"Any word on casualties?"

"Not yet."

"They're copying al-Qaeda," McGarvey said. "They'll want to bring down a second."

"That's what everyone up here is thinking," Otto replied. "It's all hands on deck."

"We'll pack."

"One of our aircraft is on the way, just about the only thing other than military in the air for now."

NINE

The Gulfstream 280 touched down at Joint Base Andrews across the river from Washington just at dawn. The pilot had apologized that the small jet, which only seated four comfortably, was all that was available.

"Lots of VIPs needing to get somewhere," he said.

Otto had sent a Company car and driver for them, and on the way up to Langley he spoke to them via a video screen in the backseat.

"I didn't want to bother you guys until now, figured you would need the sleep," he said. He was a tall, somewhat thin man, with long red hair that he usually tied in a ponytail, and the same sort of unusually wide head and open eyes that made him somewhat reminiscent of Einstein. A lot of people in the cyber world—on both sides of the legal fence—thought he was the smartest man on the planet. Everyone, including McGarvey, and the top brass at the

Agency, had a great deal of respect for him, and some of them a little fear.

"What do the overnights look like?" McGarvey asked.

"None of it any good, except that the Bureau came up with two witnesses who thought they might have seen a man coming out of the building and walking away just before it came down."

"Anyone else get out?" Pete asked.

"No."

"What about this man who made two people remember him?"

"They were on Fifty-seventh half a block west of the building, and they said that the man stopped on the corner of Fifty-seventh and Ninth and watched the entire show. After that they don't know what happened to him."

"Descriptions?"

"Tall, wearing a dark suit," Otto said. "One of them said he was blond, maybe a Scandinavian; the other said his hair was definitely dark and short, like a military buzz cut. But supposedly they weren't very coherent, especially the woman."

"How'd it come down?" MGarvey asked. "Looked like an explosion on the fourth floor."

"No evidence of explosives have been found to this point. But two sets of cell phone videos that haven't been released yet that were taken just before it collapsed showed the entire structure swaying back and forth."

"Was it windy?" Pete asked. "Those kinds of buildings always sway in the wind."

"An inch or two, but the Bureau's counterterrorism branch shared both videos with us. Our forensics people agreed with the Bureau's chief engineer—a PhD by the name of Endicott—that at the time the structure failed it was more than ten feet from vertical."

"Not the wind, what about the counterweight at the top?" McGarvey asked.

"Endicott claims that would be impossible under normal circumstances."

"Hardly normal. I want to talk to him."

"We're trying to set up a joint meeting with their people and ours sometime later today. Page asked you be included."

Walt Page was the director of the agency, and a politically connected man—like almost every DCI before him. And like most high-level leaders in just about every intel agency in the U.S., he was not a career intelligence officer. Though he and McGarvey had an on-again, off-again relationship, he was bright enough to understand that sometimes a maverick—like McGarvey—was just the person to send to the front of the firing line.

"How about survivors?"

"None yet, but they're still digging through the rubble. Fortunately there weren't that many people in the building. Fourteen workmen, making final touches on a half dozen floors; George Callahan, who was the building's developer, and his executive assistant, Melissa Saunders; four officers in the security center on the fortieth; and four chamber orchestra musicians from the New York Philharmonic, plus all the guests."

"Were they in the lobby?" Pete asked.

"The penthouse. The grand opening wasn't to be until next week," Otto added.

"They were having a private party for whoever bought the place. A hundred fifty million, I read," McGarvey said. "Heavy hitters."

"Khalid Seif and his girlfriend were celebrating. He was a UAE offshore banker, worth about thirty billion or more."

"How many at the party?"

"Seventy-seven, including Callahan and his assistant.

All of them except for that woman, and the mistresses and wives, multibillionaires from all over the world. Players here for the art auctions. They were supposed to be flying out today on their private jets to Cannes for the end of the film festival. From there it would have been the Grand Prix at Monaco next week, and then Basel in mid-June."

"What are the dates for Cannes and Monaco?" McGarvey asked.

"Last day of Cannes is the twenty-second, which gives us five days, if I'm reading you right. And the Monaco race is exactly two days later."

"A week, at most, for these people to make the circuit and then get back here."

"For what?" Pete asked.

"For building two here in New York to come down," Otto said. "Another pencil tower possibly, but just as likely any skyscraper with lots of people inside. At least a hundred or more buildings in Manhattan. Problem is, there's really no foolproof way to protect them all. And I'm betting it'll happen right after Monaco. It'd give the players time enough to regroup so that they'd start thinking they're invincible again."

"I'll need a couple of bulletproof passports and ID sets that'll get past the French," McGarvey said. He had a history with the DGSI—France's secret intelligence service—that wasn't all good. He wasn't persona non grata there, but he was close.

"If you're talking about the tall guy in a dark suit, it's a long shot. And an even longer shot—if it was him—that he'd show up in Cannes or Monaco."

"If it is him—and you're right, it's a long shot—he'll have to show up and mingle with the players, or at least be somewhere nearby. He'll want to convince at least a few of them to come back to the States for another grand opening. And the rest will have to follow, as a matter of form."

"There are fifteen pencil towers," Otto said.

"Doesn't give us much time—you to get all the information you can from the Bureau, and me and Pete to poke around New York. Maybe we can put some pressure on this bastard."

"Doesn't sound like he's the kind of operator who would work for ISIS," Pete said.

"No, but someone wants us to think this was an ISIS attack."

"Saudi Arabia," Otto said. "Their people were involved in nine-eleven."

"And they would benefit the most by having ISIS taking the blame," McGarvey said.

"They took credit for it," Pete said.

"Wasn't them, I'd bet just about anything on it. The risk would be way over-the-top. They'd have a whole hell of a lot more to lose than gain."

Page, who looked more like a successful New York banker than a spymaster, met with McGarvey, Otto, and Pete but no one else from the Company, not even Marty Bambridge, the deputy director of operations, or Carleton Patterson, the Agency's general counsel, who'd been in that position for as long as anyone could remember.

"Thank you for coming," he said. "If you've watched the reports on television and Otto has filled you in, you know just about everything we know to this point."

"I have a few ideas," McGarvey said.

"I'm sure you do. We're having a joint meeting here with the Bureau and the NYPD; you can share your thinking."

"Miss Boylan and I are going up to New York to poke around for ourselves. We'll need use of a Gulfstream, and all the intel you can share."

"I'll give them a précis of everything that comes from

this afternoon's meeting, and anything else that my darlings pick up," Otto said. His darlings were his computer programs, which monitored just about every electronic database in the world, 24/7.

"I don't imagine that you want Marty or even Carleton in on what you're planning."

"No, I don't want to have to stop and explain myself," McGarvey said. "We don't have that much time."

Page was surprised. "You have someone in mind already?"

"A possibility. And they'll try to bring down a second building, just like nine-eleven."

"God almighty."

TEN

Kamal's magnificent home was on a large property that overlooked the bays of Monaco, Golfe Bleu and Roquebrune. He'd bought the ten-thousand-square-foot house under the name Roger Harcourt, four years ago, for something over seventy-five million euros, and had an interior design team from Copenhagen completely redo every single room—there were five master suites—plus eight hundred square meters of terraces.

The entire project, which included an infinity pool, had taken nearly a year and an additional two and a half million euros, which strained even his secret bank accounts. But he looked at the place not so much as a home, but as an investment. If the time ever came for him to go to ground, which he thought might happen, the blind sale would finance him for years to come. In the meantime he was living large.

He'd flown first-class from New York to Paris, and from

there to Marseilles, where he took the train to Monaco and a cab to his house. He was a bit weary, but not tired; he'd managed to get a decent night's sleep crossing the Atlantic.

Tomorrow he would take his Bentley convertible down to Cannes, where he had VIP passes to all the showings and events at the film festival. And then two days later back here for the Grand Prix.

He needed an invitation to the next penthouse party in New York—the one in the pencil tower near the UN—which he meant to bring down the same way he destroyed AtEighth.

ISIS supposedly wanted the same symmetry as al-Qaeda had achieved with the Twin Towers.

He couldn't go again as Seif so he had to invent a new personality for himself. Someone who would be of enough interest to the players gathering at Cannes and Monaco to be asked along as a guest. Or at the very least as someone of curiosity. Maybe even of some help with the one thing multibillionaires admired and lusted after the most: more money.

The only way he figured that would happen would be if he was accepted by the players.

His house and the entire cliff-side property was safeguarded by electronic and visual sensors so that by the time the cabby dropped him off at the main entrance, his houseman, Yves Germaine, was waiting at the door.

"Good afternoon, sir, your trip was fruitful?" he asked.

He was a slightly built man in his early fifties who'd been valet to an Englishman in London, until the man died. Kamal had picked him from the service listings, and after a brief interview hired him just after this house was finished. He was formal and discreet.

"Very," Kamal said, handing over his single bag. "I'm going to the casino this evening and afterwards dinner. To-

morrow I'll be transferring to the Majestic for two days."
They would be the first two steps toward his acceptance
into the elite group.

"I'll lay out your evening clothes. You're already packed
for Cannes."

"Thank you. I'll have a shower now."

"Pardon me, sir, but you have a gentleman waiting for
you on the terrace."

Kamal's anger spiked. This was the first time in three
years that Germaine had disappointed him. One of his firm
standing rules from the start was that no one was ever to
be allowed into the house. "Who is he?"

"He identified himself as a comrade in arms at Sandhurst. Showed me several photographs of the two of you
together. In uniform. Some deshabille."

Kamal immediately knew who it was, and how extraordinary that he had come here.

"Shall I send him away, sir?"

It was a small chink in his anonymity here, which quite
possibly now had been destroyed. He didn't let his anger
show. "No, we're old friends. I wasn't expecting him, and
in the future I don't like surprises."

"I understand, sir. Will you be needing service on the
terrace?"

"I'll call if I need it," Kamal said.

The houseman took the bag back to Kamal's master
suite and Kamal went out to the southeast balcony, where
his Saudi control officer was sitting.

"Sa'ad, I'm surprised to see you here," Kamal said.

The Saudi intel officer turned. "But I shouldn't be surprised that you know my name," he said. He was a second
cousin in the royal family and he looked it; his complexion was dark, his nose prominent, his eyes deep.

"Nor, I suppose, should I be surprised that you know
about this place."

"One can't be too careful in our business," Sa'ad said.

Kamal leaned against the Lexan railing next to the stairs that went down a level to the pool deck. The Med this afternoon was a deep blue, and nearly flat calm. A mega-yacht just offshore was heading south, possibly from San Remo, even Genoa or farther north. The flag was Liberian, which meant nothing. The yacht was heading to Cannes.

"Congratulations on New York. It has had the desired effect."

"It got their attention."

"Indeed. Your first payment has posted in PSP."

"I'll check later."

"But there may be a problem."

"Yes?"

"There is a growing sentiment that ISIS was not behind the attack."

"Your timing having them accept blame was wrong. It's not my problem."

"You are correct on both counts. We may have to delay the second attack."

"Why?"

Sa'ad got up and came across to the railing. He stared at the yacht. "Jian has apparently canceled his housewarming until after Monaco. In fact he may not even inspect the place."

Jian Chang was the leading real estate mogul in all of Hong Kong, in part because he had the wholehearted sup-port of Bejing and in a larger part because he was brilliant. He had bought the penthouse at the Tower near the UN for $210 million, sight unseen. He'd supposedly said that George Callahan was a Wild West snake oil salesman, and Callahan had agreed.

Nonetheless Jian had written a check for the full amount, or at least his LLC had paid for the condo, which was the highest residence anywhere in the entire western hemisphere.

"So what?" Kamal asked.

"ISIS wants to make a statement against Western greed."

"When the second building comes down it will make a statement, whether or not a few dozen multibillionaires go down with it or not."

Sa'ad spread his hands. "Collateral damage, just like yesterday."

"Yves," Kamal said, without raising his voice.

His houseman appeared almost instantaneously at the open slider. "Sir?"

"We would like a bottle of Krug."

"I have one chilling, sir."

Sa'ad looked beyond Kamal, as the houseman disappeared. "How much does he know about you?"

"Nothing important. About as much as I really know about you."

"Would you bet your life on it?"

"No, but I'd bet his life on it. What are you doing here?"

"I've brought a message that perhaps you have done enough. The Americans will react in the fashion we want them to. They will coordinate an all-out attack against ISIS and its leadership. Not a coalition strike, but surgical hits with SEALs, just like against Osama in Pakistan in retaliation for nine-eleven."

"You've come to call me off?"

"To stand down. Your final payment will be posted within twenty-four hours. You've done a man's work."

"I'm not finished."

"You are."

The houseman returned with the champagne in an ice bucket along with two Fabergé crystal flutes, also chilled. "May I pour?"

"Leave us," Kamal said.

When the houseman was gone, Kamal poured the wine.

When Sa'ad had a drink he smiled faintly. "There are some things in Saudi Arabia that people cannot enjoy," he said.

"Do you know what will happen on May twenty-ninth?"

"In nine days."

"UNICEF's International Youth Day has been moved up from August. More than twenty-five hundred children will be at the General Assembly building in the evening. Music from around the world, dancers, clowns, magicians."

"Less than one thousand feet from the Tower," Sa'ad said.

Kamal made a call to an encrypted number in Atlanta. It was answered on the second ring by a man whose voice was distorted by the sloppy algorithm.

"Yes."

"Have you completed the list of my possible purchases? I'll be coming to see you in a few days."

"I'll be ready by the time you arrive."

ELEVEN

The message on Sa'ad al-Sakar's encrypted cell phone was simply one word: "Come."

It was after mid-night, the soft spring Mediterranean early morning balmy as the Greek-registered cargo ship the *MV Spiros* tied up at the Turkish port city of Iskenderun just a few kilometers from the border with Syria.

Their cargo was a mix of cell phones, computers, televisions, and even small refrigerators; air conditioners, fans, and two dozen portable electric generators. All of it Chinese, a fact of the withdrawal by the Russians from the area.

Sa'ad was a man in his early forties with the dark complexion, flashing eyes, and good looks of a young Omar Sharif, the onetime Egyptian actor. He'd been married briefly to a Saudi girl he'd met at UC-Berkeley, where he'd been studying English and international relations.

But after graduation when he'd been recruited by the Saudi intelligence agency he'd been told that the marriage would have to end. He could never bring his wife home. She'd been too Westernized. She wore no head scarf and in the States she'd even had a driver's license.

"For the first year your position in the General Intelligence Presidency will be relatively minor," the spokesman for the recruiting board had told him. "You will receive training, of course, in cryptography, weapons—an entire host of what we call tradecraft."

They'd met in a windowless room in an anonymous building on Riyadh's west side. The three men seated at a table wore Western dress slacks and open-collared white shirts. Sa'ad had not been offered a seat.

"Your real education will begin in the second year—if you last that long—when we will ask your complete devotion to the family," the older man seated in the middle said. His hair was white, his attitude brusque. "To your family."

"I myself am a royal," Sa'ad had said, a little hotly. But he had been young and just out of college. Rash then. Not yet tempered.

"Your cousin is a bin Talal, yes, we know this. If you did not have the blood you would not be here."

"I understand."

"Nor will you ever marry anyone outside of the family, do you also understand this?"

He was in love with his wife, Sarah. But he'd known that this day was coming. When he'd left to go back for what he told her was a job interview at the Banque Saudi Fransi, she'd told him flatly that she would never go home.

"I'll follow you to foreign postings if you get them, but I will not live in Saudi Arabia."

Sa'ad loved her, but his choice had been simple, and one he never regretted.

He'd learned a couple of years later that she had divorced him and married a German chemical engineer and was living in Berlin.

Getting off the ship he was met by a Toyota and driver. He tossed his one bag in the backseat and got in front with the clean-shaven man who was dressed in jeans, army boots, and a khaki military shirt, buttoned up at the elbows.

Without a word they drove inland toward the hills until twenty minutes later they came to a ramshackle old two-story house behind tall concrete-block walls in a neighborhood of similar buildings. They were admitted through a metal gate, and a young man with a scraggly beard directed Sa'ad upstairs.

Abu Safwan al-Rifai, the ISIS sub-commander for security and intelligence, was talking on his cell phone when Sa'ad showed up at the door. A Kalashnikov assault rifle leaned against the table. The man was young, in his middle thirties, with a slender face, well-trimmed beard and mustache, dressed in clean and pressed military khakis.

They'd never met face-to-face. Their only contacts had been by cell phone, by Internet for money transfers, and twice through couriers—once in Paris and again in Brussels. But Sa'ad had studied the man's dossier, what little there was of it, and a pair of photographs.

At this point al-Rifai was on every Western intelligence agency's Most Wanted list. His being here was a great risk, as was Sa'ad's presence.

He broke the connection and pocketed the phone. "Why has the second building not been brought down?"

They spoke English.

"The party for Mr. Jian has been delayed. The entire city is on high alert. The American authorities expect that a second attack will come at any moment and they are waiting for it."

"Then let it come."

"I have told my operative to proceed with caution."

"You have told him to stand down!" al-Rifai shouted, spittle flying.

"My superiors think that it's for the best."

"You're cowards."

"There are other considerations," Sa'ad said.

From day one with the GIP, when he'd chosen the service over his wife, he'd known the life he would have. The international travel, the intrigue, the freedom to act so long as in the end he was proven right. He'd always supposed that some of Sarah's independence and rebelliousness had rubbed off on him; that, combined with his royal lineage, had lent him a certain creativity that his superiors found troublesome at times.

But he knew that he was considered among the GIP's brightest and best. He had the family connections, he had the education, and the flair, and when he'd accumulated enough experience with as few mistakes as possible he would rise to the top of the intelligence agency, or very near it.

This operation, however, was beginning to have all the earmarks of a disaster in the making.

"There are no other considerations, you fucking coward!" al-Rifai shouted.

Sa'ad turned around and went to the door.

"You will be implicated if you turn back. Riyadh will be implicated. The second building will come down."

"And ISIS will be blamed. Is that what you still wish?"

"Yes. We want the infidel bastards here. On the ground, not with their drones or Russian jets. Live bodies that we will destroy."

"I understand."

"This operation ends now," his control officer, Colonel Fares Mustafa, had told him after AtEighth went down.

"May I be told why?"

"No."

They'd met at the compound of one of the bankers Sa'ad supposedly worked for.

"We believe that there may be unintended consequences. Saudi Arabia is no longer involved."

TWELVE

McGarvey and Pete were let into the double-wide mobile home parked on Fifty-seventh just east of Ninth Avenue that was being used by Homeland Security's National Incident Management System. Fifteen operators manned telephones and computer terminals dealing with incoming reports from more than two hundred investigators on the ground.

Fifty-seventh and Fifty-sixth between Ninth and the Avenue of the Americas were closed down, and according to Otto's take from the meeting at Langley would remain so for several months, perhaps longer, until all the rubble had been cleared away and the on-site investigation was completed.

Six gigantic mobile cranes were lifting away sections of the AtEighth building as they were cut loose, and an army of bulldozers was scooping up rubble and loading it into dump trucks to be hauled across the river to a forensics investigation dump site.

Allan Frankel, the lead NIMS commander, had only agreed to talk to them after a call from his boss, who had met with Walt Page at the Langley briefing. He was a solidly built man with a salt-and-pepper crew cut and a completely no-nonsense air. He had retired as a navy four-star just two years ago and he was accustomed to giving orders and expecting them to be carried out instantly. But he also listened to his staff and was receptive to new ideas.

He was standing at his desk studying a sheaf of blueprints. The trailer seemed to be in a state of pandemonium, people talking all at once, phones ringing, printers spitting out reports, two fax machines running steadily.

"Are you the people from the CIA?" he asked.

"Just a couple of questions and we'll get out of your hair, Admiral," McGarvey said.

"Come with me."

They followed him outside, and halfway down the block to within twenty yards of the base of AtEighth, what little was left of it. Only a few girders stuck up from what had been the fourth floor. Everything above had fallen to the ground, but just about everything below seemed to be more or less intact.

Even the glass front doors, by some quirk of happenstance, had not been broken. The media had honed in on the doors as a symbol of what had happened. Unspoken, of course, was the possibility that if someone had been standing in the doorway when the building came down they would have escaped death.

"We began removing the sections that landed on Carnegie Hall, which fortunately had emptied out a half hour earlier. So far we've found six bodies, what was left of them, in the auditorium, custodians, we believe."

"Any survivors?" Pete asked.

"We want there to be survivors as badly as everyone else does. Staff says there could be as many as four or five fixed plant operators in the basement, but to this point we haven't gotten to them. It's been less than thirty-six hours."

Huge crowds along Ninth and the Avenue of the Americas had gathered behind police barriers, but television news crews from at least a dozen local and foreign countries had been allowed to set up at various spots within the barriers, along either side of the collapsed tower. Overhead several helicopters swept slowly back and forth, the pilots careful to avoid midair collisions.

"There's not much of it," Pete said, her voice low and slow. She was caught up in the enormity of the moment.

"The building was only fifty feet on a side," Frankel said. He was holding something back.

"How about inside the tower?" McGarvey asked. "There was a party in the penthouse."

"That part of the structure was several hundred feet beyond Carnegie Hall. There were no survivors. But it'll be some time before all of the bodies are identified, even working from the guest list. There was no fire, but you have to understand that all those people were badly beat up."

"What about the fortieth floor?"

The admiral's face darkened. "That was our second major objective. It landed in the middle of the block just past Broadway. Our crews got it open about an hour ago, and I've already sent my report directly to the president."

"No survivors?" McGarvey asked, knowing the answer.

"No."

"Four of them, dead before the building landed?"

"Yes," Frankel answered carefully. "But that's as far as I'll take that line."

"Shot to death?" McGarvey pressed.

"Two of them were shot in the head. We can't be sure about the other two, their bodies were too badly crushed."

"Thank you," McGarvey said. "We'll let you get back to your work now, but do you mind if we take a look around?"

"Yes, I do mind, Mr. Director. It's too dangerous for now. But I want a quid pro quo. How did you know the security people had been shot?"

"It was just a guess, but someone spotted a man in a dark suit possibly coming out of the building just before it came down. He may have walked up the block and stopped at the corner of Ninth to watch."

"ISIS had a man inside the building, is that what you're thinking?"

"Someone was there."

"To do what, exactly? Why kill the security team?"

"To shut down the interior surveillance equipment. Shut down the telephones and the elevators. They were all on the ground floor, right?"

"All except the service elevator, we found it on what had probably been the twentieth. The car itself was ejected from the structure and was lying on its side about twenty feet from the main debris path."

"He probably used that elevator to get to the ground floor, but why did he send it up to the twentieth?" Pete asked.

"Depends on what was in the car," McGarvey said.

"The body of a young woman. The EMTs said that it looked as if her neck had been broken."

"She probably discovered him on the elevator, so he killed her, took the elevator down to ground level and then sent it back up before he walked away."

"Mother of God," Pete whispered.

"What about the counterweight?"

"It crashed through the front of a restaurant on the corner of Fifty-sixth and the Avenue of the Americas. A lot of casualties. Ended up buried thirty feet beneath the basement."

The building was electronically hardened from hacking by someone on the outside. Otto wanted the hard disk drives from security's mainframe and from the computer that controlled the building's systems, as well as the modem that answered systems commands to control the tuned mass damper. McGarvey told Frankel as much.

"We should have the first two before the end of the day, but the equipment controlling the counterweight will take a major excavation. In any case the Bureau's counterterrorism branch will have the first crack."

"Good enough," McGarvey said. Otto was close with the Bureau's technical people and they would almost certainly ask his help with the retrieval of data and its interpretation.

"No signs of explosions?" Pete asked.

"No, and it's driving a lot of people nuts. No one knows how the building came down."

"The counterweight's computer was sabotaged."

"The engineers say something like that could not have caused the collapse."

"Witnesses on the ground said the entire structure was swaying so badly the structure failed at the fourth floor."

"They say that's impossible."

McGarvey looked at the tangled debris field, girders sticking out of the air, desks, beds, couches, and seemingly endless bits of people's lives in scattered piles along a clearly defined line more than fifteen hundred feet long.

"Tell that to the relatives and friends of the people whose bodies you're recovering," he said, and he and Pete walked off.

"That was a little harsh," she said.

"They need to get their heads out, because it's going to happen again."

THIRTEEN

Kamal, dressed in an impeccably cut tuxedo, but with a pink ruffled shirt, arrived at the Casino de Monte-Carlo shortly before ten in the evening. His eyes were black now, as was his hair, and his skin was darkened a couple of tones; that, along with a neatly trimmed goatee, made him almost completely unidentifiable as the man in New York.

He handed over his Bentley to the valet and just inside he had to show his passport. Locals were not allowed to gamble here. This time he was traveling under papers that identified him as Pablo Valdes, a businessman from Mexico City.

He had come to the casino tonight to show his face. To announce that he was on the scene. Perhaps not a major player, but a player nevertheless. Someone new. Someone with money and therefore of some interest.

The real Valdes had disappeared in Colombia three weeks ago. It was speculated that he had gone to ground because the Colombian military, in cooperation with the U.S. Drug Enforcement Agency, were hot on his trail across South America and even as far north as Panama. It was also rumored that he had been shot to death by agents of a rival druglord from Afghanistan.

In fact Kamal had tracked him down in Cartagena, shot him and his two bodyguards to death. He had driven

Valdes's body to a remote spot in the countryside, where he'd buried it. By the time anybody found and identified the man, the towers project would be finished.

The casino was busy this evening, and first he went to the cashier and established a house credit account in the amount of one million euros, then with a one-hundred-thousand euro stack of plaques he went to the bar and ordered a beer.

If any of the staff had found his ruffled shirt garish they showed nothing outwardly. But he'd made his first move, to be noticed.

Sa'ad had been intrigued when he'd been told of Kamal's plan at their meeting in Paris. "There's nothing officially I can do for you," he'd cautioned.

"I may need some on-the-spot intel over the coming days."

"Call the usual number, I'll keep it open. But you won't be able to show up again as Khalid Seif. I assume you have something worked out for your second appearance."

"The problem is getting invited to the Tower at its grand opening. Jian Chang has bought the penthouse and Callahan Holdings will be conducting an open house for him as planned."

"Even after AtEighth's destruction and Callahan's death?"

"Money is an irresistible salve for even the worst of wounds. I'm not sure who'll be taking over from him, but so far as I know the party will go on. Delayed, perhaps, but nothing ever stops those people. Their egos wouldn't allow it."

"I'll find out who it is," Sa'ad said.

"Good, in the meantime I'm going to get close to whichever of the players show up at Cannes tomorrow. Toss them a bone that at least some of them might not be able to resist.

All I need is one willing to listen to me, and from there I'll work on getting an invitation to Jian's party."

"You're not one of them, unless you're bringing money. A lot of it. We'd like to know what you have in mind."

"Really?"

"Yes."

Sitting at the casino bar drinking his beer, Kamal remembered picking up on the mistake, though he'd not mentioned it. To this point from the beginning eight years ago, his only contact with Saudi intelligence was Sa'ad. Their contracts had normally been at arm's length so that nothing would come back to the royal family. Sa'ad worked more or less independently of the General Intelligence Presidency, the GIP. But he'd said that *we'd* like to know. *We,* not *I.*

It was a possible signal that the time had come to get out of the business. Or at least disentangle himself from Riyadh. His house was worth at least one hundred million, even on a forced sale, and along with another fifty invested in various real estate holdings through PSP, Seif's bank, he would have enough to live a reasonably comfortable life under a new identity somewhere.

At least until he found another employer.

"I'm nowhere near being a multibillionaire, but I have something to offer them that no matter how much money they have, they won't be able to resist."

"What's that?"

"More money, of course. An almost unlimited amount of it."

"Go on."

"Pablo Valdes."

"The Mexican businessman whose file you wanted. We didn't have much because he's never been a person of interest to us. We were able to get some back-burner details from friends, but beyond that nobody knows much about him."

"The man was in the drug business in a very large way."

"Was?"

"Yes. But he wasn't a dealer or supplier. He never ran any of the big cartels, especially not the ones in Mexico and Colombia and the underground one in Cuba that some people are convinced was a creation of the government as a foreign cash cow."

"What was he?"

"A banker, essentially the same type of creature as Khalid Seif. He worked with just about every drug cartel in the western hemisphere, all of them with the same problem, how to get rid of all the cash they were generating. No one pays for an ounce of marijuana or cocaine or heroin with a check or credit card. It's a cash-only business. Tons of drugs head north across the border into the U.S. and literally tons of cash moves the other way."

"He launders the money," Sa'ad said. "It's a common problem, and so far as we know a lot of people are in the trade. Restaurants, real estate offices, art dealers, diamond merchants but most often banks. It's common knowledge. The business is simply too diverse to shut down."

"You forgot to mention space agencies," Kamal said. "Roscomos."

"The Russians?"

"Did you know that it takes four 747s, fully loaded with pallets of cash, to fly to Moscow just for a down payment to buy one of their surveillance satellites, and much more to launch the thing into orbit from where it can watch all of the northern Caribbean from Hispaniola and Cuba plus the southern U.S. border, especially Texas, New Mexico, and Arizona?"

Sa'ad chuckled. "The Americans have been going crazy trying to figure out that the cartels always seem to be a step ahead of them. There've been rumors, of course, about satellites, though not too many people believed it. Mostly the DEA has been finding and closing down surveillance posts up in the mountains in Arizona and New Mexico."

"A diversion," Kamal said.

"How do you know this?"

"He told me before I killed him."

Sa'ad shook his head. "In any event his face is well known."

"Which face?" Kamal asked. Each time Valdes's photograph showed up in a newspaper or magazine article, it was different. And there were no videos of him.

Sa'ad accepted the point. "So you're going as Valdes, and you're going to offer them a service. What exactly?"

"The discount for laundered money is from fifty to sixty percent. Valdes paid the Russians one hundred million, and they gave him the satellite and its launch and returned fifty million into a Channel Islands bank account for business transactions, of which Valdes kept ten and transferred the remaining forty into legitimate banks in Mexico and elsewhere. No cash changed hands except with the Russians. Multiply that by factors of ten or more and after a time it becomes serious. Plus the cartels not only get forty million on each transaction, they also got the satellite."

"Serious enough for the players to buy in."

"Yes, and I'm the one who sets it up and runs the deals. The players don't have to do a thing. I send them the cash, they move it around to their various businesses, and return fifty percent to me."

"Serious money."

"Worldwide more than two hundred billion euros," Kamal said.

"Perhaps I should pass this along to the royal family. One of the princes is at Cannes, and he'll certainly be in Monaco."

The thought had occurred to Kamal earlier. Sa'ad wasn't the only one in the GIP who apparently knew about him. Perhaps as a last gesture he'd stick it to the royals and let Sa'ad take the blame. But he didn't want to be looking over his shoulder for the rest of his life. If he did this final op and then dropped out of sight, the Saudis wouldn't come looking for him.

"It's not necessary," he said.

Sa'ad nodded. "Perhaps you're right. But I could provide you with an introduction. Someone at the edge of the royal family—actually married to one of the cousins. And there are other considerations."

"Go on."

"His name is Alyan Al-Hamadi, an embarrassment to the family, but sometimes useful to us as a sort of unofficial emissary. A message boy. If he were to get hurt, it would provide an excuse to end the marriage and get rid of him."

"How will you arrange the meeting?"

"He'll meet you at the Majestic's brasserie, Fouquet's. If that's the route you wish to take. But in addition to your operation, you would be doing the family a personal favor."

"I want to stay anonymous."

"I understand," Sa'ad said. "I'll give him your work name."

Kamal finished his beer and ordered another. He left the bar and wandered past the slot machine salle, where patrons were dressed in T-shirts, shorts and flip-flops, back to the private salons, which had a dress code and where minimum bets started at ten thousand euros and very often climbed to one hundred thousand or more.

This evening he was going to lose one million. He was going to create some attention, that if he wasn't exactly a player, neither was he a pauper.

FOURTEEN

Otto had managed to book McGarvey and Pete into a suite at the Plaza, at Fifth Avenue and Central Park South, less than a half dozen blocks from the downed tower. The place was overbooked because of all the American and foreign journalists, but a sudden problem with the hotel's computer opened up a suite. Their room overlooked the park, but arriving Pete had noticed that the side of the building facing southeast was covered in dust, as were other nearby buildings.

The reminders of the aftermath of 9/11 were everywhere. Nearly every television channel showed almost constant replays of the tower coming down from a dozen different angles and distances, just as they had when the trade towers went down.

At this early stage the death toll in the building was estimated at 103, including the four officers in the fortieth-floor security center, and an estimated 409 on Fifty-seventh, in Carnegie Hall, and in the restaurant where the counterweight had landed.

Otto called five minutes after they had checked in. Pete answered and put it on speakerphone as McGarvey got a beer from the mini-bar.

"How's it going up there?"

"Seeing it firsthand is unbelievable," Pete said. "But Frankel seems to know what he's doing."

"No signs of any explosions, sabotage of the support columns?"

"None."

"Then that just about nails it," Otto said. "The tuned mass damper took it down."

"Frankel says the engineers tell him that's impossible," McGarvey said.

"Dan Endicott, one of the Bureau's people, says the same thing. Swore up and down the building's framework shouldn't have failed. Too many safeguards."

"How'd he account for the swaying?"

"He admits he can't. But he and his people are working on it."

"Did he or anyone else have any other theories?"

"No. But my little darlings have a very high confidence that short of very well placed explosives—for which no evidence has been found so far—the mass damper was the cause."

"You said that the building was hardened to electronic interference," McGarvey said. "The building's computer systems could not have been hacked from outside."

"Some of them could have, through the connections between the security center and the NYPD, fire department, and New York City's Office of Emergency Management. I'm looking through their computers, but nothing's come up over the past forty-eight hours, so I'm taking it further back. But the tuned damper is on a completely different system. Totally independent of everything else in the building, and completely hardened. If it was hacked, and that's my best bet to this point, it had to have come from inside the building. Possibly even inside the systems room a hundred feet from the top."

"The elevators were shut down, all of them on the ground floor. The four men in the security office were shot to death, and the body of a young woman was found in the service elevator, which had stopped on the twentieth floor. Her neck had been broken: The EMTs who recovered her body said it looked as if the damage in the collapse had been done to her body after she was dead."

Otto was silent for a long time. "The bastard who was spotted leaving the building, and then stopping on Ninth to watch it come down, he did it."

"The man in the dark suit," Pete said. "ISIS sure as hell doesn't do things that way. It's never been their style. And they claimed responsibility way too fast. It's back to the Saudis, has to be them, just like Mac suggested."

"Do you have a list of everyone at the party?" McGarvey asked.

"Yes."

"And their backgrounds?"

"Yes."

"Anything stick out, anything out of the ordinary, anything unusual, an anomaly, something that doesn't fit, a chess piece on a checkers board?"

"Give me a sec, I'll run a differences search."

Pete took the beer from Mac, finished it, and went to get another. Before she opened the can, Otto was back.

"Differences in net worth, but the poorest had at least three or four billion. Not the four guys in security or the workmen still left in the building, or Callahan's assistant, but Callahan Holdings is worth eighteen billion, and he was the majority owner. Three of them did not have yachts, but Alex Barkin was the only one of them who didn't own a jet. He was a venture capitalist, net worth around thirty billion. No chauffeur, he prefers to drive a pickup truck. All them hang out on the so-called circuit—art auctions, film festivals, grand prixs, those sorts of happenings—except for Barkin and for Khalid Seif."

The American Alex Barkin was well known not only for his wealth but for his eccentricities, but Seif was a new name to MGarvey and he said so.

"Turns out it was his condo, his party," Otto said. "He has controlling interest in PSP, which is a United Arab Emirates offshore bank. In fact he did business with every one of the players in the room that night."

"What else?" McGarvey asked.

"Holy shit!" Otto exclaimed after a moment. "It's him. He's the man in the dark suit."

"Do you have photographs?"

"That's just it. None exist, except for the one in his UAE passport. I'm going to that site now. Give me a minute."

"He'd have no reason to bring down the building and kill all those people," Pete said.

Otto was back in two minutes. "His passport photograph is missing. But I can tell you that he never travels anywhere. This was his first time to New York. He's never been to Cannes, or Aspen, or Monaco, not even Davos for the World Economic Forum."

"No one at the party had ever seen him before," Pete said. "They did business with the man, but they didn't know what he looked like. Still doesn't give us a motive. A guy like him wouldn't be working for the Saudis."

"Because it wasn't Seif," McGarvey said. "I'm betting that the man in the dark suit had already killed him."

"And his girlfriend who flew in with him," Otto said.

"Flew in where?"

"LaGuardia on his private jet, then by helicopter to the East Thirty-fourth Street heliport."

"How'd they get to the building? Not by taxi. Talk to whoever met the chopper, and find out if someone picked them up. And call Callahan Holdings, see if they sent a car and driver, unless Seif arranged it himself," Mac said.

"I'm on it. What are you thinking?"

"I think that Callahan's people sent a limo for Seif and his girlfriend. I think our man has a source of good intel who passed him the name of the driver. I think he killed him and picked up Seif at the heliport himself, killed the banker and his girlfriend, stashed their bodies somewhere, and made his way to the party. He wouldn't have wanted to drive around town with the bodies, so he left them somewhere close."

"What else?"

"Who's running Callahan?"

"A woman by the name of Nancy Nebel. She's the CFO."

"I want to talk to her."

"Tonight?"

"As soon as possible, because I think the next building will happen soon."

"There're lots of skyscrapers in Manhattan," Pete said.

"A pencil tower."

"Fifteen so far, and more in the works."

"When does Callahan's next project open?" McGarvey said.

Again Otto was silent for a longish time. "I'm not sure, but the building has already received its certificate of occupancy."

"What's this one called?"

"Just 'the Tower,'" Otto said.

"That's number two."

"How do you know?"

"Symmetry. They're copycatting al-Qaeda's attack on the World Trade Towers. They want to take down two towers—just like bin Laden's plane hijackers did on nine-eleven."

FIFTEEN

Otto called back a half hour later. "NYPD is searching for a black Caddy Escalade. I talked with the FBO at the heliport who met Seif and his girlfriend at eight-thirty. Said the driver showed up fifteen minutes earlier."

"Did he give you a description?" McGarvey asked.

"Tall, fair-skinned, distantly pleasant. And he was wearing a dark suit."

"No reason for you to talk to the chopper pilot or Seif's air crew. Get someone from the Bureau over to the heliport with an Identikit, and when you come up with a likeness give it to one of your search engines. Look for near matches with every known contractor. This guy has to be connected. He's almost certainly taken other assignments, possibly for Saudi intel."

"But you don't think it'll be that easy."

"No, he's too good. But it's a start. Even the best make a mistake now and then."

"What's next?"

"What about Callahan's number two?"

"When I told her what direction we were taking she agreed to meet you anytime, anyplace. 'To get the bastard who did it,' she said."

"I want to talk to her tonight. See if she can come over to the Plaza. The Rose Club, it overlooks the lobby."

"I'll call her now," Otto said.

They were dressed a little informally for the hotel—Pete in a pair of slacks and a white silk blouse, and McGarvey in pressed jeans, an open-collar shirt, and a black blazer—but almost all the print and media journalists here were working and dressed down as well. A 9/11 tragedy had happened all over again; no one cared how they looked.

McGarvey checked his Walther, a round in the chamber, and reholstered it under his jacket at the small of his back.

"You're not expecting trouble here in the hotel, are you?" she asked.

"If this guy has good resources, which I have to believe he has, then he'll have already gotten a whiff that someone is looking down his track. He's killed Callahan and now maybe he wants to get close to Nancy Nebel to find out what precautions her company is taking."

"Okay, so let's say that he's going to try to bring down the other Callahan building. The Tower over by the UN. It would make sense if he was trying to copy nine-eleven."

"He'd definitely want to get to Nebel. But he'd also have to figure out how to get invited to the penthouse party, if he means to bring the thing down the same way as At-Eighth," McGarvey said.

Otto called just as they were leaving the room. "She'll be there in fifteen minutes."

"Do we know what she looks like?" McGarvey asked.

"I sent a couple of photos to your cell phone. Five-seven, slender, narrow face, short blond hair."

"We'll watch for her."

In the elevator McGarvey opened the photos Otto had sent. In one the woman was wearing a fairly low cut evening gown, a glass of champagne in her hand, and in the other she was dressed in riding clothes, astride a horse in what could have been Central Park.

"She's an attractive woman," Pete said, looking over his shoulder.

"Forty?"

"Well-put-together fifty," Pete said.

The Rose Club was an elegant space on the mezzanine level. Furnished with upholstered chairs and couches grouped around tables, Persian carpets on wood floors, floor-to-ceiling bookcases along the back wall, it opened to the ornate lobby below. A half dozen other people were having drinks.

McGarvey ordered a bottle of champagne and three glasses. From where he sat they had a direct line of sight to the main entrance.

When the Callahan CFO walked in, she looked nothing

like her photographs. She was dressed in baggy khakis and a red Lacoste polo shirt, her hair mostly covered by a baseball cap. Not bothering with the elevator, she'd taken the stairs.

McGarvey watched the entrance a bit longer, but she'd not been followed by anyone. He and Pete stood up.

Nebel spotted them and came over. "You must be McGarvey," she said. They shook hands and Mac introduced Pete, then they all sat down.

"Your man said that our building was sabotaged," she said. "We already knew it. What I want you to tell me is that you know who did it and that you're hot on his trail." Her face was a study in newly etched lines, and she looked as if she hadn't slept in months.

"We have some pretty good ideas," McGarvey told her. "Champagne?"

"No." She motioned for a waiter and when he came over she ordered a martini, one olive, straight up. Her manner was brusque, but her voice was soft with a slight hint of the South.

"But right now we have something to tell you that won't be pleasant."

She managed a wry smile. "Just about anything after what happened last night would be pleasant."

"The people behind this are planning on bringing down another building," McGarvey said.

"ISIS, just like nine-eleven. But so far no one has been able to tell me anything about how AtEighth was brought down. They're all so goddamned panicked, they can only tell me how it didn't happen."

"The tuned mass damper."

"Impossible."

"Its program was hacked."

"The system is hardened."

"Not from the inside," Pete said.

The woman's martini arrived, but before the waiter could leave, she drank it down and handed back the glass. "Another."

"Someone at the penthouse party?" Pete asked.

"No reason for any of them to do anything like that. No motive for suicide if that's what it was," Nebel replied.

"The man shot the security officers to death, then went up to the machinery room, where he hacked the computer, then went downstairs and walked away," McGarvey said.

Nebel sat back. "I didn't think the sort of people who're attracted to ISIS were all that bright." Something else occurred to her. "But why tell me this? Your man said that you needed help. With what?"

"Do you have a guest list for your new building's penthouse grand opening party?"

"I don't know if Mr. Jian will want to have a party," Nebel said, but then she stopped short. "Jesus Christ, they're coming after the Tower, is that what you're trying to tell me?"

"We think it's a possibility," McGarvey said.

"But why us?"

"We don't know."

"We'll delay the opening. Technical difficulties."

"He'll wait you out," Pete said.

The waiter came with the second martini, but Nebel didn't touch it. "I'll get the National Guard to surround the building. Check everyone's credentials."

"Won't do much for your clients' peace of mind," Pete said. "Not for that building, and probably not for your other projects."

Nebel looked away for a moment, overwhelmed with what had happened and what she was hearing. "George really wanted me to come to the party. Lots of heavy hitters who hadn't bought yet. Wanted me to work the room." She laughed a little. "Use my charm. I reminded him that I was a CFO, not a salesperson, and he let it go."

Pete wrote one of Otto's e-mail addresses on a cocktail napkin. "Send the guest list to this man. He's the one who contacted you this evening."

"I'm going back to my office now, we're contacting all of our AtEighth clients, as well as the families of the ones who lost their lives. I'll have the list sent immediately." She got to her feet. "Seven days," she said. "That's how long you have to catch this bastard. Keep me advised, please. But I won't hesitate to the shut the entire building down if you haven't put him behind bars. Or killed him."

"Can you get us invited to the party?"

"Maybe posing as service staff, if that's what you mean."

"We want to be there as guests, just like everyone else."

"Sorry, Mr. Director, but a lot of people know who you are—or were. And you're definitely not one of the players—they all know each other. The list is small."

"Then I'll have to offer them something they want," McGarvey said.

"They have everything they could possibly want," Nebel said. "Just about nothing in the entire world would be too expensive for most of them. But it's not so much the toys—the yachts and planes and houses and buildings—or the size of their bank accounts that means the most. Money is only how the game is scored. And it's the game that means everything."

When she was gone, McGarvey phoned Otto and told him everything.

"What's next, Kemo Sabe?"

"Pete and I are flying back to our apartments in Georgetown and packing for the film festival in Cannes, and then Monaco for the Grand Prix. The contractor impersonated a man who no one had ever met face-to-face, and he'll have to do something over-the-top to get himself invited to the grand opening. That'll be his mistake."

"He might expect you or someone like you to show up."

"Build us a legend and get us the same accommodations as he's likely to get," McGarvey said. "And we'll see if we can't put a little pressure on him. I want to get to Cannes by tomorrow afternoon or early evening."

SIXTEEN

Kamal, posing as the druglord Pablo Valdes but traveling to Cannes under the passport of Angel Castillo, had kept his British tone, but he wasn't going to take on the mannerisms of a high-born Brit. He wanted his audience to see nothing more than a Mexican who spoke with an affected accent.

He pulled up at the Hotel Barrière Le Majestic a little before noon, and handed his Bentley over to a valet, while a smartly dressed bellman took the three Louis Vuitton suitcases out of the trunk.

At the desk he handed his second Mexican passport and his American Express platinum card to the clerk, who smiled politely, but not as effusively as he had for the internationally famous movie stars who'd checked in over the past days. Kamal noticed it, but didn't let on.

"I'm terribly sorry, Mr. Castillo, but we were not able to give you either of the penthouses, but we have our lovely Double Prestige Terrace Sea View Suite, which I think you will find satisfactory."

Kamal smiled. "That will do nicely," he said, and he thought how easy it would be to reach across the counter and snap the condescending bastard's neck.

He signed for the suite, and the clerk handed over a key card. "Have a pleasant stay, Señor Castillo."

Kamal gave a five-hundred-euro bill to the bellman. "Take my bags up, but I'll do the unpacking myself."

He left the hotel and walked directly down to La Croisette, which was an elegant promenade just above the beach. He was dressed in hand-stitched loafers, no socks, white linen trousers, a soft yellow button-up short-sleeved silk shirt, and expensive sunglasses.

He wanted to blend in as quickly and smoothly as possible, and this was a place to see and be seen.

The day was warm, a slight breeze coming off the Med. The beach and promenade with its shops and restaurants were busy with well-dressed people, wealthy people who moved as if they belonged to this time and place, as was their due.

Near the end of the walk was Festival Hall, where most of the film events were held, and the summer casino. A dozen mega-yachts were moored in the harbor, but not as many as had been expected. Not many water-skiers were out and about, either, and only two sailboats farther offshore made their way north toward one of the many little coves that could be accessed only by water.

He got a sidewalk table at a small café, where just like in the busy hotel lobby and on the promenade, the general mood seemed subdued. It was too soon after the attack in New York for most people to be upbeat.

"There'll be parties, of course," Sa'ad had told him. "These people are too pragmatic. What is done is done, the past cannot be changed. Billionaires tend not to be overly sentimental."

"And what about al-Hamadi, will he be at the parties?"

"Almost certainly. The man is a complete boor. But everyone tolerates him because he is an errand boy. He brings them bits and pieces, sometimes interesting, and usually amusing."

"Like the court jester."

"Exactly."

"What time does he want to meet?"

"He'll leave a message. But because of his wife he has an overinflated opinion of himself. When he's out of the country he acts as if he actually is a royal, so he'll expect you to dance to his tune."

"Who does he think I am?"

"A Mexican druglord posing as a millionaire businessman from Mexico. He may think that he's a part of the family and his wife does provide him with a decent allowance so that he can play the part and not be too much of an embarrassment to her and her family, but he wants more. He thinks that by being your partner, of sorts, he will become wealthy on his own. He'll love the intrigue of your traveling under fake papers."

"He's greedy."

"In the end isn't that what drives us all?"

No, Kamal wanted to say. But the Saudi wouldn't understand.

The waiter came and Kamal ordered a pastis. As he waited, three young women came up from the beach in string bikinis, their small breasts bare, jackets over their shoulders, wearing large sunglasses and broad-brimmed straw hats. They crossed the promenade and headed north, totally unself-conscious. This was Eden, and it was their time.

As it was his time, Kamal thought.

His drink came and sitting one leg over the other he watched the flow of traffic; the younger passersby seemed unconcerned about anything outside of their immediate world, while the older understood what had happened again in New York. Stock markets around the world had taken deep dives, security at airports and border crossings had been beefed up, and in Turkey and Iraq attacks against ISIS positions had been seriously ramped up.

The word on the street and in the news media was that ISIS was mounting a copycat operation. Like al-Qaeda on 9/11, they wanted to bring down two buildings, and possibly attack the Pentagon again and the White House. Almost no one in the media was questioning that ISIS was not sophisticated enough for such attacks, especially after Paris and Brussels. AtEighth had come down and that was enough for just about everybody to believe that more was to come, and the only way to stop it was by taking out the terrorist organization's leadership.

Kamal phoned the front desk of the Majestic and asked if there were any messages for him. The operator connected him with the system, and al-Hamadi came on, his voice heavily accented. "Castillo, you're a man I want to speak to. This afternoon. Fouquet's. One o'clock."

It was nearly that time now. Punctuality, or lack thereof, was a tool.

He signed for his bill, then went up to his room, where he splashed some water on his face and watched the goings-on down on the beach for a full half hour before he left.

He got back downstairs at a quarter after one, and the maître d' brought him to a table by a window that looked out to the lobby. Alyan al-Hamadi, dressed in shorts and a bright Hawaiian shirt, sunglasses perched on top of his head, looked up. He was irritated.

"Señor Castillo, you're late," he said petulantly. He was a short man, somewhat overweight and soft-looking. His complexion was mottled and his Arabic nose was prominent, as were his lips and the bags under his eyes. He smelled of some overly sweet cologne.

"My name is actually Pablo Valdes," Kamal said, sitting down.

Al-Hamadi was drinking champagne. The bottle was sitting in an ice bucket at his side. It was no accident that the label side faced Kamal.

"A Krug Clos d'Ambonnay," Kamal said. "I certainly hope it's a ninety-six."

Al-Hamadi looked a little crestfallen. "You certainly know your wines."

"I'm in the business of money. Serious money for serious men."

"How serious?"

"Five billion for a start."

"Pesos?"

"Dollars."

A flute was sitting in front of Kamal. Al-Hamadi motioned for the waiter, who came and filled it.

Kamal took a sip. "Good," he said. "But of course you've had the ninety-six Boërl and Kroff brut. The Drappier family's contribution."

"Of course," al-Hamadi said. At nearly four thousand euros for a magnum, it was the second-most expensive champagne in the world.

Kamal had tasted it only once, two days ago in the penthouse of AtEighth. "I've yet to try Chapuy Goût de Diamants." At 150,000 euros it didn't matter how the outrageously priced wine tasted. Ordering a bottle was a statement all in itself.

Al-Hamadi started to say something, but Kamal, tired of the little game between them, waved him off.

"Only a fool would waste that kind of money on a simple bottle of wine when there are so many other ways to deal with the issue of money."

"Five billion dollars is serious money."

"Yes, it is, my friend. But I must caution you, that it

would only be the beginning. I have a stream of cash coming my way—actually, a monumental river of cash—that somehow has to be dealt with."

"For a profit," al-Hamadi said, almost licking his lips.

"Beyond your wildest imaginings," Kamal said. "But of course I wouldn't place the entire burden on you alone. I'll need to be introduced to the right people so that we can spread the responsibility. For each transaction that you help me arrange you, of course, would get a commission, one equal to my own. We would be partners."

"Explain to me how this works."

"It's actually quite simple. I send untraceable cash to you, and you return fifty cents on the dollar to me in solid securities bonds, real estate, even positions on the futures market, or derivative and credit default swap trades."

"Money laundering," al-Hamadi said. "We take the risk and you get legitimate returns."

"Yes, you take the risk as well as a share in the fifty percent profit."

SEVENTEEN

Kamal was to meet al-Hamadi again, this time in the lobby at five. The man had taken the bait as Kamal had thought he would, given Sa'ad's description of him as a fool who loved nothing more than being at the center of a good intrigue.

They would be taking a speedboat out to the 380-foot yacht *Glory,* the fourth largest moored in the harbor. Owned by Tom Hammond, a flash trader who made the bulk of his fortune on the dot-com and real estate booms, and then credit default swaps and in the derivatives market. His net worth was somewhere in the fifteen to twenty billion range. Definitely a player. A man who trusted his own judgment above all others and who was not afraid to take risks, sometimes even on legally questionable ventures.

A half hour before going down, a sharply dressed bellman delivered a registered mail envelope with the return address of Callahan Holdings. Actually it had probably been sent by Sa'ad through a remailing service in New York. It was a partial list of the people who were invited to the penthouse party in the Tower seven days from now if it wasn't called off.

Sitting down on the balcony that overlooked the sea, he went through the list of names and brief backgrounds of the six people Saudi intel had been able to come up with on such short notice.

He was amazed that Sa'ad had taken the enormous risk. If the operation were ever to be traced back to the Saudis, it could very well mean the end of them not only as a viable sovereign state but as a major supplier of oil.

The man had definitely gone out on a limb but for what reason Kamal couldn't fathom at the moment. Unless it was nothing more than ambition. Sa'ad was making his bid for a major coup inside the GIP. If he succeeded his rise would be written in gold; if not, he would face a firing squad.

Hammond's name was there, along with the name of Jian Chang the richest man in Hong Kong, with an estimated net worth of $35 billion. No other man owned more real estate there and in China, and it was he who had bought the penthouse in the Tower for $210 million.

The others on the list included Susan Patterson, Hollywood's most famous producer, with a net worth of around two billion.

Courtney Rich, aptly named as the CEO and largest shareholder of IBEX, the leading drug research corporation in the world, with laboratories in Switzerland and the U.S. and with sprawling factories in India and Brazil. Including stock, she was worth in excess of fifteen billion euros.

Viktor Shepelev, the Russian vodka king and close personal friend of Putin's, who had his fingers in just about every major corporation, and a number of government entities, including Roscomos, through which the real Valdes had arranged for the purchase of the satellite and its boost into orbit.

Kamal looked up for a moment. He wasn't sure if the Russian and Valdes had ever met, or even talked on the phone. From what he'd managed to get from the Mexican money launderer no such meetings were ever made. All of the money exchanges were done at arm's length, almost exclusively by computer, and by agents who arranged the trucking of money pallets marked *Médicins sans Frontières* from Los Angeles International or Chicago's O'Hare for flights to some African country or another. Once out of U.S. airspace the flights were diverted to Moscow.

One of the plus sides of the system was that most of the money from the street sales of the drugs ended up in Los Angeles or Chicago. Shipping it out of the U.S. disguised as medical supplies meant that the cash wouldn't have to be taken across the Mexican border.

But he couldn't be 100 percent certain if the two men had met, or had talked on the phone.

If they had, Kamal decided, Mr. Shepelev would have an unfortunate accident.

The most surprising name and précis on the list was that of Louis Martaan, the French Grand Prix driver who was currently ranked number one in the world. At only twenty-four he was the chief driver for Team Mercedes. No net worth was listed for him but he owned what had to be very expensive condos in Monaco, Paris, and Stuttgart.

Included in the package were photographs printed on nonglossy computer paper of each of the six. Both of the women were beautiful in a distant sort of way, in their late forties, early fifties. The men were ordinary, except for Martaan, who was so young and good-looking, with dark eyes, full lips, and a lean but muscular body, that he was almost pretty. Two of the photos showed him with gorgeous young women draped all over him.

Kamal memorized all the information, and studied the photographs so that he knew he would have no trouble recognizing any of them in person. He tore all the pages, along with the envelope, into little pieces and flushed them down the toilet.

The other issue that bothered him was why the party at Jian Chang's penthouse was apparently going ahead as planned and had not been canceled. These people were billionaires—not idiots. Unless they thought that they were bulletproof. It was something he meant to find out over the next few days.

At precisely five, Kamal, dressed in khaki slacks, an open-neck white shirt, and a British-cut navy-blue blazer, went down to the still-busy lobby. Al-Hamadi, dressed almost exactly the same, showed up five minutes later, a broad smile on his dark, pudgy face.

"It's a good thing, you and me," he said, beaming.

"What is?"

"Being partners. I did my homework this afternoon." He put a finger to the side of his nose. "I'm able to smell money, and the more of it there is, the sweeter the smell. You and I will be rich."

"I already am, and you have your wife's money," Kamal

said, though he didn't know why he was being irascible, except that the Saudi irritated him.

"It's not enough for either of us," al-Hamadi said, ignoring the insult. "But you're an interesting man. No clear photographs of you exist anywhere. I know some people in Riyadh, and they checked for me. They wanted to know what my connection was with you. I told them we were gambling friends. They told me to be careful."

"And what else?"

"That you were a common drug dealer, and said that you had the habit of killing people who got in your way."

"Did you believe them?"

Al-Hamadi laughed. "There was no reason for them to lie to me."

"The GIP?"

Al-Hamadi was startled for just a moment, but then he nodded. "But I can't imagine that you'll want to kill me as long as we're making money together. I'll arrange the introductions, starting this evening aboard the *Glory*, and you'll propose the deals."

"Fair enough," Kamal said. It was almost too easy, but Sa'ad had been a help. In the end it would be a blessing to the royal family if al-Hamadi were to cease to exist.

"It's only a couple of blocks, let's walk," al-Hamadi said. "I have a few questions."

It was the first intelligent thing the Saudi had said. "I may not have the answers yet. First I'll need to establish a relationship."

They left the hotel and walked down to the promenade. The beach was much less busy than it had been earlier this afternoon. A lot of the people had returned to their hotels to clean up and get dressed for the cocktail parties leading up to the VIP events at Festival Hall and aboard the yachts. Afterward there would be lavish dinner parties, and around midnight even more cocktail parties.

None of the players, nor the people around the fringes, got much rest during the circuit. But even at the art auctions and festivals and races and yacht runs and the Concours d'Elegance in Pebble Beach business got done. These people never neglected their fortunes.

"Tell me a little something. Give me just a fig, and maybe a little honey. I'm a Bedou in the middle of the desert. I have water which you need, what will you give me in return?" the Saudi asked.

"Who among your friends are involved with cash businesses?"

"I don't know. Maybe Susan Patterson, she owns a couple thousand screens in the U.S. Movie theaters. Ticket sales I imagine are mostly in cash."

"She produces movies."

"Yes."

"Then her next movie, according to box office receipts, will be a major hit, taking in double what was expected."

It took just a moment for al-Hamadi to get it. "You pump money into the theaters for tickets not sold. The owners will know."

"I never met a man who turned down free money."

"What's to stop Susan from keeping the money?"

"There wouldn't be another deal. She'll send us back fifty cents on the dollar in the form of stocks, maybe bonds, anything negotiable other than cash. I'll give my people thirty percent, which leaves twenty for you and I to split."

Al-Hamadi stopped. "Ten percent isn't much."

"Once we get started, we'll be laundering upwards of ten billion dollars."

"Fifty million a year for each of us. As I said, not much."

"Per month. Every month."

EIGHTEEN

It had been late by the time McGarvey and Pete reached Washington, got out to their apartments in Georgetown, and packed for Cannes. They stayed the night at Mac's place while the Gulfstream was being serviced.

Pete had trimmed Mac's hair and had used one of her hair tint kits to take away the gray. She'd picked up a pair of nearly zero-strength black-framed glasses from a drugstore for him, and she took a reasonably subdued red bow tie from her purse and gave it to him.

"Better learn how to tie it without looking in a mirror," she said. "It's your new signature."

During his brief career as head of the CIA he had limited his exposure in the media as much as possible, never granting an interview. But he'd understood her reasoning. Someone could remember his face. And just the slight changes Pete had worked would, with any luck, make him reasonably anonymous to just about anyone who didn't personally know him.

They were in the CIA Cadillac Escalade headed back to Joint Base Andrews before dawn.

Their Gulfstream was refueled and ready to fly when they arrived. A final walk-around had been done by a mechanic and a new crew had shown up, checked the weather over the Atlantic, and filed a flight direct to Orly in Paris, and from there down to Mandelieu, the airport five kilometers west of Cannes.

The food service crew had just finished stocking the galley when McGarvey and Pete handed over their bags, which were loaded aboard.

The captain, Fred Gratto, and his copilot, Jack Turner, were both ex-navy who worked as contract crew for the

CIA. Tom Toynbee was their flight attendant, who promised them a nice dinner and a couple of nearly flat beds.

Gratto gave Mac a second look. "Should be a smooth flight, Mr. Director," he said. "Nice tie, sir."

Otto showed up with a package of materials. "I'll need about five minutes before you spool up," he told the pilot. "In the meantime we'll need a little privacy."

The crew left the aircraft and walked across to the operations center.

"You're not coming with us, are you?" McGarvey asked.

"No, I have to get back to the Campus, my darlings are chewing on the origin of the ISIS claim to Al Jazeera, and the Saudi connection. Pete sent me your new look and I wanted to give you your ID along with a list of the players already invited to the Tower party. Plus the names of a few of the hangers-on, one of whom might be our man."

"Any of them stick out?" Pete asked.

"A Saudi by the name of Alyan al-Hamadi. He's married to one of the cousins in the royal family—a distant cousin. From what I've picked up he spends a lot of his wife's money in the casinos and over the past couple of years here and there on the circuit. Thing is he acts like a royal, and is a general pain in the ass to everyone in Riyadh, including his wife, who apparently is happy whenever he's gone."

"Does he work for the GIP?" McGarvey asked.

"It was my first thought, but I haven't been able to dig up anything solid yet. He comes across as harmless, sometimes running little errands."

"Too harmless?" Pete asked.

Otto shrugged. "Unless our suspect tries to come across as one of the players—which I think might be next to impossible—he'll want to somehow attach himself to the group."

"Why?" Pete asked.

"He'll need an invitation to the penthouse party in six days, same as us," McGarvey said. "But no one is going to invite him unless he can give them something they need.

"Okay," Pete said. "But it won't be some nickel-and-dime scheme. It'll have to involve something serious—something that these people will think is serious."

"I'll see what I can come up with. In the meantime I have the Identikit image that the Bureau's people worked out from the descriptions of the driver who picked up Khalid Seif and his girlfriend at the heliport."

Otto opened it on a small tablet and two identical images side by side came up on the screen. Both showed a good-looking man perhaps in his thirties, fair skin, a dark mustache, dark intelligent-looking eyes. He erased the mustache from one of the images with the swipe of a finger. Lightened the hair, adding a little gray at the sides. Placed a few wrinkles at the corners of his eyes and mouth.

The final image looked the same as the untouched one, but different enough so that a casual observer would never suspect they were the same man.

"The heliport FBO said that he was around six feet tall, lean build, and spoke with a British accent. Which might not mean a thing. But I'm checking all the British schools."

"Try Sandhurst," McGarvey said. "I'm betting that he had military training, maybe even combat somewhere."

"Why not British intelligence?" Pete asked.

"I think the man's been under fire. If we're right, he went up to the counterweight room and hacked its computer. But he kept his shit together long enough to take the service elevator to the ground floor, kill the woman, send the car back up to the twentieth floor for whatever reason, and then walk a block away and stop to watch the building come down."

"Nebel says the woman was Callahan's assistant. Melissa Saunders. Had her MBA from Harvard and she was an up-and-comer. Not married, parents in Minnesota somewhere."

"He's a Nero," Pete said. "Played around while Rome burned."

"Good enough name for now," McGarvey said. "What else?"

"I worked up your passports, driver's licenses, family photos, plus your presence on the Internet. You're Joseph Canton and Toni Borman, bloggers on a site called politicsnow.com. For the past two years you guys have been analyzing geopolitical events and passing along your take not only about what's going on, but what it all means. Where it's been, and why, and where it's going and why that should matter."

"You've done something like that for me before."

"Pakistan, and it opened the right doors at the right time. Our targets sat up and took notice. This time the players are starting to look your way. Tar sands in Canada and the Keystone pipeline are of great interest to Saudi and Russian oil. They're listening. The deal with Iran is having an effect on North Korea, and a number of players have financial interests in both countries." Otto pulled up the site on the tablet. "My darlings have come up with a few thousand posts. You might want to browse through them. But I've not taken any position that you haven't already taken." He grinned. "It's you, Kemo Sabe: truth, justice and the American way."

"There's more," Pete said.

"Yes. Louise says that I'm becoming an old hen. But I've always been that way."

Louise Horn was Otto's wife, and a perfect match for him. She was a genius who'd once worked for the National Security Agency and National Reconnaissance Office jointly with the CIA on satellite deployments, positions, and product. To this day she knew the proper procedures and programs that opened security to her so that she could use the spy birds on a very limited basis. It had sometimes been an asset for her husband and for Mac, and now Pete. If they wanted a real-time look down at just about anywhere on the planet in a wide range of frequencies—radio, microwave, infrared, and visible light—she could provide it.

By the same token she had become mother to them all. Calling Otto an old hen was like the pot calling the kettle black.

"You both are," McGarvey said.

"But she has a good point. These people—the players—control a significant portion of all the wealth on the planet. They can direct entire armies with a simple phone call. If they wanted you and Pete dead, it wouldn't be of any more importance than if they swatted a mosquito. A simple nod and so much shit would fall down upon the two of you that there would simply be no defense."

"It's always been that way," McGarvey said, and he got an almost overwhelming feeling that Pete was directly on the firing line. Again. It was his own doing, and there wasn't a thing he could do about it.

Pete was looking at him, an odd expression on her face. "A penny," she said.

"Maybe you should hang back and help Otto at this end. When the time comes we may have to move fast up in New York."

"If I stayed here you'd have to have a girlfriend in Cannes, otherwise you'd stand out. That's not going to happen."

Otto stood up and shrugged. "Watch yourselves, guys. These people don't play by the same rules as we do. F. Scott and Hemingway were right, after all."

An antique Chris Craft inboard speedboat, its wood hull and deck gleaming in the lowering sunlight, its Chevy 158-horsepower inboard gurgling, was waiting for them at the dock in the old port just past the Palais des Festivals. Already a crowd had gathered for the showing of a movie at the Palais.

"If you want tickets I'll get them for you," al-Hamadi said. "But the real money is anchored in the harbor."

Two sailors, in white ducks and traditional striped shirts, helped them aboard then released the lines and they headed out toward Hammond's motor yacht *Glory.* Three-hundred-eighty feet at the waterline, she had been built two years ago by the Italian shipyard Codecasa in Tuscany.

She wasn't the largest mega-yacht of the dozen in the harbor, but she was sleeker than most of them. Only the *M/Y Anna,* supposedly named after Tolstoy's heroine Anna Karenina, built for Viktor Shepelev, with its almost completely glass, crystal, and diamond interior, was more over-the-top.

Many of the players thought the Russian's yacht was so glitzy that it was tacky. A few had said publicly that the man had more cash than class. But none of them ever declined an invitation to party aboard, nor did anyone ever fail to invite him and his current mistress.

The term was *Neo kulturny,* "without culture." The old Soviet hardliners embraced it, but the new oligarchs were ashamed, and they tried to do whatever they could to rise above the distinction. Shepelev, for all his wealth, was no exception.

Which in Kamal's mind made the man ripe for picking.

Hammond's yacht was smaller but classy by comparison.

Several small runabouts were tied to the *Glory,* fenders protecting the hull of the larger vessel. As Kamal and al-Hamadi approached, a small Bell helicopter appeared from the west, probably St. Tropez, and set down on the ship's forward helipad. A man and a woman got off, and when they were clear the chopper headed back the way it had come.

"Tom is holding a private screening of one of the finalists," al-Hamadi shouted over the roar of the engine. "A movie that's not even been seen here yet, and afterwards a surprise."

"It's good that you were invited," Kamal shouted.

The Saudi dismissed the compliment with a gesture, and he looked away.

A minute later as they approached the aft boarding platform, the Chris Craft's engine dropped to an idle, and al-Hamadi looked back.

"I know what I am to these people, Mr. Valdes. An amusement, and not much more. But from time to time I bring them a tidbit, a fig and some honey, so I'm useful. I'm not a royal, but still I'm of some value."

"I didn't mean it the way it sounded," Kamal said, humoring the man.

"It doesn't matter. You're another tidbit I'm bringing them. But be very careful of these people. They have more power, and ruthlessness, than you can imagine."

"The men who run the drug cartels are not known for their kindness or understanding."

Tom Hammond, who was in his late forties, but who looked and acted like one of the California dot.com boy geniuses, which he had been, his short blond hair mussed, dressed in tattered jeans, a *WSJ* black T-shirt, and flip-flops, stood next to an attractive woman with high cheekbones and puffed-up lips, dressed in a black bikini, a white gauzy beach jacket, and diamond-encrusted Hermès sandals.

They were greeting their guests as they came aboard and inviting them into the salon or up one level to the main sundeck. Already there were at least two dozen people plus crew present, and more were arriving by speedboat and helicopter.

A four-piece jazz combo was playing somewhere above, and smartly dressed waiters and waitresses mingled with trays of champagne and hors d'oeuvres.

"The gentleman is Tom Hammond and his hostess is Susan Patterson, the Hollywood producer," al-Hamadi said as he and Kamal approached. "They've become a thing ever since she dumped her husband."

"Alyan, we heard that you were in town. Glad you could make it," Hammond said and they shook hands.

"Wouldn't miss one of your parties," al-Hamadi said. He gave Susan a brief peck on the cheek.

"Pablo Valdes," Kamal said, offering his hand. "Alyan and I are engaged in a little business, and he asked me to tag along. I hope you don't mind."

Hammond hesitated only a moment, but then he shook hands.

"But your accent is English," Susan said.

"Eton," Kamal said, offering his hand. "My father owned vineyards in Sonoma and thought that I should lose my California-Mexican accent and learn some manners while doing it. So he sent me off."

"It worked," she said, and held out her left hand.

Kamal lifted it and lightly brushed his lips across her empty ring finger.

Hammond gave him an odd look. "Welcome aboard, please enjoy yourself. Perhaps we can have a talk later. Alyan sometimes comes up with interesting possibilities, one of the many reasons we enjoy his company."

"At your service," Kamal said to both of them.

He and al-Hamadi got a glass of champagne and went up to the sun-deck, where they moved to the aft rail that looked down on the boarding platform. Fifteen or twenty people were gathered, some standing, others seated at tables or on lounge chairs. They were drinking and talking, but their laughter seemed subdued and even artificial to Kamal, because of the downing of AtEighth, he supposed.

"What was that all about?" al-Hamadi asked. He was nervous.

"Weren't Tom Hammond and the woman the sort of people you wanted me to meet?"

"I mean with Susan. He caught what you were doing."

"It was her game."

"Hammond is dangerous."

"So is she, and I'm guessing that she's already bored with him and wants to play another game."

"With you?"

"With us. You've opened the deal, and in the next twenty-four hours or so I'm going to close it. She and her movie revenues will be our first, and Tom Hammond will be our second."

Al-Hamadi gave him an odd look. "With care, or you could jeopardize everything I've worked for."

"And what exactly is that?"

"Independence."

TWENTY

It was seven in the evening in Paris, when the Gulfstream touched down at Orly airport. Pete had only picked at her dinner and was still asleep, but McGarvey had stayed awake most of the way, and Otto had stuck with it at Langley.

Mac's phone buzzed. It was Otto.

"You've gotta be close to Paris."

"Taxiing over to the private terminal for refueling."

"We caught a couple of breaks. I sent some stuff to Hanks and he's sending someone to meet you." Bob Hanks was the CIA's Paris chief of station.

Toynbee brought Mac a Bloody Mary.

"NYPD found two bodies in a Caddy Escalade—the same one the heliport FBO said picked up Seif and his girlfriend. They'd both been shot twice, one shot apparently postmortem in the side of the head."

"Where was it parked?"

"In a private garage in the Meatpacking District, purchased on February tenth by an LLC under the name Attenborough. A passport under the name Roger Attenborough, heavyset guy with a square face, was found on the front seat, along with a black necktie. The car was dusted, but so far the Bureau's come up with nothing."

"I'd be surprised if they find anything. Our Nero is almost certainly on no one's records anywhere. And if he's ever been on file he's made the effort to change or erase his vitals."

"Seif's passport, wallet, and cell phone were missing. The GPS location has it somewhere in the rubble of AtEighth. He wants us to believe Seif's body is still inside."

"He bought a little extra time. What else?"

"Attenborough checked into a suite at the Grand Hyatt two days before the tower came down, and checked out the morning after. He listed his home in London with a number near Knightsbridge and paid for it with a platinum Amex. But it turns out it's an accommodations address, nothing more. Attenborough was a one-off cover ID."

"Did we get a description from any of the hotel staff?"

"The cops are checking, but a lot of businessmen come and go from there so it's possible he didn't stand out in anyone's mind. But the Bureau's shared their Identikit likeness with the NYPD, and they've printed copies. With any luck they'll come up with a refinement or two. Whatever we get I'll send to you on your phone."

"How about al-Hamadi?"

"That's another break. He's at Cannes, has a suite in the Majestic, but he's leaving tomorrow or the day after."

"Monaco?" McGarvey said.

"Yes. But you might not have enough time at Cannes to run him down. Monaco might be better. He's booked for three days at the Hermitage."

"Can you get us rooms at both hotels?"

"Already done. I would have booked you suites, but for now you're just online journalists, not billionaires."

"How about after Monaco?"

"My guess is that most of them will show up for the art fair in Basel in a couple of weeks, and then Aspen starting the twenty-fifth of June."

"Is the grand-opening penthouse party at the Tower still on?"

"Still the twenty-ninth. Nebel wanted to give us more time, and evidently Jian wasn't in any hurry to come to New York."

"Children's Day at the UN is still set for the same day."

"That's right, and the General Assembly building would be right in the path if the Tower came down," Otto said. "Maybe we can have Nebel push it back another week."

"Nero will just adjust his timetable. If need be we'll evacuate the building the day before if we haven't caught the bastard by then," McGarvey said. His lack of sleep was beginning to catch up with him.

Almost as if he were a mind reader Toynbee came from the galley with a cup of coffee and exchanged it for McGarvey's untouched Bloody Mary.

They reached the VIP terminal and the captain shut down the engines. Toynbee opened the door.

Bob Hanks himself was waiting outside the main entrance along with two other men, one of them in a customs officer's uniform. McGarvey didn't recognize the man in civilian clothes who was chatting with Hanks, except he was almost certainly a French cop or more likely an intelligence officer.

"We just pulled up. Hanks is here, along with a customs officer and another guy in civilian clothes. I'm guessing DGSI, and he's carrying a shoulder bag."

"Major Pierre Galan. You don't know him, but he knows about you."

"How?"

"My guess would be that Marty gave him a courtesy call."

"Covering his own ass," McGarvey said. It was not totally unexpected. He and Bambridge had a history, most of it not outstanding.

"He'll want you to turn over your real passport, for which he'll give you a one-week card to remain in France, same for Pete. And he'll want both of you to surrender your weapons. Bob has been briefed and he's carrying a subcompact Glock for Pete and a Walther for you. Suppressors and three magazines of ammunition for each. But if you're caught carrying there's nothing he could do. It'd have to be bumped up to the ambassador, who'd pass the buck to State. Nothing we couldn't handle, but it could slow you down."

"The hatch is open and the customs officer and Galan are coming over," McGarvey said.

Pete was awake. "I heard most of that," she said.

"DGSI. They'll want our real passports and weapons. We're here on vacation."

"Honeymoon," she said.

Toynbee stepped aside to let the two men through the hatch. They both did a double take when they saw McGarvey.

"Monsieur McGarvey, I presume, and Mademoiselle Boylan, I am Pierre Galan. You are not welcome in France," he said. He was a narrow-shouldered man with a Gallic nose and sharp, angular features. He was not smiling. "Especially you, sir, in disguise."

"Are we being kicked out?"

"You will have one week, no longer. Are either of you armed?"

"We both are," McGarvey said.

Galan frowned. "Why are you carrying weapons into France?"

"You know my background, so you know I usually don't travel unarmed, and you'll know why."

"I want your weapons and passports. In exchange you will be issued receipts which you can reclaim once you leave France."

McGarvey took his Walther from the seat pocket in front of him, along with the two spare magazines of ammunition and the silencer, which he handed over to the officer, then dug his real passport from his shoulder bag and handed it over too. Pete did the same.

The customs officer was impressed.

"Who were you planning on going to war with?" Galan asked.

"Nothing more than defense," McGarvey said.

"Suppressors are illegal in France."

"And in the U.S."

Galan stuffed the things in his shoulder bag and the customs officer handed Mac and Pete their temporary visa cards.

"Stay out of trouble," Galan said. He gave them a hard look and he and the customs officer left.

Galan said something to Hanks, then went into the terminal. When he was gone the Paris COS turned to Mac and Pete.

"Mr. Director," he said. "Miss Boylan." He was an ordinary-looking man in a business suit, his tie loose. He could have been a banker or an estate manager somewhere. He was a good if lackluster rep in the Company. Steady.

"Otto Rencke called and said that you'd agreed to help," McGarvey said.

"Just an equipment run, nothing else," Hanks said. He took two pistols out of his trouser pockets, and suppressors and magazines out of his coat pockets. "I assume you have good papers."

"Company generated."

"Are you staying in Paris?"

"No. As soon as we're buttoned up we'll be gone."

Hanks hesitated for just a moment, but then he shook their hands. "Good luck, guys, and I mean it. Especially if you're here because of what the bastards did to us again in New York."

TWENTY-ONE

By nine all the guests had arrived aboard the *Glory*. Besides the drinks and hors d'oeuvres, a buffet supper had been laid out in the main salon. Gradually most of the players and their girlfriends had wandered upstairs to the theater to see the movie that was expected to win the top prize for best drama. This was its first showing in Cannes; everyone else would have to wait until tomorrow.

Others had dispersed throughout the ship, some in pairs at the railings, talking business. A few couples had found empty staterooms where they could have a little privacy and still watch the movie, which was being piped to flat-screen monitors just about everywhere.

Al-Hamadi was somewhere with Hammond, distracting the man for an hour or so at Kamal's request.

Susan Patterson, drinking a glass of champagne, was leaning against the starboard rail just forward of the main salon, watching the traffic along the Esplanade Georges Pompidou, and the lights of the city and the villas in the hills above.

"Looks like a fabulous jewel box," Kamal said coming up behind her.

"Yes, it does, rather," she said without turning around. Her accent was now British.

Kamal had brought a bottle of Krug, and he filled her glass and refilled his, then set the bottle on the deck. "I didn't know that you were British," he said.

She looked at him as if she were trying to memorize his face. "I've been to London a few times, did some work at Pinewood Studios," she said, smiling. "But I was a pretty good actor once upon a time." Now she spoke with an Arab accent.

Kamal was startled but he didn't let it show. "I'm sorry that I've never seen one of your pictures."

She brushed it aside. "You wouldn't have," she said, switching back to American Midwest. "They were mostly what we call chick flicks. Sappy love stories set in Victorian England, a couple in ancient Persia. The boy has long beautiful hair, his shirt open, and the damsel is always in need of rescuing. Silly, actually."

"But I think you liked the work."

"I loved it, but all that came to a halt once I started to make serious money. And the secret of that is to start with fifty or a hundred million, and the first billion isn't far behind." She looked again toward the shore. "But having that kind of money is a responsibility all of its own. Ask Bill and Melinda or the people here tonight."

"I have a proposition for you," Kamal said. He didn't think that beating around the bush with this woman was the right course. She was too smart, and probably streetwise.

"Every player aboard knows that you're here with a deal that they can't resist. Alyan was practically licking his lips from the moment he showed up with you."

"Perhaps it was a mistake, me coming here."

"Are you kidding? What does a billionaire want more than anything?"

"Money."

"Yes," she said. "Wait. Valdes. Mexico. Not a drug runner, but I think you're involved."

He let her work it out.

"My guess is you launder their money. It's a big problem for them. Sales in the States are brisk, and getting bigger. But it's cash only. A few hundred million a year? A lot of it through banks in London, which is why your accent."

"A few hundred billion, and just now London has come under a lot of scrutiny. But I did go to Eton as a kid."

"Tom might agree to take a slice, he has some pretty good bank connections. And of course Viktor owns several banks in Vladivostok, Novosibirsk, Krasnoyarsk, and other dreadful places like those. So will Jian Chang, who's got the morals and scruples of a hungry lion standing over a baby gazelle."

"Shepelev and Jian aren't here tonight."

"No, but they'll probably be at Basel and almost certainly Aspen. And Jian of course will be in New York for his party."

"I thought the party had been called off."

"He's about the richest person in our little group of misfits. When he calls, no one refuses."

"Misfits?"

She laughed. "Spoiled children. But we work hard."

"I never thought you didn't," Kamal said.

Susan laughed again, but this time with a bit of irony. She was a billionaire, but just on the fringe of this group. In some ways she was considered fluff by her male counterparts. It had been the same in the movie industry. She had a nice body, a photographable face, and she knew how to speak her lines. But she also knew how to make a deal.

"Okay," she said. "Let's talk. I'm assuming it'll have to do with ticket sales. Most of the theater managers have been fucking me for years anyway, so they're not above a little larceny."

Kamal started to answer her, but she put a finger to his lips. "Bring the bottle," she said, and she turned and inside the salon took the stairs down.

She and Hammond shared the owner's palatial suite aft, but she used a key card to get into an adjoining suite. "Tom has his private domain whenever he needs it, and when I'm aboard this is mine."

The much larger than king-size circular bed was in the center of the space, a white silk headboard at one end. A huge bathroom with a Jacuzzi and all the other amenities, done in gold, was forward, and a large walk-in closet aft.

She put her glass down on a sideboard, then took off her beach jacket and bikini. Her breasts were small and taunt, her belly flat, and the hair from her pudenda had been removed. She'd had very good plastic surgery, because although she was pushing fifty she had the body of a twenty-five-year-old.

Kamal undressed and joined her, kissing her neck, and her nipples, and finally her inner thighs. He took his time with her. Twice she cried out, her back arched, her head thrown back, her eyes closed.

"Now," she said, her face flushed.

Kamal entered her, slowly, lingered for a long moment, her body thrumming beneath him, and then began to make love very slowly. He thought about the moment he saw the life going out of one of his victim's eyes. Sometimes agony, but almost always surprise when they realized it was over, and there was nothing they could do about it.

It was the same now. Her eyes were open, looking into his, her lips parted.

He was insane, but at moments like this he reveled in the fact.

She wanted him to come to orgasm first, he could see it on her face, feel it. He smiled, and slowed his pace, until at some point she finally closed her eyes again, arched her back and let go, a tremor racing through her body.

"Christ," she said after a long time.

He moved away from her, got out of the bed, and filled their glasses with the still-cool wine, then propped his pillow against the headboard, the same as she had, and got back into bed.

They sipped their wine for a while in silence, until she looked at him.

"Did you ever meet Nenet Akila?" she asked.

She was the Egyptian movie studio owner he'd met in the AtEighth penthouse. He was startled, but he did not let it show. "No."

"She would have loved you."

"Would have?"

"She's dead now. In the pencil tower that went down. We were friends."

"I'm sorry."

"Yeah, me too," Susan said. She finished her champagne and held out her glass. "More, please, and then we'll talk about how you plan to make me even richer than I already am."

"With pleasure," Kamal said. "More than you can possibly imagine."

They both laughed.

TWENTY-TWO

McGarvey came awake the instant Pete touched his cheek. "Al-Hamadi is waiting for us downstairs," she said.

The room in the very busy Majestic that Otto had somehow managed to get for them was on the fourth floor, and had a surprisingly decent view of the harbor. They'd left a message with al-Hamadi that a friend of the Saudi's wife had asked that a confidential meeting be arranged as soon as possible. No one was to be told because a great deal of money could be on the line.

They'd had dinner in the room, and by eleven McGarvey had taken a quick shower and laid down on the bed to get a few hours of sleep. It was eleven-thirty now.

"How'd he sound?" McGarvey asked, sitting up.

"Pissed off. Wanted to know who the friend was, and what it had to do with his wife."

McGarvey went into the bathroom and splashed some cold water on his face. "Did he mention anything about money?"

"No, but he called us. And when I told him that we were political bloggers from the States he didn't hang up."

McGarvey looked at Pete's image in the mirror. "I think that our man has a dirty little secret that he might be desperate to keep from his wife and her family. Maybe he wants his independence from her. Maybe he wants to be his own man. With his own money."

Pete was grinning. "I think we owe Otto a thank-you."

"For a lot of things."

"How do you want to play this?"

"Where does he want to meet?"

"The Gallery bar downstairs."

"At Fouquet's," McGarvey said. "I've been there once. I want you to go down first and get a seat at the bar if you can. Or someplace where you can see the entrance. I want to know if anyone's watching al-Hamadi and especially if anyone reacts when I show up."

"Do you want me to take the Glock?"

"From this point on neither of us is going anywhere unarmed." McGarvey turned around. "Watch yourself, Pete. Especially your six. If Nero is here it's because he wants an invitation to the party at the Tower. I expect he's very good, and that means he'll be super-aware of his surroundings."

"Do you think that he might have used al-Hamadi as a conduit?"

"The Saudi does seem to be the weak link. Maybe too weak. Step lightly."

Pete kissed him on the cheek, got her purse, and left the room. She was dressed in fashion jeans, boat shoes, and a peasant blouse. Because of the way she looked she would be a distraction for just about any straight man in the room.

McGarvey waited five minutes before holstering the Walther under his blazer at the small of his back. He stuffed a smartphone that Otto had transformed into an encrypted satphone, without changing its outward appearance, into his jacket pocket and took the elevator down.

The hotel was still very busy, traffic heavy on the Croisette. Parties would be going on all across the city until dawn. Tomorrow was the last day of the film festival, after which it was off to Monaco for the race on Sunday.

The Gallery was filled almost to capacity. Pete was sitting at the far end of the bar, where she had a view of the entire room. A barman was just serving her a glass of red wine, and when McGarvey caught her eye she nodded slightly, then looked away. So far as she could tell nothing was wrong here for the moment.

McGarvey recognized the Saudi from the photos Otto had come up with. He was seated in an armchair facing an empty chair across a small table. McGarvey walked over.

"Mr. al-Hamadi, thank you for agreeing to talk to me on such short notice. I'm Joe Canton, I run a blog called politicsnow. Maybe you've heard of it?"

"No," al-Hamadi said crossly. "Sit down."

McGarvey took the chair.

"Now what the fuck is this all about? A friend of my wife's sending you here with a message? What message? And who the hell are you?"

"Joe Canton."

"Fuck you. Who sent you?"

"It's about money, a great deal of it, and I was told by someone who's connected in a very loose way with the royal family that you would be the man for me to talk to." McGarvey shrugged. "Of course if you're not interested . . ."

"Wait. What's this have to do with my wife?"

"Nothing, actually. I told a little lie, it was the only way I thought that you would agree to talk to me."

"She's not involved?"

"Not in any way except that her family's position makes you an important man in certain circles."

Al-Hamadi was still suspicious, but "money" would be the magic word, according to Otto.

A waiter came and McGarvey ordered a Heineken.

"I'll give you five minutes," al-Hamadi said. He was drinking champagne, a bottle of Krug in the ice bucket.

"Bitcoins."

Al-Hamadi poured a glass of champagne. "I know nothing about them."

"It's a volatile market, but with the right moves it can be cornered."

"Small-time, I'm guessing."

"Potentially billions U.S."

A flicker of interest came into al-Hamadi's eyes, but he shook his head. "Sounds like a scam."

"A bitcoin is a virtual unit of money. But it exists only on the Internet. The customer bargains for a price per coin from a holder, who can be anyone. Once a deal is made, the buyer makes a bank transfer to the seller, who sends the bitcoins online. The new owner stores them in what's called a virtual wallet."

"What good are they? I mean, can you walk into a Mercedes dealer and buy a Maybach with them?"

"At some dealerships, yes. But the customer could sell the coins and use the cash."

"I'm still not sure that I'm following you."

"All these wallets filled with anything from a few thousand dollars' worth of bitcoins to, in a few cases, millions are not regulated by any government anywhere. Almost like flash trading or credit default swaps on the market. Regulators can't get a real handle on them. Peer-to-peer transactions for goods, services, or the transfers of cash."

"I'm still listening."

"The market values have been all over the place. In 2011 one unit sold for thirty cents U.S., jumping within days to thirty-two dollars, before settling on two. A couple of years later they topped out at two hundred fifty plus, before dropping back to fifty. But they've been as high as twelve hundred U.S."

"No way of predicting something like that."

"Doesn't have to be predicted, just manipulated."

Al-Hamadi emptied his glass and poured another just as McGarvey's beer came.

"So far as I understand we're talking mostly small change."

"At this last issue, what they call halving, there are twenty-plus million bitcoins circulating. The word on the street is that number is set to double in six months, and double again six months later."

Al-Hamadi said nothing, but it was obvious he was trying to get a grip on what he was being told.

"At a thousand per unit, we're talking about twenty-one billion for now. Double that in six months and doubling again in another six months begins to get very serious. At that point I have to believe, as do my subscribers, that governments will have to step in."

"If you're proposing that I invest in something like that, the answer would have to be no."

"I'm suggesting that we corner the market."

"The Hunt brothers tried it with silver and lost their shirts."

"You're not listening. If we can get a flash trader involved, the bitcoin unit price could be manipulated down to a couple of hundred dollars, maybe less. Once that happens we could buy a very long position, and when the unit value went back up to the thousand-or-more range, we'd dump the entire lot."

"The profit would be staggering," al-Hamadi said.

"I came to you because you have the connections."

Al-Hamadi came to his senses. "And you?" he asked.

"I have the method and the audience."

TWENTY-THREE

It was one in the morning when the phone in Susan Patterson's cabin chimed. She had gotten dressed in jeans and a T-shirt after she and Kamal had made love for the second time. He had a foot in the door. It was a first step.

The phone chimed again. "Are you going to answer it?" he asked.

"It's Tom," she said, sudden color coming into her face. "Hello," she said from across the room, and the call was answered on speakerphone.

"Whenever you two are ready, come to my office."

"You son of a bitch. You were watching."

"You knew that I would be, and you gave a wonderful performance."

"Who's left aboard?"

"A couple hangers-on. No one really important, at least not for the moment."

Susan looked at Kamal.

He nodded. "I wanted your attention, sir."

"You have it," Hammond said.

"Hang up," Susan said and the connection was broken. She finished her glass of champagne. "He's jealous," she said.

"Of us?"

She laughed. "Just the money part. He's miffed that you didn't come to him first."

They went to Hammond's large office, all decked out in wood paneling and monogrammed carpeting, but no paintings or any other objects d'art. Three walls were adorned with large flat-screen monitors, a couple of which showed the various stock markets and trading floors around the world on split screens. Another showed worldwide weather, another translated and summarized headline stories from dozens of newspapers and television networks in all the important countries, and still another showed what apparently were search engine feeds from various intelligence agencies. One on a back wall showed Susan's stateroom.

Several fuzzy photographs of Pablo Valdes were displayed on one of the screens.

"Not very good likenesses," Kamal said. "But then I've never been fond of publicity."

Hammond's large desk was in the middle of the room. Along one wall was a grouping of a couple of easy chairs, a white leather couch, and a glass-topped stainless-steel coffee table. Everything in the room was stark, ultra-modern Italian and at the cutting edge of high-tech.

They sat down across from each other. Hammond offered them coffee, which they declined.

"Business, then," he said. "You're apparently dealing with a much larger problem than I suspected existed. Of course I've never been involved in the business, so my knowledge has been limited. Until now. You mentioned a hundred billion per year?"

"Several hundred billion per year and just now growing at a nearly unmanageable rate, primarily from the U.S."

"Are you saying that you're the only money launderer?"

"There are others, but on much smaller scales."

"Money laundering," Hammond said, and several headlines came up on one of the screens. One listed a large column of reports from the UN Office on Drugs and Crime, and another, datelined London, named that city as the main center of money laundering in the world.

"A number of banks there are coming under fire," Kamal said.

"So you came to us," Hammond said. "What did you offer Alyan?"

"A finder's fee."

"What exactly have you offered Susan, by way of profit for the risk she'd be taking? You were whispering in her ear so I didn't catch that part. Did you know you were being watched?"

"I thought that it was a possibility," Kamal said. "Fifty cents on the dollar. For every one billion I'd send her in U.S. dollars—mostly ones, five, tens, and twenties—she would return five hundred million in negotiable bonds and other securities that she would purchase from her own money."

"You're taking a big risk, manipulating ticket sales," Hammond said to her.

"No different than some of the other financial dealings in show biz," she said. "You and I talked about spreading the costs of promotion on any one movie across to as many low performers to cut the net profits for the major hits. Padding movie tickets sales—which still is mostly a cash business—will be relatively easy."

"Credit card ticket sales are increasing."

"We'll offer discounts for cash."

Hammond turned back to Kamal. "What do you do with your five hundred million profit?"

"Thirty goes to the cartels and twenty comes to me."

"If I bought in, sixty would stay with me. You could still give your partners their thirty, and your cut would be reduced to ten. Still not a bad day's work, especially as it's us who would shoulder most of the risk."

"No," Kamal said. He got up and turned to Susan. "Are we still on?"

"Yes."

"Mr. Hammond, thank you for your hospitality this evening. This is a lovely ship."

Hammond waited until Kamal had reached the door. "How will I receive the cash?"

Kamal hesitated a second before he turned back.

"Pallets of cash containing anything you list them to contain will be flown anywhere you want them to be flown. Or, containers filled with whatever you say they are filled with will be shipped anywhere you want them to be shipped. How you deal with the cash will be up to you. But I assume that you have a sufficient number of offshore shell companies that could handle the influx. Keep it off the regulators' radars. Right now I'm told that there are opportunities with the Greek government for the right player."

"Your payment?"

"Immediately on receipt. Derivatives, credit default swaps, negotiable bonds."

"Real estate?"

Al-Hamadi had gotten him in the front door with Susan and with Hammond. "I'd like to talk to Mr. Shepelev about his banks, and with Jian Chang about hotels in Hong Kong."

Hammond pursed his lips. "You aim high."

"I think diversity is for the best, don't you?"

Hammond let it ride for a beat. "Neither of them are here now nor will they be in Monaco. But Viktor will almost certainly be in Basel, and Chang will be in Aspen, and of course we'll all be in New York."

"New York?" Kamal asked.

"Chang's bought a condo in one of the new pencil towers. He'll be throwing a party."

"Yes, Susan mentioned that. But I would have thought that after what just happened he would have canceled. They say it was an act of terrorism. Another nine-eleven."

"Homeland Security and the Bureau are all over it. I'm told that the CIA is on it too."

"You have a good source of information."

"Yes, I do. So unless you're the easily frightened type, you can show up in New York and I'll introduce you around. For diversity's sake, as you say."

"I'd like that very much."

Susan got up. "I'll walk you out," she told him.

"Are you going up to Monaco for the race?" Hammond asked.

"I wouldn't miss it," Kamal said.

"Where are you staying?"

"The Hermitage, of course. Is there anyplace else?"

Hammond laughed. "My yacht. But then to make money you have to spend it."

Kamal walked out with Susan. They paused for moment in the passageway.

"Where are you staying tonight?" she asked him.

"The Majestic."

"Mind if I tag along? I could drive up to Monaco with you."

"As long as we don't only talk business," Kamal said.

Susan laughed lightly. "Well, maybe just a little," she said. She went back to Hammond's office. "Be a sweetheart, Tom, and have my things sent over to the Majestic."

TWENTY-FOUR

McGarvey stood at the open window looking across the Croisette at the anchor lights of the yachts in the bay. It was midnight and still traffic was busy. He'd overheard someone in the bar say that for the film festival week no one in Cannes went to bed except for sex.

He was bone weary, yet he couldn't sleep, even after he and Pete had made love after their meeting with al-Hamadi. He was too keyed up.

Pete came up behind him. "Penny," she said.

"We're missing something," he said. He'd been chewing on the anomaly ever since Otto had phoned with the news that the bodies of Khalid Seif and his girlfriend had been found in the garage.

The UAE offshore banker had been a close enough physical match to the Identikit images they had of the man who'd killed him that the assassin had been able to infiltrate the penthouse party. That added to the fact that Seif apparently had never met face-to-face with any of his clients, and photographs of him were practically nonexistent, made Nero's entry easy enough.

He explained all of that to Pete.

"Then what's the problem?"

"If he wants to bring down the Tower near the UN the same way he did AtEighth, he'll have to be invited to Jian's penthouse party. But masquerading as who? Seif is dead."

"Nero is here for just about the same reason we are: to get enough attention that we're invited to the Tower party. It'd make us a part of the group. On the fringe, but still allowed to tag along because we're of some use."

"And he'll have to be doing the same thing."

"He's either on one of the yachts or in this hotel," Pete said. "And he'll probably be at Monaco tomorrow. But we might have another problem."

"What's that?"

"Al-Hamadi. I don't trust him, and I don't think he is who he says he is."

McGarvey had used his phone to record his conversation with the Saudi, and Pete had played it back twice. But she hadn't voiced her doubts until now.

"Did you pick up something?"

"I don't know, just a hunch. But I'd bet just about anything that he's a fake."

"Maybe he works for Saudi intelligence to keep an eye on the princes who hang out with the players."

"Could be that simple."

"Then why did he bother to listen to me?"

"Exactly."

McGarvey got his phone and called Otto's universal number, which would automatically find him wherever he was. In this case it was at home in McLean.

Louise answered. "Hi, Mac, how's it going?"

"We got al-Hamadi's interest. He's going to take your bitcoin proposal to Hammond."

"How about that. By all accounts he's one of the greediest bastards in that rat pack."

"They're not all that bad."

"No, but the rotten ones are lowlifes. Lots of cash but mostly no class other than glitz."

McGarvey hadn't heard her this worked up since Katy and Liz had been murdered. "Where's this coming from, Louise?"

"The collateral damage on the ground when the tower fell. They weren't a part of it, just like the people in the towers on nine-eleven. When's it going to end, Kirk?"

"I don't know. Maybe never. All we can do is deal with the here and now."

"How's Pete holding up?"

"I'm glad she's here," McGarvey said.

"Good," Louise said. "Otto was just tucking in Audie. Here he is."

Otto came on. "She's just fine," he said before McGarvey could ask about his granddaughter. "What's up?"

"We made contact with al-Hamadi, who's taking the bitcoin idea to Hammond. And Nero is here, I'm sure of it."

"One hundred percent sure?"

"No. But I'm betting that he'll be at Monaco tomorrow, then Basel and probably Aspen."

"It'd have to mean he's made contact as well. He'd have to be one of them, or offering them a service they can't refuse. Just like you."

"The point is he'll be staying at the best hotels. Almost certainly here at the Majestic and then the Hermitage at Monaco. Probably Les Trois Rois in Basel and the St. Regis in Aspen. But he has a problem."

"Yeah, once he's in with the players he'll have to stick with the same name he's using right now. I'm on it."

"While you're at it, I want you to take a closer look at al-Hamadi. We think that he's too good to be true."

"Saudi intel?"

"It's possible."

"Sit tight, this might take a half hour or so," Otto said and he rang off.

McGarvey stared at the yachts for a long moment or two. He was still missing something.

"I'm going for a walk," he said. "You can come along if you want."

"Wouldn't miss it for the world."

They dressed in jeans and polo shirts, and when they went downstairs the lobby was still fairly busy with people drinking champagne and talking animatedly. Pete recognized several American movie stars, one of them a gorgeous young blonde, nearly naked, draped all over a man who had to be in his fifties with a potbelly and a terrible hairpiece.

"Beauty and the beast," Pete said.

"That's what they used to call you and your interrogator partners."

Pete laughed. "That was different. Anyway, they don't call me that anymore."

"Why's that?"

"They know that you'd shoot them."

McGarvey had heard the same thing, though he'd never mentioned it to her. "The former director's girlfriend?"

"Something like that."

They left the hotel and walked down to the Croisette and farther down to the beach and the water's edge. The sea was calm this morning, only small wavelets washing onto the mostly pebble *plage*. The sky was clear and filled with stars that overpowered even the city lights, and other couples were walking arm in arm.

"Nero has to know that New York in on high alert, so if he's going to bring down another tower he'll have some plan that we haven't guessed yet," McGarvey said, thinking aloud.

"Maybe it's misdirection," Pete said. "Maybe while we're surrounding the Tower he knocks another one down. There're fourteen others in Manhattan. Unless he's specifically after Callahan."

"Otto's found no connection."

"Then why AtEighth?"

"I've been asking myself the same question. And why al-Hamadi?"

"You're still looking at a Saudi involvement."

"The same as nine-eleven."

"But there's no motivation."

"ISIS."

"We've already taken out some of their leadership," Pete said. They stopped and she turned to him. "Look, the Saudi coalition has already made significant hits on ISIS. Taking out AtEighth, and if Nero actually takes down the Tower—which at this point looks unlikely—what would it gain them?"

"I'm not sure," McGarvey said, and Otto called.

"Fifty-seven matches between the Majestic and the Hermitage in Monaco. Eighteen if you include Basel and nine plus Aspen."

"Anyone who stands out all the way to Aspen?"

"That far out all of them are well-knowns," Otto said.

"But there are a few matches between Cannes and Monaco that I'm still working on. Other than that, *nada*. Sorry, Kemo Sabe."

"Unless I push it, and see who pushes back," McGarvey said.

TWENTY-FIVE

Al-Hamadi was sweating like a pig, his breathing sharp and shallow, and the more he tried he could not achieve an orgasm. But it wasn't his fault.

None of the sluts aboard Hammond's yacht had given him the time of day, so he'd been forced—as often happened—to come back to the hotel and hire an expensive call girl for a couple of hours. Ten thousand euros. The most he'd ever paid but her bloodline was supposedly Persian royalty.

He was fucking an Iranian princess, but it was giving him absolutely no pleasure.

Ever since he was a fat boy in private school in Jeddah on the Red Sea he'd developed a love affair for all things Western: American baseball and football, instead of cricket and soccer. His roommates, who'd buggered him all the way through the fifth and sixth forms, had introduced him to the old American television series *Dallas*. Texas was an oil-rich desert filled with royalty, the same as Saudi Arabia.

He imagined himself as the patriarch of a vast ranch, surrounded by wealth, privilege, and beautiful willing women.

He had a decent enough head on his shoulders to study international law, but never the follow-through to pass any bar exam after he'd graduated near the bottom of his class.

Nevertheless he'd been hired as a minor functionary in the Ministry of the Interior, for the simple reason the state did not want to throw away the money it had spent on an education that his mother could not afford after his father had been killed in an oil field accident.

No one liked him, so he'd been shunted to duty at the United Nations in New York as an assistant to the cultural attaché. To everyone's surprise, including his own, he'd blossomed for the simple reason he was good at ingratiating himself with people. He played the buffoon who made people he dealt with feel superior. He was a gofer, willing to do or get or arrange just about anything someone wanted.

For a time he'd earned the nickname the Concierge, until his sixth year, when he met his wife, Nouf. She was an intellectual, a wallflower working as a translator—Arabic into English, French, Italian, and German. She was on the short side, a little chubby, like Alyan, but she had royal blood. A cousin to the Abdulaziz line. Much higher up than his own lineage. The ultimate of ultimates on the family tree. Nothing short of Saudi Arabia's historical leadership.

They'd fallen in love, he the smooth talker and she the desperate woman with no real prospect for marriage despite her royal line.

One year later in Riyadh, they married. He went back to work at the ministry and she spent her time translating books, while he gambled, drank, and chased whores on her share of oil money.

His satphone on the table across the room buzzed softly.

The call girl rolled over to him, her fingernails gently caressing his limp penis. "Are we done, sweetheart?" she asked. Her voice was as husky as her complexion.

Al-Hamadi batted her hand away. "Get the fuck out of here," he said, getting out of bed. "The next time I want a fucking cow I'll go to a farm."

"As you wish."

He got to the phone on the third ring as the woman gathered her clothes and purse and went into the bathroom and closed the door.

The call was encrypted, but the caller ID came up with his home phone.

"Darling," he answered.

"Get rid of your whore and call me back," his wife said, and she hung up.

After the woman left, al-Hamadi ordered a bottle of Krug, but he waited until it was brought up and a flute was poured for him before he returned his wife's call.

"I don't have time for your miserable excuses, so save them," she said.

"Okay."

They'd come to an understanding a few years ago. He was what he was—and her money helped support him—and she was who she was with the ambition to move up in the royal family. He enjoyed his freedom and she enjoyed taking the odd assignment from time to time and pointing her husband in the direction someone—though she'd never told him who—wanted him to proceed.

"Are you alone?"

"Yes."

"We want you to do something as soon as possible. This morning would be for the best."

"I'm listening," al-Hamadi said. He never denied her. She had the money and the position.

"The American you met with. We don't know who he is or what he wants, but he must be eliminated. Or at the very least distracted."

"Distracted from what?"

"It doesn't matter," Nouf said impatiently. "From his

present course, from whatever! He is an unknown. We do not like unknowns."

"May I be given more information?"

"No. Just do it."

"Okay, sweetheart," al-Hamadi said. "I should be back after New York."

But the line was dead.

He made a telephone call to a contact in Marseilles and laid out the operation.

"I have people nearby, but there must be a bonus for such short notice."

"Agreed," al-Hamadi said, and gave the man the details.

TWENTY-SIX

McGarvey and Pete had just got back to the hotel when al-Hamadi came out of the elevator and over to them. He seemed to be excited about something.

"I called your room, but you didn't answer," the Saudi said.

McGarvey introduced Pete by her work name.

"Nice to meet you, Miss Borman."

"The pleasure is mine, Mr. al-Hamadi."

He nodded. "I need to borrow Joseph for a half hour, if you don't mind."

"Of course not," McGarvey said. "I'll be up in a bit," he told Pete.

"I'll be around," she said, and she walked off.

Al-Hamadi took McGarvey's arm and they left the hotel, crossed the Croisette, and went back down to the stony beach, heading away from the harbor, where most of the night's activity was still happening. It was much darker in this direction. And deserted.

"I talked to Mr. Hammond about your bitcoin idea, and he's intrigued. Said it was his second offer today."

"Is that unusual?"

"For guys like him, it's common. Something you're not."

McGarvey pulled up short. Two men had come down from the Croisette. "So what are we doing here at this hour of the morning?" he asked. "What's so urgent?"

"Mr. Hammond wants me to find out more about you. His people checked your blog, but nobody ever heard about it until yesterday."

"I've posted for two years."

"That's what they told Mr. Hammond. But they'd never heard of you."

"Maybe he should hire some people who know what the hell they're doing."

The two men, both of them built like Sherman tanks, wearing black jeans, T-shirts, and dark jackets, came directly over. Al-Hamadi didn't seem to notice.

"Or maybe I'll just back out and find someone else," McGarvey said, watching the men out of the corner of his eye as they approached.

"So what are you two guys, arm in arm, puftas or something?" the slightly larger of the two on the left asked in heavily accented English. It was a mistake. They couldn't know that McGarvey was an English speaker.

They'd stopped about ten feet away. By his dark, rough looks and the accent, McGarvey guessed the bigger one to be either Corsican or French Algerian. Muscle for hire.

"You have a choice," McGarvey told them. "Either turn around and crawl back into whatever sewer you came out of. Or get on with it. Actually, I'd prefer the latter, because I have a couple of questions for you."

Al-Hamadi stepped a few feet away.

McGarvey glanced at the Saudi, but the man didn't seem overly concerned.

"*Putain, américaine,*" the other one said. It meant, roughly, "fucking American."

There was still enough traffic above that getting into a gunfight would only summon the police. McGavey didn't want it.

The two men pulled old-fashioned knives out of their pockets, flipped out the blades, and separated before coming at him. It was a second stupid mistake.

At the last moment, McGarvey dodged left, grabbed the nearest guy's arm, and swung the man around so that the other man plowed straight into the knife, the blade burying itself in his chest.

Mac stepped back and drove his doubled-over knuckles into the first man's neck, badly bruising his larynx.

The man staggered backward and dropped to his knees.

Al-Hamadi suddenly darted forward and kicked the man with the knife sticking out of his chest directly in the temple.

"Bastards," he said. He yanked the bloody knife out of the man's body and turned to the one McGarvey had put down. "I'll show the sons of bitches."

McGarvey had to forcefully stop him. "I want one of them alive."

"They're scum."

"I want to know who hired them."

"They're common street criminals. Cannes this time of year is good pickings."

"Let's find out," McGarvey said. He took out his Walther, screwed the silencer on the muzzle, and bent down beside the first man, who was coming around.

"I didn't know you were carrying a gun," al-Hamadi said.

"You're right, this time of year Cannes is good pickings.

It'll be the same in Monaco tomorrow." He started to reach into the man's jacket pocket, but the Corsican grabbed his wrist.

McGarvey turned his pistol around and smashed the butt into the man's nose, blood immediately gushing, and he let go of Mac's wrist.

"Who sent you?"

"Fuck you," the man croaked.

"Once again, who hired you?"

The Corsican said nothing.

McGarvey was aware of al-Hamadi hovering over him with a knife in hand.

"Your partner is dead, and I don't have a reason to let you walk away from here, except maybe for you to take a message back to whoever sent you."

The Corsican glared at him.

McGarvey opened the man's jacket and felt the inside pockets, but they were empty. Patting him down he came up with a wallet and passport. The man was an Algerian after all. His passport gave his name as Samir Madyan. He had a little more than a thousand euros in the wallet.

"A lot of money, Samir. But I think I'll let you keep it. Sooner or later whoever hired you to take me out will find out that you failed, and they'll want to know about their money. Maybe they'll want you to try again."

The Alergian's eyes shifted to something over McGarvey's shoulder.

"Wipe the knife down, your fingerprints are all over it," McGarvey told al-Hamadi. He was ready to roll left and bring his pistol around.

"I never thought of that," the Saudi said.

McGarvey turned back to the man on the ground. "If I ever see you again, I'll kill you, do you understand?"

The Algerian nodded, but said nothing.

McGarvey got up and stepped back as he unscrewed the silencer, pocketed it, and holstered his pistol.

They hadn't attracted any attention so far, but it wouldn't last. And once the body was discovered the police would be called. Unless his partner carried it away.

On the way back to the hotel al-Hamadi was subdued. He kept wiping his hands with a handkerchief.

"You might want to tell Hammond that the bitcoin scheme I offered is off the table. I'll take it to someone else. He'd best stay away from me—and that includes you—because it looks like I'm on someone's hit list."

"They were just ordinary criminals. Street thieves."

"No," McGarvey said.

"What do I tell him about your blog?"

"Nothing."

He told Pete what had happened, and then phoned Otto. "I think it was al-Hamadi who hired those guys. Otherwise it was too much of a coincidence. He might be working for Saudi intel after all. Find out what you can about him."

"Well, whoever he works for wants you dead," Otto said. "I'm on it."

Monaco Grand Prix

Kamal drove his Bentley up to the Hermitage in Monaco. It seemed strange to be so close to his real home like this, but there was little if any danger of anyone recognizing him. Monégasques were not a particularly neighborly people. If you wanted your privacy no one ever questioned it.

Susan had stayed with him last night, but in the morning she decided that she would make her own way to Monaco. He assumed she'd be aboard the *Glory*.

Sex was good with her, but it was just sex, nothing more. He decided that when the time came he would get a great deal more pleasure killing her than fucking her.

Hammond had offered to let him come aboard the yacht, but he'd said he had to take care of a few errands. Privately.

He and Hammond had spoken on the phone first thing in the morning. "I can offer you privacy aboard, if you wish."

Kamal had chuckled. "Sorry, but I've already had a taste of your notion of privacy."

Hammond had laughed too. "That was strictly business."

"Isn't everything?"

"We're having another party this evening, and then of course the race tomorrow afternoon. Will you be joining us?"

"For the race, certainly, and afterwards I'd like to continue our discussion."

"I won't be going back to my office in New York until

Monday or Tuesday, but then I'll be in Basel on the eighteenth. Viktor should be there too."

"How about Mr. Jian?"

"Aspen for a day or two then of course his party at the Tower."

"I'll see you tomorrow, then."

"Lunch aboard at noon," Hammond said abruptly. "Someone on the dock will direct you."

He hung up.

Inside Kamal registered under the Castillo identification and was shown to his suite, both balconies of which overlooked the principality and the harbor. He gave the bellman five hundred euros.

When the man was gone he opened the complimentary bottle of Krug, poured a glass, and went out to the expansive southeast balcony, big enough to easily accommodate a dozen or more guests for a reception.

He had no errands in his own town, of course, he simply needed the time to be alone. It was sometimes rare while he was in the middle of an operation. He'd never enjoyed stakeouts, or waiting with a sniper rifle someplace secure until his subject came into a decent sight line.

Almost always he was face-to-face with the people he killed, or at the very least nearby. He loved the final look in their eyes when they knew that no one could save them. That alone was worth even more than the money.

But sometimes like now he needed a break in the action. Time to sit back and reassess his progress.

In the distance to the south a large white yacht with a broad blue swath from high on the bow sweeping to the stern where it met the waterline—almost like a large wave— was heading north. It was the *Glory*. Antibes was a distant blur in the haze twenty-five kilometers away, but Beaulieu and Villefranche were much closer. The view from the decks on this beautiful day had to be magnificent.

Being rich was a good thing, he decided. But being su-perrich, like Hammond and the other players, came with too many problems. In part because most of them thought that their wealth made them invulnerable. Made their opinions and judgments sure things. Their tastes some-times set fashion trends.

The house phone chimed, but he ignored it as he watched the oncoming yacht. A speedboat pulled a pair of water-skiers just to the north of the harbor entrance. And way out in the Med, toward Corsica, a much larger boat, either a car ferry or a cargo ship, was inbound probably for Mar-seilles.

The streets had been blocked by safety barriers along the entire three-and-a-third-kilometer Formula One course, which followed the waterfront for a distance before entering a tunnel and then, after a very fast straightaway, climbing up into the town and the famous Fairmont hairpin turn.

It was the slowest race in the entire F1 circuit and in the Triple Crown, which was here, the 24 Hours of Le Mans, and the Indianapolis 500 in the States. It was also the most dangerous of them all.

The phone chimed again a minute later, and Kamal went inside. It was al-Hamadi, both times with the same message. He was also staying here in the hotel, and not aboard the yacht.

"Call me as soon as possible. This is urgent. You may have competition coming your way." He left a number.

Kamal went back outside and used his KryptAll En-crypted TSCM Counter Surveillance cell phone to call Sa'ad's secure access number. The Saudi intel officer an-swered on the second ring.

"Yes."

"Al-Hamadi may have become a problem," Kamal said.

"Tell me."

"We're both here at the Hermitage. He's left me a

message that I may have competition coming my way. Do you have any idea what the man is talking about?"

"Have you already met with Hammond?"

"Yes. He's interested."

"Enough for Jian Chang to invite you to the party?"

"At this point it seems yes."

"Then the only thing I can think of is that Alyan might be playing more than one string with Hammond. You and whoever else he's talking about. He could very possibly want you to engage in some sort of bidding war where he would come out the winner."

"Should I kill him?"

"Eventually yes, but not right now. See what he's talking about and we'll go from there."

"He's a fool."

"Indeed he is."

Kamal pocketed the phone, poured more champagne and, using the house phone, returned al-Hamadi's call. "Come to my suite now."

Al-Hamadi showed up two minutes later dressed in jeans, boat shoes, and a Team Mercedes T-shirt. He seemed to be all out of breath as if he'd run up a couple of flights of stairs. But Kamal got the impression that the man was acting.

They went out to the balcony, where Kamal poured the Saudi a glass of champagne. They didn't sit down.

"He says his name is Joe Canton, a blogger on a site called politicsnow. But I checked, and no one heard of him until a couple of days ago. The problem is that he's posted at least two years' worth of blogs."

"So what?"

"He came to me with a scheme to corner the bitcoin market."

"And you took him to Hammond?"

"Yes. And Tom is definitely interested. There're only twenty-one million of them, but if the price rises to a thousand U.S. or more each, the money would be significant."

"What's the problem?" Kamal asked. His radar was singing but he was careful not to show it.

"The problem is I asked him to take a walk with me on the beach last night. Tom had a few questions he wanted me to ask. But before we got fifty meters a couple of bastards came down from the Croisette to rob us, or something. I don't know. But they were big and tough-looking. They meant business."

"What happened?"

"They came at us with knives, and Canton took care of both of them. He pistol-whipped one of them, and he stabbed the other one to death. We just left them there on the beach as if nothing unusual had happened."

"Canton's a professional?"

"I'd bet almost anything on it."

"An American cop?"

"Maybe from Treasury here looking for you," al-Hamadi said.

Kamal was sure that the man was lying, but about what, exactly, and why, he didn't know. But he was going to find out.

TWENTY-EIGHT

McGarvey and Pete had an early breakfast in their room. They were taking the train up to Monaco in time for lunch at the Hermitage. In the meantime they watched the local television broadcasts on Orange S.A., Canal+, and Canal+ Cinéma, which mostly covered the film festival. But there was nothing about the incident on the beach last night.

The *Nice-Matin* newspaper came with their breakfast, but like the TV broadcasts its headlines were almost exclusively about the festival. No mention was made about crime of any sort in Cannes.

"No one wants to disturb the rich and famous," Pete said, not at all surprised.

McGarvey phoned Otto. It was a little past one in the morning in Langley but Otto was still at his desk.

"There's nothing on TV or in the local newspapers about last night."

"There wouldn't be," Otto said. "The Police Municipale are treating it as a suicide. Apparently there were no witnesses, only the dead body on the ground with a knife wound in its chest."

"Al-Hamadi kicked the bastard in the side of the head."

"It wasn't mentioned."

"Anything about me or Pete on the DGSI's mainframe?"

"Nothing yet. But if they catch wind that you guys are involved they might send someone up to start sniffing around. You might want to think about getting out of Dodge ASAP."

"We're heading up to Monaco in a couple of hours."

"You told al-Hamadi to let Hammond know that your bitcoin offer was off the table. But by now Hammond has to know about last night. He'll have to guess that you're not who you say you are, especially if al-Hamadi tells him how you handled the situation. He might think that you're a cop."

"If he does he'll have to wonder why I approached him the way I did," McGarvey said. "But I don't think he'll just let me walk off. His curiosity will get the better of him."

"And his greed," Pete said, turning away from the television.

Otto heard it. "You're talking about tons of money. He's going to want more."

"I'm counting on it. In the meantime, what have you come up with on al-Hamadi?"

"Nothing more than we already knew. If he's working for Saudi intel he's deep cover. Probably not even a paper trail. Just a control officer who he reports to verbally, who in turn makes his reports verbally to his supervisor."

"Makes him an important operator."

"I have a gut feeling that his charter is to keep tabs on the royals, so that they can be reined in when they get themselves into trouble."

"If that's the case he must be a busy man. But his cover is damned good. From what I've seen he plays the role of the fool very well. But we haven't encountered any royals yet."

"They were all over the place at the festival and they'll be in Monaco for the race," Otto said. "There're at least two of their yachts in Monaco and a third, plus Hammond's, on the way."

"Then why the hell is al-Hamadi bothering with me?"

"Because for the moment it seems as if his target is Hammond, for some reason."

Something suddenly came into McGarvey's head. It was tradecraft pure and simple. Anomalies. Look for the one possibility, or set of possibilities, that no matter how unlikely would open an entirely new avenue. Murphy's Law: Out of five things, the one that would do you the most harm is likely to be the next to happen. Or: If everything seems to be going well, you're probably running into an ambush.

"Nero's here and he's using al-Hamadi for the same reason we're using him. He's looking for an invitation to Jian's penthouse party."

"He'd have to have a good source of intel."

"He had it in New York to target Seif and masquerade as him."

"The same ploy won't work again."

"He's offered Hammond, or someone like him, a moneymaking scheme, of course. Something that would appeal to Jian."

"It would have to be something so big that a guy like Hammond couldn't or wouldn't want to handle on his own," Otto said. "Fringe."

"Nero is here for one reason—to get an invitation to the Tower. For now it's his Achilles' heel. In the meantime do you have any updates on the Identikit? Someone from the Bureau was going to talk to possible witnesses."

"All the new stuff is contradictory," Otto said. "It only takes a day or two for people's memories to start getting fuzzy. The first image is probably as close as we're going to get. And no one downtown is recommending distribution even of that version."

"How about his general build?"

"All over the map, Kemo Sabe. We're back at square one. If someone looks like he doesn't belong . . . well, you know what to do."

They finished packing and McGarvey was about to call the bellman when the house phone rang. It was al-Hamadi.

"I thought that you'd be up here in Monaco by now."

"We're taking the noon train," McGarvey said.

"That's not necessary. Mr. Hammond will send a car for you."

"I told you last night that my offer is off the table."

Al-Hamadi hesitated for a beat. "About last night, I never thanked you."

"For what?"

"Those bastards could have killed us both. You reacted almost like you were a cop or something."

"I was in the Air Force OSI for a few years a long time ago. Old training, I guess, doesn't die." The Office of Special Investigations was the air force's counterintelligence, criminal investigative, and protective services agency.

"I thought it must have been something like that. Those guys didn't have a chance."

McGarvey didn't answer.

"Mr. Hammond is still very interested. And from what I understand so is Ms. Patterson."

"Who the hell is she?"

"A Hollywood big deal. She and Hammond are a thing."

"No."

"I'm trying to help here."

"I don't give a shit," McGarvey said. "Just stay the fuck away from us."

"Hammond has talked with Viktor Shepelev, who wants to buy in."

"I have a couple of other people already interested."

"Not these kind of people," al-Hamadi said, and he almost sounded desperate.

"I want people with balls, because that's what it's going to take to corner the market."

"I'm talking about a fantastic finder's fee."

McGarvey laughed. "I'm not interested in a finder's fee. You don't have a fucking clue. I'm in this one hundred percent. I know the play, I know the moves, I know the timing."

"Maybe I'll recommend that Hammond and the others do this thing on their own, and you can go screw yourself."

"Be my guest, and when it falls apart because none of them knows what they're doing, you can be the fall guy." McGarvey hung up.

Pete was grinning. "That was probably the worst sales pitch I've ever heard. Unless you really meant to blow them off."

"What are you talking about? I thought I was being charming."

"Fuel to the fire?"

"Something like that."

TWENTY-NINE

The run up to Monaco was only twenty-five miles by train, the route scenic. They stopped briefly at Antibes, then Nice for nearly ten minutes while a couple of passengers helped an old woman aboard and to her seat. They didn't pull out of the station until she was settled.

"Merci, merci, mes petites," she kept saying to the pair of helpful young men.

"You don't see that every day," Pete said.

"This is France," McGarvey said.

"You lived here once upon a time."

"Yes, and so did Otto. It was good for a while, but then it got bad."

"Bad, how?"

"Just bad," McGarvey said, thinking back.

In fact almost every place he'd ever lived for any length of time had gotten bad. Even Washington and the Beltway and beyond. A friend of his had died in an attack at a Georgetown restaurant. His son-in-law had been gunned down, his wife and daughter killed in a bomb blast, and even Pete had nearly lost her life in an op.

It had been the same in Florida, where he'd been the target of a couple of assassination attempts.

And on the *plage* last night.

"A penny," Pete said, breaking him out of his thoughts. He realized, for the first time, that though Pete often used the expression—so had Katy.

"Are you carrying?"

"Yes."

"Don't go anywhere without it."

"You've already said that."

McGarvey held up a hand. "I don't want to lose you. Watch your six, I mean it."

"I'm frosty, boss."

"Christ." McGarvey had to laugh.

The train station was in the hills just above the old Sainte-Dévote Chapel, below which was the busy port of Monaco. Hammond's yacht was a half mile to the south, angling in toward the entrance between the breakwaters.

Outside they got a cab to take them to the Hermitage. Traffic wasn't busy until they reached La Condamine, the business downtown of Monaco. Traffic here was impossible because of all the people in town for the week, and because important sections of the streets were blocked off for the race.

"And it will be three weeks before all the barriers have been removed and life can get back to normal," their driver told them. "But no one complains, *hein*."

"The money is good," McGarvey said, stating the obvious.

The driver looked in the rearview mirror to see if the American was pulling his leg, but then smiled. "Except from the Brits. Most of them are tight."

Otto called. "I ran down the guest lists from the major hotels in Cannes and Monaco, and came up with nothing of any real interest except for a Mexican by the name of Angel Castillo. But the guy checks out okay. He runs a small stock brokerage company in Mexico City. Just a one-man operation, but he's accredited on the Bolsa." The Bolsa Mexicana de Valores was Mexico's stock exchange.

"Is he registered at Basel or Aspen?" McGarvey asked.

"No. And before you ask, that name didn't show up at any of the top-ten hotels in Manhattan going back three months."

"Castillo is out, but Nero is here. I can damned near feel him."

"Problem is, nobody knows what he looks like, except the ones who were at AtEighth when it went down. But I've come up with something else, and I don't even know if I should mention it."

"Everything is on the board," McGarvey said.

"I'm still following up on the possibility that the Saudis are involved. I've eliminated any government-sanctioned operation. If something like that ever got out the royals would become pariahs. We're talking about the murders of a lot of seriously rich people and blaming it on ISIS. The blowback would be intense."

"Nothing would come of it. The families of the nine-eleven victims sued but the court dropped it for lack of strong enough evidence to overcome Saudi Arabia's sovereign immunity."

"My darlings are starting to pick up whiffs of someone called el Nassr, 'the Eagle.' That could be his actual surname, but I'm betting that it's a designator. A code name. The GIP likes that sort of ambiguity."

"What's the context?"

"It popped up when a German politician was found murdered in bed with his mistress. Both of them were shot in the head twice, once at short range. The same insurance shots as Nero's. The German was leading a campaign to control OPEC's pricing policies, which would have had a direct effect on Saudi oil production. Anyway, the BND had a brief reference to a Saudi national who might have gone by the code name Eagle. They didn't take it any further."

"Any others?"

"Nothing concrete. One reference in Caracas about an incident in Maracaibo when a series of drilling platforms went up in flames. It was eventually declared an industrial accident. But one line in an early report said something to the effect that 'It was as if an Eagle, its talons spread wide, swooped down for an attack.'"

"Thin," McGarvey said, but the two references resonated.

"At this point we don't have anything else. Are you expecting Hammond to call?"

"I'd bet good money that he will. And does the name Patterson—Ms. Patterson—a Hollywood big shot, mean anything to you?"

"Hold on."

McGarvey glanced at the driver, who seemed to be concentrating on getting through traffic, and then to Pete, who had caught his gesture. She shook her head, the movement very slight.

Otto came back. "Susan Patterson, a Hollywood producer worth a couple of billion. She was in just about the same league as Nenet Akila, who was killed when At-Eighth came down. They were friends, or at least nodding acquaintances."

"An interesting connection."

"I wouldn't take it any further than that. All these people run in the same crowd."

"Keep us posted," McGarvey said. "I think I'm going to throw another stick into the pack of dogs. See which one yelps."

The driver dropped them off at the Hermitage, one of Monaco's premier hotels. They checked in under the same work names as they had used in Cannes, and were shown to their decent junior suite, which had its own balcony that looked down on the harbor and the section of the racetrack along the waterfront.

When they were alone, McGarvey explained what Otto had come up with, including the hint of someone with the code name el Nassr.

"I don't think the cabby was paying much attention," she said.

The house phone on the coffee table rang and Pete went across to answer it.

"This is Mr. Canton's suite," she said. She put it on speakerphone.

"I'm Tom Hammond. If he's floating around there, I'd like to have a quick word with him."

Pete held out the phone. She was grinning.

McGarvey answered. "I'm surprised to hear from you," he said.

"Alyan told me about your unfortunate adventure last night."

"Unfortunate for them, not me."

Hammond laughed. "I'd like to talk to you about your project."

"I have someone else interested."

"We're just coming through the breakwater now. Should be squared away within the hour. Can I expect you?"

"I'm not interested in your parties, Mr. Hammond, just business."

"Of course, but I think that you and Ms. Borman would enjoy the race from my boat tomorrow better than from your balcony," Hammond said. "One hour?"

"Sure," McGarvey said.

He hung up and Pete gave him a fist bump.

THIRTY

Kamal was sitting on the balcony having croissants and dark coffee so he wouldn't have to endure what the Americans called a buffet lunch aboard Hammond's yacht, which was just now gliding through the breakwaters. It wasn't the largest here but it was close. He'd seen an interview with the American, who claimed that he wasn't in competition for the biggest, most expensive things on the block—the yachts, the houses, the cars.

"Or the most expensive women?" the interviewer had asked.

Hammond had gotten up and walked off the set. A few days later the interviewer was fired.

Kamal had done the research on the handful of targets he needed to turn in order to get invited to Jian's party at the Tower. Hammond had turned out to be an interesting man, but so were most of the other players on the circuit. Even the bland ones—the Gates and the Buffets—were egocentric. They all shared the same characteristic: they believed in themselves.

Ego was a weakness that could be exploited, unlike his own, which he figured he had under perfect control.

But his chief concern at the moment was the blogger Joe Canton, whom al-Hamadi had warned him about. To this point he was an unknown.

He phoned Sa'ad again and explained the situation. "Could he be working with Alyan?"

"I doubt it. And I also doubt that he's a U.S. Treasury agent as Alyan suggested. The American government doesn't do business that way."

"He was attacked on the beach last night. Your doing?"

"No. We think it was random."

Kamal didn't think so, but he let it ride. "He's not who

he claims to be. His blog posts supposedly go back two years and yet no one heard of him until a couple of days ago."

"You're going aboard Hammond's yacht for the race?"

"Yes."

"Good. If Canton shows up and you get the chance to take his picture, send it to me."

"I don't want to come face-to-face with the man this close to the operation."

"On the contrary, my dear friend, it's exactly what you must do," Sa'ad said. "Talk to him, find out what he's all about. And if need be, kill him."

Kamal saw the logic. "Especially if he shows up at Basel or Aspen."

"It's unlikely that the Americans know about you, unless you were sloppy in New York."

It was an insult, but Kamal let it go. For now.

"Canton is nothing more than someone else coming to Hammond with a deal."

"I'll take care of it."

"Do."

Kamal finished his coffee and retrieved his weapon kit in a zip-up leather case and brought it back out to the balcony.

Wilson Combat pistols were loosely modeled after the old U.S. Army Colt .45 1911A1, the official sidearm well into the nineties when the military switched over to the Beretta 92F. But the Wilson pistols, which came in a wide variety of models, had it over the Colt and Beretta in reliability and especially in accuracy.

After New York he'd decided to switch from the Glock to the Wilson in the 9mm Ultralight Carry Sentinel version. It only had an eight-round magazine, but it had an accuracy guarantee of an inch and a half at twenty-five yards. It was something Kamal had verified on his own.

There was nothing wrong with the Glock, but it was nowhere as accurate or reliable.

The gun was clean, but he disassembled it, cleaned everything again with odorless gun oil, and put it back together. He took the bullets from both magazines and made sure everything was ultraclean before loading both mags and seating one home in the butt of the pistol. He cycled a round into the chamber, ejected the magazine, and loaded one round before seating it home again. Nine shots now.

He was just wiping down the suppressor when Susan Patterson breezed out onto the balcony. "Going pheasant hunting?"

On instinct alone Kamal snatched the pistol and turned and pointed it at her.

She stopped short and held up her hands. "Whoa, I don't even like pheasant." She was startled but she was more amused than frightened.

"How'd you get in?"

"I told one of the maids that I was your lover. Still, it cost me three hundred euros before she would let me in."

Kamal watched her eyes. She wasn't lying; either that or she was damned good at it.

"Would you mind pointing that thing somewhere else?"

He lowered the pistol and laid it on the hand towel he'd spread out.

She came over and sat down next to him. She was wearing a white pantsuit cut low in front and back, with a broad black belt around her narrow waist and a Versace baseball cap, diamonds in the bill. She looked stunning and she knew it.

"Why are you here?" Kamal asked.

"In the first place, to seduce you where Tom can't get his rocks off by watching. And then to take you back to the yacht for lunch." She reached out for the gun.

"Don't. It's not a toy."

She pulled her hand back. "I didn't think it was."

"You know who I am and what I'm doing here."

She nodded. "You have enemies."

"More than you can guess."

"You weren't carrying that last night. Why now?"

Kamal hesitated. Killing her would be satisfying, but not here and definitely not now.

"You're expecting trouble," Susan said. "Is it something that Tom should know about? Something that's going to follow you to the ship?"

"I won't know everybody aboard."

"I can vouch for most of them. And I can guarantee you that the average billionaire might be ruthless but they aren't homicidal. And neither are their wives nor girl-friends. No one wants to start trouble and cut themselves off from the golden goose."

"You sometimes travel with bodyguards."

"Only to some public events."

"Guns bother you."

"Any sort of violence bothers me," Susan said. "Espe-cially after nine-eleven and then last week in New York."

"Do you think something like that will happen again?"

"Maybe not another building coming down. But some act of terrorism, like Paris and Brussels and Orlando. And just about everyone I know thinks the same thing."

Kamal smiled and nodded. "So do I."

"Okay," she said after a moment. "I like having you around as a bodyguard, as long as you're not a magnet for trouble."

"I'll do everything in my power not to be," he said.

They made love in the large bed, the big windows open to the sea breeze. The first time on the yacht she had been wild, biting and scratching and moving so quickly it was as if she was trying to prove something, trying to get it over as quickly as possible, to assert her control.

But this time she was willing to let Kamal take the lead. His lovemaking was slow, and gentle and deliberate, hitting all the correct notes.

During the entire thing he watched her eyes each time she opened them, no guile there. How her nostrils flared. A small bead of perspiration on her upper lip. Her erect nipples, the small rash on her chest between her breasts, the four-inch scar high on her left shoulder.

When she came it wasn't so frantic either; rather her satisfaction came in long, slow waves that seemed to ripple through her entire body.

It would be the same, even better, when he killed her, he thought as his own pleasure peaked, and he almost laughed out loud.

THIRTY-ONE

There was no direct route on foot to the harbor from the hotel, because of the closed race circuit, so McGarvey and Pete had to take a cab. People were everywhere, and from the pits the high-pitched screams of the F1 engines being tested overpowered just about every other noise. And from the expressions on the faces of some of the people they passed, the sounds could have been a powerful aphrodisiac.

"Have you ever been to one of these things?" Pete asked.

"Not this one, but I was at Spa in Belgium a few years ago, and when I was living in Switzerland I went down to Germany for the race at Nürburgring. Lots of people, lots of noise, lots of parties all centered on the drivers. Just about all of them young and arrogant."

"And lots of money."

"That too. But in those days the races were all about fatalism. Young bucks putting their lives on the line, and the women flocking to them."

Pete smiled. "Not my type." But then she changed the subject. "Do you think Nero will be aboard?"

"On Hammond's yacht or someone else's."

"He wants an invite to Jian's party, so maybe he's in Hong Kong now. Or maybe with Callahan's people buying a condo in the Tower."

McGarvey had thought about those possibilities and several others. But the Bureau was all over the place in New York, and Nancy Nebel, who was now the acting CEO of Callahan Holdings, was cautious. She'd admitted to Otto that there'd been plenty of cancellations. They were refunding millions in deposit monies without question.

The company was taking a serious hit because of At-Eighth, but business would come back. Even downtown, One World Trade Center was as busy as the Twin Towers had been. Only now the security was much tighter.

"Nebel's vetting everyone—even if they're only showing a mild interest," McGarvey said. "And from what Otto told me about the players, Jian is one of the most standoffish of them all. He never goes anywhere without a security detail, and he almost never comes to Monaco or any of the art festivals."

"He's not a party boy," Pete said.

"Not from what Otto has learned. The guy is all business."

"I would have thought that a couple of hundred million for a penthouse in New York was over-the-top. Not much of an investment."

"He knows real estate, so I suspect he's looking to make a profit."

"Which leaves Hammond and people like him the most likely avenue for an invitation to the party."

"The same reason we're here."

"You expect our guy?"

"If al-Hamadi is who we think he is, and if Nero is working for the GIP like Otto thinks, then it's a good bet he'll be here at least for the race tomorrow," McGarvey said as they pulled up at the docks.

"The thing is we don't know what he looks like," Pete said.

McGarvey paid the driver and they walked down to the port security post, where they had to show their passports. "We're here at Mr. Hammond's invitation," he said.

One of the two officers went inside and checked the monitor for the *Glory*'s guest list. When he came out his attitude had changed.

"You may proceed," he said, handing back their passports. "Would you like a ride?"

Several golf carts were parked to the left. McGarvey was about to say they'd walk, when a man in his early twenties, dark good looks, came from across the street. He was wearing the coveralls of Team Mercedes, and racing shoes.

"Louis Martaan," he offered, ignoring the port security officers. "If you guys are going out to Tom's boat you can ride with me. I'll drive." At the moment he was the number-one ranked driver on the Grand Prix circuit. His temper was as legendary as his driving, and when he was in the mood, so was his charm.

"Not too fast," Pete said.

"Not until tomorrow," he said, grinning.

He handed Pete into the passenger seat of one of the golf carts, and as soon as McGarvey got in, he took off.

"Are you going to watch the race with Tom and the others?"

"If we're invited," Pete said.

"You will be," Martaan said.

"I thought you'd be tuning up your engine or something?"

He laughed. "The suspensions, but the lunches Tom serves are much better than the terrible German slop we get."

When they reached the yacht, Martaan raced up the gangway without waiting for them.

"He's not Nero," Pete said whimsically.

"Good thing," McGarvey said.

Pete looked at him. "Why?"

"He's too good-looking for me to shoot."

At the head of the gangway a young woman with white shorts and a blue T-shirt was waiting for them. "If you'll come with me, sir, Mr. Hammond is waiting for you in his office."

"Sexist," Pete said under her breath.

"Mingle," McGarvey said, and he followed the young woman.

Hammond was sitting on the edge of his desk looking up at one of the monitors that showed the aft pool deck where tables and chairs had been set up for lunch. A couple of dozen people were already there, including Pete, who was talking to a woman in a brief white bikini, a gauze beach jacket thrown over her shoulders.

"Courtney Rich," he said. "CEO of IBEX, a stock trading company." He turned to McGarvey. "It's like betting on horses, you know. She started out on her own and made a hit because she knows what she's doing and she's not afraid to take calculated risks."

"It can't have been that easy," McGarvey said. All these people talked about was money.

"She's hired a lot of really good people, and she listens to them."

"Smart woman. And attractive."

"So is your Ms. Borman. Your lover?"

"None of your business," McGarvey said.

Hammond smiled. "No," he said. "Your blog is a scam."

"Yes, it is."

"A cover for what, Canton, if that's your real name?"

"It's not, but I'm not going to tell you a cover for what, except that I'm looking for someone. And that it's personal."

"I suspected something like that after Alyan told me what happened on the beach. You don't believe the attack was random?"

"No."

"Or who directed it?"

"The man I'm looking for."

Hammond stared at the monitor for a long time. "The bitcoin deal you offered, is that also a scam?"

"No. In fact if you're interested I'll have someone contact you with the details."

Hammond chuckled. "I'm sure that Treasury would love it if I broke that bank. And now you want me to tell Chang about the deal so that you can get invited to his party at the Tower, and put it to him face-to-face."

"Something like that."

Hammond smiled. "Are you that good a salesman?"

"I'm here."

"Aren't you worried about another attack like AtEighth?"

"I hadn't really thought about it," McGarvey said. "You?"

"Chang will have a lot of security. Almost never goes anywhere without it. If he doesn't postpone his party—which he hasn't yet—it means he thinks it'll be safe. I'll get you invited, and afterwards I might just take a serious look at your bitcoin notion. In the meantime, enjoy my ship. Mingle but don't try to sell anyone else anything."

"I appreciate it," McGarvey said, and he went to the door.

THIRTY-TWO

McGarvey got a Heineken, no glass, at the bar on the forward deck and went back to the pool, where a guitarist was playing something classical and melodic. A few more people had shown up, most of them in swimsuits.

Martaan was sitting against the aft rail talking to a group of four women, all of them young, beautiful, and scantily clad. He said something and they all laughed; one of them touched his arm.

A lunch buffet had been set up just inside the main salon, where other tables and chairs had been arranged. Already some people had helped themselves and were eating.

Waitresses in white shorts and blue T-shirts circulated with trays of champagne. Others brought various wines and mixed drinks from the bar.

McGarvey took a spot opposite the race driver from where he could see just about everybody. He estimated there were at least thirty people already here and more coming from midships, where the gangway entrance was placed.

A few of the faces were vaguely familiar to him, people he might have seen on television. But all of them had one obvious thing in common: they were comfortable here in the midst of so much wealth. This was their due. And he didn't blame them, though some of them were arrogant pricks.

He had to smile.

"You're the man with Pete?" a woman behind him said.

McGarvey turned. She was Courtney Rich, the IBEX CEO. Up close she obviously wasn't a young woman, possibly in her midforties, maybe fifty, but her figure was trim, her face almost movie star perfect, and even her neck and the backs of her hands, which were telltale signs of a woman's age, seemed flawless. She'd spent a fair amount of money to look that way.

"Joe Canton," McGarvey said. They shook hands.

"Lovely girl. But I don't think she quite trusts you here. She seemed a bit nervous."

"There was an incident on the beach in Cannes. A couple of muggers tried to take me down. She's a little skittish."

"You seem to have emerged intact."

"I was lucky."

"No one here will try to mug you, though if you've come to Tom with a deal, someone might try to rob you."

"I'll keep that in mind."

A man and woman came from midships. They were dressed in street clothes, not for the pool. The woman was a former movie star; now a producer, though McGarvey couldn't remember her name. But the man she was with instantly got his hackles up. For a moment it was almost as if he were looking at himself in a mirror. The eyes were familiar.

They came over.

"Courtney, when did you get into town?" the woman asked.

"Just last night." They hugged briefly. "This is Joe Canton, here, I think, to offer Tom something spectacular."

"Susan Patterson," the woman said. "And it's a small world."

"Angel Castillo," Kamal said, shaking hands with McGarvey. "Tom's an interesting man, don't you think?"

"And bright," McGarvey said. "Men like him usually attract all sorts of people."

"Gentlemen, no business until after the race tomorrow," Courtney said. "This is party time."

McGarvey held up his hand. "The only competition will be on the circuit tomorrow."

"Promise?"

"Scout's honor."

"Good enough," Courtney said.

Kamal smiled pleasantly. "I'm sure that we'll have a chance to talk later. Nice meeting you."

"And you," McGarvey said.

Kamal and Susan walked away.

"Who is he?" McGarvey asked when they were out of earshot.

"I don't know. Some friend of Tom's from Mexico City, showed up in Cannes, I was told. He's brought something to do with a terrible amount of money. It's why super-bitch is hanging on so tightly."

Courtney looked past him. "Here comes your Pete," she said. "Just watch yourself because if you're talking serious money with Tom, Susan will come after you next."

"What's she to Tom?"

"They're each other's flavor of the month, didn't you know?" Courtney said and she walked off.

"Lots of sharks here, and not just the ones in the water," Pete said. She had a glass of champagne.

"They're game players, but they're the only ones who know the rules."

"What do you think of Courtney?"

"I got the feeling that she might be one of a handful of people here without an agenda."

"Just here for the fun. I got the same impression. What about the has-been movie star and her handsome stud?"

"Angel Castillo, the Mexican stockbroker Otto told me about. He was at Cannes."

The two of them had joined Martaan and his fan club.

"You have that look," Pete said. "Talk to me."

"He's killed people."

"How do you know that?"

"It's in his eyes."

"The thousand-yard stare?"

"More than that. Something calculating. Like he was lining up his next shot."

Kamal turned and glanced at them. McGarvey nodded and Kamal smiled and returned the gesture.

"Hammond's not stupid," Pete said. "If Castillo is trying to arrange a deal he'd be vetted."

"Right," McGarvey said, but he was far from convinced, and Pete read that much from his expression.

"What's our next play?" she asked.

McGarvey took out his phone and called Otto. "We're aboard Hammond's yacht and I've just met Castillo. I want you to dig deeper."

"Do you think he's a candidate?"

"I'm not sure, except that most Mexican stockbrokers don't speak with an English accent."

"Can you see him from where you're standing or sitting?"

"He's about forty feet from me."

"Is Pete with you?"

"Right next to me."

"Turn to her so that your phone is pointing toward him." McGarvey did it.

"Got him," Otto said almost immediately. "Three decent photos, one really good one."

"Soon as you come up with something let me know."

"What's your confidence?"

"Just a hunch," McGarvey said. "Ten percent."

"Good enough for me," Otto said and he rang off.

McGarvey pocketed the phone. "Otto took a couple of pictures of him."

"What's next?" Pete asked.

"I think we'll push him a bit and see how he reacts."

THIRTY-THREE

Kamal and Susan Patterson were seated at a table near the aft rail, with Courtney Rich and the race driver. McGarvey and Pete got their plates from inside the salon and went to Kamal's table.

"Mind if we sit with you?" McGarvey asked.

"Of course not," Courtney said.

A waitress came with a tray of champagne and Martaan got a fresh glass.

"If your team manager catches you drinking booze this close to the race, he'll have a fit," Courtney said.

"Why do you think I'm having lunch here?" Martaan asked, grinning. "And he'd do more than have a fit, as you say."

"What's the fine for drunk driving in a Grand Prix race?" Pete asked.

The race driver raised his glass. "Death," he said, and he drained it.

A dark mood suddenly came across Courtney and Susan, and they looked at each other.

"I don't think that Monsieur Martaan got to be number one by driving with alcohol in his system," Kamal said.

"I wasn't thinking about the race," Courtney said.

"What, then?" Susan asked.

"AtEighth. Friends."

No one spoke. The hum of conversation around them on the pool deck was soft until a woman laughed, the sound at that moment out of place, almost hysterical.

"Did you know many people there?" McGarvey asked.

"I knew most of them," Courtney said.

"I was supposed to be there, but I got stuck in L.A. and couldn't make it," Susan said.

Courtney reached across the table and placed a hand on Susan's. "The worst of it is that no one has heard anything. The cause is still up in the air."

"It was no accident," Pete said. "I'd be willing to bet anything on it."

"The engineers are thinking that it was an explosion on one of the lower floors," Kamal said.

"Whatever, it was, terrorists did it," Courtney said.

Kamal shrugged. "ISIS is claiming responsibility. And they may be fierce fighters but they don't have the sophistication that bin Laden and al-Qaeda had."

"Are you suggesting it wasn't them?"

"On the contrary, there's no reason to believe it wasn't them," Kamal said. "All I'm saying is that they could have gotten into the building somehow, planted explosives on one of the lower floors, and set a fuse or something."

"They would have been caught on the building's surveillance cameras," Courtney suggested. "But there's been absolutely no word on that issue."

"The investigators may not have gotten to the cameras yet," McGarvey said, watching for a reaction from Kamal. "And they don't tell us everything. Never do."

"Or if they have, they're not saying anything about it."

"You would have thought they'd have plastered the dirty bastards' faces all over the television and newspapers," Susan said.

"Or the Internet," Kamal said. "Have you heard anything from your subscribers?"

McGarvey suppressed a smile. "Lots of ideas but nothing solid."

"Do you think it'll happen again?" Susan asked.

"I haven't heard anything that makes any sense," McGarvey said.

"I'm asking, because I've been invited to Jian's penthouse party."

"So have I," Courtney said. "And just about everyone else aboard this ship will be there too."

The sense of gloom settled even heavier on the table.

"I'm sure that the building will be heavily guarded," Kamal said.

"It'd be physically impossible to guard every skyscraper in Manhattan," Courtney shot back. "It seems to me that the sick motherfuckers are after us."

"Why?" Pete asked.

Courtney was angry. "Someone's always got a hard-on for rich people. They think we're all crooks. Robber barons, sucking all the money away from the poor so that we can guzzle Krug on the deck of a mega-yacht."

"The only flaw in your thinking is that the poor generally don't have any money to suck away other than their 401(K)s and pension plans," Tom Hammond said behind them. "Lots of municipalities and even states are dipping their toes into those ponds." He was dressed in white linen slacks and an open-collar shirt, the first four buttons undone. He had a bottle of champagne he was drinking from.

"You know what I'm talking about," Courtney said. "Someone's coming after us because we're the greedy Western capitalists."

"Am I included?"

"We all are. And just now the symbols of our success are the outrageous buildings going up in New York."

Hammond laughed. "And yachts like this one. And our

jets, and our fifty-two-bedroom compounds, and the circuit, so we can be with people to whom we don't owe an explanation. Courtney dear, please don't tell me that you're turning into a Gates. Spending your money to feed and house the poor. So much philanthropy he doesn't have time to work."

"But every year he's worth more money."

"If you're so ashamed of your money, why don't you give it all away and find a job?" Hammond asked.

Everyone within earshot laughed. The dark mood was broken.

Courtney dismissed him with a gesture.

"So, Señor Castillo, have you and Joe Canton had a chance to talk?"

"Not, not so far. But his blog is interesting," Kamal said. "More geopolitics, I think, than local."

"But I've heard of Señor Castillo in an indirect way," McGarvey said. "I'm looking for investment possibilities, and I was given your name along with others."

"The Internet is that lucrative?" Kamal asked.

"Around a million U.S. a week from my subscribers, and it's growing. And what better company than this to discuss what to do? And at this moment the Bolsa seems to be doing well."

If Kamal was surprised, McGarvey didn't detect it.

"I can be of some help. Perhaps after the race, maybe before Basel, we can get together."

"I'd like that, just one-on-one."

"Of course."

"Will you be at Jian's housewarming?"

"I don't know," Kamal said.

"You'll be my guest," Hammond said. "As will Joe and Ms. Borman. If the three of you will be in New York."

"In that case I wouldn't miss it," Kamal said.

"Nor would we," McGarvey said. "Now if you'll excuse

me for a moment." He got up but motioned for Pete to stay at the table.

He was hoping that Otto would get back to him with something. His feeling that Castillo wasn't whom he presented himself to be was much stronger now. The man was a liar and an egotist, it was in his eyes, in the set of his mouth, like he thought every other person at the table was inferior to him.

In the salon he got another beer and then went forward to the bow, where he leaned against the rail and looked at the town and the hills behind it.

For a time he and Katy had considered moving here. She'd even contacted a real estate agent who sent her the package of legal and financial documents they'd need to complete before they would be allowed to relocate. The minimum opening balance in a checking account was five million U.S., not particularly onerous, but the prices of even tiny apartments were in the multimillion-dollar range. And no apartment in the principality, unless it was furnished, came with anything. No kitchen appliances, no floor coverings, no curtains, not even light fixtures or plates on the wall sockets. What you bought was a shell with a balcony and windows.

In any event McGarvey didn't think the French intelligence service would have been happy about him showing up as a resident in Monaco. And the service had a great deal of influence on the principality when it concerned foreign, gun-toting intel officers.

He'd explained it to Katy, and although she wasn't overly upset, she was vexed. It was one more roadblock in their lives because of who he was.

"Are we prisoners in our own country?" she'd asked at one point.

"No, but Monaco and especially France might not be such a hot idea."

Hammond joined him at the rail. "Well?"

"Señor Castillo is an interesting person."

"Should I do business with him?"

"I don't know. That decision's yours."

Hammond was silent for a beat. "Is he the man you're looking for?"

"I'm not sure," McGarvey said.

T H I R T Y – F O U R

One of the stewards came onto the forward deck but respectfully stopped ten feet from Hammond.

"Excuse me," Hammond said and he went to the steward, who said something to him that McGarvey couldn't hear.

The steward left and Hammond came back. "I have to leave. Business. But please, enjoy yourself."

"We will, thank you."

"And will you be joining us for the race tomorrow?"

"I think so."

"Good," Hammond said and he went into the salon.

From where McGarvey stood he watched the billionaire take the stairs down.

Leaving his beer on the rail, McGarvey went into the salon and started downstairs, but one of the young women stewards was coming up.

She smiled. "May I help you, sir?"

"Tom asked to have a word with me. Said he'd be in his office. But this is my first time aboard."

"I'll show you."

"That's not necessary. I know it's below somewhere, just point the way."

The steward looked uncertain. "Down two decks, the first door starboard side."

"Thanks, you're a doll," McGarvey said, and he passed her.

Two decks down a corridor paneled in gleaming teak, thick carpet underfoot, and fine paintings on the bulkheads, ran the length of the yacht. McGarvey stopped at the first door on the right side and was listening, when a heavyset man came down the stairs.

He looked more like a bodyguard than a steward, and he had a look of suspicion etched into his features. "May I help you, sir?" he asked.

"No," McGarvey said. He knocked on the door and went inside.

Hammond was perched on the edge of his desk. He and al-Hamadi, who was seated on the leather couch, looked up in surprise, and, in Hammond's case, fleeting anger.

The bodyguard came to the door. "Is everything in order here, sir?" he asked.

"Yes, Karl, we were expecting Mr. Canton."

McGarvey closed the door. "Sorry to barge in on you like this, but I spotted Alyan coming aboard and I thought he might have come to talk to you, either about me or Señor Castillo."

Al-Hamadi looked like a deer caught in headlights, but Hammond's expression was unreadable.

"Despite the size of this ship, it's actually quite small in comparison to any of my houses. And I value my privacy above just about anything else."

"I understand and apologize," McGarvey said. "I'll just collect Toni and we'll leave." He turned to go.

"Yes, we were talking about you and Castillo, both of you here offering me business deals, one of which is not strictly legal."

It was quite an admission. But it was unlikely that Hammond would ever be caught out by any law enforcement agency anywhere. Almost none of his business dealings were completely transparent. And in many cases, according to Otto, his businesses were at arm's length.

"Both of us came to you through Alyan?"

"Yes."

"In Castillo's case, how?"

Al-Hamadi looked to Hammond, who simply nodded.

"More or less the same way you did. He heard about me somewhere, probably at one of the casinos here in France, or perhaps Vegas or South Africa. There's that sort of circuit. Said he wanted to talk to Tom about a deal."

"What kind of a deal?"

"I can't say."

The pool deck was displayed on one of the monitors. Kamal and Pete were talking, and it was obvious that Susan Patterson wasn't particularly happy about it. But Courtney seemed to be enjoying herself.

"I haven't had time to do my homework on you, Canton. You admit that you're not a blogger, but are you a cop? Maybe U.S. Treasury?"

"I'm a civilian. And I can guarantee that I'm not employed by any agency in Washington."

"But you were a cop at one time?"

"Air Force OSI."

"So Alyan says. But I guess that you're a contractor, then. For whom?"

"I'm not that either."

"But your proposal to me is still on the table?"

"Nothing's changed," McGarvey said. "Castillo isn't his real name."

"It's no business of yours," Hammond said.

Al-Hamadi was clearly nervous.

"Castillo is a small-time stockbroker on the Bolsa in Mexico City," McGarvey said. "At least that's who he claims he is. But he's not connected enough to offer you anything of interest."

"Again it's no concern of yours."

"It becomes mine if my name is ever associated with his."

"Such a connection will never come from me," Hammond said.

"I'd still like to have an invitation to Jian's party. I'd like to offer him a piece of the action."

"You and Ms. Borman will be my guests."

At the door McGarvey turned back. "I'm not sure we'll be aboard for the race tomorrow. But we'll be in Basel. The Grand Hotel."

"Les Tres Rois," Hammond said. "I wish you luck unless you booked last year."

Back on the main deck Pete was waiting just forward of the gangway. A few of the guests had already left, but most of them were still aboard.

She started to say something when McGarvey appeared at the salon's sliding-glass doors, but he motioned for her to hold it.

"I've had enough partying for today," he said. "Let's go."

They hitched a ride on one of the golf carts back to the head of the docks, and from there caught a cab back to the Hermitage. But McGarvey held his silence until the cabby dropped them off at the hotel.

Upstairs in their room he went to the house phone and turned the instrument over. But if it was bugged it wasn't obvious.

"All they do is drink and talk about money," he said. He started around the room examining the lights, and the mirrors and paintings hanging on the walls.

"Can you think of anything more interesting?" she asked from the bedroom, where she checked the phone, the headboard, and mirrors and pictures.

They didn't have proper electronic bug detection equipment, but McGarvey figured it was worth the effort. If they found something it would be a signal of sorts that someone was looking at them and wanted them to back off.

The room was apparently clean and when they were finished they took the elevator down.

McGarvey called Otto and told him what had happened and about their search.

"Send Pete back upstairs and leave her phone in the room. I'll check for bugs."

McGarvey got out in the lobby and Pete went back up.

"Castillo is a blind," Otto said. "Someone by that name is registered on the Bolsa, but he's not made a trade all this year."

"Doesn't make him Nero."

"No. But he's got something to hide."

"And Hammond and al-Hamadi are helping him."

"My darlings are still checking for a match, or even near misses with his photos. But if Hammond is helping him, it can only mean that there's serious money on the table."

THIRTY-FIVE

"Attractive woman, Pete," Susan said.

"Not bad," Kamal replied absently. There'd been something about Joe Canton that didn't ring true, especially in light of what al-Hamadi had told him.

"She's obviously in love with him," Courtney said from across the table.

"That's nothing but a feminist myth," Martaan said rising. "There's no such thing as love."

"Not even a mother for her son?"

"Especially not," the race driver said, and he left.

"Pre-race jitters," Courtney said. "I've seen it before. All of them get it."

Kamal got up. "Don't go anywhere, I'll be right back," he told Susan and he went forward into the salon and took the stairs down two decks.

He knocked on Hammond's office door, which opened immediately.

"I thought you might be coming to see me," Hammond said.

Al-Hamadi was seated on the couch.

The image on one of the screens was of the pool deck. They'd seen everything.

"Joe Canton and the woman with him are fakes," Kamal said. "I think he could be a cop."

"That's a possibility," Hammond said. He shrugged. "He was interested in you and how you and Alyan met, and why."

Kamal sat down in one of the chairs and crossed his legs, to calm his nerves. He'd expected someone like Canton. Once the real Pablo Valdes had dropped out of sight the American DEA and Treasury department had been alerted. But he hadn't expected anyone to come this far so soon.

"Did you reveal my real identity?"

"Of course not," Hammond said. "In fact I vouched for you."

"Thank you for that, but aren't you taking a risk, doing business with me?"

"Not at all because he's not looking for a Mexican money launderer."

"Who then?"

Hammond laughed. "He says he doesn't want to be associated with riffraff."

Kamal laughed too. "His bitcoin scheme is a stretch. Alyan gave me a couple of the details."

"But not illegal," al-Hamadi said.

"Maybe impossible. Maybe he's pulling a scam on you."

Hammond was staring at him. "Why?"

"He could be U.S. Treasury."

"My people have found no connection between him and any law enforcement agency."

"But he and his woman are not bloggers."

"No," Hammond said. "But I'm told that his bitcoin scheme could work. We're looking into it. But in the meantime he and his woman will probably show up for the race tomorrow. Will you be here?"

"Wouldn't miss it," Kamal said getting up. "If he contacts either of you gentlemen again, would you let me know?"

"Of course," Hammond said, but it was obvious he didn't mean it, and just as obvious that he wasn't hiding his lie.

"I would be careful," al-Hamadi said. "He's a dangerous man."

"Has there been any word about the two men who attacked him?" Kamal asked. "That might give us a clue who he really is and what he's after."

"Nothing," Hammond said.

Susan was waiting for him in the salon. "What was that all about?" she asked.

"He wanted to know more about my deal."

"Leaving me out isn't fair. I've already told you that I wanted a part of the action."

"That might not be for the best right now. It's what I told Tom."

"Why?"

There were a lot of people in the salon. None of them was paying attention to him or Susan, but he was starting to feel uncomfortable, as if someone were looking down at him through a microscope as if he were a bug. A bug with a deadly sting.

"Later," he said.

"Good, let's go back to the hotel, I've got something for you."

Kamal made a show of brushing a finger across her cheek. They were lovers, and he wanted to make sure everyone knew it. It made him one of the players, or at least one of the hangers-on. "You're in the deal, but you don't have to pay for it with sex."

She laughed but it was strained. "I've never paid for anything with my body."

Kamal shrugged. It was a lie. She'd started out as a movie star, short on talent but not looks. "I apologize." Killing her in the end would be good.

"Accepted. But I do have something for you that I think will be helpful."

"A hint?"

"Later, as you said. It'll be a fair exchange, what I have for what you told Tom. Strictly business."

They held their silence until they got back to the hotel. On the way up to his suite Susan watched his face.

"You're the first Hispanic I've ever run into with a British accent," she said.

"My dad sent me to school in England."

"Porque?"

"He never told me, and he hung himself when I was in the middle of my first year."

"Did your mother explain it to you?"

"I never knew her, and the housekeepers couldn't help. Anyway, he left enough money for me to finish school."

"You must have missed him."

Kamal laughed without humor. "I was glad when I'd heard he was gone. In fact, Hammond reminds me of him."

"How?"

"He must have had friends at the AtEighth party. But he doesn't seem to be overly upset."

"Tom doesn't have friends. Only people he either fucks or does business with, or both."

Upstairs Kamal entered five sevens and an asterisk on his cell phone and walked through the suite and out to the balcony. There were no alarms. The place wasn't bugged.

"Checking for messages," he explained.

Susan poured them champagne from the fresh bottle of Krug that housekeeping had left in an ice bucket.

"What'd you tell Tom?"

"I think Canton is a cop, probably works for the American DEA or U.S. Treasury, something like that. But Tom said his people didn't think so."

"Here looking for you? If he is a cop."

"Tom vouched for me."

"Because of the deal you've offered him. Money's more important than friends."

"Is that why you were fucking him?"

"Only partly," she said. "Mostly it was out of boredom, until you came along."

"With my deal."

"Could there be any other reason?" she asked. "Anyway, I have something for you. What's your cell phone number?"

He gave her the one unsecure number of the three in his SIM card, the only one that would show up if his phone was hacked.

She called it, and when it chirped he answered. It was a text message.

MAYBE THIS WILL HELP

Along with the message were two decent photographs of Canton, one in profile, the other with him standing at the forward rail, Hammond to one side.

"I took these when he wasn't looking."

THIRTY-SIX

McGarvey and Pete walked down to a sidewalk café and got lucky with a table facing the racetrack near the entrance to the tunnel, the harbor just on the other side. His nerves were jumping all over the place. He was sure that they were being watched, but by whom he didn't know.

The waiter came and they ordered coffees.

Pete picked up on his mood. "What's up?"

"I think someone's doubled back on us," he said.

He scanned the yachts across the way, and closer, the people walking past. To the south many of the balconies on the apartment buildings facing the track had people. During the race tomorrow every balcony would be crammed.

But for now there was nothing out of place that he could see. No cameras on tripods, no parabolic dishes for listening to conversations over a great distance. No glint of binocular or spotting scope lenses on any of the rooftops. No helicopters slowly circling overhead with someone hanging out an open hatch. No passerby in a suit coat that was cut slightly large in the chest to conceal a pistol in a shoulder holster.

"Castillo, or whoever he really is? Or Nero?"

McGarvey turned to look at her. "If Nero's here, and I think he is, he's come to get an invitation to Jian's party but not necessarily from Hammond. And he's not alone, I'd bet anything on it."

"A woman, like Susan Patterson?"

"Maybe, but he's also got an organization behind him. Someone who led him to al-Hamadi, or to someone else who could get him an audience with one of the players."

"Nero would have to be posing as someone interesting enough to catch the attention of people like Hammond."

"That's the point," McGarvey said. "Castillo doesn't have anything to offer."

"Then why'd Hammond agree to meet with him? Why was he invited on the yacht? And what is the Patterson broad doing draped all over him? It doesn't make any sense from my seat in the bleachers."

Their coffee came, the waiter leaving the small *addition* slip under McGarvey's saucer.

Otto phoned, and he sounded all out of breath like he usually did when he was excited. "There's a bug in your television set. Audio and visual. Pretty neat."

"Nero?"

"Maybe, but I'm betting the DGSI put it there."

"Because of the warning we got when we showed up in Paris?" McGarvey asked. "That doesn't make any sense. And they would have to know our work names."

"I haven't figured that one out yet, but they could have connected you with the dead guy on the beach in Cannes. There was nothing about it in the news, or on the service's mainframe."

"They know about me, but they also know about you, so they're keeping it off their computers for now."

"Yeah, and there's more," Otto said. "The pictures you took of Castillo have turned up to be a dead end. He doesn't show up in any databases I've been able to search, and my darlings are pretty thorough. And that's something all in itself. Everyone leaves a record. Driving licenses, passports, school graduations."

"He speaks with a British accent, my bet is that he went to school there as a kid."

"Accents can be faked."

"If that was the case he'd be speaking with a Mexican accent, it'd make more sense. And Hammond had to have picked up on it. Which means Castillo had a good explanation."

"One that Hammond's people would have vetted," Otto said. "I'm on it."

"What about the bug in our room?"

"I left it so watch what you say. But they already know that you checked in under work names, and they probably followed you out to Hammond's yacht, so they have to be curious about what you guys are really doing there."

"Has the DGSI taken it any further?"

"If you mean to Page, I don't know. But I can check."

"Don't. But I won't be surprised if Walt calls me at some point."

"What're you going to tell him?"

"Enough to have him get the French off my back at least until Monday."

"Okay. In the meantime I'll try to find out what Hammond knows about Castillo that would want him to do business."

After their coffees they went for a walk back in the general direction of the hotel, but never so far away from the Med that it was out of sight. Once again McGarvey was reminded of his dead wife. They had sailed in the Gulf of Mexico and out to the Bahamas. But that was gone now, and although Pete was at his side, and he thought he was falling in love with her, it wasn't the same.

Nothing could ever be the same because of everything

else that had happened in his life. He was in constant fear for Pete's safety.

He told her everything that Otto had found, and not found, and the new search for whomever Castillo had presented himself to be to Hammond.

"If he's brought a deal, it'd have to be worth some serious money," Pete agreed. "A hundred million?"

"More."

"Okay, so we have to find someone—presumably from Mexico—who's dealing in that kind of money."

McGarvey had it all of a sudden and he phoned Otto. "Drug cartel money laundering."

"I'll get back to you."

"What if that turns out to be another dead end?" Pete asked.

"Basel is next."

"But if Nero has already got an invitation to Jian's party, wouldn't he just fade back into the woodwork?" she asked.

"Good point."

"This'll have to be coordinated with Homeland Security, the Bureau, and the NYPD."

"And that's exactly what I don't want to happen. If they put shooters all over the place, I'd be able to spot them and I'd turn back."

"Unless Castillo isn't Nero," Pete said, continuing to play devil's advocate. "He could be one of the hangers-on. Even one of the wait staff or a workman. Even a cop or one of the players' bodyguards. He got into AtEighth by impersonating Khalid Seif, a man all of them had worked with but no one, apparently not even Callahan himself, had ever seen in person. The list isn't endless, but it's nearly so. Question is, what would you do if you were him?"

"I don't know yet, but I'd find a way."

"Yes, you would."

Otto got back to him. "Pablo Valdes. *Numero uno* in the business. But it's just a name, no clear photographs and no police record; even our DEA has nothing much on him."

"What kind of money are we talking about?"

"In the tens of billions, more," Otto said. "Tempting to a guy like Hammond and some of the crowd he runs around with."

"It's just about the same way he got into AtEighth."

"Still doesn't mean a thing, and it doesn't prove that he's impersonating Valdes and in turn presenting himself as Castillo."

"Only Hammond would know that," McGarvey said.

"Nero impersonated Seif, a man no one had ever seen. And he may be doing the same thing as Valdes. It's gotta mean he has a damned good source of intel. He didn't do this on his own."

"Back to the Saudis again?" McGarvey asked.

"Possible, but there won't be anything that would stick. I haven't found anything on their mainframe on el Nassr, but something might show up on Seif and Valdes. Maybe routine background checks."

"We're going back out to the yacht to watch the race tomorrow," McGarvey said. "See if you can find out anything by then."

"Will do," Otto promised.

Before they got back to the hotel McGarvey explained everything to Pete. "It's a deal that Hammond might buy into. He's willing to take a look at Otto's bitcoin scheme, why not money laundering?"

"Could explain why the Patterson broad is hanging all over Castillo," Pete said. She grinned. "Maybe someone should ask *her*."

THIRTY-SEVEN

Kamal suggested that they have dinner in the hotel's La Vistamar on the terrace overlooking the harbor. It had one Michelin star, and Susan accepted immediately.

She phoned the yacht and had some fresh clothes, including a cocktail dress and decent shoes, sent over to the hotel.

"I'll just jump in the shower, if you'll be a dear and make reservations," she said. "If they give you any trouble use my name."

When she was in the bedroom suite Kamal called the restaurant on the house phone and booked them a table for two. Even using Susan's name, nothing was open until nine, two hours from now.

Out on the balcony he phoned Sa'ad, who seemed impatient, almost angry at being disturbed again.

"I'm late," he said. "Be quick."

"Joe Canton, the American who's brought the bitcoin scheme to Hammond, could be a cop looking for me."

"Yes, I know. But if you can't complete this operation cleanly then I want you to back away. In any event, half of the objective has been accomplished with the desired effect. There's even talk in Congress about joining with Russian forces in Syria. Our problem could be solved that easily."

"I want to walk away intact."

"Walk away if that's what you want. But the other half of your fee will be forfeited."

"Intact," Kamal said. "I'm not going to spend the rest of my life in prison somewhere. Or watching over my shoulder for someone coming up behind me."

Sa'ad did not reply for a longish moment. "What are you saying?"

"I want to finish, but I need some information."

Again Sa'ad held his silence for a beat. When he came back he was cautious. "Nothing will be traced back to us," he said. "You know this. If you fail we will wash our hands of you."

"Behind sovereign immunity?"

"If it comes to that. But you're not stopping?"

"No," Kamal said. Strictly speaking he didn't need the money, though it was going to be very expensive to go deep. But in point of fact if a dozen buildings with people in them needed to come down he would be happy to take on the satisfying work.

"As you wish. What help do you need?"

"I have two photographs of the American. I want to know who he is."

"Was he aware that you had taken them?"

"No."

"Are you sure?"

"Yes," Kamal said.

"I won't be able to look at them until later tonight or sometime tomorrow. But if I come up with something, I'll call you."

"Thank you."

"In the meantime, don't do anything stupid."

Kamal's grip on the phone tightened. Killing the Saudi intelligence officer would be a thing of joy—foolish, but satisfying. "I'll wait for your call."

"Will you be aboard Hammond's yacht for the race?"

"Yes."

"Will your American and his woman be there as well?"

"Almost certainly."

"Send the photographs."

Kamal sent them.

"I'll try to get back to you before then," Sa'ad said, and he hung up.

"You're a man of many mysteries," Susan said from the doorway. She was drying her hair with a towel, but she was naked, her body still glistening.

Kamal turned around. "Do you find that appealing?"

"I find money appealing. Who did you send the photos to?"

"A research service in Amsterdam."

"Hackers?"

"They're the only ones who know how to come up with information the old-fashioned away. By stealing it."

"My name wasn't associated?"

"No. But would it matter?"

"You're a money launderer. Canton and the arm candy with him probably work for the DEA, Treasury, or maybe even the FBI. I'm not worried about them, of course, but the people who run the cartels you represent aren't interested in law and order. Someone crosses them and they kill them. They're even worse than the ISIS crazies."

Kamal smiled. "As long as you're with me, you're safe."

"What are you talking about?" she asked. Her voice was level but he could see stress in her eyes, in the set of her mouth and her posture. She was frightened. This was something that she didn't know if her money could protect her from. She was vulnerable.

"I'm providing them with a necessary service," Kamal said. "Simply put, they won't fuck with me as long as I'm solving their problem for them."

She looked at him, searching his face, obviously trying to gauge his sincerity. For all her money, she was little more than an insecure little girl.

"What time are our reservations?"

"Nine."

She went to a house phone and called the desk. "A package is coming for me from the *Glory*. Hold it at the desk until I call for it." She hung up and turned back to Kamal. "We have an hour and a half."

"Time enough," he said, and he went with her into the bedroom. Making love to her was more than sex for him. Each time she was in the throes of orgasm he imagined killing her. His hands around her throat, crushing the wind from her. Watching her eyes bulging. Watching her lips turning blue.

He would be on top of her, between her legs, his bulk holding her thrashing body from escape.

He pulled off his clothes as she laid down on the bed, his erection almost painful.

She was beautiful in life, but when the time came she was going to be gorgeous at the point of death.

Susan wore a white cocktail dress, the front cut so low that whenever she moved to either side the nipples of her breasts were momentarily exposed. Even in Monaco, one of the most hedonistic places on the planet, she turned heads.

Kamal wore an Armani tuxedo and ruffled shirt but no tie. He too turned heads, and both he and Susan knew the effect they were producing.

When they were seated at a table next to the balcony's rail, the maître d' handed them menus, but Kamal declined.

Two waiters were there.

"*Oursins* first," Kamal told them. "Caviar, perhaps *potage d'oignon,* lobsters au gratin, and wine."

"Yes, sir," the head waiter said. "And may I recommend a fine wine?"

"No. We'll have a bottle of Boërl and Kroff Brut. Very cold."

Even the head waiter was impressed, though he didn't

show it. The single bottle was priced in the range of twenty-five hundred dollars, plus the restaurant's markup.

"Keep a second bottle on ice, please."

"Splurging, are we?" Susan asked.

"But it's not my money."

THIRTY-EIGHT

The house phone rang at eight in the morning, and McGarvey, who had gotten up an hour earlier and was on the balcony looking at the harbor, picked it up. "Yes?"

"M. Canton, this is the desk, your car is here, sir."

"I didn't order a car."

"It has come to take you to the harbor."

"We'll be a half hour."

"The driver did not mention Mme. Borman."

"Thank you," McGarvey said. He got an outside line and telephoned the *Glory*.

A woman answered. *"Oui?"*

"This is Joe Canton, I'd like to speak with Mr. Hammond."

"Oui, une moment, monsieur."

Hammond came on almost immediately. "You're an early riser."

"Yes, I am. Did you send a car for me?"

"No. Do you need one?"

"It's not necessary. Just a mix-up at the desk."

"We'll see you and Ms. Borman at eleven then. But no later or I'll have to send a helicopter to the hotel to get you through the mob."

Pete came out in shorts and a T-shirt. "Who was that?"

"The desk called and said my car was waiting, but when

I called Hammond he didn't know what I was talking about."

She had a cup of coffee and she put it down. "Let's go see who's interested in us. Maybe it's Nero."

"The car was sent for me, not us," McGarvey said. "And I have a feeling it's someone from the DGSI. I want you to stay here and if I don't show up or at least call, let Otto know what's happening."

"I'm not going to stay here and let you get yourself taken out."

"Yes, you are. If it's Nero or someone he's sent, I'll handle it. In the meantime our plane is waiting in Cannes. Just get the hell out of France."

Pete was worked up. "Goddamnit, Kirk, this isn't right and you know it."

"If both of us are taken down, there'll be no one to show up at Jian's party. One of us has to be there, and *you* know it."

"Christ," she said.

He gave her a hug. "Don't count me out yet."

She gave him a bleak look, but nodded.

He got his jacket, and the passport card Major Galan had issued, but left his gun.

Two large men in business suits, no ties, were waiting for him in the lobby, which was not very busy at this hour of the morning. No one was checking out on the day of the race.

McGarvey walked directly over to them where they stood just to the left of the doors. "Gentlemen, you're my ride?"

"Yes, sir," the taller of the pair said. He discreetly showed his DGSI identification. "Major Galan has a few questions for you."

"How did you find me here?"

"Are you armed, sir?" the agent asked.

"No."

They stepped aside and McGarvey went out ahead of them to a dark blue Citroën C-Elysée parked in front, the rear passenger-side door open. The car was sleek and fast, and not many years ago had competed in touring car races in Germany.

Major Galan was waiting in the backseat. "Get in, please," he said.

"Am I under arrest?" McGarvey asked.

"That will depend upon you."

"What about Ms. Boylan? She'll wonder where I've gone."

"She'll be told to leave France when her visa card expires. And we'll inform Mr. Page what action we've taken here."

McGarvey got in. The two officers followed and they drove off.

"Where are you taking me?"

"To police headquarters here, and if need be, back to Paris."

"My things?"

"I'm sure that Ms. Boylan will see to them."

"May I telephone her?"

"No."

Monaco's Sûrete Publique police headquarters was located in the middle of the race course on the Rue Suffren-Reymond. Police parted the crowds and opened the barriers for them to pass through.

They went into the building through the sallyport where prisoners were brought for booking, and from there directly back to an interrogation room. McGarvey was searched before he sat down at a small table across from Galan.

"You and Ms. Boylan did not come to France for the film festival or for the Grand Prix," the major said. "Why are you here?"

"I'm following a possible lead to the destruction of the pencil tower in New York."

"You should be in Syria."

"That's a possibility."

"What about Ms. Boylan's presence here?"

"She's acting as my cover."

Galan considered this for a moment. "Have you had success?"

"Not yet."

The major took two photos out of a file folder and passed them across to McGarvey. One of them was of a burly bare-chested man on what looked like an apartment balcony, and the other of a man in slacks and a polo shirt in front of what looked like a nightclub. They were the ones from the beach.

"Do you know either of these men?"

"No."

"Both of them were seen in Cannes," Galan said. He passed another photo across. It was the dead man on the beach. "You were seen with another man who we've identified as a Saudi Arabian national leaving the Majestic Hotel and walking down to the *plage* shortly before this body was discovered. Did you see or hear anything?"

"No. But from the looks of it the wound was either caused by a knife or a gunshot."

"Actually, what killed the man was a blow to the side of the head from a blunt object."

"Fingerprints, DNA?"

"No."

"You know who I am, and what I've done in France, and at least once *for* France, so you have to know this is not how I've ever worked," McGarvey said, and he shoved the photographs back to the major. "These guys look like street thugs."

"They are. We're looking for the second man, who with the proper persuasion might give us a description of the man who did this."

"And maybe what they were doing on the beach at that time of night."

Galan held his silence for a beat. "Looking for you, I suspect."

"When you catch up with him, I'd like to ask a couple of questions. Because if someone sent them after me, it meant they knew who I was and why I was here, and were watching the hotel."

"Their timing was wrong, is that what you're telling me?"

"It looks like it," McGarvey said. "What now?"

"Your air crew is standing by at the airport in Cannes. They've been instructed to leave French airspace as quickly as possible as soon as you're aboard."

"And Ms. Boylan?"

"She has the remainder of the week to stay in France."

THIRTY-NINE

Pete telephoned Otto from the room. As usual he answered on the first ring, even though it was in the middle of the night on the East Coast.

"The French police hauled Mac away a half hour ago, and he hasn't called me yet," she said. Her thoughts were jumping all over the place.

"How do you know it was the cops?"

She told Otto about the telephone call and Mac's instructions that if he didn't return or at least call her, to get out of France. "I got downstairs right behind him, in time to see him get in the backseat of a car and drive off. The plates were government."

"Okay, hold on."

Pete took her phone to the balcony and looked out over the harbor. If Castillo was in actuality their Nero she couldn't just pack up and return to Langley. At least not until she had something new to take back with her.

Otto was back in under a minute. "Okay, it was the cops. I talked to Captain Gratto in Cannes. He was ordered to make the plane ready for immediate takeoff. It sounds like Mac is being kicked out. Did they say anything to you?"

"Nothing."

"I'll call Gratto again and tell him to declare an emergency. It'll give you time to pack up, rent a car, and get down there."

"I'm not leaving."

"What are you talking about? You have to get out."

"I'm going out to Hammond's yacht for the race."

"Goddamnit, Pete, if the guy posing as Castillo is in fact Nero, you wouldn't stand a chance."

"Nothing's going to happen aboard a yacht filled with people."

"I'm not worried about that part. It's afterwards."

"I still have my gun and the one Hanks gave Mac."

"With all due respect, you're a damned good interrogator, but not much of a field agent."

"I'll take the TGV up to Paris first thing tomorrow. Get me a reservation on an early evening flight back to Dulles."

"If I have to, I'll call the French police and tell them that you're armed and need to be kicked out of France."

"Don't do it," Pete practically shouted.

"Shit," Otto said, resigned. "Keep your phone with you, I'll monitor what's happening." He hesitated. "Mac's going to kill me. And you."

"I know," Pete said. "Gotta go."

Pete got dressed in flared jeans and a white peasant blouse that was long enough to cover the subcompact slim-line Glock pistol Hanks had brought for her, the holster tucked in the waistband. The magazine held only seven rounds plus the one in the receiver, but the .45-caliber load had good stopping power. She didn't bother with the silencer or extra mag. If it came to a shootout, she wanted it short and noisy so that help wouldn't be long in coming.

She didn't carry a purse, only the French visa card, a couple hundred euros in cash, and her Amex gold card, plus the cell phone in her back pocket.

She didn't bother calling the yacht for a helicopter to come pick her up. She wanted some time to think about her options. Otto was right, she wasn't the best field officer in the pack, but she was learning by leaps and bounds tagging along with McGarvey. And the lesson she was focused on now was taking care of business.

Because of the dense crowds it took the cab more than a half hour to get down to the harbor, where she caught a golf cart out to the yacht.

Hammond had evidently been alerted because he met her at the head of the gangway and pulled her aside, as two others came up behind her. "Joe is running late?" he asked.

"Actually, he's on his way to New York. Business. But he wanted me to stay for the race and assure you that whenever you want to buy in, he'll have his pro contact you with the details."

"Pro?"

"Yeah. His name is Otto and there's no one better anywhere on the planet. And that's not bragging, believe me."

Hammond gave her an odd look. "I thought that was just a cover."

"In this business, cover stories have to be real."

"Who do you work for?"

"Ourselves," Pete said. "Now, what does a girl have to do around here to have a drink and get something to eat?"

"The pool deck or topsides, where the race will be easier to watch," Hammond said. "But you know your way around." He kissed her cheek, then went into the salon and took the stairs down.

Courtney, champagne in hand, met her on the pool deck. "You're becoming quite the regular," she said. "Where's Joe?"

"On his way to New York by now, I think," Pete said, shrugging. She snagged a glass of champagne from one of the waitresses.

"I see," Courtney said, arching an eyebrow. "But I don't think that either of you came to watch the race."

"Did Tom say something to you?" Pete asked.

"Only in the vaguest of terms."

Kamal came from the starboard side of the yacht, a glass of champagne in hand, and he walked to the aft rail and looked toward the city.

Courtney followed Pete's gaze. "Be careful, honey."

"Yes?"

"He's a dangerous man."

"Aren't they all?"

"Not like him, or like your man. They're both cut of the same cloth, I think."

Pete was startled and it showed.

"Maybe on different sides of the fence, but the same nevertheless."

"How about his girlfriend? Is she dangerous too?"

Courtney laughed. "She's a slut, but a shrewd one. She's with Angel because of the deal he's offered Tom."

"What deal would that be?" Pete asked.

"Why don't you ask him yourself? Here he comes."

Kamal was smiling pleasantly. "Ladies."

"Got to go," Courtney said and she went into the salon.

"I don't think she likes me," Kamal said. "There's a problem between her and Susan."

"She might be jealous," Pete suggested.

"Of what?"

"The deal you've offered Tom. Courtney believes that Susan is being cut in, and I think she probably wants some of the action."

"Deal?"

"That's what I heard."

Kamal looked past her. "Where's Joe this morning?"

"He had to get back to New York, but I wanted to stay for the race."

"I thought that you were a couple."

"If you mean married, the answer is no. We're just partners."

"Here to offer Tom a deal of your own?"

"Something like that. Do you want to swap proposals? There's room for both of you."

"I'll have to think about it," Kamal said insincerely.

Susan came out from the salon, dressed again in a stunningly tiny black string bikini and a gauze pool jacket. As soon as she spotted Kamal with Pete, her face lit up in a smile that was more grimace.

"I wondered where you had gotten yourself to, darling," she said, accepting Kamal's kiss on the cheek. She gave Pete a once-over. "Slumming, are we?"

"Are you?" Pete asked her. She turned back to Kamal. "Anyway, think about it."

"Think about what?" Susan demanded.

Pete turned and went into the salon to get another glass of wine and something to eat. One for the Christians, zip for the lions.

FORTY

Major Galan rode with McGarvey down to the airport at Cannes, the same two operatives who had showed up at the hotel also tagging along, one of them driving as before.

"I won't feel comfortable until I see you safely in the air, Mr. Director," the French DGSI officer admitted.

By now Pete would have contacted Otto, who would had found out that McGarvey was being deported. He counted on her being bright about it and taking the train directly to Paris and flying home from there. But in the back of his head he didn't think it was going to work out that way.

"Why's that?"

"Wherever you go you have the habit of leaving behind a trail of bodies. It's a history France does not want. We have mounting troubles of our own."

"Immigrants," McGarvey said. They had been Europe's biggest problem for several years now.

"Yes, too many of them left over from Syria. ISIS, some of them, proved after Paris."

The morning was beautiful, and back in Monaco the race would be starting soon. McGarvey could only hope that at the very least Pete had stayed put at the hotel and had not been foolish enough to go out to Hammond's yacht. But the more he thought about it the more he was certain it's exactly where she was. Pushing at Nero, galling him into making a move.

"I'd like to let Ms. Boylan know where I'm going. She'll be worried."

"I'm sure that M. Rencke will have already informed her. In any event she knows that you have been detained. She followed you down to the lobby and came to the door as we drove off. The license plates on this car are of the government."

McGarvey held his silence, working out his options.

"Is she in some danger?" Galan asked.

"I don't think so."

"The man on the beach targeted you, we're sure of it, though not why nor under whose employment. Should we be concerned that they may come after her?"

"It's not likely," McGarvey said.

"In any event if she works with you, she must be a capable woman. But until or unless she breaks a French law she will be free to come and go as she pleases. Until her visa card expires, when her passport will be returned to her."

They rode along the scenic A8 autoroute, traffic very light because of the race.

"I read some of your files," Galan said. "Not all of them, of course, but enough to understand that you are a dangerous man and that you would not have brought weapons into France unless you were in pursuit of someone. Perhaps we could be of some assistance, if you will tell us why you came."

"We're looking for the man who brought down At-Eighth."

Galan was impressed. "You think he is here in France, in Monaco, working for ISIS?"

"We think it's a possibility."

"But you're not sure."

"No."

Galan thought about it for a longish moment. "But why would he come here?"

"We're not sure about that either."

"Maybe we can help, if the request came through channels from Langley. Your director could call mine."

"I'm not employed by the CIA."

"That's what I was told you would say," Galan replied.

The Gulfstream was parked in front of the VIP terminal at Mandelieu airport just west of Cannes.

Galan got out of the car with McGarvey and handed him a sealed package. "Your weapons along with Mme. Boylan's, and your passport. Do not come back to France unless you make your intentions known, you come unarmed, and you ask for permission. Is any of this unclear, Mr. Director?"

"No," McGarvey said.

"Then I wish you luck with your investigation—whoever is directing it. America did not need another disaster such as this one. Obviously ISIS has mounted a copycat operation."

"That's what we think."

"Then *bon chance,* and if there is anything France can do to help—and believe me I have been authorized to tell you this—make the request through channels."

They shook hands, and as soon as McGarvey was aboard, and the aircraft buttoned up, Gratto taxied to the runway, and they were airborne within a couple of minutes.

When they were at cruising altitude and heading north to Prestwick, where they would refuel, McGarvey went forward to the cockpit.

"Change of plans. I want you to drop me off in Geneva."

"What about Ms. Boylan?"

"I'm going back for her."

"Yes, sir," Gratto said, grinning.

Back in his seat Mac phoned Otto. "Tell me that Pete is on her way to Paris."

"She's aboard Hammond's yacht," Otto said. "Nothing I could say would stop her."

It was exactly what McGarvey knew she would do. "If Castillo is Nero, and he's our guy, he'll kill her if he gets the chance."

"Don't count her out, Mac. She pretty capable. Anyway, her cell phone is on and I'm monitoring her conversations. So far it's just been a pissing contest between her and Susan Patterson."

"I'm on my way to Geneva, from where I'll get back to Monaco."

"It'll have to be by car, you've already missed the one TGV to Marseilles. But it's less than three hundred miles, so you should be back early this evening. Did Galan return your pistol?"

"Yes," McGarvey said. "Can you set Pete's cell phone to vibrate instead of ring?"

"Done," Otto said.

"What's happening right now?"

"She's talking to a woman; my darlings say ninety-eight percent Courtney Rich, about the race. They've met one of the drivers, and Ms. Rich is worried about him. Says he has a death wish."

"Anyone else with them?"

"Background noise, but no, and definitely not Castillo unless he isn't talking."

"Put me through to her."

Pete's phone vibrated and she answered it. "Yes?"

"It's me. I'm in the air on my way to Geneva. Can you talk?"

"It's Joe, on his way to New York," she said.

"Sweet," a woman said.

A moment or two later Pete was back. "I'm on the starboard deck, no one's nearby. Castillo is on the pool deck with the Patterson broad. From what I've been able to figure out she's not all that happy with him."

"I want you to get the hell out of there right now. Go back to the hotel and don't let anybody in, not even room service. I should get to you sometime early tonight. Do you understand?"

"We don't know he's Nero."

"We don't know he's *not* Nero, for Christ's sake, Pete."

"You're right, and that's one of the things we came here to find out."

"Goddamnit, you have to start listening to me."

"I'm either part of this endeavor—part of your life—or I'll just turn away and say the hell with you."

McGarvey didn't know what to do. He could see the limo carrying his wife and daughter blown apart right in front of him. His wife was not an operative, but his daughter had been. And they were both dead.

"If she leaves now, Nero—if it's him—will know that something's up," Otto broke in. "And all the locks in any hotel anywhere won't stop him if he's our guy."

"I'll keep people around me until it's time to hole up in our room," Pete said. "And trust me, Kirk, anyone trying to get through that door will be dead."

FORTY-ONE

Each time the racing machines entered the tunnel, and seconds later emerged with an almost impossibly loud scream then disappeared, Hammond's guests on the yacht looked up with some interest. But as soon as the four lead cars bunched up in a tight group were gone, they went back to their talk.

Kamal, sitting with Susan and two other couples on the pool deck, spotted the American woman talking with Courtney, who seemed to have adopted her. He would have bet almost anything that the Americans were not who they presented themselves to be. In fact, the more he thought about it he was nearly certain that they had somehow found out about him, which was why they were here.

But that was nothing more than a hunch, an instinct for survival that the drill instructors at Sandhurst had drummed into their heads. "Develop your instincts, learn which of your hunches is based on fact—no matter how insignificant the fact might seem to you at the time. Might save your life."

Susan leaned closer to him. "Do you want to fuck her?" she asked softly enough so that the others couldn't hear what she'd said.

"She's not my type, but it might be interesting," he said, turning to her. "Would you mind terribly?"

"Not unless you offered her a part of your deal. The boardroom is already crowded enough with me and Tom and the possibility of Viktor and Jian."

"She's obviously not a player, so it's not likely she could buy in for any significant portion."

"Obviously," Susan said. "So what are you looking for?"

"I'm not sure. But there's something odd about her and the man she came with."

"Do you think they're on to you?"

Kamal forced himself not to demand what she meant. "I doubt it, but they want something, and I think Tom knows more about them than he lets on."

Susan smiled. "Tom knows more about everything than he'll ever let on."

The lead cars came through the tunnel, the positions

unchanged, except for number four, a McLaren, which had dropped back, a small amount of smoke trailing from the engine.

It was only the fifteenth of seventy-eight laps and this was the first trouble.

"Martaan is still in the lead," Susan said, watching the cars until they'd turned out of sight around the curve. "Just about everyone here thinks that there's a good chance he won't survive the race."

Both couples, whom Kamal and Susan had mostly ignored, drifted off.

"Why's that?"

"He's too much in love with his stardom."

"Weren't you?"

"Of course, but then, I wasn't doing something that had the potential of killing me," she said. She glanced up to where Courtney was talking with the American woman.

Kamal followed her gaze.

"I could help you with her," Susan said.

"Do you mean a ménage à trois?"

Susan chuckled. "If that's your style, it's okay with me."

"I doubt if she'd be willing."

"A little coke to calm her down, and then a popper or two to bring her up. Might get some interesting answers from her, along with the sex. Maybe find out who she really is. Could be fun."

"Tonight?"

"Right now. We can use my stateroom. Tom would probably get his rocks off watching us."

Kamal was amazed despite himself. She was the shallowest, most hedonistic woman he'd ever met. He had thought how good it would be killing her in the middle of sex, but now he wondered if it wouldn't be even more interesting to let her live for a while. If for no other reason than to see what other incredible things she was capable of.

"How would you proceed?"

"Watch," Susan said. She snagged one of the crew passing with a tray of champagne and got two glasses. "Is she looking at us?"

Kamal glanced at the upper deck. Courtney and the American were looking the other way. "No," he said.

Susan poured something into both of the champagne glasses. "Look and learn," she said, standing up.

"You've drugged both drinks," Kamal said.

"I can handle it," Susan said. "Maybe the broad can't." She slapped him very hard on the face. "You motherfucker!" she cried at the top of her voice, then picked up both glasses and stomped off.

A few of the people around the pool looked over and chuckled, but then turned back to the race. Susan Patterson had a reputation.

Tom Hammond came from the salon and sat down at Kamal's table just as Susan reached Pete and Courtney.

"Susan puts on a good show," Hammond said. "What's the drill this time?"

"She's trying to arrange a ménage à trois," Kamal said.

"One of her favorites. But let me guess, it was your idea because you don't trust either the woman or the man she came with."

"They could be DEA."

"I don't think so, but they're not bloggers either. They came to me with a deal to corner the bitcoin market. Might be something you'd be interested in. Long-term, I think. But they're talking a fair sum of money."

"It's a thought," Kamal said.

The American woman had taken the glass of champagne.

"It would get you close enough to find out what they're really up to—besides the bitcoin idea, I mean."

The American woman wasn't drinking.

Kamal turned his attention to Hammond. "This is a game to you."

"Isn't it to you?"

"No."

The American woman, a slight smile on her full lips, was listening to Susan, who had turned animated.

"Pablo Valdes has disappeared," Hammond said.

"Yes, I have."

"The Mexican army thinks that you're in the mountains somewhere near the U.S. border."

"Then it's a good thing that I'm here, and in a few weeks I'll be in New York," Kamal said. In fact Valdes's body was in the mountains one hundred miles west of Ciudad Juárez.

The American woman held the champagne glass up to the light, then smiled and tossed it over the side.

Susan shrugged, downed her drink, and tossed the empty glass overboard. She said something, then walked away.

"I don't think that's exactly how she planned it," Hammond said.

"I'd like you to do me a favor."

"I don't do favors."

"I'll give you two extra points on the deal."

"What do you want?"

"I have to leave in a bit, but I'd like you to keep Ms. Borman here until after the race, and for as long as possible after that."

"What are you planning?"

"I won't know till I do a little research."

"We have computers and satphones aboard that you could use."

"I appreciate the offer, but some things are best left private."

"Will we see you tomorrow? We're taking a run out to Mallorca."

"I'll see. But I could always chopper out to you."

Kamal managed to get off the yacht without Susan or the American woman spotting him. He took a cab back to his suite at the Hermitage. Almost the moment he walked in Sa'ad was on the phone.

"You need to go to ground as soon as possible."

"What are you talking about?"

"We think that it is a possibility that the man in the photographs you sent me is Kirk McGarvey, onetime director of the CIA. He's in disguise, but if it is him, and you go against him, you're a dead man."

Mega-yacht Run;
Mallorca

FORTY-TWO

Callahan Holdings CFO, and now acting CEO Nancy Nebel, got off the private elevator on the 110th floor, and paused in the entry vestibule for a moment or two. It was a few minutes after eight in the evening. This was Jian Chang's penthouse—two floors of luxury connected by an escalator.

The unit, which had sold for $210 million sight unseen, was the most expensive condo in all of North America.

"And that's just the beginning," George had told her.

AtEighth was nice but this pencil tower was even more luxurious: "Like comparing the *Lusitania* with the *QM2*," he'd said. "But much better things are coming."

She'd seen the plans, of course, not only for the next three towers, but for Grand Soleil, a mixed-use building in Midtown, that would rise more than three thousand feet above Park Avenue South.

And Frank Lloyd Wright's original scheme for a sky-scraper that would rise 5,280 feet into the sky, a full mile, had been George's ultimate plan. He'd been worried that some sheik in the Middle East, Dubai, or the UAE would beat him to the punch.

Such a monstrous building would never—could never—make a profit, and Nancy had told him just that.

"Of course not, sweetheart," he'd said. The words were condescending, but his meaning wasn't. This project would be all about prestige. Not only for the company, but for New York, for the U.S.—hell, for the entire western hemisphere.

She hadn't bought it, but George had been a consummate salesman, and convincing the board, though not easy, was the sort of a challenge he'd always loved. And he'd won the fight. The building hadn't been named yet, nor had an architectural firm been selected. The concept had started as nothing more than something inside George's head, and a few sketches he'd made on a legal pad. It had only advanced to a fanciful model in the Callahan lobby.

She remembered when he'd first showed it to her. The sketches had taken her breath way. "It looks like it's about ready to take off straight up," she'd said.

"Maybe we'll call it Star Ship."

"We're talking about, what, five billion dollars?"

"More," he'd said, but he'd been a dreamer and figures like that never bothered him.

Li Huan, who was Mr. Jian's number-one assistant, came down the escalator with an attractive Occidental woman whom Nancy didn't recognize. They were deep in discussion. The penthouse had been furnished only to the extent of kitchen appliances, treatments for the sixteen-foot floor-to-ceiling windows, and the wood, tile, and carpet on the floors, plus the magnificent handcrafted light fixtures and chandeliers, most of which were studded with diamonds, many of the individual stones five carats or more.

Except for one hanging in the exact middle of the condo from the second-floor ceiling through the soaring atrium, whose value was more than $15 million. Some of its stones—diamonds, rubies, emeralds—were in the ten-carat range, but had cost Jian nothing, because they had been in his family for a dozen generations.

"Ah, Mrs. Nebel," Li said, spotting her.

He and the woman came over. "Everything is in order here?" Nancy asked.

"Of course," Mr. Li said. "Please meet Mr. Jian's curator of collectibles, Ms. Kelley Conley."

Nancy shook hands with both of them.

"You've built a beautiful residence, congratulations," the young woman said. She was American, from California somewhere.

"Thank you, I hope Mr. Jian will like it."

"I can guarantee it," Kelley Conley said. "But we were so sorry to hear of the tragedy of AtEighth. What a horrible thing to occur so soon after nine-eleven."

"I can assure you something like that will not happen here. Our security will be bulletproof."

"But unobtrusive, I would expect," Li said.

"Of course."

Li took a heavily embossed sheet of Jian Chang's letterhead from his breast pocket and handed it to Nancy. "This is Mr. Jian's guest list. Seventy people in all—mostly couples. But you may notice four names that may not be familiar to you."

Nancy scanned the list. Almost all of them were players—men and a few women who were billionaires. The four names at the bottom were of men she'd never heard of. One of them Russian or Ukrainian, Two western—possibly British or U.S. citizens—and one German. She looked up.

"The four are Mr. Jian's personal security people. They will be armed."

"I think you'll need authorization from the New York Police Department."

"Governor Bestman was kind enough to provide the authorization," Li said.

Bestman's name along with his wife's were on the list. It was a shrewd move on Jian's part, inviting the governor to the grand opening. And Nancy had to smile inwardly. With the governor here security would be especially tight.

Completely different from AtEighth, she thought, but then, we learned from our mistakes lest we be doomed to repeat them.

"Mr. Jian asks that the list not be published in any media, including the Internet, until the day after the party. The guests on the list have already received their hand-written invitations."

"Will there be any last-minute additions?"

"No," Li said. "And as soon as possible I would like to have a list of every person who will be in residence."

"This penthouse will be the only residence occupied."

"Excuse me. I meant to say that I require a list of every person who will be in this building that evening, no matter in what capacity."

"Security staff, and the rest workmen putting finishing touches to the various condominiums. Plus myself and perhaps one or two other representatives of Callahan Holdings."

"Security personnel and you and your staff, yes; workmen, no," Li said. "Surely a delay of twenty-four hours will not be a detriment to your work in progress."

"What about the catering staff, the bartenders, the servers?"

"Thank you for your efforts in this regard, but we have already taken care of the arrangements."

"Will you need help with the furnishings?"

"No," Kelley Conley said. "And now if you will excuse us."

Nancy was a little hurt. She wanted to be thought of as something more than a real estate salesman. And way in the back of her heart she was worried, despite Li Huan's assurances, and the collectibles curator's attitude, smug and certain as only a young person's could be.

"Then I'll look forward to meeting Mr. Jian in four days."

"And he wishes to finally meet you," Li said.

Nancy left the penthouse and took Jian's elevator down to the ground floor, where the two Bobs—Marston and Whiteside—manned the front desk and acted as doormen/security officers. They were dressed in gray slacks, white shirts, and dark blue blazers, embossed with the Tower's emblem—the figure of the impossibly tall building of glass and aluminum standing out against a light blue background—on the left breast pockets.

"Who's on duty opening night?" Nancy asked.

"Down here, we are, ma'am," Whiteside said. "Plus two others."

"Good. I'll give you guys a list of all the guests, with their photographs. We'll have a drill the day before, but that evening no one, and I mean no one who isn't on the list, and who you personally cannot positively identify, will be allowed inside. And I don't give a damn if it's the president of the United States."

"Yes, ma'am," Marston said. "There will not be a repeat of AtEighth here. We can guarantee it."

But his assurances were not comforting.

FORTY-THREE

Dan Endicott rode over to CIA headquarters with Thomas Held, the chief of the Bureau's counterterrorism branch. It was early, but the Company had scheduled a second Joint Task Force meeting at eight-thirty in the morning in the auditorium—called the Bubble because of its shape. As with the meeting just after AtEighth came down, no agenda had been posted. But everyone who'd been invited knew the only topics on the table would be who had brought the pencil tower down, how had they done it, and how to prevent a second attack.

It was a quarter after when they showed their credentials and were passed through the gate. Access to the Bubble was through an underground tunnel from the Original Headquarters Building.

"What are you going to tell them, if you're asked?" Held asked.

"McGarvey thinks he knows what brought the building down, but the architects don't want to admit it's possible," Endicott replied without looking at his boss.

It was a pretty day, but the drive up to the OHB was ominous to Endicott. Another attack could hit them any day now. In Manhattan, almost certainly, and Midtown, somewhere near AtEighth, was his guess. But he felt that he was missing something, that they all were missing something important.

"The beams broke between the fourth and fifth floors, but there's been no evidence found so far that explosives were used," he said.

"Witnesses on the ground say that the entire southeast corner between those floors blew outwards," Held countered.

"That's when they failed from stresses beyond their design parameters. And more than a dozen witnesses said that the building was swaying so far off center that they knew it had to come down."

"It's consistent with small shaped charges on those beams," Held said. He was playing devil's advocate and Endicott knew it.

"Just what they all want to hear, because it's the simplest explanation."

"Occam's razor. The simplest explanation usually tends to be the right one."

"Only this time it could be wrong," Endicott said.

It was something he hated to admit, because everything within his engineering background told him that the tuned mass damper at the top of the tower could not have brought the building down. Yet the witnesses plus the several cell phone videos showed the tower was off center by at least ten feet before it came down. Plus, to this point, there was no evidence of explosives at the base.

They parked in the visitors' lot, and inside the OHB they were given badges, and were directed to the tunnel.

"We've been here before," Held told the security officer.

"Yes, sir."

"The real question is what's the Agency doing to track down the ISIS people who authorized the attack and bring them in?" Endicott said in the tunnel.

Three other men and one woman in NYFD uniforms were just ahead of them.

"And do what, torture them?"

"You're damned right. And when we get what we need, put a bullet in their head."

"Revenge?"

"Call it what you want, but we didn't offer bin Laden a trial. And no one on this side of the pond seemed to mind."

The Bubble, which could hold more than five hundred people, was state of the art in design; media presentation equipment, including a projection screen that came up from the floor, and a lighting system to allow for color television cameras and digital motion picture recordings, were first class. Large plaster disks on the inside of the dome looked futuristic, but actually served as acoustic enhancers.

Only the first few rows were occupied with about fifty people, some of whom Endicott recognized from the

Bureau and from the governor's commission on crime. Others were in the uniforms of the New York fire and police departments, the coast guard and navy; plus Air Force General Thomas Dixon, who was the director of the National Security Agency, was present.

A short man with narrow shoulders and a dark complexion came to the stage. He was dressed in an ordinary dark blue suit, white shirt, tie knotted properly.

"My name is Martin Bambridge, I'm the deputy director of the Central Intelligence Agency's National Clandestine Service. Thank you for coming today; we have a lot of work ahead of us, so I won't keep you long."

Bambridge stepped aside as the projection screen rose from the floor. Almost immediately several images of AtEighth came up, showing the building from several angles, plus two from the air as it was when still intact.

"Some of these images you will have already seen," Bambridge said. "Some are advertising shots, including videos, many of them digitally enhanced by us. Others were taken by witnesses with cell phones from various angles, most of them at street level, but a few from buildings to the south and west—out of the damage path."

The screen split into a montage of views from four separate angles that were projected in slow motion.

At first nothing out of the ordinary seemed to be happening.

"Tourists taking pictures. Obviously nothing professional."

The building began to sway, slightly at first, slowly drifting farther to the southeast, then back to the northwest, with each pass. Some of the images became shaky as the cameramen or -women knew what was happening and were frightened.

Someone on the sixth floor of the Hearst Building just

across the avenue caught the explosion between the fourth and fifth floors of AtEighth.

The motion on that image stopped.

"Watch carefully," Bambridge said.

He used a remote control to advance the scene frame by frame, until a full minute and a half later the pencil tower fell to the street.

The lights, which had dimmed, came up, and Bambridge stepped back to center stage. "No residue of any type of explosive has been found in the rubble.

"Then what brought it down?" someone in the second row called out.

"Our Directorate of Science and Technology has come to the same conclusion that the FBI's counterterrorism's Special Agent Dan Endicott has arrived at. If there was an explosion it was of a type that we are not aware of. The building's structure failed between the fourth and fifth floors because the tuned mass damper system on the top floors of the building operated out of sync with the wind, and in the end created a harmonic oscillation beyond the engineers' design specifications."

Bambridge put two slow-motion images back up on the screen; one showed the extreme displacement of the top of the building, and the other a steady image of the fourth and fifth floors.

When the top of the building finally came back to the southeast, displaced by ten feet or more, the area between the fourth and fifth floors blew out and the building did not swing back, it toppled to the street.

When it was over, the auditorium was deathly still.

"Do you believe that ISIS may have instituted a copycat operation—the same as nine-eleven?" Endicott asked. "Targeting a second building?"

"We think that it's a possibility."

"In Midtown Manhattan?"

"The idea is being given strong consideration. The special investigative branches of the NYPD and FD are working up a list of the likely targets."

Someone else in front started to ask a question, but Bambridge held up a hand.

"Let me finish. Precautions will be put in place within the next twelve hours. But quietly and secretly. Nothing anywhere in or near Midtown must in any way appear out of the ordinary—except of course for the continuing cleanup work along AtEighth's damage path. If our efforts were to be discovered, the perps would simply bide their time."

Endicott stood up. "What is the Agency doing to find the terrorists? Do we have boots on the ground in Syria, or the other ISIS strongholds?"

"Yes."

"Can you be more specific?"

"Not at this time," Bambridge said. "There will not be another nine-eleven."

"AtEighth coming down was close enough," someone in front said.

FORTY-FOUR

Pete stood at the aft rail above the pool deck sipping a glass of champagne and watching the race, which was in its last eight laps. Television coverage was being piped throughout the yacht on monitors just about everywhere, including the upper salon. To this point, the race was one of the deadliest in years. Two cars had tangled with each other and crashed somewhere out of the hairpin curve while accelerating, both drivers killed instantly.

The race had been stopped for more than a half hour, and the next three laps were run under a yellow caution flag.

Al-Hamadi came up to her. "I'm looking for Angel, have you seen him?"

"Find Susan and he won't be far behind, or vice versa," Pete said.

"And Joe seems to have disappeared as well."

"He's on his way to New York. Business. How about you?"

"If you mean after the race, I suppose I'll stay aboard for the run down to Mallorca. Will you be joining us? Could be interesting."

"I haven't been asked."

"That can be arranged. I'm sure that Tom would want to talk to you about your bitcoin deal. He seems to be interested."

"How about you?"

Al-Hamadi smiled. "I'm really not one of the players. Mostly just an errand boy. If it works out with Tom, he'll give me a finder's fee."

"I thought you were connected through your wife and the royal family."

"As I said, Ms. Borman, I'm merely an errand boy."

Pete thought that it was an extraordinary admission for him to make. Unless he was after something. "Did Pablo send you?"

Al-Hamadi's eyes narrowed. "Who is Pablo? I'm not familiar with the name."

"Pablo Valdes, the chief money launderer for most of the Mexican drug cartels."

"I don't know him."

"Sure you do, as Angel Castillo."

"If you're correct, then we both know what sort of a deal he's offered Tom."

She shrugged and turned to watch the race as the first

two machines, Martaan still in the lead, made it through the tunnel. "A lucrative one."

"And very dangerous for anyone who gets in the way."

"Are you warning me?" Pete asked, turning to him.

"We know that you and Joe are not bloggers. My guess would be either the American DEA or Treasury department."

"You think we're cops?"

"Yes, with no authority here."

"We're not bloggers, but we're not cops."

"Then what?"

"Let's just say that we're gathering material for a story about the super-rich."

Al-Hamadi started to object, but Pete held him off.

"When AtEighth came down a lot of ordinary people lost their lives, but so did some of the richest people on the planet. Interest in the U.S. has spiked. People want to know what happened."

"Do you think ISIS is going to try to take down another building?"

"I don't know, but right now any story having to do with the rich and famous is worth money."

Al-Hamadi chuckled.

Pete couldn't read from his expression if he believed her or not, and she was going to ask him who he thought she was, when a woman down on the pool deck cried out. Everyone was gathering around the TV monitor.

Ashore in the distance, a dark plume of smoke rose up into the sky.

Pete turned and went to the monitor in the upper salon, where a dozen people were on their feet. Someone had turned up the sound.

The images showed a huge ball of flame in the middle of the track, and the announcer was saying that there was absolutely no chance that Martaan could have survived.

A replay showed Martaan's car coming into a turn at what was obviously too fast a speed, the number-two machine just ten or fifteen meters behind. Suddenly the Mercedes's front right wheel and entire strut assembly collapsed. Almost instantly the car went airborne, over the barriers and into several parked cars, two pickup trucks, and a van, everything going up in a massive ball of flame, followed by a tremendous plume of black smoke.

"How many lives have been lost is still unknown at this point, but at least eight people who were trackside in or near the vehicles are certainly dead, as is Louis Martaan, the Team Mercedes driver, ranked number one on the F1 circuit."

Firemen were shooting retardant foam into the flames.

The images on the monitor went back to the moment leading to the crash, and then in slow motion, the front right of the Mercedes collapsing and the machine flipping up and crashing into the parked vehicles.

"For God's sake, turn it off," one of the women said, and one of the men switched off the monitor.

"It's a dangerous sport," al-Hamadi said just behind Pete.

She turned to him. "It's not the only dangerous game," she said, and left the salon.

Hammond and a number of other people were watching a monitor just inside the salon at the gangway. He came out as Pete started down.

"Are you leaving?" he asked.

She looked up at him. "I've had enough for now."

"He was young."

"And immortal."

"They all are," Hammond said. "And stupid, a lot of them. Brash. Arrogant. But very good at what they do."

Pete nodded. "Thanks for inviting us aboard."

"Will you and Joe be at Jian's party?"

"If we're still welcome as your guests."

"You are," Hammond said.

No cabs were available at the head of the dock, but Hammond had sent a car to take her back to the Hermitage. The driver said nothing, and Pete was appreciative for the silence on the half-hour drive.

Everyone in the hotel was subdued. Music that normally played on the speaker system had been shut off, and the few people in the lobby were glued to their iPhones and iPads, connecting to various media outlets covering the aftermath of the crash.

She went into the mostly empty bar, where she got a club soda with a twist. The television over the bar was off, and she was glad of it.

Taking her drink over to a table by a window, she phoned Otto. "He was a nice kid," she said.

"They all are," Otto said. "Are you okay?"

"I'll live," she said. It was one of Mac's expressions that she'd picked up without even thinking about it.

"No trouble getting back to the hotel?"

"None."

"Was Nero still on the yacht when you left?"

"If he was I didn't see him."

"Go to your room right now and stay frosty till Mac gets there. He's coming back for you." Otto said. "I shit you not, Pete, you gotta listen this time."

"Right," Pete said. She hung up, finished her club soda, and took the elevator up to the fifth floor.

The moment she opened the door and stepped inside, she smelled Kamal's cologne and she knew that she had made a big mistake. She reached for her pistol, but Kamal was right there, gun in hand, the silencer on the muzzle almost obscene.

"I won't kill you unless you force me to do it," he said.

Pete figured the odds, and stayed her hand.

FORTY-FIVE

Kamal sat in an armchair that he had pulled into the middle of the sitting room, giving him a perfect sight line to anyone at the door. He held what looked to Pete like an old-fashioned Army Colt .45, but smaller. There was no possible way that she could outdraw him.

Not yet.

"I assume that you were reaching for a pistol under your blouse, which means, of course, that you are not a writer looking for material on the rich and famous, as Alyan said you told him."

"May I sit down?" Pete asked, nodding toward the couch.

"Certainly," Kamal said. He raised his pistol. "But first remove your weapon and place it on the floor to your right."

Pete did as she was told, but carefully and slowly, bending down to place it on the floor. She hoped that Otto was still monitoring what was going on around her.

She went to the couch, less than ten feet from Kamal, and perched on the arm. "Okay, Mr. Castillo, or whoever you really are, what's next?"

"Who do you think I am?"

"I think that there's a good possibility you're Pablo Valdes."

"How do you know that?"

"I don't, but it's our best guess so far."

"The CIA's best guess?"

"I don't work for the CIA."

"But Joe does," Kamal said. "Or should I say Kirk Mc-Garvey."

Pete hid her shock. "He teaches Voltaire at a college in Florida."

"But you and he are working together, and you showed up here to see me."

"Yes, we traced you here."

"How?"

"You dropped out of sight, and we thought that it was likely you got out of Mexico before the army found you. But the money you launder piles up pretty fast, so we figured you would have to find a way to deal with it. It's what you offered Hammond."

"Don't insult my intelligence," Kamal said. "There's no possible way you could have traced me to this specific city, on that specific yacht out there."

"We were the lucky team. There are others in Moscow and Paris and Zurich. Lots of other places too. It was a full-court press."

"Who do you work for?"

"Treasury, of course."

"You have no jurisdiction here."

"True, but we found you, and Mr. McGarvey is on his way to inform our boss. And from there I expect that the Prefectures of Police here, and across the border in France, will be notified, as will the DGSI in Paris."

"What to do," Kamal said, a slight smile playing at the corners of his mouth.

The gesture just then was troubling, and Pete braced herself to dive behind the couch and somehow make it to her gun.

"Leave, of course," he said. "First thing in the morning would be soon enough. It'll take that long before your people can gain the cooperation of the police here. But then

I suppose I should have some insurance. Perhaps I could persuade you to come with me."

"That would be more trouble than you can imagine."

"I could kill you."

"Which would interest the cops here to no end."

Kamal thought a moment. "You're right," he said.

Careful to keep the gun trained on Pete, he used his cell phone to call someone. "When are you leaving?"

Pete hoped that Otto was quick enough to catch the call.

"I'll be delayed, perhaps as long as twenty-four hours," Kamal said. He broke the connection and pocketed the phone.

The man was a professional, Pete had to give him that. But he didn't seem to fit the mold of a crazy working with ISIS to bring down buildings. Certainly he was no jihadist. More the type who would launder money in the billions with no compunctions.

"Again the question is: What to do?" he said.

Pete couldn't help herself. "You could always stick that gun up your ass and pull the trigger."

Kamal was amused. Keeping the gun on her, he got up and went to a house phone. "Eight-ten. I need my automobile. Please have it out front immediately."

This did not sound good. Pete measured the distance to her pistol lying on the floor.

"No, I'm not checking out," he said and hung up.

"How do you plan on getting me through the lobby?" Pete asked.

"You'll come willingly."

"Not likely."

"Then I'll shoot you dead, and slip away in the confusion. By the time the police arrive I will be long gone. And trust me, Ms. Borman, or whatever your real name is, that would be much easier than you could imagine." He smiled.

"Eyewitnesses."

"Almost always unreliable."

"Almost," she said.

"You may pack a suitcase or leave as you are."

Pete opted to leave as she was. When the maid came to clean the room she would report that things had been left behind and the desk might report it to the police. Worst-case scenario, they would place everything in storage.

But she still had Otto.

Kamal picked up Pete's Glock and pocketed it. "May I have your cell phone, please?"

"No."

He held out a hand, and reluctantly she gave it to him, praying to whatever gods that Otto was still monitoring the situation.

With one hand he awkwardly removed the back of the phone, pried out the battery, and removed the SIM card. Still his aim never wavered. He pocketed the card and battery, and the phone and its back plate.

Otto would know that they were leaving, but he wouldn't know to where. The only possibility was that he was calling the police now.

Kamal removed the silencer, put it in his pocket, and stuck the pistol in the waistband of his trousers beneath his jacket.

Pete was ready to spring at him, but he read something of it from her eyes.

"Believe me, dear, I don't need a pistol to kill you."

She believed him.

Getting off the elevator in the lobby, Kamal took Pete's arm, and together they walked out of the hotel to where a Bentley convertible, its top up, was waiting.

"You may drive," he told her. "I'll give you directions."

By the time Pete got behind the wheel, Kamal had tipped the valet and climbed into the passenger seat. "Let's go home, shall we?"

FORTY-SIX

McGarvey had just crossed into France in his rental Peugeot and was heading south on the A41, when Otto called all out of breath. Traffic was heavy as it usually was this time of the year, but the day was too pretty for what he was certain Otto was going to tell him.

"He's taken Pete."

"How?"

"He was waiting for her in your hotel room, and she didn't have a chance from the get-go," Otto said. He explained everything he'd heard through Pete's cell phone. "He used the house phone to have his car brought around, and they left."

"To where?"

"I don't know. He had her phone, and it just went dead. Must have taken out the battery and probably the SIM card."

"Call Gratto and have him get the Gulfstream back here."

"It never left. I had him stand by in case you needed to get back in a hurry."

"Good thinking. Hack the hotel's system and see what kind of a car he was driving."

"I've already done that too. It's a three-year-old Bentley Continental GT Speed Convertible, metallic blue. Paris plates, but the address is an accommodations listing. A dead end. He could be taking her just about anywhere."

McGarvey got off the highway and took the on-ramp back to Geneva. "There's no way he'll spend a night somewhere with her. If it's too far he'd have to kill her and ditch the body. I'm betting it's someplace close. Maybe even right there in Monaco."

"He needs more information."

"If he thinks that she suspects he's Nero, he'll kill her for sure."

"There's more," Otto said. "He knows your name."

"Christ."

"But it sounded as if she convinced him that you and she worked for Treasury, and along with a lot of other teams were on the trail of Valdes."

"That fiction won't last long. If he knows who I am, it means he has a pretty good source of intel."

"Photographs of you were in a lot of newspapers and on a few television news shows, and your disguise wouldn't fool a decent facial recognition program."

"That's not the stuff I'm worried about. It's what I've been involved with after I left the Company. If he knows that, he'll know that Pete and I don't work for Treasury."

"I'll put something on Treasury's mainframe. If his source can hack that deeply he might be convinced that you guys are after Valdes."

"Better do the same with everybody else. The Bureau, Homeland Security, any system you can reach."

"That'd be all of them, Kemo Sabe. I'm on it," Otto said. "What about asking the DGSI for help?"

McGarvey had considered it. "That would end up in a shootout that no one would win. Especially not Pete. This guy has no intention of being taken, especially not alive."

"Finesse."

"Something like that."

"But, Mac, I don't know where to start looking."

"He's made a mistake somewhere. We'll find it."

The Gulfstream was spooling up when McGarvey got back to Geneva's airport, and it was ready for takeoff after he'd returned his rental car and took a shuttle across to the VIP terminal.

Toynbee was waiting with a cold beer when he came aboard.

"Otto says we're returning to Cannes," Gratto said from the cockpit. "ATC will want us to file a flight plan, but if the DGSI gets wind of us coming back, they'll want to know why."

"File one for Cannes, and at the last minute head out into the Med and file for Genoa."

As soon as he was strapped in, they taxied out to the active runway and took off, heading directly to the Italian city, which was less than a hundred miles from Monaco. Even before they reached cruising altitude McGarvey got back on the phone to Otto.

"Assuming I'm right and Nero has gone to ground somewhere nearby, it could very well be his home base."

"If that's the case he'll have no other choice but to kill Pete."

"Not until he finds out what she knows, and not if I get there first. He was aboard Hammond's yacht, which probably means he's got money, which also means that he's damned good at what he does. He gets paid well."

"Big bucks to bring down AtEighth, and even more for a second one," Otto said. "ISIS can afford it."

"Could be that simple. Or, it's someone with a good reason to make us believe that they're behind it."

"And deep enough pockets to afford someone like Nero," Otto said, picking up the direction McGarvey was going. "He's driving a Bentley, and it's not a rental, so his home base will be a good one."

"Find out who bought what and for how much over the past several years. It'll have to be a private house or a villa. Maybe something off the beaten path. No snoopy neighbors."

"Might he have staff? Someone to look after the place when he was gone?"

"If he does it would probably be someone English. A valet, cook, house cleaner. A man probably. Someone versatile."

"Why British especially?"

"I'm betting Nero, if that's who Valdes is, was educated as a kid in the UK, and I have a strong feeling he attended Sandhurst. Might even have graduated."

"Fuck," Otto said. He almost never used the word.

"What?"

"Sandhurst, you mentioned it before. Said you had a hunch. Just a mo."

He was back in under fifteen seconds. "My darlings picked up on it two days ago, but I was too damned busy to pay any attention. Besides the KIAs, accidents, and natural causes, we only found one who dropped out under odd circumstances. His name was Kamal al-Daran, parents immigrated to England when he was just a kid. Put him in the best schools including Eton and then Sandhurst, where he graduated near the top of his class at both schools. Sandhurst was ten years ago. Puts Nero at about the right age. Anyway, he went on leave and took the *QM2* to the U.S. Somewhere in the mid-Atlantic he apparently fell overboard. His body was never found, end of story."

"It's him," McGarvey said. "Get everything you can, especially photographs."

"There's more," Otto said. "His parents emigrated from Saudi Arabia. Maybe they want us to fight their battles against ISIS instead of spending more of their own money. They were probably involved with nine-eleven, though it was never proven. They hid behind sovereign immunity. But this now sure as hell fits the pattern."

"If he's on an op for the GIP, his intel would be first rate," McGarvey said. "And it's more than likely that the two guys who tried to take me out in Cannes were work-for-hire muscle."

"It fits."

"Let me know what you come up with," McGarvey said.

"What do you have in mind?"

"I'm going to push a little, see what happens."

"In the meantime, Pete."

"Find out where he lives and I'll take care of it."

"Watch yourself, Mac."

Hammond answered on the second ring.

"Joe Canton. I'm trying to contact Mr. Castillo, but apparently he's checked out of his hotel. Is he aboard?"

"No," Hammond said. "I thought you were in New York."

"I'm halfway across the Atlantic right now," McGarvey said. "Any idea where I might find him?"

"Not a clue. But he said he would catch up with us in a day or two. We're leaving for Mallorca in the morning. Will you be able to get back and join us there?"

"Wouldn't miss it for the world."

FORTY-SEVEN

Sitting on the Monaco terrace finishing a late dinner of chilled lobster salad, croissants, and a bottle of Krug, all served by Kamal's manservant, the entire setup seemed surreal to Pete. The magnificent view of Monaco Bay, the fabulous house, the lovely meal, and even Yves, who had attended them, was ominous. The calf being fattened before the kill. Even worse, Kamal had become the perfect gentleman once they had arrived.

"Nice place you have here," she said.

"Unfortunately I'll have to find another home soon."

"Mexico?"

"Perhaps in time, but for now the army would very much like to catch up with me. Shot while trying to escape."

"You don't seem overly concerned."

"Money has its uses."

Pete took a sip of her wine. She'd never tasted Krug before but she decided that it definitely lived up to its reputation. "I suppose I could mention to Yves that you have kidnapped me."

Kamal raised his hand, and the valet appeared at the slider.

"Yes, sir?"

"Ms. Borman has something to tell you."

"Yes, ma'am?"

"Did you know that your boss launders drug money for the Mexican cartels?" Pete said.

"No, ma'am, I've never asked."

"And are you aware that he's kidnapped me, and it's very likely that he'll kill me before the evening is over?"

"No, ma'am," Yves said. "Would there be anything else?"

"Perhaps some coffee and cognac in a bit," Kamal said, and Yves left.

Pete was impressed despite the situation. "Where did you get him?"

"From a listing's service. He's discreet."

"I'll say."

"Let's talk about the relationship between you and Mr. McGarvey."

"We're partners."

"You stayed in the same hotel room, only one bed. Lovers?"

"None of your business."

"Ah, but this evening everything is my business. It was you two who approached me, not the other way around. I want to know why."

"I've already explained who we work for and why we came looking for you. The Mexican government has asked for our help, and since most of the cocaine the cartels supply comes to us, we agreed."

"And if you have me believe you, Mr. McGarvey is already halfway across the Atlantic to report to your boss that you have found me."

"Yes."

"Why not just make a phone call? If you two are right, and I am really Pablo Valdes, then I'm sure the Prefecture of Police here could be induced to help arrest me."

"I don't know the answer to that, except that you seem to be a friend of Tom Hammond's and Susan Patterson's, and Monégasques respect money above all else."

"Indeed."

Their coffee and cognacs came, but Pete declined the liquor. The two glasses of champagne had already given her a slight buzz, and she was certain that she'd be needing all of her wits about her before the evening was over. Her only hope was that Mac was on his way back to Monaco and that somehow Otto had pulled another rabbit out of his technological hat and found out about this place.

"It's really quite a nice cognac," Kamal said.

"I've had enough. I'm not what you would call a big drinker."

For several minutes they sat in silence, the early evening beautiful, the lights of Monaco splashing across the bay. Somewhere in the distance she could hear a siren, but then it faded. They were in another world here, for all intents and purposes isolated. The feeling grew that her situation was becoming more ominous with every passing minute. No matter what magic Otto conjured up, it wouldn't be possible for Mac to get here in time.

"What's next?" she finally asked.

"That will depend entirely on your level of cooperation," Kamal said. He raised his right hand and the valet instantly appeared.

Pete wondered if the man had overheard their conversation.

"That will be all for this evening."

"Yes, sir."

"We will be wanting our privacy."

"Of course, sir," Yves said and he left.

"Who do you and Mr. McGarvey work for?"

"Treasury."

"And you believe that I am Pablo Valdes."

"Yes."

"Are you two lovers?"

"None of your business."

Kamal smiled and nodded. "Then perhaps we shall become lovers this evening. Talk like lovers. Tell each other our secrets."

"Right," Pete said.

Kamal got up and took a pistol from the waistband

under his shirt. He screwed the silencer on the end of the barrel. "Let's retire, shall we?"

"Or else you'll shoot me?"

"Of course."

Pete got up. "May I take the cognac? Maybe I'll have some after all."

"By all means," Kamal said.

Pete looked toward the sea. The house was perched at the top of a rocky slope with a few scraggly trees that led down to a cliff. She figured it wasn't much more than a twenty-foot drop from there but she couldn't tell if was to the water or a beach or rocks.

"To the sliding doors at the end of the terrace, please," Kamal said.

Pete went ahead of him, feigning a little unsteadiness. The glass sliders were opened to a large bedroom suite. Dim lights in the ceiling, meant to look like a starry sky, cast a soft glow.

She stopped, and looked again toward the sea. The drop from the terrace to the sloping ground was maybe ten feet or a little more. Workable, she decided, if she didn't break an ankle in the fall, or if Nero didn't shoot her somewhere vital. But she was counting that he wouldn't want her dead until he found out the real reason why she and Mac had come here.

"Now what?" she asked.

"Go inside, take off your clothes, and lie down on the bed."

"Are you going to rape me?"

"I don't think so."

"Torture me?"

"If need be, but I've always found that when people are naked they become vulnerable to the mere suggestion of pain."

Pete suppressed a smile. He'd made a mistake. Whoever

he was—Nero or someone else—he definitely wasn't a money launderer for the Mexican drug cartels. An intelligence operative or a field officer, trained in the military and working freelance for some intelligence or special operations organization such as the Russian Spetsnaz, or perhaps the Iranian secret police—what was once known as SAVAK.

The problem for her was that those kinds of agencies weren't in the business of destroying buildings and killing innocent civilians and blaming it on a terrorist group.

She leaned against the rail, raised the cognac, and took a deep draft, but didn't swallow it.

"Christ, Christ," she sputtered, spewing the liquor down the front of her blouse.

Kamal's aim wavered.

"I'm going to be sick." She dropped the snifter and as it shattered on the tile floor, she rolled over the edge and dropped to the rocks below.

FORTY-EIGHT

As soon as he crossed into France, McGarvey slowed down to just ten kilometers over the speed limit. He couldn't afford to be stopped now by the police. The flight down from Geneva had gone without a hitch and renting a Fiat at Genoa had been easy under his Canton ID, which Galan hadn't taken from him.

Otto hadn't called back yet, which was worrisome, and twice Mac had started to phone him, but both times he stayed his hand. When Otto had something relevant he would call.

The fact that Nero, or whoever the hell he really was, had waited for Pete in the hotel room and had taken her at

gunpoint did not prove he was the one who had taken down
AtEighth, even though just about everything in McGarvey's gut told him they had found the bastard. But it did
prove that he was someone of interest, that he was willing
to go to such extreme lengths to protect his freedom.

Mac's biggest fear was for his own sanity. He had vi-
sions of finding Pete's body, and he didn't know how he
could handle such a thing again. And if Nero had killed
her, the man would never see the inside of a courtroom,
let alone a prison cell. Nor would the people he worked for.

It was less than ten miles from the Italian border to
Monaco, and he drove straight to the Hermitage and got
lucky with a parking spot across the street. Traffic was still
heavy but the people were subdued. He had heard on the
radio about the deaths on the race course, especially of
Louis Martaan, the number-one driver.

At the front desk he asked about his room, but the clerk
was a little confused. "But, Monsieur, you have not yet
checked out. Is this what you wish?"

"Of course not, but I've lost my key, may I have another?"

He had to show his passport, but the clerk gave him
another key card and he went upstairs and listened at the
door. There was no sound from within.

He pulled out his pistol, unlocked the door, and pushed
it open.

Pete's scent hung on the air along with another mascu-
line scent he did not recognize. An easy chair had been
placed in the middle of the sitting room, with a direct sight
line on the doorway. Nero had waited here for Pete to get
back. A fifty-euro note to any of the maids plus the story
that he and Pete were secret lovers would have been enough
for them to open the door for him.

The only troubling point was why hadn't he shot her to
death as soon as she was inside and the door closed. Why

the questions, and why take her down to the lobby and out to his car? A dozen or more witnesses, including the hotel's staff, would be able to testify that they had left the hotel together.

Pete's clothes were still in the closet and in her roll-about, and her purse was on the couch, where she had probably tossed it. Her phone was gone as was her pistol, but not the silencer nor the extra magazine of bullets.

He packed up everything, including the rest of his things, so that when it was time to get out and make the dash back across the Italian border, they'd be ready.

Pete was coming with him.

McGarvey left the hotel and walked half a block to a small bustling sidewalk café where he took one of the remaining seats from which he could watch the front of the hotel and his rental Fiat across the street.

The mood everywhere in Monaco was dark, but no darker than his.

Otto finally called a half hour later. He was excited. "I found a good possibility. A place right on the sea just a mile or so from where you are now. A guy by the name of Roger Harcourt, a Brit, bought it four years ago for seventy-five million euros. Building permits were taken out for a complete renovation the week after the closing. I monitored the phone system, but there've been no calls in the last two months."

"He uses a cell phone," McGarvey said.

"I checked. No cell phone registered to Harcourt or Castillo. And of course there'd be none for Valdes. And there's more."

"There always is."

"He has a fairly sophisticated surveillance system in place. Motion and infrared detectors. Sensors and alarms on all the doors and windows. And it looks as if even though a door or window is open, anyone passing through will also set off an alarm."

"Every time he walked through a door alarm bells would start ringing?"

"I'm guessing there's a recognition system. Plus the alarms are silent and are not connected to the police or any security service. I can look at them, but I can't hack them. You show up and he'll know about it immediately."

"Does he have a staff?"

"One man. Yves Germaine, born in France, educated in England. No police or intelligence agency records in England, France, or here."

"He's clean."

"Yes, and so apparently is Harcourt."

"Then why did he take Pete?" McGarvey demanded. None of it made any sense.

"Nothing points to him not being Valdes," Otto said. "So maybe he wants to know what proof you have, and what you've told the Mexican government. It could be as simple as that."

"He'll kill her if he's convinced she's from Treasury."

"Not if you show up, providing you don't start a gun-fight."

McGarvey laid a ten-euro note on the table for his coffee and headed toward his car. "What's the phone number?"

"You're going out there?"

"Of course, but first I'm going to warn him."

Otto gave him driving directions. "Watch your step, Kemo Sabe, I shit you not. If this guy is Valdes or Nero, either way, he's got Pete as a hostage."

It took less than fifteen minutes for McGarvey to find the place, just off the A8 down a narrow paved road that led toward the sea and past four other properties. No lights shone on any of them.

He switched off his lights as he pulled to a stop at the last gate before the road ended. From what he could see through the steel bars of the double gate in the concrete wall the house was very large, and sleekly modern.

Turning around so that the car was facing back to the highway, he switched off the engine and pocketed the keys. The windows were down and the night was still except for an occasional truck on the highway above, but that was more than a hundred yards away, the sounds very faint.

He tried the phone number, but it rang only once before it went to a recorded message in French: *This number is not in service at this time.* It went dead.

Otto came on. "Try it again."

This time it rang eight times before a man answered. "Yes."

"I would like to speak with Mr. Harcourt," McGarvey said.

"I'm sorry, sir, but Mr. Harcourt has retired for the evening."

"Tell him that Joe Canton wishes to have a brief word. He knows me."

"I'm sorry, sir."

The line went dead.

A moment later Otto made it ring through again.

This time the man picked it up after the second ring. "I will call the police if you persist."

"Mr. Harcourt wouldn't want that," McGarvey said. "And tell him that I'd also like to speak with Mme. Borman."

FORTY-NINE

Kamal was getting tired of the game. He stood ten feet from the edge of the cliff at the extreme north end of his property and cocked an ear to listen, but there were no sounds on the night air except for the gentle wave action below on the rocks.

His cell phone was connected with the surveillance system, and he had tracked the woman's heat signature as she crisscrossed the route along the cliffs first to the south and then here, looking for a way out. But the only way was either to jump to her death on the rocks below, or come up past or through the house. The tall concrete walls were topped with nearly invisible spikes only three inches tall, but spaced one inch apart. The spikes were electrified. Anyone who managed to somehow climb to the top would come in contact with them and be instantly electrocuted.

She was here now, hanging over the edge of the cliff. He could see her heat signature rising in the nearly still air.

"I have you on surveillance," he said. "Infrared. And your choices now are simple. Either hold on until you get tired and fall to your death. Or climb up and we'll go back to the house."

Pete did not reply.

"I have all night, you do not. And for what it's worth I promise I will not shoot you."

His phone chimed in the talk mode, and Kamal switched from surveillance. It was Yves from the house.

"Yes?"

"Mr. Canton is at the front gate, wishing to speak with you and with the woman."

"Just a moment."

He switched to the surveillance cameras on the front wall. A small Fiat was parked on the road, facing back toward the highway, but not blocking the gate. Someone was behind the wheel, but it was impossible to tell who it was. He switched back to the phone. "Tell him I'm sending the woman out."

"Yes, sir."

"Mr. Canton has somehow traced you to my home, and at this moment is at the front gate asking to talk to the both of us. So now, as you can see, it would be impossible for me to shoot you even if I wanted such a thing. Which I never did."

Still the woman did not reply.

Kamal was irritated. He was of two minds: Kill the woman here and now, then let McGarvey in and kill him too. "We don't have all night. Your boyfriend is waiting at the gate."

He switched back to the infrared mode, but the woman's heat signature had moved. He started to turn when she came at him with a large rock in her hand, swinging it directly toward his head.

He managed to deflect the blow, but it landed on the shoulder of his gun hand. His entire arm went numb and he dropped the pistol and moved back.

She made no sound as she came at him again, only a slight smile on her half-parted lips.

In that instant Kamal knew that she would kill him, no questions asked, and be glad of it. He'd never seen such determination in a woman's eyes—in any person's eyes.

This time he managed to step aside as she swung at his head. He grabbed her arm with his good hand, pulling her nearly off her feet so hard that she dropped the rock. Letting go and shoving her away he backhanded her in the face, and she went down hard on her ass. Still she made no sound, nor did the look in her eyes change.

He picked up his pistol with his left hand, and aimed it at her head, his finger on the trigger.

She didn't move, almost as if she were willing him to shoot.

He held for a longish moment.

"Shit or get off the pot, we don't have all night," she said. "As you say, my boyfriend is here, and he'll tear you a new asshole. You can count on it."

"Crude, darling."

"That's not the half of it."

He lowered his aim and stuffed the pistol in his belt. Pete started to get up, but he gestured for her to stop.

"I don't need a gun to kill you, and you can count on that." He called the house. "Tell the gentleman at the gate that I'm sending out his woman, unharmed."

"That's it?" Pete said as he broke the connection and pocketed the phone.

"That's it," he said. He reached out a hand to help her back to her feet, but she batted it away. "You'll want to put some ice on your face; I hit you a little harder than I intended."

"We're not going to stop," Pete told him, getting up.

"I'm not who you bastards think I am," he told her.

"Who do we think you are?"

"A businessman."

"Someone who launders drug money," Pete said. "Spare me."

"Like it or not it's a business, and not one that I started. Nor would there be any such business as ours if your people didn't have such a big appetite for our product. The land of the free and the brave. Spare me, Ms. Borman, or whoever the hell you really are. Your government is holier than thou, always has been. But look at your record. Look at it. Vietnam, and Laos, and Cambodia. Your CIA selling drugs to finance its wars. Or Iraq. You left the place destroyed and for no good reason. And afterwards what did the people have? No reliable water supply, no electricity.

Almost no infrastructure. And did you rebuild? Of course not."

"Nice speech."

Kamal stepped aside. "Go," he said.

"We're not finished. Guaranteed."

"If either of you come at me again, I'll kill you. Guaranteed, as you say."

Pete glanced up at the house.

"There's a path around to the right. It'll take you to the driveway. I'll have the gate opened for you."

Pete looked at him for a long beat. "Don't ever come to the States," she said. "We'll be waiting for you." She turned and headed up to the house, favoring her right leg as she walked.

Once she was out of sight, Kamal went up to the house, entering through a rear door on the left. Yves was waiting for him at the head of the stairs in the rear hall just off the Monaco terrace.

"I'm leaving," Kamal told him. "I'll probably be gone for at least three weeks. If you'd like, once you have the place buttoned up you may take your vacation."

"Yes, sir. Is there a specific date when you want me to return?"

"I'll let you know. But you will receive full pay and benefits at least through the end of the year if I'm delayed."

Yves nodded. "A pleasure, sir, working for a gentleman."

"The pleasure has been mine."

Kamal got two spare identity kits, including credit cards and passports, one Canadian, the other Swiss. Back downstairs in the seven-car garage, he got onto his MV Agusta motorcycle.

He opened the garage door on his side and phoned Yves upstairs. "How far is the woman from the gate?"

"Seventy-five meters."

"Open it."

Not bothering with the helmet, Kamal started the bike, revved it a couple of times, and then shot out of the garage. It was capable of reaching two-hundred-plus miles per hour; the mechanics had removed the speed limiting devices for him.

When he flashed past the woman he was doing eighty. He brought the bike up on its rear wheel, and made the corner onto the road in front of the Fiat as McGarvey was getting out.

But then dropping the wheel and leaning well forward he accelerated with just about everything the bike had to give, sincerely hoping that McGarvey and the broad would turn up in his gun sights again—no matter how irrational that would be for all of them.

FIFTY

McGarvey had his pistol out and was taking a bead on Kamal's back as the bike flashed by when Pete shouted at him not to take the shot.

He lowered his gun as she reached the gate. She was limping and in the light from the spots on the wall, he could see that her arms were scratched up, and the side of her face was red and puffy.

"There's a good chance the guy isn't Nero," she said, coming into his arms. "He could have shot me in the head, but he didn't."

She wanted to cry, it was obvious to McGarvey. "Are you okay?"

"I'll live," she said, managing a smile. "Let's get out of here, I need a shower."

"What about his man?"

"He'd be a waste of time. I don't think we'd get anything useful in the short run."

On the way back to the hotel, she told him everything that had happened from the time she got back to their room and the man was sitting there, gun in hand. "I didn't have a chance."

"Otto got most of that until your phone went off-line."

"He took out the battery and the SIM card," Pete said. "But how did you get back here so fast?"

"Otto had Gratto stay behind in Geneva, and when Nero or whoever the hell he is—and I'm still betting that he's our man—took you he called me and I drove back and had them fly down to Genoa. He's waiting there for us."

"He's Valdes, I'm about ninety percent sure of it. But how did you know where I was?"

"Otto traced the house to an Englishman by the name of Harcourt, and said it was a pretty good bet. Anyway, he was right again."

When they reached the A8 and turned left, Otto called. "How is she?"

"Banged up but in one piece. She's betting Harcourt is not Nero. Thinks he's Valdes after all."

"As of a couple of hours ago the Mexican army hadn't run him to ground. Which may or may not prove a thing. So what's next?"

"We're coming home. Call Gratto and tell him to prep the plane. We'll be there in an hour."

"Make it an hour and a half," Pete said.

Otto heard it. "Will do. But the question still stands: What next? Marty's found out that you and Pete are in France. I don't know how, but he has, and he wants some answers."

"Set up a meeting with him in Walt's conference room. Get the Bureau's lead man along with Callahan's CEO, and anyone else you can think of. But keep it small. Nero—whoever this guy is—has got a good source of intel. Too good, so let's keep the need-to-know list to a minimum."

"What time?"

"We should be back first thing in the morning."

"Everyone's going to want to know if you still think he's going to try to hit us again," Otto said.

"Count on it," MacGarvey said.

"Shit."

"Yeah."

Two police cars, their blue lights flashing, were parked at an angle in front of the Hermitage, hemming in the Agusta motorcycle.

"Maybe our problem is solved," Pete said.

McGarvey continued past, and as soon as he could he turned around and headed back the way they had come. Parked to one side was the same Citröen in which he had been taken to the airport at Cannes. The same two men who'd come with Major Galan were standing by.

"I see it," Pete said as they drove by. "Or do you think they came for us?"

"The cops probably nailed Nero for speeding. But Galan found out that I was back and he came to arrest me."

McGarvey checked in his rearview mirror.

"Did they spot us?"

"One of his men got in the car and might be calling the good major."

"So much for my shower," Pete said.

They reached the Italian border and the same uniformed officials on both sides who had checked McGarvey through earlier just waved him across. If Major Galan's people had recognized him, they hadn't alerted the French border people yet.

"Maybe they just wanted to get rid of us," Pete said.

No one was behind them, and McGarvey watched in the rearview mirror as the officer on the French side went back into the crossing post.

Traffic was light on the Autostrada and they made good time, reaching the airport outside of Genoa in just under one hour. Gratto had the jet on the tarmac in front of the general aviation terminal, and as soon as McGarvey and Pete arrived he spooled up the engines.

The man at the terminal who had arranged for the rental car signed for its return, and they went aboard and were airborne in less than ten minutes.

"We'll stay out of French airspace," the pilot said.

"Good idea," McGarvey told him. "And thanks for standing by."

"Our pleasure, Mr. Director."

As soon as they were at cruising altitude, Toynbee came back with a brandy for each of them. "This'll start you out while I'm fixing dinner."

He returned a minute later with an ice pack for Pete's face. "I hope the bastard who did that to you gets cancer and dies a long, painful death."

Pete grinned. "Thanks. Me too."

Dinner was filet mignon, a baked potato, a small salad with bleu cheese dressing, and a good Bordeaux. McGarvey inhaled his, and Pete wasn't far behind him.

Toynbee laid the seats at the back of the small cabin as flat as they would go, and brought out small pillows and blankets for them.

"Dessert?" he asked. "I promise, just like the steaks, not out of a can."

"Sleep," Pete said.

"You too, Mr. Director? I'll wake you an hour out. Someone will meet us there to take you home."

It was a few minutes after four in the morning local when they were on final approach to Andrews before Toynbee woke them.

"Sorry, guys, but I didn't have the heart to wake you any earlier," he said. "Mr. Rencke agreed with me. He said the meeting has been scheduled at nine."

McGarvey felt gummy, but better than he had for the last couple of days. The ice pack had helped with Pete's face, but she still looked battered, and his anger spiked again. "You look good," he told her.

She smiled. "Liar. But I'll take the compliment."

Toynbee came back with coffee. "This oughta help a little."

"Do you want to marry me?" Pete asked.

"My wife might take exception, but sure, if you clean up first."

The landing was smooth, and an armored Cadillac Escalade with two minders was waiting for them.

"Compliments of the DCI himself," Toynbee told them.

At the open cabin door Gratto turned in his seat. "This isn't over yet, is it," he said as a statement, not as a question.

"Not by a long shot," McGarvey told him. "Thanks for the ride."

"Where to next?"

"Mallorca."

FIFTY-ONE

Kamal took the TGV up to Paris first thing in the morning, about the same time as Hammond slipped his moorings and headed for the leisurely overnight run to Mallorca. A half dozen other mega-yachts made up the fleet, and Hammond had promised Kamal a stateroom would remain open for him as long as he wished.

Sa'ad was waiting for him at the Deux Magots, the lunch crowd of tourists just starting to fill the place. The GIP major did not look pleased.

"Let's go for a walk," Kamal said, and he turned and headed across the street without looking back.

Sa'ad caught up with him just as they passed the entry to the Métro. "Are we taking the subway?"

"No, too many ears."

"Why did you call me from Riyadh so suddenly? What has happened?"

"I came head-to-head with McGarvey's woman."

Sa'ad stopped short. "You stupid man. It's a wonder you're still alive."

"I think I convinced her that I'm a money launderer. A businessman."

"I'm washing my hands of you, and that order was given directly by the palace to my boss. I'm here only as a courtesy to a man who has already given us great service."

"No," Kamal said.

"I know that you are an atheist, nevertheless I'm telling you to go with Allah. But if you insist on continuing, our intelligence might have to be shared with the CIA. It would be out of my hands."

It was what Kamal had expected, and it was exactly why he had called for Sa'ad to come to Paris. "Including the fact that you hired me to take down two buildings, including AtEighth?"

"You can't prove any of that."

"I think that if you give me up, they'll find my numbered accounts at PSP. It wouldn't be outside the realm of possibility for them to trace the dates and amounts back to the GIP."

"Not likely. And in any event it would prove nothing. We might even send operatives to kill you."

"Except that I was on a Saudi Arabian–approved mission, and the blame was to go to ISIS. And the point is that I'm still active. I've not completed my orders."

"Your orders are to stand down," the agent runner said angrily.

"Repeat that," Kamal said, taking his phone out of his jacket pocket. He dialed a number with his thumb, and pushed *send*. "Our conversation has been sent to an anonymous remailer that you will never find."

"You're a dead man."

"You'll have to catch me first. And of course you really can't call the Americans for help. There would be too many questions."

Sa'ad glanced around. The street and sidewalks were crowded, but the two of them were all but anonymous here. He started to reach beneath his jacket.

Kamal knew that he had won. "Here in the middle of Paris in broad daylight?"

Sa'ad hesitated.

"I'm only doing what you wanted me to do in the first place. That has not changed."

"Is it more money you want?"

"No."

"Then what? I don't understand."

"I want the contact number reactivated. And I'll need

to know what security precautions are being taken to stop the next tower from going down."

"My God, man, you can't be serious."

"Very serious. The second tower is coming down with or without your help. But it'll be a hell of a lot easier if you'll cooperate with me. Our careers are linked. You and I are brothers. If I fall, so do you."

"The blame will never come back to the palace."

"No, just to you and me. Rogue operators, working completely on our own."

Sa'ad took a long moment to work out the ramifications. "If it's not about the money, then why?"

"You wouldn't understand."

"Try me."

"For the pleasure of the thing."

Sa'ad absorbed it. "You're insane."

"Totally. But don't confuse that with stupidity."

"Maybe a bullet in the back of your head would be the best for both of us."

"It's too late for that."

After leaving Sa'ad, Kamal booked a ticket on the TGV from Paris to Barcelona and took a cab to the busy Gare de Lyon train station, where he had a late lunch of two *bières ordinaire* and a *croque-monsieur* grilled ham and cheese sandwich.

He used his travel app to contact the Grand Hotel Central, one of the best hotels in the Spanish city. Booking a suite for just the one night under his Castillo identification, he waited until the absolute last minute to board the train for the six-and-a-half-hour trip.

Sa'ad had sent no one for him. Or at least he'd not been able to pick out anyone from the thinning crowd on the platform.

He found his first-class compartment as soon as they'd pulled out of the station. An attractive woman in her mid-to-late-forties was seated across from him. She was obviously Parisian; her medium chestnut short hair was mussed just outside of perfection, and her blouse, its long sleeves pushed up to her elbows, the tattered but slim-fitting jeans and high-heeled shoes, plus a Hermès print scarf, were casually elegant. *Dans le vent,* the French said. "In the wind." "In fashion."

"Good afternoon, mademoiselle," he said pleasantly.

"Madame," she corrected him.

He inclined his head slightly. "*Pardon,* I didn't notice a ring."

A few minutes later they were moving through the outskirts of Paris, and he telephoned the Hermitage and spoke to the day manager.

"This is M. Castillo. I'm checking out, and I'll need you to do two things for me."

"Of course, monsieur. Will you be settling your account with the American Express platinum we have on record for you?"

"Of course, and please add a forty percent tip for your staff, and accept my apologies for the incident with the police last night."

"Thank you for your generosity, and think nothing of the incident. Now, how may I personally be of service, M. Castillo?"

"Firstly I would like the valet to place my motorcycle in storage for the time being."

"It's already been taken care of, sir."

"And I would like my things packed and sent by air to the Grand Central Hotel in Barcelona, to arrive no later than six this evening."

"Of course, though we may have to employ a private aviation service."

"I'll leave that to your good judgment."

"Yes, sir. Will there be anything else?"

"For the moment, no."

The attendant came for his ticket, followed by a steward from whom Kamal ordered a decent bottle of champagne.

"Dom Pérignon, sir?" the young man asked.

"Will you join me?" he asked his compartment mate. "It will certainly make the journey, and perhaps dinner a little later, go more quickly."

"Yes, please," she said.

"Two glasses," he told the attendant.

When he was gone Kamal offered his hand, which the woman took. "Angel Castillo."

"*Oui,* I couldn't help but overhear," she said. Her voice was soft and husky and she smiled at the corners of her eyes and lips. "Denise Theroux. Are you Spanish?"

"Mexican."

"I've never met a Mexican before."

"Then I'll give you the short course why we're superior in so many ways."

She laughed.

FIFTY-TWO

They dropped Pete off at her apartment in Georgetown, one of the minders staying with her, while the other was to drive McGarvey over to his place.

"We'll be back in a half hour," McGarvey told her.

"I'll need more than that, and then you're taking me to breakfast. We have plenty of time. And we need to talk."

McGarvey's minder was Benny Barton and McGarvey

had seen him before. He and the other minder, Sam Mc-
Guire, were ex-SEALs, and looking at them there was
nothing spectacular to see. But they were trained killers
and worked as a team. Marty had sent the best.

"What's the word on Campus?" McGarvey asked.

"They're going to try to bring down another one,
Mr. Director. But the word is that no one wants to believe
it."

"Any guesses on which one and when?"

"Something on East Fifty-seventh."

"Why there?"

Barton looked at him. "It's where the first one was. And
it's where the money is, sir. Would you buy into the neighborhood now?"

"No."

"Neither would anyone I personally know. Those kinds
of places are mostly for people who want to thumb their
noses at the rest of the world. Like the prince out east
somewhere who has a two-hundred-bedroom mansion.
Who the hell needs two hundred bedrooms, and ten swim-
ming pools, and a staff of two hundred?"

"I don't know."

Barton was suddenly sheepish. "Sorry, sir. I'm not some
do-gooder who thinks nobody should be rich, but those
who are have to share everything with the poor. But Jesus,
how much is too much?"

"No apologies necessary," McGarvey said. "But I can
think of a few who do good with their money. Bill Gates
and his wife, for instance."

"You're right, sir. But you asked why target places like
the pencil towers? It's the same as the trade towers on nine-
eleven. To the kind of people who gravitated to al-Qaeda
and now ISIS we're Satan, New York is hell on earth, and
those buildings are the devil's symbols. They have to bring
them down. And maybe they won't stop at just two."

"That's a cheery thought."

"Just doing what they pay me for, sir."

At his apartment, which was just a few blocks away from Pete's, McGarvey shaved and took a shower. He repacked his bag with some fresh clothes including a jacket, a tux in its hanging bag, and the last two clean passports and ID kits from his go-to-hell stash. Major Galan had returned the Walther, even the silencer, and two mags and ammunition.

Neither he nor Pete would walk around unarmed. And he was going to try his damndest to convince her to stay either here or at worst up in New York to lay the groundwork for what he knew was going to turn out to be practically a search for a needle in a large stack of needles. Manhattan had a lot of tall buildings.

They just had to figure out which one was next and mount a full-court press.

Otto phoned him on the way over. "How're you guys doing?"

"We could use a little more sleep, but right after the meeting I'm headed to Mallorca to catch up with Hammond."

"I just talked to Pete; she says she's packed and ready to go. Meeting's here in one hour. You guys can grab a quick bite in the cafeteria, and afterwards Louise says you guys are having dinner here and spending the night. Audie wants to see you, and anyway, Gratto and his crew need to get some rest before they head across the drink again."

McGarvey could sometimes bulldoze Otto, but he'd never been able to get past Louise, especially not if they held up the trump card: Audie, his granddaughter.

Barton called two minutes out, and when they pulled up Pete and her minder came out of the building. McGarvey

got in the backseat and she climbed in with him as Mc-
Guire loaded her bags into the rear area.

The minders' heads were on swivels as was McGarvey's,
but nothing seemed out of the ordinary. Within forty
seconds of stopping they were on the way to Langley.

The two housekeepers had been briefed. If it was Nero
at Cannes and aboard Hammond's yacht for the race, and
again at the Hermitage, where he had taken Pete at gunpoint, then the man had good intel. Good enough that he
would know McGarvey and Pete were back in D.C., and
send someone to pick them off.

"So where are we going to breakfast?" Pete asked.
She had taken a shower, fixed her hair, and had put on a
little makeup to cover the redness on the side of her face.
She looked fresh and eager.

"The cafeteria. Walt wants to get the meeting started."

"Peachy. Anyway, Louise called and invited us for dinner and a sleepover. Promised we wouldn't have to be in
separate beds."

"Good."

"Audie will be there. Sweet kid, she calls me Auntie Pete
and then laughs. Louise says that she's bright and knows
a lot more than we give her credit for."

McGarvey looked away for a moment.

"They're doing a good job raising her," Pete said.

He turned back. "Better than I could have on my own."

Otto met them with their passes at the elevator in the VIP
garage. He went up with them to the cafeteria across from
the covered walkway that overlooked one of the inner
courtyards. Just outside the windows was the Kryptos
statue, with four encoded messages cut into the copper
plates. Three of the messages had been decrypted several
years ago, but it wasn't until recently that Otto had cracked

the fourth. It had helped with an op that Mac had been in the middle of.

Looking haggard, his eyes puffy and bloodshot, his long hair flying all over the place, his tattered jeans and CCCP sweatshirt a little dirty where he'd spilled Coke or something down his front, he was happy to see them.

"I'm not sure who Castillo really is, but I don't think he's Nero," Pete said.

"And I don't think he's Valdes," McGarvey said. "Gut feeling."

They went down the serving line, got bottles of water, Pete a ham and egg sandwich, and Mac and Otto chile with beans and a couple of tortillas. The food was surprisingly not bad.

"That's good enough for me," Otto said as they took their seats. The place for breakfast lunch, dinner, and around midnight for breakfast again was usually busy but at this hour it was mostly deserted.

"So assuming Castillo is neither Valdes nor Nero, what's next?" Pete asked. "We're going back to Mallorca to Hammond's yacht? But we can't just shoot the guy for kidnapping me."

"I'm going to press him," McGarvey said. "You're going to New York to help the Bureau and NYPD investigators. We need to know what Nero's next target will be, and his timetable."

"You're talking about the Tower at the UN," Otto said. "If that's the place then his timetable is UNICEF's children's day in the General Assembly Building four days from now. Thirty-five hundred kids from around the world will be there. And it's only one thousand feet from the building, which is nearly twice that tall."

"We can't surround the place, because he'd just delay the attack until we backed off, which we'd have to do sooner or later," Pete said. "Whoever the hell Nero is. We don't have any clear pictures from AtEighth, no fingerprints from the Caddy he used to pick up Seif. No DNA. Nothing. We're in the dark. Just guessing."

"If it's Castillo and his target is the Tower across from the UN we have to stop him," McGarvey said.

"I hope to God that you're wrong. But if you aren't, and he manages to actually do it, the average American will be even more frightened for their security than they were after nine-eleven," Pete said.

FIFTY-THREE

Otto brought them up to the DCI's private conference room on the seventh floor of the OHB fifteen minutes before the regular meeting was to begin. Walt Page, Marty Bambridge, and Carleton Patterson, the CIA's aging general counsel, were the only three there at the moment.

Tall windows overlooked some of the other buildings on campus, and beyond them the woods to the south. The long oval table could seat a dozen comfortably, and the room was equipped with the latest flat-screen 3-D technology that did not require glasses. The equipment could bring up everything currently on the Company's mainframe, including the most current intelligence information for all of their sources everywhere in the world.

Otto had designed the system, which had been installed just last year.

"Welcome back in one piece," Page said from the head of the table, and he motioned for the three of them to take their places to his left.

Bambridge nodded, but said nothing. He and McGarvey

had never gotten along, but in the past year or so they had come to an understanding not to get in each other's way.

But Patterson, now in his late seventies, who had been with the Company seemingly forever, was a different story. He'd always been like an uncle to McGarvey and a friend to Otto, and he had taken an instant liking to Pete the first time he'd met her with McGarvey. Only this time he wasn't smiling. "I take it you've brought nothing definitive back with you, my dear boy."

"Except the one we're calling Nero for the moment, could be the man masquerading as Pablo Valdes, masquerading as Angel Castillo."

"Yes, Otto's kept us abreast of your progress," Page said. He'd spent an important part of his career as the CEO of IBM, and he looked the part.

"I'm afraid that you're playing with fire this time," Patterson said. "Evidently your Nero has befriended Tom Hammond and a number of other influential people."

This wasn't like Patterson, who always recommended caution, but who had never been timid.

"That's because the man has offered Hammond, and probably Susan Patterson, a large stake in the Mexican drug cartel money-laundering business," McGarvey said, and he knew where this was heading. "That at the very least deserves our attention."

"Your information has been turned over to the DEA and to Treasury," Bambridge said.

"And Homeland Security, just in case my hunch is correct?"

"They've been informed, as has the NYPD, the Bureau's counterterrorism agency, the New York National Guard, and every other agency involved on the chance that there'll be another attack," Bambridge said. "But we have not mentioned the man who is traveling under the name Castillo to anyone other than the DEA and Treasury."

"We think that you're going down the wrong path," Patterson said. "Even if Castillo is the drug launderer, it's officially none of our business." The faintest of smiles momentarily creased the corners of his mouth. He was saying something different than what he thought.

Bambridge sat forward. "Look, let's call a truce here, okay? We think that you may be right, that whoever took down AtEighth will try to take down another building. Possibly another of the pencil towers on East Fifty-seventh. Everyone is on board and security is tight. No one wants the bad guys to back off until the security people finally stand down, which they would have to sooner or later."

McGarvey knew where this was going as well. Bambridge was nothing if not predictable, which was the same direction the CIA had been heading over the past few years. "What's your point, Marty?"

"Castillo-Valdes is a dead end. Instead of chasing after him we would like you and Ms. Boylan to stay here and concentrate on New York. If you have evidence or even a gut feeling—something we've all come to respect here—then by all means work on defending the Tower by the UN. I'm sure that Ms. Nebel, Callahan's acting CEO, would be more than happy to put you and Ms. Boylan on the staff as security people. It would get you inside the penthouse for Jian Chang's party. It would put both of you in a perfect position to stop such an attack, if from what I understand that is the date of the attack. But consensus is a building somewhere on East Fifty-seventh."

"It make sense from where I sit," Page said.

It was worse than McGarvey thought it would be. "How many people have you shared this with?"

"The need-to-know list is small and it will be kept that way," Bambridge said.

"Everyone has to be kept out of sight, or he'll back off," McGarvey said.

"Don't you mean 'they'?" Bambridge asked. "ISIS?"

"Him," McGarvey said. "And I'll tell that to everyone else at the briefing."

"The appropriate people have already been briefed," Page said. "I wanted to hear where your investigation had led you. Henri Regent and I spoke last night." Regent was the director general of France's DGSI. "It was unofficial of course, but he asked that you be kept out of France."

"I won't be going back there anytime soon, unless Nero returns to his house in Monaco for some reason."

"Then you will go to New York?" Page asked.

"Yes," McGarvey said. "Now, if you gentlemen will excuse me I have work to do."

He started to rise but Pete put a hand on his arm, and he sat back down. He knew what was coming just by the look on her face. He could have written the minutes for this entire meeting without ever attending.

"Nero was registered in one of the suites at the Hermitage in Monaco," she said. "But he spent most of his two days and nights on Tom Hammond's yacht, from where he and the others could watch the race. As did Kirk and I."

"Do you mean the man identifying himself as Castillo?" Bambridge asked. "The one you think is really Pablo Valdes the money launderer?"

"Whoever. But most of the time he was either shacked up with Susan Patterson, the Hollywood producer, or talking in private with Hammond."

"How do you know this?" Page asked.

"This is all a game to Hammond, and to the woman," Pete said. "He's toying with the guy as he was with us. Tossing the dice just for the hell of it, to see what possible combinations come up. We offered him a scheme that would let him corner the bitcoin market. He would buy in low, and then drive the prices up by several thousand percentage points and dump it all. His profit would be enormous. In the billion-dollar-plus range."

"He wouldn't have bought anything so outrageous," Bambridge said. "He's smart enough to know such a thing would be impossible."

"Actually quite easy," Otto countered. "You just need some decent seed money. A hundred million or so."

"Why would you offer him something like that?" Page asked.

"To see if he would bite," Pete said. "Which he did. And because of it, an invitation to Mr. Jian's party, which we got."

She looked at McGarvey, who nodded for her to continue. In for a penny, in for a pound.

"We also wanted to see if he'd share this with Valdes, which he did, and to see what Valdes's reaction might be."

"And?" Page asked.

"Somehow the French found out that Mac was there in Monaco, so they arrested him and put him on the plane. Told him to get out."

"But not you," Bambridge said.

"No," Pete said. "After Mac was gone, Valdes kidnapped me at gunpoint, and took me to his home less than two miles away. Right on the sea, very nice. Otto was able to trace it not to Valdes, but to a British citizen by the name of Harcourt. Mac came back for me, but I'd already gotten out of the house and was on the run."

"If we're to believe you, it's nothing short of insanity," Bambridge said. "If he wanted to prove he was Valdes he did it. He's not your so-called Nero."

"I'm pretty sure that was his thinking," Pete said.

"Proves my point."

"That's just it, Marty, if he really is Valdes, why kidnap me? There's no reason for it. He's not a wanted man in France, and even our own Justice Department hasn't indicted him."

Patterson sat forward. "Do you have a clear photograph of your Nero?" he asked McGarvey. "From AtEighth?"

"No."

"Fingerprints, DNA, his voice recorded and perhaps analyzed?"

"Nothing."

"Just a hunch?"

McGarvey nodded. "Just a hunch."

FIFTY-FOUR

All afternoon on their way to Barcelona, Denise talked about herself—about her attorney husband who had at least two mistresses, about their apartment not far from the Champs-Élysées, and their two country places, one a villa in the hills above St. Tropez and the other a chateau near Versailles. But not once did she ask about him, which raised Kamal's antenna.

They came to the outskirts of the Spanish city, and she smiled. "You are a very good listener, Angel. Thank you for that."

"You don't sound very happy," Kamal said.

"I'm sorry, but I merely had to vent. It's been a long time. A lot of pent-up emotions." She smiled again. "The last hours have been all about me. So why are you traveling to Barcelona and from where?"

"From Monaco, where I watched the race, and here to catch a yacht."

"Glamorous, but the race was a very sad affair. Martaan was just a baby boy."

"But arrogant."

"You met him?"

"Yes," Kamal said. "What about you, why have you come to Barcelona?"

"To get away for a few days, perhaps longer. And do some browsing in the art galleries. I own a shop in Paris, and lately the craze is all about Spanish art. Whimsy, like the stuff at Friendly Fairy and the photo art at Kowasa and Alonso Vidal. Personally I despise it all, but my well-heeled customers—mostly mindless women with nothing else to do except spend their husbands' money—love it."

Kamal couldn't decide about her. Either she was one of the mindless women she'd just disparaged, or she was a splendid actress: But to what purpose?

"There I go again, talking about myself," she said.

"I'm staying tonight, at the Grand Central, but I'll be leaving sometime tomorrow."

"I overheard that too when you were talking to the Hermitage. As it turns out I'm staying at the same hotel. I always do when I come here. Perhaps we could have dinner together, and I'll listen while you talk."

"I can't think of spending my evening anywhere else," Kamal told her. At the very least he would have a chance to find out who the hell she was.

"Galant."

They shared a cab to the hotel in the city center, and he stood just behind Denise as she checked in with a Chase card, with her name on it. She was booked into a superior room, and the desk clerk summoned a bellman to take her single bag upstairs.

"We hope that you enjoy your stay, madame," the clerk told her.

"I'll meet you down here in the City Bar in fifteen minutes," she told Kamal. "I'll make reservations for us at Comerc 24 at nine. I'm told it's a good restaurant."

When she was gone, Kamal presented his Amex platinum. He'd booked a loft suite, which overlooked the ancient Roman walls that had once surrounded the city.

"Your bags have arrived, sir."

"Very good. Do you know of the restaurant the lady mentioned?" he asked the clerk.

"Yes, sir. It has a very good reputation, but she may be optimistic if she believes that she'll secure a reservation on such short notice."

"I have a feeling she usually gets what she wants."

"Yes, sir."

The bellman took Kamal's bags upstairs. "Shall I unpack for you, sir?"

"It's not necessary," Kamal said and he gave the man a hundred-euro bill.

The suite came with a complimentary bottle of Cava, the Spanish champagne. But it had always tasted like carbonated sugar water to him, even after the marginally drinkable Dom on the train.

He phoned Hammond's private number on the *Glory*. Susan Patterson answered.

"Who is it?" she demanded. She sounded angry.

"Me," Kamal said.

The phone was silent for just a moment, but when she came back her tone was much lighter, though she was still demanding. "Where the hell are you calling from?" she said. "Close, I hope."

"Barcelona. Are you in Mallorca yet?"

"Anchored off Palma with the others, and we've been here forever."

"I thought they were your friends."

"They're boring as hell," she said.

"Then leave."

"I want to see you first. I'll have Tom send the helicopter. It's not much more than a hundred miles or so. You can be aboard in time for dinner."

"Not until morning. I'm going to have something to eat here at the hotel."

"Eat something or someone?" she said.

"That's crude. Why the anger?"

"He and Alyan are practically joined at the hip. The bastards are hatching something, and I'm not included."

"Do you think that it involves me?"

"A hundred percent. I need you here to insist that I'm dealt back in."

"And if I don't? Insist?"

"I'll make you a proposal that you won't be able to refuse," she said. "What time do you want the chopper?"

"Eight."

"You might have to go out to the airport to catch it. I'll have someone let you know."

The restaurant was crowded; some of the tapas were fine, others marginal and most of the diners were tourists. It wasn't his kind of place, and Denise couldn't stop talking about herself. She was almost pathological, and yet he had the growing feeling that her prattling about nothing was an act. But still to what end he couldn't fathom, though he thought it important that he did.

By eleven they were back at the hotel, a different staff on duty now at the front desk, and no one paid any attention to them.

He went up to her floor. At her door she asked if he wanted to come in for a nightcap and he agreed.

"There's wine on the sideboard, help yourself, and give

me just a minute," she told him, went into the bathroom and closed the door.

Kamal engaged the safety lock, and without a sound took up position just to the right of the door. The woman had been too obvious this evening. She was here with a purpose.

She came out a few moments later, a small Glock pistol with a silencer in her hand.

Kamal took it away from her and shoved her back into the bathroom. She didn't make a sound.

"Who sent you?" he asked.

"A friend, who instructed me to delay you here," she answered, not at all frightened.

She was a field officer, and that's what had bothered Kamal. "For how long?"

"Twenty-four hours."

"Then what?"

"I wasn't told."

"Do you know who I am and who I work for?"

"You're a freelance. That, and you were ordered to stand down but refused."

"Stand down from what?"

"I wasn't told that either. My orders were simply to detain you."

Kamal nodded. "How can I refuse?" he asked. He kissed her and she kissed him back. "Why don't you take off your clothes and get in the shower? I like the water hot. I'll open the wine and join you."

He turned around and tossed the pistol on the couch, then took off his jacket and went to the sideboard to open the wine.

The water began to run as he got the wine open. He turned around as Denise, naked, got into the shower.

Putting the bottle down, he got the pistol from where

he had tossed it and went into the bathroom just as she was adjusting the water. She started to turn and he fired one shot point-blank into her right temple. She collapsed without a word. No insurance shot was needed this time.

He shut off the water, wiped his prints off the pistol, and put it in her right hand.

Of course the police would figure out that it hadn't been a suicide, but by then he would be long gone. To New York.

FIFTY-FIVE

Louise had made a traditional American dinner for them—roast beef, mashed potatoes, and creamed corn—which turned out to be Audie's all-time-favorite meal. Just three, she was a precocious kid; not only was she bright, she'd spent more time with adults, including trainees at the CIA boot camp, than with children her own age.

Otto had promised that would come to an end when she enrolled in a school for the gifted. She was smart but she needed to be socialized.

McGarvey and Pete went to bed early, shortly after Gratto called and said they would be ready to take off at or just before dawn for the crossing to Barcelona. From there they would chopper out to Hammond's yacht.

"Us showing up will be a shock to Nero, or whoever the hell he really is," Pete said, lying next to him.

"Nothing we could do to him aboard the yacht, though it'd make for an interesting scene seeing him face-to-face again. Especially with you in the mix."

McGarvey realized that he'd been so convinced that the man posing as Valdes was in actuality their Nero that he hadn't really considered any other possibility. "Maybe he is nothing more than a money launderer for the cartels, but he put his hands on you."

Pete rolled over to him, and in the dim light he could see that she was smiling. "We can sleep on the way over," she said.

They got up around four-thirty, and after McGarvey was ready, he went into Audie's room and pulled up her covers and gave her a kiss on the forehead. She was the spitting image of Liz, her mother, who in turn had looked like Katy, her grandmother. Seeing her sleeping brought back a host of memories, some wonderful, like Katy sitting in their gazebo on Casey Key, but others almost impossible to bear, like watching the car they were riding in going up in flames.

Otto had the coffee on and was waiting in the kitchen for them. "All set, then?" he asked.

"I don't know what we're going to find on Mallorca, but if Nero is there I'm going to push him hard," McGarvey said.

"And if not?"

"We'll come back to New York and try to figure out what his next move will be. But we're going to need some damned good intel. It's a safe bet he won't be going back to Monaco, and he'll have to travel to New York either by commercial airliner or a private jet."

"As anybody."

"Set your darlings to search for passport photos."

"Or for anything unusual or unexplained," Pete said. "He was shook up enough in Monaco to grab me. That was his first mistake. Mac showing up so quickly rattled him enough that I think it's likely he's going to make another mistake."

"Take care," Louise said at the kitchen door. "We want you back. Audie needs her grampy father, and maybe a grammy mother."

"I'll drive you to Andrews," Otto said.

They lifted off shortly before six in the morning toward the sun. Gratto figured with a decent tailwind, they would touch down at Barcelona's El Prat airport around six in the evening.

Once they were out over the Atlantic, McGarvey phoned Hammond aboard his yacht. It took a minute or so for the man to be summoned, and in the background there was music.

"Hammond."

"Joe Canton, I'm on my way back. I hope the invitation to come aboard still stands, because I have some more information for you. That is, if you're still interested."

"I'm very interested, and when I spoke with Chang and Viktor they also wanted in."

"Good. I'll be in Barcelona around six this evening."

"Will Ms. Borman be coming with you?"

"She'll be meeting me in Barcelona."

"Good. I'll send my helicopter to pick you up at the airport."

"Make it seven your time. I have a couple of things to take care of first."

"Seven it is."

McGarvey went up to the cockpit and explained the situation with Hammond's helicopter. "Soon as we touch down, I want you to take on some fuel, and get the hell out of there. But don't go far. We may need to get back in a hurry."

"I'll do you one better. I think I can duck out of sight inside a service hangar till you need us."

They touched down just past six local, where they went through Customs and Immigration at the VIP terminal. Since they had come in aboard a U.S. government aircraft, and would be met by a helicopter to take them onward to Mallorca, their overnight bags and persons were not checked, only their passports were stamped.

An EC135 helicopter, painted blue and white just like Hammond's yacht, showed up ten minutes after Gratto got the Gulfstream out of sight.

Al-Hamadi jumped out and took two bags from the cargo space as McGarvey and Pete approached.

"You're leaving?" McGarvey asked, shouting over the engine and rotor noises.

"My wife wants me back. Some small crisis or another."

"Will you be at Mr. Jian's party in New York?"

"Wouldn't miss it for the world."

"Is Mr. Castillo aboard yet?" Pete asked.

"He was supposed to helicopter out this morning, but he called at the last minute and told Tom that he had business somewhere in Mexico," al-Hamadi said. "Maybe you guys can help liven things up. Nothing's been the same since the race. And less than half the yachts showed up. It's like an extended funeral."

"A bad year," Pete said.

"Yes."

Al-Hamadi nodded and headed across the apron to the VIP terminal.

"What do you want to do?" Pete asked when the Saudi was out of earshot.

"If we don't at least make an appearance we might get

bumped off the list for Jian's party," McGarvey said. "It's something I don't want to happen."

"If he's Nero after all, he's probably already on his way to New York."

The flight out to the yacht took less than an hour. A lot of people were aboard, though not as many as had been for the race. Pete went looking for Susan Patterson to see if she could find out where Valdes had gotten himself to, and McGarvey was directed below to Hammond's office.

The billionaire was lying facedown on a padded table while a model-pretty young woman, topless, was giving him a massage. Vivaldi's "Four Seasons" was playing.

"Welcome aboard," Hammond said. "Was New York productive?"

"Not as well as I'd hoped."

"You'll do better at Chang's party. I think we're all going to need some cheering up."

Hammond reached around and patted the girl on the butt. "Thanks, darlin', enough for now."

The girl put on a gauzy top, wiped her hands on a towel, and left them.

"I was hoping Castillo—or should I say Valdes?—would be here. I wanted to talk to him about buying in."

"He thinks that you and Ms. Borman work for either the DEA or Treasury. And Ms. Bormon says she wants to write about rich celebrities."

McGarvey smiled. "Neither, but we're here for the same reason he is. To make money. We'd like a piece of his action. Unless you're taking it all."

"I always leave plenty of room at the trough."

"Happy to hear that. He and you were the only reasons

we came out this evening. That, and I wanted to give both of you a secure e-mail address and password to a site where you'll be given a bitcoin prospectus."

"I'll look at it tonight."

"You can always reach me at the same address. And my satphone has a very good encryption algorithm."

"Are you at least staying the night?"

"We have to get back, if your pilot will return us to the airport."

Hammond glanced at one of the monitors. Pete and Susan Patterson seemed to be in deep conversation. "Probably for the best that you two leave. Susan can be a vindictive bitch when she thinks she's being challenged."

"I'll see you at the party," McGarvey said, but Hammond had turned his back and was already on the phone with someone.

Mac let himself out, and went to rescue Pete.

FIFTY-SIX

Kamal sat alone at the bar in the anonymous Renaissance Paris Vendôme Hotel, barely tolerating a split of ordinary Dom Pérignon after an unimaginative dinner of lobster and pommes frites.

Of course the fare was not the hotel's fault. He had ordered the pedestrian food and drink to go with the Prestige single room he'd booked. He was abstaining from the amenities he'd enjoyed for a very long time because he was preparing to go off the radar. He needed to fade into the woodwork; for all practical purposes, disappear off the face of the earth.

McGarvey and the woman were looking for him. He was certain they suspected that he was behind taking At-

Eighth down, and that he would try to destroy another. There was no other reason that the former director of the CIA would have shown up. Certainly not for anything so simple as money laundering. Of course, they couldn't know what building, nor could they know his timetable. But they thought he was coming.

He could no longer count on the support of the GIP and his contact, Sa'ad al-Sakar. Not only had his flow of information been cut off, Sa'ad had actually sent the stupid woman to kill him.

His money stream had been cut off as well. But that was of very little concern to him. In the first place he had plenty of money to last a lifetime, and second, money or not, intel or not, he was going through with his original plan. Something he had given a lot of thought to after McGarvey's woman managed to escape.

The bartender came and poured him another glass, emptying the split. "Another, monsieur?"

"Yes, please."

He'd taken the early morning train back to Paris, and as soon as he'd arrived, even before he checked in at the Vendôme, he'd had the cab driver stop at an electronics shop where he'd bought a cheap tablet computer.

He set it up with the hotel's wi-fi connection, and first searched the Spanish news outlets for stories about a woman found shot to death at the Grand Central. But there had been nothing. To this point the cops were likely treating her death as a suicide.

Next he searched the U.S. news outlets for stories about the downing of AtEighth. Nothing new had turned up, except that some of the columnists and a few military analysts working for the TV networks were warning about another attack. A copycat of 9/11.

ISIS was chief among the suspects, especially after the attacks in Paris a year and a half ago, though al-Qaeda was being mentioned as well. But those were attacks from abroad.

Paris and Brussels had finally begun to settle down after the trouble; nevertheless the new immigration laws were tougher than ever. Anyone with a Syrian or Iraqi passport was immediately suspect, and unless they could show a spotless record and perfect papers, they were either turned back at the border or arrested. And it was nearly the same in the U.S.

In Paris, the 10th arrondissement was the city's biggest headache, with a population well over one hundred thousand and a growing number of immigrants. It was the most ethnically mixed neighborhood anywhere in France, and possibly the most dangerous, aside from a couple of areas in Marseilles.

Kamal signed for his bill and took a cab to the Gare de l'Est, in the 10th. From there he walked a half dozen blocks to an area of small sidewalk cafés. But it wasn't until he'd passed five of them, with all the tables occupied, that he found one with a couple of empty spots and he sat down.

Sweet spices and cooking oil and a dozen other scents he'd never encountered before, filled the night air. No one looked at him directly, but he was out of place here, and he was sure that he was being watched.

When the waiter, in dark slacks and a white shirt buttoned at the collar, came, Kamal ordered a sweet tea. For a long moment the waiter just stared at him as if he were a dangerous bug.

Kamal took out a small Star of David medallion meant to be hung on a chain around the neck and laid it on the table.

The waiter stepped back a pace.

Kamal took out a short piece of black electrician's tape, attached it to the medallion, and shoved it across the table.

This time the waiter gave him a quizzical, but entirely unfriendly, look then turned and walked back inside.

A hush came over the half dozen sidewalk tables. Everyone stared at him, wishing he would get up and go, or drop dead on the spot.

A man in ordinary street clothes came out with Kamal's tea. "What do you want here, monsieur?" he asked in French.

"A name."

"What name?"

"Of a friend. A man willing to continue Allah's work in America."

"I don't know what you're talking about. But for your own safety I would advise that you leave immediately."

"Do I look like a gendarme?"

"Oui."

The man had brought the *addition* on a small slip of paper.

Kamal took out a pen and wrote an international number on the back of the slip. It was one of the accommodation numbers he used, this one in Ankara. It would go blank without the use of a onetime password.

"Tell them it is for Emile."

The man did not touch the paper.

Kamal laid a ten-euro coin on the table, and got up and left without looking at any of the other patrons.

After two blocks he knew that he was being followed, and it was exactly what he'd wanted to happen. He had gotten someone's attention.

He was creating a traceable trail to ISIS.

Instead of heading toward the train station and a safer part of the neighborhood he quickened his pace and turned deeper into the district, ducking into the Bastille Métro entrance, from where the Canal Saint-Martin ran underground to the République Métro station.

Away from the lights of the station Kamal sped up, ducking into a maintenance alcove a hundred meters farther along.

Two men in dark shirts, black jeans, and sneakers were

right behind him. They had a five-day growth on their faces, but they looked as if they were barely into their twenties.

Kamal stepped out as they hurried past. "I thought it was two old women following me, but now it turns out you're merely boys," he said in Arabic.

They pulled up short and spun around.

"Fucker," one of them said.

They pulled knives and separated, coming at him from the right and left. It was a mistake.

He stepped lightly to the left, grabbed one of the boys by the knife arm, spun him around, and smashed him face-first into the black stone wall.

The other one was on him in an instant, but stopped short when Kamal turned to him.

"Stupid, actually, when I came as a friend with a message."

"You won't leave here alive," the kid said.

"If you persist it will be you and your friend who die here. But that's up to you."

The kid didn't know what to do.

"If I was a cop my fellow officers would be all over this place by now."

"You lie."

"I'll spare your lives. Go back to the café and tell them to call the number."

"If I don't?"

"You will, because there's a good chance you'll end up martyrs fighting against the Great Satan."

The kid was uncertain.

Kamal stepped into him, snatched the knife from his hand, and threw it into the canal. "I can wait until some-one else comes, and perhaps they will not be stupid, be-cause there's also a very good chance that you'll earn a great deal of money for the cause."

Still the kid didn't know what to do.

"Inshallah," Kamal said, and he walked away.

PART
FIVE

New York City,
Tower Down

McGarvey was taken by how fast things seemed to have settled down. According to Gatto as they came in for a landing, air traffic across the country—including New York—had returned to near normal.

"Guess after nine-eleven we became pros," Toynbee said.

"It'll make it easier for Nero," McGarvey said.

"Nero?"

"The guy who's going to try to take down another tower."

"Shit. Has this been all about him? Cannes, Monaco, Genoa?"

"Yeah."

"But we haven't nailed him yet?" Toynbee asked. He was clearly disappointed.

"We will," McGarvey said. "Guaranteed."

After they had touched down at Andrews and taxied over to the navy's hangar that the CIA occasionally used, Gatto wanted to know if they were finished with the op.

"You can stand fast for at least twenty-four hours, but then we'll have to get up to New York," McGarvey said.

"Our pleasure, Mr. Director."

McGarvey didn't want minders who would slow them from this time on. He *did* want someone to come after him, though he didn't think anything serious was going to happen until he and Pete started poking around New York. The UNICEF thing at the UN was set for three days. It was their and Nero's timetable.

In the meantime, according to Otto, the Bureau's anti-terrorism people along with the NYPD were covering just about every tall building on East Fifty-seventh plus the more obvious ones around the city—among them the new World Trade Center and the Empire State Building.

Otto was waiting for them with the same old battered Mercedes 300SD turbo diesel he'd had even before he and Louise were married "You don't want minders so you'll have to put up with me. Anyway, I needed to talk to you before we got out to Campus."

"Georgetown first," McGarvey said.

"I figured that you guys would want to get to your places before business."

They went through the main gate and took the Beltway south around the city. It was the long way but Otto said that he needed a little time to explain the situation here in Washington as well as up in New York.

"Everyone is practically shitting Twinkies. Everyone thinks that everyone else is off their rocker, including—or maybe especially—you and Pete. But I think that I finally figured out how ISIS cells are communicating with each other." He thumped the back of his hand on the steering wheel. "I'm so stupid, it was right there all along staring me in the face, and I didn't see it until last night."

"One step at a time," McGarvey said. He was riding shotgun.

Pete, in the backseat, touched Otto on the shoulder. "You dress like a ragpicker despite Louise's help, but you're anything but stupid."

"They're talking to each other in the same old way before Paris, only this time it's in 3-D and more subtle.

PlayStation Five A now. Warriors for God, and they flood the program with places they're going to hit. Targets all over the world. Paris, Brussels, and New York again; Washington, Chicago, Ankara, Istanbul, London, Madrid, Moscow. Name the city or airport, and they'll hit it. Detailed plans. Dates, times, personnel, weapons, expected casualties."

"It's like they're intentionally flooding the game with bogus dates and targets," Pete said.

"Right. So far almost all of the hits have been nothing but background noise, designed to keep everyone running around like chickens with their heads cut off."

"Almost all?" McGarvey asked.

"Two days ago a Turkish airliner bound for Tehran had engine problems so it went back to the terminal and offloaded the passengers. When it was on the way across the field to a maintenance hangar, about the same time if it had taken off on schedule, and would have been at thirty-five thousand feet, a bomb exploded in the cargo hold. That one was in the game, and it happened."

"What's the ratio?" McGarvey asked.

"For every actual event, one hundred are posted," Otto said. "And that's been going on for eight months now."

"Long enough that everyone's all but backed off," Pete said. "No way to cover every possible threat."

"But you've found the key," McGarvey said.

"I think so. There've only been four other targets that were hit in the last year or so, one on Turkey's border with Syria, two on Saudi Arabia's northern border with Iraq, and AtEighth. In each of the game's scenarios the bad guy was a Pakistani."

"That makes no sense," Pete said. "ISIS has no beef with Pakistan."

"It doesn't have to. It's just a key."

"What about New York again?" McGarvey asked.

"That's the bad news. There've been bogus PlayStation attacks in San Francisco, the Mall of America near Minneapolis, and the cruise ship port in Tampa. No Pakistani names, and no mention of New York."

"Yet," Pete said.

"Something like that takes planning," McGarvey said. "If they were going to hit New York it would be in the game, if Otto was right."

"There's more bad news," Otto said. "I had to pass this along to Walt this morning. Matt Braun's people were on it within a half hour." Braun was chief of the CIA's Directorate of Science and Technology. "For the moment everyone's backed off on the idea that ISIS will mount a nine-eleven copycat op one day from now on the Tower or any other target in Manhattan."

Traffic was heavy as usual for a weekday, and the sky was overcast, spreading a gloom over the countryside. Otto was glum.

"Sorry, Mac," he said.

"Who else knows about this?" Pete asked.

"The French and Brits, of course. And just about everyone else with a vested interest."

"Including Pakistan?" Pete asked.

"Yeah."

"They're wrong," McGarvey said. He could feel Nero in his gut. He could see the operation going down, just as he could see the Tower at the UN crashing and killing the children gathered at the General Assembly.

"I'm not sure, Kemo Sabe," Otto said.

"I've done things alone before, I can do it again."

"Don't talk stupid," Pete said from the backseat. "Tell us what you want to do and we'll do it, goddamnit."

"Nero will come to New York. He'll be at Jian's party and he'll bring down the Tower unless we stop him."

"ISIS is saying nothing," Otto said.

"This has never been about ISIS. It's Saudi Arabia. They want us to fight their battles. Going against fellow Muslims, even ISIS extremists, makes them look bad in the eyes of a lot of neighbors. And it was the Saudis who looked the other way when al-Qaeda hit us on nine-eleven."

"Assuming you're right, what do you want me to do?" Otto asked.

"Within twenty-four hours of AtEighth coming down, ISIS claimed responsibility. First find out if there was any inkling of the attacks on the PlayStation site."

"I've already checked. There was nothing."

"Then try to verify if ISIS actually was involved, or if their claim was made through a channel they've never used before. Run it back to the source."

"And?" Otto asked.

"I'll try to convince Walt I'm right."

"Won't happen."

"Pete and I are going to New York on the assumption that I'm right," McGarvey said.

"Gives you guys one day with no help," Otto said.

"We have you."

FIFTY-EIGHT

They met again in the DCI's private conference room just off his office. The table was set for an early lunch, and Walt Page, Bambridge, Patterson, and Matt Braun had already arrived by the time McGarvey and Pete were shown in. Otto had gone directly to his darlings to see if Castillo, Valdes, or Harcourt, whoever Nero really was, had been making any waves in the past twenty-four hours.

McGarvey had taken off the glasses and bow tie, and had dressed as he usually did—jeans, white shirt, black blazer. There no longer was any reason to walk around in any sort of a disguise, even a weak one.

The mood wasn't as somber as McGarvey had figured it would be. But nobody was smiling.

"Welcome back again," Page said. "I think both of you know Matt."

"We've worked together from time to time," McGarvey said. He and Pete took their seats.

"I thought we'd first cover a couple of issues, and then have lunch. Prime rib today."

"Good. We want to take care of a few things here, and in the morning we're heading back to New York."

"At this point you might be wasting your time, Mr. Mc-Garvey," Braun said. He was a short stocky man, with an almost perfectly square face and chin. He looked like one of the private eyes on the cover of a thirties pulp magazine.

"Otto said that you and he were working together on the PlayStation idea."

"That was really good. I would never have caught it on my own. But it tells us pretty clearly that ISIS is not planning an attack in New York, or at least not anytime soon. Looking back to the Paris and Brussels attacks, all the signs were there months beforehand. It's just that no one was seeing it."

"Had Otto figured it out then, there wouldn't have been any attacks," Marty said. He was confident.

"ISIS didn't bring down AtEighth," McGarvey told them. "Nor will they will try to bring down any other building in New York."

"Your Nero, the one who you didn't stop, not even in Monaco after he had taken Ms. Boylan at gunpoint?"

"I had no proof at that point."

"But he kidnapped your partner and threatened her with

death. I would have thought that such an act by itself would have been cause for you to arrest the man. Or maybe shoot him."

"What's your point, Marty?"

"My point is this: The man who has gone under several aliases already—something unusual for a wealthy man, if the house in Monaco *is* his, and who gets invited aboard the yacht of a multibillionaire—is no terrorist. But I think you were justified in believing that he might actually be Pablo Valdes, the Mexican drug-money launderer."

"Just another alias to get him close to Hammond with a deal."

"Well, the Mexican army found a body they think is Valdes's in the mountains not far from the border with Arizona. They're keeping it quiet for now in the hope that the cartel bosses will be so desperate to do something with all the cash that keeps pouring in that they'll make a mistake. So who is this guy? And why did he go to Hammond with a deal that he couldn't actually make?"

"For the same reason we offered Hammond a deal," Pete said.

"Which was?"

"To get invited to Jian Chang's housewarming party in the penthouse at the Tower. One day from now."

"And did you get an invitation?" Marty asked.

"Yes, and we'll be there."

"Just out of curiosity, my dear girl, what was the deal?" Patterson asked. Unlike Bambridge and Braun he didn't seem so confident. But then, he had known McGarvey a lot longer than anyone else in the room.

"A way to corner the bitcoin market. Jian himself is interested, as are a couple of others who'll be at the party."

"Not possible," Braun said.

"Ask Otto," Pete said. "He'll explain it to you."

Braun shut his mouth.

"So what's next?" Page asked.

"Nero is going to try to take down the Tower. Pete and I will be there to stop him."

"You'll be going as a private citizen," Marty said. "But Ms. Boylan will not be going with you."

"Why's that?" Pete asked.

"Because you're an employee of the Agency, in my directorate, and I'm ordering you to stay at your desk and resume your duties."

"I quit," Pete said.

"You can't."

"I just did. And if you want, I'll put it in writing and e-mail it to you."

Marty was getting hot. "If need be I'll have you placed under house arrest."

"Hold on," Page said. He and Patterson exchanged a glance. "Kirk has served this agency before any of us—except for Carleton—were here. He's given it just about everything, nearly his life on several occasions, and the lives of his wife, his daughter, and his son-in-law. He had your desk, Marty, and even mine for short stints. But mostly he's operated out there by himself, often without any official sanctions."

"Always with a pile of bodies in his wake," Marty said. "France never wants him to come back."

"They would have welcomed him with open arms three days before Paris if he'd had a hunch the attacks were going to take place," Page said.

"So we just let them walk out of here and do whatever they want to do in New York?" Marty said.

"No one believes I'm right," McGarvey said. "Not the Bureau and especially not the NYPD. But if you can convince them that another attack is possible, have them send up a couple of high-flying drones, but no one on the ground.

No snipers on rooftops. Nothing like that. He'd spot them and back off."

"But what if you're right, my dear boy?"

"I hope I'm not," McGarvey said. He'd always had the same thought when he came up against his hunches.

"But let's assume that you are. And it's just you, Ms. Boylan, and a couple of drones. What if you fail?"

"If we let everyone on board it'll become a free-for-all and he'll back off until we stand down. Two months, six, a year, two years. He has more patience than we do."

"ISIS doesn't," Marty said.

"It's not them."

"Who then?"

"Saudi Arabia," McGarvey said. "Nero is a contractor for the GIP."

"Christ," Marty said softly. "You're crazy."

"You'll have your drones, we'll take care of that part," Page said. "But there won't be a word to anyone from this agency unless you ask for help. And I won't accept your resignation, Ms. Boylan. Kirk will need all the help he can get in New York. And afterwards you'll continue to be a valuable asset."

"Yes, sir," Pete said.

"Good. Now let's have lunch."

McGarvey rose, and Pete did so right after him. "We'll take a rain check, Mr. Director. We're flying up to New York first thing in the morning, and we have a lot to do here beforehand."

"Good hunting, Mr. Director," Page said. "And Ms. Boylan. We'll have lunch on Saturday when you get back."

Downstairs Otto buzzed them into his office. "How'd it go?"

"About how we expected," McGarvey said.

"Marty was an asshole as usual?"

"He's just trying to do his job the best he can. And it's not an easy one, I've been there."

"Page gave you the go-ahead?"

"Promised us lunch when it was over," McGarvey said. "We're flying up first thing in the morning. Arrange a meeting for us with Nancy Nebel and Dan Endicott at the Tower. But ask them both to keep it quiet for the time being. They can decide what to do after we talk."

"They're bound to ask why."

"Stonewall. This has to be totally under the radar."

FIFTY-NINE

Kamal sat at the bar at the Atlanta airport Holiday Inn sipping a Michelob Ultra to wash away the taste of a simply wretched dinner of something they called macaroni and cheese and a hamburger. He had gotten into the country without fanfare under a U.S. passport in the name of Howard Ramsey, had rented an ordinary Chevrolet Impala from Budget, and had driven over to the least notable hotel he could think of that still had relatively decent service. No one would expect him to be in a place such as this. At least not for now.

This was not his ideal city; he'd never particularly liked or felt comfortable in the American South, and yet the contact number he'd left in Paris had been called, and a code name of al-Dhib and an Atlanta phone number had been left.

His only concerns were McGarvey's resources at the CIA. By now they most likely had good photographs of him under his Castillo persona, and face recognition programs might be able to pick him as a possible from the passport photo.

Before he'd left Paris he'd cut his hair short and dyed it blond, to match the passport photo and California driver's license. He also picked up a pair of drugstore glasses with cheap frames, also shown in the photos. The change wasn't startling, but combined with the way he walked hunched over as if he suffered from back pain, and the ordinary off-the-rack suit he'd purchased, he was no longer Castillo or Valdes.

There were less than twenty-four hours until the children's day gathering at the UN, and at this point he needed to meet with al-Dhib, he needed a weapon, and he needed to get to New York without coming face-to-face with McGarvey or the woman.

Back in his room by seven he went online and found the addresses of several gun dealers, including the Atlanta Gun Emporium on Virginia, just a couple of miles from the hotel. Its posted hours, Monday through Saturday, were from nine to nine.

He got directions, and taking five thousand U.S. dollars from his suitcase drove over. The Emporium was housed in a huge warehouse-type building, with just about every model of every legal firearm on display.

A few customers, all of them men, were in the section of long guns, but only one clerk was behind the counter in the area filled with pistols. The man had long stringy hair and wore a hunting vest, a big flashy diamond ring on the pinkie finger of his left hand.

He looked up as Kamal approached. "What can I do for you?"

"I need a pistol. Semiautomatic. Something that fires a nine-millimeter round, with a decent magazine capacity."

"If you're talking price I have the standard Beretta 92 FS. Same pistol the army used to use. Easy to disassemble, damn near jam-proof." He took the weapon from inside one of the glass cases and laid it on a red cloth on the counter.

"Too bulky," Kamal said.

"Something smaller. Subcompact?"

"Yes."

He went to another glass case and took out a small pistol that Kamal immediately recognized.

"This is a Glock 43, subcompact slimline. Fires the nine-by-nineteen round, and the magazine capacity is only six rounds. But it's a sweet personal defense weapon. And in the right hands it would do the job nicely."

He handed the gun to Kamal, who made a show of feeling its weight, and turned and pointed it at the mounted head of a wild boar. It was almost like handling an old friend.

"I'll take it, along with two boxes of hollow points, three magazines, and a quick-draw underarm holster," he said, laying the gun on the counter.

"Good choices, sir. I'll just need to see your driver's license and have you fill out a form, and you can come back in three days."

"That's a problem."

"Sir?" the clerk asked, but he didn't seem surprised.

"I need it now. One thousand dollars."

The clerk considered it for a moment. He turned and went into a back room. Kamal was about to leave, when the man came back out.

"Little problem with the surveillance cameras. Had to back them up five minutes, then turn them off. You were saying?"

"Fifteen hundred."

"Three thousand."

"Seventeen fifty," Kamal said. "In cash, now." He took the money from his pants pocket and began counting it out on the counter.

The clerk shrugged. "Twenty-five hundred."

Kamal hesitated a moment, but then counted out the rest.

The clerk produced a small nylon ripstop bag with no logo from under the counter and loaded it with the pistol and other things. He handed it over, along with a receipt for two boxes of .22 short rounds, and a packet of targets. "Happy hunting," he said.

Leaving the Emporium, Kamal drove a standard detection and evasion route. After a half hour he was certain that he hadn't been followed, and made his way back to the Holiday Inn.

Upstairs in his room he disassembled the Glock, making certain that the firing pin had not been removed, that the springs in the three magazines were in working order, and that the ammunition had not been tampered with.

He loaded all three mags, seated one in the pistol's handle, cycled a round in the chamber, and added the replacement in the mag. With the lights off he sat at the window, from where he could watch the front driveway into the hotel.

A few cars disappeared under the overhang for several minutes while the people registered, and then reappeared, going to parking spots.

Everything was normal. Nothing unexpected had happened since he'd entered the States.

He laid down for a couple of hours' sleep, awaking at exactly midnight. He listened to the lack of sounds from out in the corridor then checked the window again. The parking lot was quiet.

Powering up his laptop, he pulled up a detailed street map of Manhattan on which prominent buildings were highlighted. Empire State, Chrysler, 60 Wall Street, 125

Greenwich Street, One World Trade Center, 8 Spruce Street, and a half dozen others, including AtEighth, which was still shown intact.

He highlighted four in various locations around Central Park, including 432 Park Avenue, which had opened a couple of years ago and was for a brief time the tallest residential building in the city, until others, including AtEighth and the Tower at the UN, had risen.

After a quick shower, he got dressed, donned the holster and pistol under his left arm, repacked his bag and left it by the door.

Using his cell phone he called Sa'ad's contact number. It rang ten times before the Saudi GIP officer finally picked up.

"I'm surprised to hear from you."

"Denise is dead."

"I thought as much," Sa'ad said after a slight hesitation. "Foolish of you to have sent her."

"Where are you?"

"Paris, but I'm going to New York," Kamal said.

"You're cutting it close if you mean to continue."

"McGarvey suspects who I am. So the less time I spend in the city, the less likely he'll be in a position to stop me."

"But you'll both be at Jian's party."

"Perhaps not," Kamal said, and he gave it a moment to sink in.

"I don't understand," Sa'ad replied.

Kamal hung up and called the number for al-Dhib.

"Yes," his contact said.

"I'm coming to see you now."

"I was told to expect you. Are you here in the city?"

"Yes."

"Was it you in Paris?"

"Yes," Kamal said.

"Is it beginning?"

"It's what I need to talk to you about."

SIXTY

"The question is why are we waiting until morning to go up to New York," Pete asked on the way over to the Renckes' safe house. It was just past midnight. She was driving her BMW convertible, the top down.

They'd spent a couple of hours in Otto's office on Campus compiling a list of the most high-value targets in Manhattan. There were more than one hundred, with the Tower topping the list. Impossible to adequately cover them all, and Otto said so. Afterward they'd had dinner and went back to Mac's apartment to get a few hours of sleep.

The fact of the matter was that McGarvey had been thinking about how Nero would go about planning the attack. And he'd come up with the only reasonable solution: if Nero wanted to hit the Tower and he knew that at least someone expected that to be his next target—because of Jian's party—then he would create a diversion. Or diversions.

"Because Nero knows that we're coming after him," McGarvey said.

"And if he's Valdes, he knows we'll be at the party."

"Right. So I don't want us to get there until the last possible moment."

"Christ," Pete said, but then she concentrated on her driving.

McGarvey glanced over at her, and the realization that she had truly become his partner—an indispensible partner—struck him all at once like a ton of bricks. He supposed that it was love, but it felt more like dependence, like someone who had your six, like someone you cared for, like someone you worried over, like someone you could count on.

It was corny, but he supposed it might be a definition, among others, for love.

"Do you want a Tums?" he asked, trying to lighten the mood just a little.

"A whole bloody bottle," she said. "But the question still stands: Why the last minute? Jian's party is set for eight Friday night, one day from now, actually tomorrow. Forty hours?"

"We're going to be all over the building before the party starts."

"Yeah, so?"

"He'll be there too."

"And if he sees us he'll back off, right?"

"To try another day, which is exactly what I don't want, so we'll stay under the radar as much as possible."

Pete concentrated on her driving again for a few minutes, working it out in her mind. They got off the Dolly Madison Parkway, traffic almost nonexistent at this hour. "We're clean," she said.

"I want to keep it that way until the party."

A Cadillac Escalade with deeply tinted windows was parked in front of Otto's two-story colonial. McGarvey recognized the plates.

"It's one of ours," he said. "Hang back a bit."

He got out, his jacket loose, and approached the SUV, keeping tight against the vehicle. Nothing looked amiss up at the house. The porch lights were on, a light shone from the front entry hall, and the garage door was closed.

McGarvey took out his pistol and, holding it at his side, had just about reached the driver's-side door when the window powered down, and a man with a crew cut stuck his bare hands out, and then his head.

"Mr. Director, we're Mr. Bambridge's security detail. We were told to expect you, sir."

McGarvey vaguely recognized the man.

Another man had been riding shotgun, and McGarvey spotted his reflection in the door mirror as he came around from behind the SUV.

"Good idea, bad approach," McGarvey said, half turning so that the Walther in his left hand, but under his right, pointed center mass at the minder, became visible.

"Shit," the guy said softly.

McGarvey lowered his pistol, and turned back to the driver. "You should have opened your door. I spotted him in the mirror."

"And always check your six," Pete said from the shadows behind the Caddy. She stood, knees slightly bent, her pistol trained on the man behind McGarvey.

The driver looked serious. "You might have hit your partner," he said.

"Only if I'd missed, and I never miss," she said.

Louise opened the door for them. "Nice little drama," she said. "And before you ask, Audie is at the Farm."

"What's Marty want?" McGarvey asked.

"I'll let him tell you, because you wouldn't believe it from me."

Gatherings at the Renckes' house were always in the kitchen, at the counter with four stools, or between it and the fridge and range, from where Louise could dispense beer, wine, cognac, or something from the oven.

Bambridge, in jeans and a light polo shirt, was drinking a beer with Otto when McGarvey and Pete walked in. He turned and shrugged. "I'm pretty sure that I am the last person you expected to see here," he said.

"We have to get up to New York first thing in the morning," Mac said. "Time is tight."

"They want to take your aircraft away from you."

"They, who?"

"Doesn't matter, just SOP. But your crew mutinied, and the paperwork got lost on my desk. Far as I see it you guys have got around forty hours until Jian's party. Doesn't leave you a lot of wiggle room."

"I think I'll have a beer," McGarvey told Louise.

"Me too," Pete said.

"That's the good news," Otto said. "But the Bureau is in the middle of what could be another possible complication."

"This time in Atlanta," Bambridge said.

Louise brought them the beers.

Pete took one of the bar stools, but McGarvey preferred to remain on his feet. "I'm listening."

"I don't have all the facts. Doug Masterson, the SAC down there, is an old friend. He called me with the heads-up less than an hour ago, and I asked Otto to hack their mainframe. Doug's not going to be real happy if he finds out."

"He won't," Otto said.

"Anyway, the Bureau has been keeping tabs on people they believe might have connections with terrorist groups—right now especially al-Qaeda and ISIS. There're concentrations in places like Detroit, Albany, Pittsburgh, Minneapolis, and Atlanta. The NSA phone intercept program looks for calls with certain key words. In this particular case they were trying to get a bead on a possible ISIS front man here in the States who goes by the code name of al-Dhib. 'The Wolf,' in Arabic."

"And?"

"He's clean, even untouchable. Name's Hollis Reed. He is the senior partner in a law firm that specializes in civil rights. Outstanding citizen. Married, two kids in high school, pays his taxes on time, belongs to a couple of service clubs, and even serves on the mayor's special task force investigating police violence against blacks."

"Goes to church regularly, I suppose," Pete said.

"Not a church," Bambridge said. "A mosque right in the heart of Buckhead—Atlanta's upscale neighborhood."

Pete played devil's advocate. "Doesn't make him a terrorist," she said.

McGarvey held his silence, waiting for the "but."

"The NSA has been tracking al-Dhib's phone for the past eighteen months. They've picked up hundreds of routine calls—it's his business line, that rolls over to his cell phone."

"The number is protected by a crappy encryption algorithm," Otto said.

"But they also picked up a half dozen calls over the past month from the same man, asking for information mostly on business opportunities in Atlanta. They're code phrases, of course."

"I just finished listening to one of the calls, made tonight," Otto said. "It's Nero."

"Your Nero is here in the States," Bambridge said. "And the Bureau is going to pick him up for questioning."

"Tell them to back off, " McGarvey said.

"They won't."

"Then tell them to send the SWAT team, because if they get close to this guy, and he is our Nero, he'll kill them."

SIXTY-ONE

The law firm of Brickman, Reed, Stearns and Lipton was housed in what appeared to be an antebellum mansion, complete with a long front porch, the roof held up with Doric columns, in the Buckhead neighborhood of Atlanta's West Paces Ferry-Northside.

It was around one in the morning, traffic all but nonexistent, when Kamal drove past the building. No vehicles were parked on the street in front of the law office, nor in front of any of the other offices on the block. Most of them were architects, medical specialists, and other law firms.

His senses were on full alert, but nothing seemed out of place. The rooftops were clean, nothing was circling overhead. The window down, he stopped at the end of the block, shut off the engine, and held his breath so he could listen. Even a drone made a distinctive noise, but all he could hear was the sound of a far-distant siren. Normal twenty-four/seven for any large city.

He drove around the block and found a delivery alley that ran behind the buildings, where parking areas were set up for employees and gated entrances to underground parking were reserved for senior staff. No cars were in sight.

Pulling in to one of the slots behind Reed's building, he shut off the engine and waited a full five minutes to see if someone was coming. If the Bureau, or more important, McGarvey and his woman, had somehow discovered that he was here in Atlanta, they would move heaven and earth to get to him.

But that was impossible. The National Security Agency's telephone surveillance program was the very best in the entire world. But even that system couldn't work miracles. Reed was an upstanding citizen who'd been educated at the best schools, including Harvard. He served on the boards of directors of any number of local and a few national charities.

He was all but bulletproof, and only had become radicalized working with blacks and other minorities who'd been victimized by what he thought were federal policies that favored only the ultrarich at the expense of everyone else.

A vocal critic of ISIS and the group's brutality, Reed secretly agreed that their tactics—though too horrible to contemplate—were necessary in the very short run.

Curiously enough it was Sa'ad who'd shown Reed's file, among others, to Kamal last year in the early planning stages of AtEighth.

"In the end we will engineer their downfall," Sa'ad had promised. "Their own foolishness and arrogance will be their undoing. They will take the blame, focusing the Americans' investigation entirely on ISIS."

"Is Reed a suspect right now?" Kamal had asked.

"That one is clean, I can guarantee it."

The underground parking gate opened, but instead of driving inside, Kamal got out of the car, with his cheap tablet, and walked down the ramp to a small elevator to the right. An older Rolls Silver Shadow was parked in the slot marked REED.

Reed was waiting for him in the broad, luxuriously carpeted third-floor corridor. Expensive paintings—original, Kamal guessed—hung on the paneled walls.

"I assume that you took precautions to make certain you weren't followed," Reed said. He was a black man, tall, patrician-looking, as if he were some ancient African tribal chief dressed in linen slacks and a white silk shirt, the top two buttons undone. His hair was short and graying, his face oval, and his eyes dark and penetrating. His accent was East Coast money.

"Of course," Kamal said, startled, but he didn't let it show. All this time he thought he'd been dealing with a white-establishment type. Poor homework. A mistake.

Reed led him back to his expansive office with a view toward downtown Atlanta. "Would you like something to drink?"

"No, thank you," Kamal said. "I'll just be staying for a minute." He handed the lawyer the tablet. "I've highlighted a list of nine targets."

Reed set the tablet down on his desk. "Do we have a timetable? I ask because I have people in Manhattan and New Jersey ready to move. They just need the word."

"Are they dedicated?"

Reed laughed. "If you mean are they willing to give their lives for the cause—and all that horseshit—of course they are. They've been educated that way."

"Seven in the evening, Friday." The timetable did not matter. Reed was nothing more than a diversion for the FBI.

For a longish moment Reed showed no reaction, but then he laughed bitterly. "Totally impossible."

Kamal stepped around the lawyer and picked up the tablet. "I was told that you had the people and that you were reliable and resourceful."

"Yes, but not stupid."

"I'll get someone else," Kamal said, and he started for the door. Fact was, there wasn't anyone else. At least not in the short term. The lawyer's refusal would make his job a million times more difficult, but still—not impossible.

"Wait."

Kamal turned back.

"I may be able to mount four individual strikes."

"Six."

"Four, and that's pushing it."

Four was good. He had won. "Precisely at seven."

"Do I have discretion to which targets I'll send my people? Some may have heightened security because of AtEighth."

Kamal had picked the buildings at the greatest distance from the UN. "You have complete discretion, except that I don't want adjacent buildings hit. I want to spread the LE and rescue teams as far from each other as possible."

"I understand completely."

Kamal handed the lawyer the tablet. "One million U.S. will be placed in your PSP account within twenty-four hours. But I do not want you to wait until it shows up to activate your people."

"Trust is important," Reed said. "I understand."

"Good."

"Inshallah."

SIXTY-TWO

Kamal was halfway down the corridor to the elevator when Reed came out of his office. "A car just showed up in the alley."

"Did it stop?"

"It's down there now."

Kamal went back to the lawyer's office where the images from the building's security system were displayed on the desktop. Two men got out of a dark blue Ford sedan and walked over to the Chevy. They were wearing blue windbreakers, FBI stenciled on the backs.

"Son of a bitch," Reed said softly. "You fucking led them to me."

"If they were that sure it was me here, they'd have sent

more than two men," Kamal said. "Can you contact your people right now and get them started?"

Reed was confused, but he nodded. "I think so."

"Do it, but use my tablet, not your own phone or computer."

"It's too late."

"Give me three minutes then come downstairs. I'll need you to follow me."

"But they're going to arrest us."

"They're going to try," Kamal said. "Make your calls now."

He went to the end of the corridor and took the stairs two at a time down to the parking garage just as the two agents were coming down the ramp.

Kamal held up in the deeper shadows and pulled out his pistol. "Who the hell are you guys?" he called out softly.

One of them reached under his jacket, but Kamal shot him twice, center mass, before he could reach his weapon. The man dropped to the floor.

Kamal stepped out of the shadows, his pistol trained on the second agent, who was just pulling out his pistol.

"Very carefully place your weapon on the ground," Kamal said.

The agent hesitated. He was young, and he looked frightened.

"I will not hesitate to kill you," Kamal warned. He kept his tone of voice reasonable.

Don't accelerate a confrontation, they were trained at Sandhurst. Keep it calm. Lull your opponent into thinking that a solution might be possible, no matter how dire the situation might seem to him.

"Now, please, then you can call for an ambulance before your friend bleeds out."

The agent laid his pistol on the ground, his movements

slow and deliberate. He was desperately looking for an opening.

Kamal lowered his gun. "Now who the hell are you people? You scared the shit out of me."

"FBI," the kid said.

"I thought you were burglars or something. What are you doing here?"

"I think you know," the agent said. It was a big mistake, and he realized it almost the moment the words came out of his mouth.

"Have you called for backup?"

"They're on their way."

"No."

The agent dropped to one knee and reached for his gun when Kamal shot him in the top of his head.

The kid fell backward, and Kamal went to him and put an insurance round in his temple. Then he went to the first agent and shot him in the side of the head.

He looked up at one of the surveillance cameras. "Shut the system down, and erase everything from just before I showed up, and then get down here."

Holstering his pistol he went back up to the Ford—the key was still in the ignition—backed it into the garage, and popped the trunk.

He took their IDs then muscled the two bodies into the trunk, careful to get no blood on himself.

Reed showed up a minute later. "I'll never be able to come back. Atlanta and my life here is done for me."

"I'll show you how to disappear, and believe me, it's easier than you might imagine. Everyone will believe that you're dead, but your family will be able to join you."

"They won't leave here."

"Yes, they will, because you'll be someplace nicer than you can imagine," Kamal said. *"Inshallah."*

"Inshallah," Reed muttered.

"Did you shut off the system and do the erasure?"

"Yes, but I only managed to make contact with four of my people."

"It's enough," Kamal said.

Kamal drove the Ford over to an area of the city called the Bluff, which according to Reed was one of the most dangerous sections of Atlanta. He parked a block away from where a crowd of loiterers had gathered, and tossed one of the FBI wallets on the street, keeping the other one for himself. He went back to Reed, who'd followed him with the Rolls.

"Drug dealers," Reed said.

"Let's go back to your office, I want to get my car."

"Those were FBI guys. Won't they have called in your plate?"

"They would have asked for backup if they had."

"Someone will be waiting for us if they did."

"Then let's go see," Kamal said. "Before your pals at the end of the block come down to say hello."

Reed approached his office with a great deal of care under Kamal's instructions. No one was surveilling the place from the front, nor were there any vehicles other than the Chevy parked in back.

"We're clean," Kamal said.

"What now?"

"Park your car in the garage, and I'll take you some-place from where you can go to ground until I can arrange for a team to come pick you up."

Reed didn't answer at first. Around back he powered

open the garage security gate and parked in his spot. He turned in his seat. "I'm putting my faith in you."

"As I have in you, my friend."

Reed got out of the car and started around back to walk up the ramp to the Chevy.

Kamal reached across the seat and pushed the button to open the trunk. He got out, went around to the back, and fired one shot into the lawyer's head. The man's knees gave out and he crumpled to the pavement.

Holstering his pistol, Kamal manhandled the lawyer's body into the trunk, then took out the Glock and fired an insurance round into the side of the man's head before he shut the trunk lid.

He took the stairs up to Reed's office, where he found the surveillance systems controls, and made sure that the recordings had actually been erased. He also checked the phone log to make sure that his voice wasn't on it, then powered up the tablet and pulled up the e-mails that Reed had sent earlier. There were four of them.

By three he was well clear of the city on I-85 heading northeast toward Richmond and eventually I-95, which would take him to New York City. There he would abandon the car, in about ten hours, around one in the afternoon.

Then he would take a cab to a massage parlor, which was actually a whorehouse in the Village, where he would have something to eat and drink a bottle of Dom Pérignon if that's the best they have, have a massage and a good fuck, and get a few hours of sleep till six.

Inshallah, as the lawyer would say.

SIXTY-THREE

The Gulfstream touched down at LaGuardia shortly before eight in the morning, twelve hours before Jian Chang's party at the Tower. Nancy Nebel had sent a car for them, and as the aircraft pulled up in front of the VIP terminal the driver got out.

"What happens now, Mr. Director?" Gratto asked.

"It'll be a done deal by midnight," McGarvey said. "One way or the other."

"We'll refuel and stand by for your call."

"Give 'em hell," Toynbee told them as they got off the plane and crossed to the waiting car.

The driver took their bags and put them in the trunk. "Mrs. Nebel is waiting for you with the others, but she said that she would understand if you wanted to check in to a hotel first."

"Later," McGarvey said.

Because air traffic was already back to more or less normal, the highway leading through Queens to Manhattan from the airport was choked with rush-hour traffic. The car was a Lincoln limousine and McGarvey was sure that it was armored from the way it handled.

Callahan Holdings' office took up the top three floors of a building at West Broadway and Park Place at the edge of the Financial District and within sight of the new World Trade Center.

The driver took them through the Midtown Tunnel and pulled up in front of the office. He jumped out and opened the door for them.

"You're expected. Security will escort you up. What would you like me to do with your luggage?"

"Will we have use of the car after the meeting?" Mc-Garvey asked.

"For as long as you want it, sir."

"Then leave the bags in the trunk for now."

Four security officers, in light gray blazers, were stationed behind a desk in the anonymous lobby. McGarvey and Pete were buzzed in through the glass doors, and one of the men came around to get them. His name tag said PARKER.

"Good morning. Are either of you armed?"

"We both are," McGarvey said. "Will that be a problem?"

"No, sir. If you'll follow me I'll escort you up to the conference room."

"Just give us the floor number and we'll find our way," Pete said.

"No, ma'am. You need a security card to get past the fortieth floor."

An attractive young woman who introduced herself as Kate Sullivan, Mrs. Nebel's personal assistant, met them at the elevator. "Good morning, Mr. Director, Ms. Boylan," she said. "If you'll follow me they're waiting for you in the conference room."

A receptionist sat behind a desk in the reception area. Behind her were three frosted-glass panels showing artists' depictions of three towers. One of them was impossibly tall, tapering in stages all the way to a narrow spire at the top. It looked like a rocketship ready to blast off.

McGarvey hesitated a moment.

"Quite a concept," Kate said. "It was Mr. Callahan's dream project."

"How tall is it?" Pete asked.

"One mile—five thousand two hundred eighty feet."

"Will it ever get built?"

"If Mrs. Nebel can convince the board it will be."

They followed the woman to the conference room that was at the end of the corridor and took up the southeast corner looking toward the World Trade Center. Models of AtEighth and the Tower rose eight feet from a display table in one corner.

Nancy Nebel was seated with two men whom she introduced as Dan Endicott and Millard Greenberg. Both worked for the FBI, Endicott in the Bureau's counterterrorism section, and Greenberg as special agent in charge of the New York office. Neither seemed very happy.

"We can use your help, Mr. Director, especially after what happened overnight in Atlanta," Greenberg said. He was a large, somewhat clunky man with a round head, fleshy cheeks, and no hair. He didn't look like a cop.

"The two agents sent to the attorney's office ran into trouble?" McGarvey asked.

"Their bodies were discovered an hour ago, shot to death in the remains of their car parked in what I was told is a troubled section of the city."

"No backup was sent with them?"

"The SAC thought it wasn't necessary."

"Christ. Tell them to have the medical examiner check to see if they were shot in the head, postmortem, at close range."

"After they were dead?" Nancy Nebel asked.

"An insurance shot. It's our man's signature. What about the lawyer?"

"His body was discovered in the trunk of his car parked in an underground garage beneath his office building. He was shot once in the back of the head and again in his right temple."

"If there was a surveillance system, you'll find that it

was disabled," McGarvey said. He took out his cell phone and called Otto's number.

"This room is shielded, your phone will not work here," Nancy Nebel said.

Otto answered on the first ring. "If you're at Callahan's tell them that they have a shitty shielding system."

"Nero took out the two Bureau agents and the lawyer in Atlanta. He's on his way here."

"We did everything we could, except hold their hands."

"Their surveillance system was almost certainly wiped clean, but I want you to take a look anyway, see if you can come up with something."

"He had to have gotten the weapon there in Atlanta. I'll try hotel check-ins again and correlate them with nearby gun shops. We might get lucky."

"Keep us posted."

"Will do," Otto said, and rang off.

"Who's Nero?" Greenberg asked.

"We don't know his actual name, but he may be a free-lancer that the Saudis call Nassr. The Eagle. He's the guy who sabotaged the mass damper system which brought down AtEighth."

"Impossible," Endicott said. "The engineering is all wrong."

"What brought it down?" McGarvey asked.

"Explosives on several key structural members between the fourth and fifth floors."

"Has residue been found?"

"Not yet. Could have been something new, something my people have never seen before."

"Witnesses on the ground said that the building was swaying way off center," Pete said.

"People in situations like that tend to be unreliable. But assuming they were right, we think that one or two preliminary explosives prematurely detonated. It would have caused the building to become unstable and sway well beyond its design parameters."

"My architectural engineers agree," Nancy Nebel said.

"Have all your other buildings been checked for explosives?" McGarvey asked, knowing that he was probably beating a dead horse.

"Thoroughly," Endicott said.

"And the mass damper chamber?"

"It needs a special security pass for access," Nancy Nebel said.

"Who has them?"

"I have the only one, other than the ones in security."

"You'd bet your life and the lives of the owner and his guests that the building is safe?" Pete asked.

"With all the security measures that have been put in place, yes," Nancy Nebel said.

"I hope you're right," Pete said. "But we'd like to take a look for ourselves sometime today, before the party, and before the caterers show up."

"I'll have someone from our security team show you around whenever you like."

"Thank you," Pete said.

"I wonder why Nero took the trouble to kill our two people and the lawyer?" Greenberg asked.

"I'm not sure, a diversion probably, but I expect that we'll know sometime tonight," McGarvey replied. "In the meantime, what about all the other skyscrapers in town? Have they been checked for explosives?"

"We're working on it," Greenberg said.

SIXTY-FOUR

The limo pulled up in front of the Tower on Forty-first Street, kitty-corner from the UN across First Avenue. Crowds of tourists, among them many children with their parents here for the UNICEF celebrations all day today and into this evening, crossed when the cops held up traffic and streamed into the Plaza.

"We might be an hour or more," McGarvey told the driver.

"I'll be here, Mr. Director."

They got out of the car but instead of entering the building, they went across the street so that McGarvey could get a better idea of the line between the impossibly tall, slender building and the UN General Assembly.

"It's the children who worry me the most," Pete said. "We should have them moved away from here."

"He'd call off the attack."

"Well and good."

"He's not going to give up. He'll just go to ground and wait until the right time. Maybe when the building is filled with tenants and maybe when the president is addressing the General Assembly."

"I hate to say it, but better a bunch of politicians than children," Pete said.

"It's not going to happen," McGarvey told her. "We're going to stop the bastard. Today. Tonight."

Pete shivered. "I can feel him, you know. He's on his way, and I'm frightened."

"I know."

They went back across the street, where they were met at the building's front glass doors by a security officer in a dark blazer, a pistol obvious under his jacket. He was large, and looked fit. Ex-military, McGarvey guessed. He was extremely serious, and didn't bother to introduce himself.

"Good morning, Mr. Director, ma'am," he said.

Three other similarly dressed men with the same rigid attitude were stationed at the reception desk and communications/surveillance console.

The atrium lobby, like the one at AtEighth, soared eighty feet above the pristine white marble floor. Two sets of escalators ran to the mezzanine level where, Nancy Nebel had explained, there would be a high-end boutique restaurant by the official opening day in one month.

A thirty-foot-tall statue in clear crystal of a nude woman, her breasts partially covered by her waist-length hair, her arms outstretched over her head as if she were giving thanks to some god, hung from the center of the ceiling, itself covered with crystal panels at all angles.

The total effect was stunning.

"It's almost like being in some ancient temple," Pete said half under her breath. "Ready for the faithful to show up."

"Home sweet home," McGarvey said, impressed despite himself.

Pete laughed, but it was without humor. "Gaudy, if you ask me."

"If you're ready, I'll take you up to security on the fiftieth," the officer said. "Cathy Kennedy is chief of today's detail, she'll show you around."

"How many people on her detail?"

"Including us, three more than fifty."

"I suggest that you guys lighten up. When the perp shows up tonight and gets a good look at you, he'll do a one-eighty and disappear."

The officer cracked a slight smile. "That's the point, isn't it, sir?"

"No, it's not."

"What then, you want us to arrest him?"

"No," McGarvey said. "Either you kill him on the spot, or I will if we come face-to-face."

The security center on the fiftieth floor, with access only by the service elevator and emergency stairwells, was nearly a carbon copy of the one at AtEighth. The other spaces on the floor housed mostly electrical panels, plus the communications, surveillance, and computer mainframes.

Cathy Kennedy turned out to be a slender, almost wispy woman possibly in her midthirties with short blond hair and a pleasant oval face. Her blazer hung over the back of her chair at the center console. She was armed with a Wilson Tactical pistol in a shoulder holster under her right arm.

She introduced herself. "Happy to have your help, Mr. Director, ma'am," she said. Her voice held a slightly Southern twang. Maybe Texas. "Especially since we've been ordered to keep everything low-key." Her deep, almost impossibly blue eyes were slightly narrowed, as if she were expecting an attack to come at any moment from any direction.

"Navy?" McGarvey asked.

"Green Berets," she said, lightening up a bit.

"Afghanistan?"

"Iraq, Pakistan, Iran. Does it show?"

"Around the edges," McGarvey said. "A key card is the only way here by the service elevator?"

"Yes."

"Who has them?"

"One downstairs, one here, and Mrs. Nebel's."

"This door?" McGarvey asked.

"Entry by recognition only."

"What about upstairs?"

"The bad guy won't get to the penthouse, sir."

"He'll be on the guest list," McGarvey said. "But I meant the machinery room on the top floors."

"The tuned mass damper," Kennedy said. "Yes, sir, we were told that you believe that's how AtEighth was brought down. But the computer that ran that system was located right next to it. In this building the machinery is controlled from this floor. And we can override the system from this room."

"Can you be hacked here?" Pete asked.

"Nothing gets in or out of here except through our equipment."

Pete took out her cell phone and speed-dialed Otto.

"I just told you that your phone won't work in here, ma'am."

Otto answered. "You're in the building. Security?"

"Yeah. Send them a greeting, if you would."

"Just a mo," Otto said.

Three seconds later the image of the devil, horns and all, appeared on all the screens in the room.

"Son of a bitch," one of the techs said. He did something on his keyboard, but the image remained.

"Thanks, Otto," Pete said, and she hung up and pocketed her phone.

A moment later the image on the screens disappeared.

"You made your point," Kennedy said. "Your geek is smarter than ours. So what's next?"

"We're calling our suspect Nero, for want of a better name," McGarvey said. "He's on his way here from Atlanta, where he murdered two FBI agents and a lawyer who probably worked with ISIS. He took down AtEighth and he intends to take this place down tonight."

"Kill him before he gets in."

"That's the problem," Pete said. "Unless we manage to take him before he gets in, and he escapes, he will come back and try again once we let our guard down. Which we will have to do sooner or later."

"I'm not liking it, but I'm listening."

"Otto," McGarvey said.

"Yes?" Otto's voice came from all the speakers in the room.

"Jesus," Kennedy said.

"Send us the guest list, photos, and a précis of each of them."

"Gotcha."

One by one the list of seventy-two names, including Nancy Nebel's, plus the security staff in the building, came up. The image of Valdes appeared halfway through.

"Stop," McGarvey said. "This is our man, we think."

"You think, or you know?" Kennedy asked.

"We think."

SIXTY-FIVE

The security officer who'd escorted them upstairs was waiting for them in the corridor. Kennedy came to the door with them. "These folks would like to take a look around. Nothing is off-limits."

"Yes, ma'am."

"Let's start at the machinery room up top," McGarvey said.

"Yes, sir."

"Do you have a name?"

"Ross Parker."

"Marines?"

Parker stifled a brief grin. "No, sir. SEAL Team Six.

And I want to personally thank you for what you did for our guys last year. You saved the lives of a lot of good people."

A team of assassins contracted by a Pakistani intel officer had been sent to the U.S. to kill all the SEAL Team Six operators who'd taken out Osama bin Laden. McGarvey took them down with Pete's help and that of a German intel officer, but not before a couple of SEALs and their families had been assassinated.

"Could have been better," McGarvey said in the service elevator on the way up to the top floor.

"We do what we can, Mr. Director."

The elevator opened directly on the three-story-tall machinery room, which, except for the emergency stairwells and elevator shaft, took up the entire width and breadth of the building's 115th through 118th stories. As had been the case at the top of AtEighth the space was dominated by a massive stack of steel plates, computer-controlled by twelve hydraulic rams.

Two of the pistons moved the damper silently a couple of inches at an angle to the left to compensate for a gust of wind hitting the building, paused a moment or two, and then moved back.

Moments later it moved again to the left, this time slightly farther and faster.

"This place gives me the willies," Pete said. "Like it knows that we're not supposed to be in here."

"I agree," Parker said.

McGarvey could feel the sheer mass and power of the mechanism, even though it made absolutely no noise. Despite what Nancy Nebel and Endicott and their engineers had promised, that the system couldn't possibly bring down a building, standing here he knew damned well that they were wrong. It was exactly what had caused the destruction of AtEighth, and if Nero was successful, this place would come down in the same way. Only this time the casualties would be much worse.

Pete was looking at him. "You too?"

"We'd better stop him," McGarvey said.

"We will."

Parker picked up on it. "He won't get past the lobby. Guaranteed." The ex-SEAL grinned. "We'll even save a piece of the bastard for you, sir."

Down two floors the service elevator led to an unadorned room through a door that was a vestibule, done up in deep pile carpeting, expensive panelled walls with Chinese art, along with a small table on which rested a Ming Dynasty vase.

Just to the left was the private elevator that faced double doors lacquered in black, open now to Jian's two-story penthouse.

The building was sixty feet on a side, and sixteen-feet-tall floor-to-ceiling windows, which covered almost every wall, looked down on the Manhattan skyline north and south, and to the New Jersey countryside in one direction and all the way out to the Atlantic in the opposite.

Even the foyer just inside was wrapped around both vestibules and both elevators, windows looking out toward the ocean.

The place was furnished almost as if it were an attraction somewhere in a fantastic Disneyland, in a mix of ancient Chinese collectibles and ultra-modern minimalist Scandinavian furniture.

Workmen were busy setting up tables and serving stations for the party this evening, and a steady stream of delivery men in white coats came up in the private elevator bringing food of all sorts into the massive kitchen, liquors to the service stations throughout the 7,200-square-foot condo, and serving platters, plates, glassware, and silverware.

Everything was ultra–first class, almost too precious even to look at.

Pete was impressed. "All it takes is money," she said.

"Jian's the third or fourth richest man on earth," McGarvey said.

"And he's not afraid to spend it."

Li Huan came down the escalator from the second floor and walked directly over to them. He was tall, for a Chinese, slender with thick black hair. At this moment he was dressed in jeans and a white polo shirt.

He introduced himself. "Are you from the police?"

"We're on your guest list," McGarvey said.

Li took out his iPhone.

"Joe Canton and Toni Borman."

"Yes, friends of Mr. Hammond's. You're early. Please return no earlier than seven," he said, and turned to leave.

"We're contractors with the CIA."

The young man turned back. "Here in what capacity, specifically?"

"To help prevent another tragedy," Pete said.

Li raised an eyebrow. "Have either Mr. Hammond or Mr. Jian been appraised of your actual identities?"

"No, and it will stay that way this evening," McGarvey said.

The man started to turn away again, but McGarvey grabbed his arm and pulled him close. He smelled foreign, his scent sandalwood, Oriental, pleasantly clean and crisp.

"Will you be here this evening?" he asked.

Li tried to pull away.

"Your life might depend on it," McGarvey said. He kept his voice low so that none of the staff or delivery people could hear him.

"Of course I'll be here," he said.

"Then so far as anyone is concerned, and that includes your boss, we are Joe Canton and Toni Borman, friends of Tom Hammond's."

"I can't do such a thing."

"In that case we'll have to take you into custody and hold you overnight."

"Impossible."

"Your call," McGarvey said. "I want your word that you'll tell no one."

He shook his head.

"You silly bastard, do you realize how many people could die here tonight?" Pete said. "If this building does go down like AtEighth did, it'll land on the UN's General Assembly building, where nearly three thousand children will be."

Still the man hesitated.

Pete reached under her shirt at the base of her back for her pistol. "If I have to shoot you to keep your fucking mouth shut, I will. Believe me."

McGarvey stayed her hand. "Call the NYPD and as soon as they send someone, turn him over," he told the security officer.

"What charge?" Parker asked.

"Besides stupidity? Obstruction of justice."

"Yes, sir," Parker said. He held out his hand to Li. "Sir, if you'll just come downstairs with me."

"Wait," the man said. "This could cost me my job."

"It could cost you your life," Pete replied.

"Sir," Parker said.

He said something in Chinese half under his breath, but then nodded. "I need to be here. I'll do as you say."

SIXTY-SIX

Parker escorted them down to the Callahan sales office on the mezzanine opposite the nearly completed restaurant. Nancy Nebel was there in the conference room, along with Cathy Kennedy, Daniel Endicott, and three men.

"Kirk McGarvey and Pete Boylan are representing the Central Intelligence Agency for this operation," Nebel introduced them.

They sat down at the conference table.

"You know Dan Endicott," she said, and she introduced the other three men.

James Long, in the uniform of an NYPD captain, was operational chief for the mission. He was a man in his late forties, with a salt-and-pepper buzz cut and a chiseled face almost like a statue's. He wasn't smiling.

Nor was Bob Gilford, a captain in the uniform of the city's fire department. He was also in his mid- to late forties and he looked compact and fit despite his small size. His hair was dark and his face oval.

"Jim Whalen," the third man introduced himself. "I'm the assistant SAC in the Bureau's New York counterterrorism section, and I'll be in charge of this building."

"We'll be operating on our own for the remainder of today and this evening," McGarvey said.

"That will not happen."

"We've been invited to the party under our work names of Joseph Canton and Toni Borman, but we'll each need a security card so we can have free access to every floor of the building."

Whalen was becoming agitated. "You're not listening, but I was told to expect it from you."

"We are and will remain armed. And at no time will

anyone from any of you gentlemen's departments acknowledge us as part of any team."

"Special identification badges will be issued to everyone at the last moment, to guard against an imposter or imposters from breaking security."

"Unless our guy kills one of your people and steals his badge," Pete spoke up. "What then?"

"All of that is a moot point," Whalen said. He turned to Nancy. "I'm closing down this building as of this moment."

"You damned well better not," McGarvey said.

"It's for the best, sir," the NYPD captain said. "We can't take the risk of your perp somehow getting past our security—no matter how unlikely that may be. There'll be an estimated three thousand people at the UN's General Assembly building throughout today and until nine this evening. Most of them will be children from one hundred eighteen different countries. No, sir, we cannot take the risk."

"He'll back off but he won't quit."

"It'll give us more time to run him to ground," Whalen said.

"Not likely," Pete said.

"You say you found him."

"We weren't hamstrung by bureaucracy."

"I want this building completely evacuated within the next ninety minutes," Whalen said. "SWAT teams will establish a one-block perimeter, and the NYPD will put two snipers in each of four helicopters in the air at all times."

McGarvey took out his phone and called Walt Page's direct number. The DCI answered on the second ring. McGarvey put him on speakerphone.

"Yes."

"Give John Church a call, tell him that we've run into a snag with the local counterterrorism SAC," McGarvey said. "Name of Whalen." Church was the secretary of Homeland Security.

"What's at issue?"

"He wants to close down the building and surround it with SWAT shooters."

"It might be for the best, Mac. But it's your call."

"The bastard will be here tonight, and we're going to take him down so it won't happen again. At least not by his hand."

"I'll call him now. And I'll phone Ed Maslak as well." Maslak was the president's chief of staff.

"They need to give the order before Nero catches wind that something is going down."

"Are you with Mr. Whalen now?"

"Yes," McGarvey said, and he hit the *end* icon.

"Who was that?" Whalen asked.

"The director of the Central Intelligence Agency."

"Doesn't change a fucking thing," the SAC said. "Sorry, ladies, but it doesn't change a thing."

Cathy Kennedy was impressed. "I can have your key cards ready within the hour," she said to Mac.

Nancy Nebel was concerned. "I want to agree with Mr. Whalen that the risk is just too great, especially after At-Eighth, and yet I have to agree with Mr. McGarvey that this guy will bide his time and hit us once we let our guard down."

"You're just interested in your bottom line," Whalen shot back angrily.

"I don't have to take that fucking shit from you or any-body," Nebel said, her voice even. "And don't excuse my language."

Whalen was silent for just a beat, but then he picked it up. "We'll start by evacuating everyone in the penthouse. And I'll need a list of everyone else in the building, your staff as well as the workmen."

"I can have my people here within minutes," Long said.

"I want it kept orderly, no panic."

"I can shut the building down for twenty-four hours because of the risk of an electrical fire," the NYPD officer said. "There'll be some grumbling, of course, but we'll offer our apologies. In the interest of public safety, which in fact is the truth."

"I'll accept that," Whalen said, and he turned again to McGarvey and Pete. "I can have federal marshals here to take both of you in custody within twenty minutes. Either that or you play by my rules."

"Ross can take me back up to the penthouse, there're a few things I want to take a look at," McGarvey told the security chief. "Ms. Boylan can take a closer look at your operation, and she can see if our geek can harden your system, especially the program regulating the mass tuned damper system."

"You son of a bitch, I'll arrest you myself," Whalen said. "I want both of you out of here now!"

McGarvey gave the man a long moment to calm down. "We're all here for the same purpose, to stop another At-Eighth from happening."

Whalen started to protest, but McGarvey held him off.

"We'll give you a physical description, as well as images of our suspect. You can have a couple of your agents dressed the same as the building's security people stationed in the lobby. He comes through the front door, nail him."

"This building will be in lockdown. It's the safe bet."

McGarvey exchanged a glance with Pete, then shrugged. "Call the marshals and let's get this over with soon, so we can go back to work."

"Goddamnit," Whalen said. He pulled his phone out of his pocket at the same time it chimed. He answered it. "Whalen."

Almost immediately his face began to fall in degrees. He turned his eyes away from the others as he got to his feet.

"Yes, sir. I understand what you're saying, but I'd like to give you an outline of what we're up against here, and what I'm suggesting we do to avert a tragedy."

He listened for nearly a full minute.

"Yes, sir. But under protest."

He broke the connection, pocketed his phone, and turned to McGarvey. "We'll do it your way."

"Our way. We're just here in case he gets through the front door and makes it up to the penthouse. If he gets that far, I'll kill him."

Whalen nodded.

"And another thing, have your people on alert for diversionary attacks sometime after seven," McGarvey said at the door. "He'll try to draw off your manpower from this building."

"Christ, can you be more specific?" Long asked.

"No. But it's what I would do."

SIXTY-SEVEN

One of the girls whose nickname was Sushi woke Kamal by gently rubbing her hand up his thigh and tickling his balls with the tips of her long fingernails.

His immediate reaction was to reach up and clamp his fingers around her throat, but he made himself relax. He smiled, but kept his eyes closed.

The high-end massage parlor—all the girls were priced in the range of $1,000 to $2,000 per hour—was done up in tasteful, even subdued, brocades on the walls, deep carpeting, indirect lighting, Jacuzzi baths, and comfortable beds. Just now Vivaldi played softly.

He'd given the madam ten thousand in cash a few hours ago. "For the afternoon," he'd said. "And champagne."

"Dom is included," the attractive Japanese woman in her late forties told him. "Krug or Cristal will be extra."

"Krug, please."

"Sushi will be your full-time girl. She'll do everything for you. She is very skilled."

And she was.

Kamal opened his eyes and looked up at her.

"Would you like to make love?" she asked. She was a narrow-hipped woman in her early twenties, perhaps even younger, very possibly a college student earning tuition money. Her breasts were small, her pudenda hairless, and it had been obvious from the start that she'd never had children.

"Perhaps I'll come back another day and ask for you. But for now I would like a pot of black tea, some white toast with butter, a piece of fruit, and a bottle of water."

It was nearly six. When the girl was gone, Kamal took a long, leisurely shower, then dressed in the slacks and shirt he'd worn up from Atlanta. The jacket and trousers had been pressed, and the shirt laundered, lightly starched and ironed.

So far as he could tell his one suitcase had not been touched; the telltale on the lock was intact.

Sushi came back with his light supper. "May I serve you?"

"I would like to be left alone now, and I'll be leaving soon. But you were wonderful, and I will be back."

She lowered her eyes in the Japanese fashion. "Thank you very much."

When she left, Kamal poured a cup of tea. He strapped the shoulder holster on his left side under his arm, checked the action of the pistol, and made sure the spring in the magazine was free, before he loaded the gun.

Sitting in one of the easy chairs in the bedroom, he drank his tea, ate a piece of toast and one of the clementine oranges, a fruit he had always been fond of.

At times like these, just before an op, a calm came over him. It was almost a serenity, a trust that fate would either allow him to succeed or to fail. They were the only two options open now, because he would not turn away. If it was his fate to be successful, then so be it. But if he was going to die tonight, then so be that as well.

At six-thirty he phoned Sa'ad. "I'm ready to move. Do you have anything for me?"

His Saudi control officer was waiting for the call. It was after two in the morning in Riyadh, and yet he'd answered the phone after only one ring. "There is no dissuading you?"

"No."

"There have been some developments. I will give you a number to call."

"Who is it?"

"A friend."

"Here in New York? Working for the government?"

"In Washington. But you'll only be able to call him once, after which the number will automatically be disconnected. Once you have made that call you'll get nothing further from him, or me."

"I understand."

"My channel of information will also cease. Nor will you ever learn my actual position. Do you understand these things as well?"

"Perfectly," Kamal said. "I'll be going to ground, where no one, including you, will be able to find me. Don't try, because if I am discovered I will kill whoever you've sent. And perhaps I'll come after you from a direction you won't expect. Do you understand these things as well?"

"Yes," Sa'ad replied. "Then we are in complete agreement?"

"Complete."

The connection ended.

Kamal finished his tea and toast, then called the number Sa'ad had given him. It too was answered immediately, as if the man had been waiting for the call.

"This is al-Nassr."

"They know that you're coming."

"Has the party been canceled?"

"No. But they know about Atlanta, and they may also have guessed that you have planned a diversion."

"What about Kirk McGarvey?" Kamal asked.

"He's your major problem. The SAC wanted to close down the building, and the police and fire departments agreed. But he overrode them. He knows you're coming and what you mean to do. The advantage is his."

"Does he or anyone else know about you?"

"No."

"Are you certain?"

"Yes."

"How can you be?"

"I'm in a position to be," the man said and he hung up.

Kamal made one more call, this one to Hammond's private number.

The billionaire answered after several rings. It sounded as if there was a party going on. "Are you in town?"

"As a matter of fact I'm on the way to the party right now. Has it already started?"

"A half hour ago. Mr. Jian is very interested in talking to you despite all the onerous security."

"Are the police there?"

"If you mean are they here looking for you, no. Anyway, Pablo Valdes is dead. They're here because they're looking for terrorists, not businessmen. You're name is on the list in the lobby. Don't be long. Susan's looking forward to seeing you again."

Kamal opened the back of the phone, took out the SIM card, and replaced it with the one he'd used to hack AtEighth's tuned mass damper system. He had access now to two files in his phone: the first of the mechanical and electronic plans for AtEighth, and the other the same type of information for the Tower. Both had been supplied to him by Sa'ad months ago, and he had memorized the important parts.

Pocketing it, he sat for several minutes, eating another of the clementines.

Despite the disguise, McGarvey and his woman would recognize him almost immediately. But if they were up in the penthouse and not at the ground-floor entrance, he had a very good chance of getting past security.

He put on his jacket, took the Atlanta FBI agent's ID, and studied the picture again. The man's name was Thomas Hatchett and, looking at himself in the mirror, the match was not close, but good enough to pass muster with the people in the security center on the fiftieth floor.

Opening enough.

He left his suitcase with the madam up front. "I'll be back for it later tonight."

The woman smiled wistfully. "I think not."

"Why?"

"You have the look."

At the door, Kamal glanced back. "Then in the morning sell it for what you can."

"I'll have a buyer tonight," the woman said.

Kamal laughed. It was the funniest thing he'd heard in a month.

It was just six-forty.

SIXTY-EIGHT

McGarvey and Pete had spent the afternoon wandering around the neighborhood and then inside the UN General Assembly building, choked with children and their parents or guardians.

The mood had been upbeat, but neither of them had been able to share it.

"If we screw up a lot of people are going to die tonight," McGarvey said at one point.

"Don't second-guess yourself," Pete told him.

They got their things from the car and changed for the party, which Hammond had promised would be informal. "We dress in business attire or even black tie when it's necessary. Beyond that most of us are more comfortable in jeans and a pair of loafers."

Dressed in fresh khaki slacks and blazers necessary to conceal their holstered pistols, they presented themselves at the Tower's front door a minute before 6:45.

Ross Parker admitted them, just as two couples were boarding Jian's elevator.

"The party started early?" McGarvey said.

"The first showed up around six, Mr. Jian and Mrs. Nebel right behind them."

In addition to the four building security people, two other men dressed in FBI jackets and another three uniformed NYPD cops had taken up position well back on either side of the lobby, from where they had a good sight line on the glass doors.

"Sorry, sir, but we didn't have much to say about it," Parker said. "Mr. Whalen said that it was the absolute minimum he would accept."

"No one fitting Nero's description has shown up yet?"

"No," Parker said and he went back to the desk, where he got two red security passes. "Mrs. Kennedy sent these down for you twenty minutes ago."

"She gave us passes this afternoon," McGarvey said.

"The codes were changed. Also at Mr. Whalen's insistence."

Al-Hamadi, in jeans and a light yellow sweater, breezed in with Susan Patterson, who was wearing a stunning black pantsuit, cut extremely low in front and in back, a diamond pendant hanging from her long slender neck to the cleavage between her breasts.

They had been smiling and chatting, but when the woman spotted Pete, her smile suddenly went rigid. "Of all people I didn't expect to see either of you here."

"Just slumming," Pete said. "Same as you, though I like your costume."

One of the security officers came over with an iPad. "Your names, please?"

Al-Hamadi gave his, but Susan simply glared at the man as if he had to be a complete idiot for not recognizing her.

"Ma'am?"

"Her name is Susan Patterson, she's on the list," Pete said. "She used to act in movies."

"Yes, ma'am," the security officer said. "You may go right up."

"A little catty," McGarvey said after the pair was on the way up in the elevator.

Pete had to chuckle. "She might be rich, but she's had so much plastic surgery she's become a joke."

"A joke whose life we might have to save tonight."

"Right."

"Keep your people on their toes," McGarvey told Parker, and he and Pete took the service elevator up to the fiftieth, where Kennedy buzzed them into the security center.

"Party's started early," she said.

"We saw a couple of Whalen's people downstairs, is he anywhere around?" McGarvey asked.

"He was here forty-five minutes ago, but he got a call on his phone and he bugged out."

"Did he say to where?"

"No, but he told me to change all the security codes. Which I did on Mrs. Nebel's authorization."

McGarvey softened. "He's just trying to do his job."

"So are you two and the rest of us."

Images of the goings-on up in the penthouse were displayed on four split screens. Al-Hamadi and Susan Patterson showed up on one of the screens, and moments later another screen showed Hammond greeting them, kissing her on the cheek.

Another screen split right and left showed the east and west emergency stairwells, but the images changed every three or four seconds.

"Impossible to watch every floor top to bottom at the same time, so the system was designed to take random samples. Four-second snippets."

"Show me," McGarvey said.

They left the security center and walked down to the south stairwell, dimly lit and smelling of concrete dust and something vaguely electrical.

A red light on the camera above the floor winked and shut off four seconds later.

"Totally random," Kennedy said.

Five electrical panels secured behind locked metal doors, each about the size of a regular house door, lined the walls between the stairwells and the entrance to the security center.

"These essentially control the building's electrical and electronic systems. Our monitoring equipment, phones, air handling, fire alarms, and suppression networks—separate ones for each twenty floors."

"The tuned mass damper system topside?" McGarvey asked.

"That too," Kennedy said.

"Let's see," Pete said.

Kennedy produced a key and opened one of the doors. Inside was a monitor panel and several indicators that showed the real-time status of everything, including the wind velocity and direction for each part of the building from the ground up. A computer calculated wind loading on the structure, along with the temperature, precipitation, and even the estimated weight of all the furnishings and people at any moment.

"Right now there's a slightly higher weight distribution near the top because of the party," Kennedy said.

"From here signals are sent to the damping system to keep the building on an even keel?" McGarvey asked.

"Yes."

"How?"

Kennedy pointed to a box about the size of a hardcover book attached to the left side of the panel. A row of lights was blinking. "A simple modem that transmits the signal to the pistons controlling the damper."

McGarvey stared at the blinking lights for several moments. "Is it hardened against hacking?"

"I'm told it is."

McGarvey phoned Otto. "We're on the fiftieth floor at the control panel for the damper. Can you get to it?"

"Indirectly," Otto said. "I tried before and had to go through the link to the fire department, police, and nine-one-one. Problem is the link is vulnerable. Every time something comes in on their site I lose control and have to start over again. The system is purposely simple—almost primitive—which is its strength."

"How about right now?"

"A building fire around a Hundred-tenth on the West Side. Two alarms. The system is tied up."

"How does he get to it?"

"He'd have to be right there in front of the panel. He could mechanically hack into the control system, or even electronically, which would send the signal to the damper through the modem."

"Then what?"

"Disable the modem and then get out of there."

"That easy?"

"He has to get into the building, and then to the fiftieth, where he'd need maybe thirty seconds tops. Not so easy."

SIXTY-NINE

Kamal sat on a bench in the park across from the UN and within easy sight of the Tower. It was just seven and traffic was very busy. Children and their guardians continued to stream in by bus, others on foot down Forty-second Street. The kids were noisy, laughing and talking and running in just about every direction.

Wild animals, he thought, but not unkindly. From time to time he had realized that he was missing a great deal in his life: a wife, children, a country home, maybe horses, a sailboat, family vacations. Normal things, but different from the Saudi tradition. His countrymen were far too strict, their rules against women still oppressive, even though they got the vote.

England was a little better, the U.S. far too wild and dangerous, but France, and especially Monaco, had suited him just fine; their traditions, their respect, their food and wine suited him.

But of course all of that was over for him now. Had been in fact for some time. And after this evening he would have to go to ground for several years at least. Bin Laden had been finally tracked down and killed, but in his estimation only because the fool had surrounded himself with friends, family, acolytes, even wives.

He would disappear alone. To Thailand at first, he thought. Then as the dust began to settle, perhaps Hong Kong, which he supposed would be an irony after killing Jian, the city's richest man.

Afterward—after some plastic surgery, maybe a completely different hairstyle, skin tone, dental work, a new persona—he might buy a château in France or a manor house north of London and set himself up as an eccentric multimillionaire. With his money and changed looks there wouldn't be many questions.

F. Scott and Hemingway had been right after all: the rich were different and everyone treated them so.

An explosion somewhere off in the distance to the west, perhaps around Grand Central Station, went unnoticed by almost everyone across the street except for a cop directing traffic, and a pair of security guards at the entrance to the UN's grounds.

The cop stopped traffic, and Kamal got up and headed across the street.

"What the hell was that?" he asked the officer.

"I don't know," the cop said, when there was another explosion in the general direction of Central Park.

"Christ, not the bastards again," Kamal said, and he hurried across the street, mingling with the crowd of confused people.

The cop in the middle of the street was talking to someone on his lapel mic, his left hand still up, holding back traffic.

Horns started to blare all over the place, and a cabby who tried to make a U-turn got clipped by a school bus, blocking all the traffic in both directions on First Avenue.

Kamal headed toward the Tower, when a third explosion came from the south, followed by a lot of gunfire from a few blocks away. He guessed the entrance to the Midtown Tunnel. If they took it out he would have to use another way off the island back to LaGuardia, where he would rent a car and head south. Once again the authorities would be foolishly concentrating on air traffic and not the highways.

Sirens, what he took to be police cars then fire trucks and perhaps ambulances, came from just about every quarter.

He got to within a half a block of the Tower, when a plain gray Chevy Impala pulled up, followed almost immediately by an NYPD radio car. The FBI agents who'd been standing by in the lobby emerged, jumped into the Chevy, and took off. They were followed immediately by the uniformed cops, who piled into the police car and, sirens blaring, blasted up East Forty-seventh Street past the Trump World Tower.

Kamal crossed back to the west side of First Avenue and just as he got to Forty-seventh, another explosion, this one farther away but definitely in the direction of Central Park, and possibly even Fifty-seventh, where cleanup from At-Eighth was still going on, rumbled and echoed off the buildings.

Pulling out Hachett's FBI ID and holding it over his head, he rushed across the street to the Tower's glass doors.

One of the building's security people came on the run and opened the door for him, but he only took a cursory glance at the ID.

"Where the hell are my people?" Kamal demanded, flattening his British accent.

"Didn't you hear the shit going down out there?"

"That's why I'm here. But the idiots were not supposed to leave."

"They didn't explain anything to me, sir."

"Where's Mr. McGarvey and his partner?"

"They were on the fiftieth, but I think they might have gone up to the penthouse party."

"I want this place locked down now. No one gets in. No one."

"What about the party?"

"I'll see what McGarvey suggests, but I think we need to evacuate. I'm going up now."

"Do you need a security pass? We've changed the codes."

"No. I'll take Mr. Jian's elevator." The service elevator was too obvious, and was monitored in real time.

Kamal hurried across the lobby to the penthouse elevator, conscious that the security guard he'd spoken with, possibly even the others, were looking at him. He resisted the urge to turn around until the elevator opened and he stepped inside the car, and pressed for the penthouse.

But the guards were huddled around the console, their attention on a monitor and on the front doors.

Idiots, Kamal thought as the doors closed and the elevator started up.

He pulled the Glock out of his holster, and hiding it behind his right leg he waited patiently until the car reached the top residence level. He was indifferent. More curious than concerned.

The door opened to the plush vestibule. The black lacquered doors to the penthouse were open. Music came from within the condo, and the people he could see from where he stood inside the car were in conversation with one another, their backs turned his way.

He hesitated just a moment, willing McGarvey or his woman—especially McGarvey—to come into view. He would shoot them and take his chances in the confusion with the rest of the op.

But he stepped out of the car and went immediately to the east stairwell door, where he hesitated again at the little square window.

Time was of the essence. At any moment someone could come out into the vestibule and spot him standing there.

If it was McGarvey they would have a gun battle.

He wanted it, he almost longed for the chance, but not now. Not here.

The red light on the monitor camera winked on, and four seconds later it went out.

Kamal pushed open the door, stepped into the stairwell, and when the door silently closed he waited at the window for several seconds. But no one came into the vestibule and he started down, a fifty-fifty chance that a camera would come on when he was at each floor.

He holstered his pistol, pulled out the FBI ID, and held it over his head as he took the stairs two at a time.

He got lucky until the sixtieth floor when the camera light came on, remained lit three seconds, and then winked out.

But he'd kept his face averted away from the cameras, which on each floor were placed in the same position, pointing toward the middle of each landing. It was a mistake in the design. The cameras came on in a random pattern, but they weren't pointed randomly.

On the fiftieth, Kamal held up at the door to the service corridor. None of the elevators that were available to the residents, including Jian's, stopped at this floor.

No one was in the corridor, and the door to the security suite was closed.

The stairwell door was locked.

Kamal drew his pistol, stepped aside, and fired one shot point-blank into the door handle's lock.

SEVENTY

McGarvey was upstairs in the office adjacent to the owner's suite talking with Hammond and Jian Chang when there was some sort of a commotion downstairs.

Jian was in midsentence, asking for a clarification on what his ultimate exposure, and therefore risk, would be if he went all in with Hammond on the bitcoin deal, when Pete burst in.

"This is a private meeting, young lady," Jian said, rising from his chair.

McGarvey got to his feet. "What?"

"Four explosions so far. At least two toward Central Park and one along with a lot of gunfire in the direction of the tunnel."

Nancy Nebel appeared at the doorway, her face pale. She was out of breath. "Are they targeting someone else or is it us? Because if it is us, I need to get everyone out of here right now."

"I'll let you know in thirty seconds," McGarvey said. "Call security and have them lock the building down," he told Pete and hustled out to the balcony, from where he could look down at the party. Apparently no one was aware that something was happening around them.

Otto called before he could hit speed dial. "Your diversion is starting. Get everyone out of there."

"Stand by," McGarvey said.

Nancy Nebel was at the doorway, Jian and Hammond behind her. "Has it started like you said it would?" she demanded.

"Get everybody out of here, but no panic," McGarvey said.

"Christ, they have to know."

Jian pushed past her. "I'll take care of it."

"I'll help," Hammond said. "Tell them that there's a problem with the building's electrical system."

"Where should we go?" Jian asked. He was calm.

"Away from here, first. But we'll get them to the Baccarat, I'll get us the ballroom," Hammond said. "Can you arrange transportation?" he asked Nancy Nebel.

"Not if I'm to get everybody out."

"I'll have Li take care of it," Jian said.

Hammond, Jian, and Nebel took the escalator down to the party.

Pete held a hand over the mouthpiece of a house phone. "Everything's normal so far. But Kennedy's been alerted to the attacks. She wants to know what you want her to do."

"The penthouse is going to be evacuated, have her clear out anyone else in the building."

Pete relayed the message. "On whose authority, she wants to know."

"Mine, goddamnit," McGarvey said. He turned back to Otto. "What about the damper panel?"

"Nothing so far as I can tell. But the PD, FD, and nine-one-one are jammed, so I'm only getting through intermittently."

Pete was still on the house phone. "She says help is coming."

"Tower security's circuits just lit up like the Fourth of July," Otto said. "Kennedy must be calling everyone. It's going to make it even tougher to monitor now."

"Keep at it," McGarvey said. "Just the damper panel."

A stir was already rippling across the floor below. No one seemed to be in any sort of a panic yet, but a number of guests, drinks still in hand, were heading toward the doors.

The chamber orchestra musicians on the balcony just beyond the escalator had stopped playing.

"Will do," Otto said.

"Anything comes up that you can't control, let me know," McGarvey said, and he hung up.

Pete was looking at him.

"Get the musicians and all the staff out of here. Tell them that the party is being moved to the Baccarat."

"What about you?"

"I'm going down to the lobby to make sure he doesn't get inside."

"He knows you, so duck first and shoot later," Pete said.

"You too."

McGarvey took the escalator stairs down two at a time. Hammond and Jian had started the still-orderly exodus out the doors. The private elevator had a maximum capacity of twelve people, but already more than that had crowded in and two women were pushing their way through. But to this point it was a game, like the old party diversion called Twister in which the point was to make body contact. Naughty contact. People were still laughing.

Al-Hamadi and Susan stood to one side watching the show, champagne in hand.

McGarvey went over to them. "We're taking the service elevator down to the lobby right now. Follow me."

"Tired of your girlfriend already?" Susan said.

"Let's go."

"We'll wait our turn."

"I need your help to identify Castillo when he tries to get in. Which he should at any minute, so I need you to hustle."

"What's he to you?" Susan protested.

"Shut the fuck up, sweetheart," al-Hamadi said. "We're following Mr. Canton."

"Just across the hall," McGarvey said. He handed his red pass to al-Hamadi. "This'll get you aboard, I'll be right behind you. Wait for me."

They pushed their way through into the vestibule as Mc-Garvey took Nancy Nebel aside. "I'm taking Susan and al-Hamadi down in the service elevator. If possible I'll send it back up to you, but I may need it so hold off until I tell you."

"Is it really happening?" she asked again.

"I'm not sure."

"But you think so."

"Yes. Can you handle it up here for now?"

"No problem," she said. "Just don't futz around, okay?"

"Okay."

The service elevator doors were closing as McGarvey got to the vestibule, and he was just in time to stop them and get aboard.

Al-Hamadi stepped away from the call button panel. "I don't want to be stuck up here if the building comes under attack."

The elevator started down.

Susan stood in the corner, her champagne glass still in hand, a slight smirk on her full lips.

Al-Hamadi backed up against the rear wall of the car. His eyes were as wide as a deer's caught in headlights.

"In Cannes on the beach," McGarvey said. "It was you who sent the two guys after me."

"I was there on the firing line too. My ass was on the line."

"Who hired you?"

"I saved your life."

McGarvey slapped the man's face, rocking his head back against the wall. "Who hired you?"

Al-Hamadi was dazed. He shook his head.

McGarvey slapped him again, this time much harder. "Who?"

"I can't. It means my life."

McGarvey pulled out his pistol and jammed the muzzle into al-Hamadi's forehead. "I don't need you in the lobby. Susan has fucked him, she'll remember his face."

Susan was amused. "How can one forget a face, even lying on her back with her eyes closed?"

The moment was frozen.

They passed the fiftieth floor.

"Sa'ad al-Sakar," al-Hamadi mumbled.

"Who is he?"

Al-Hamadi shook his head.

"Answer me before we reach the lobby, or I swear to Christ you're a dead man," McGarvey pressed.

Al-Hamadi hesitated.

"We can protect you."

"GIP," al-Hamadi said, and his bladder emptied.

SEVENTY-ONE

Kamal tugged at the service panel just a few feet away from the door into the security suite, but as he had expected it was locked. He was in a hurry now, too many happenstances had developed around him. He expected a shit storm to develop at any moment.

He'd been delayed in the stairwell when Cathy Kennedy herself had come out of security and walked directly to the stairwell where he was crouching.

Turning on his heel he raced up the stairs to the switchback halfway to fifty-one.

But after a full three minutes when the woman didn't

open the door, he'd crept back down and cautiously looked through the window. The corridor had been empty.

Standing to one side, out of the line of possible ricochets, he had fired one shot into the panel door lock, the noise impossibly loud in the corridor.

Flattening himself against the wall, he'd trained his pistol toward the security door for a full sixty seconds.

When nobody had come, he'd pulled open the panel and studied the layout that he had memorized from the plans. Holding the pistol under his left arm, he took out his phone and entered the same code he'd used for AtEighth, including the last digit, and hit *enter*.

For a seeming eternity nothing happened, until the lights on the modem all began to blink rapidly for several seconds, but then settled back finally to a steady state.

The final instructions had been sent to the tuned mass damper at the top three floors of the building.

Kamal fired one shot into the modem. All the lights blinked off and he shut the panel door.

The mechanism would continue, out of sync, to move the massive weight back and forth in the precise direction of the UN's General Assembly. No power on earth could save the building now.

The Tower would come down in ten minutes, give or take.

Kamal hesitated for just a moment. McGarvey was here somewhere in the building, most likely still upstairs in the penthouse waiting for him. And it was within the realm of possibility that once the former CIA director realized what was happening he would manage to get out.

There was no way he wanted to look over his shoulder for the rest of his life, waiting for the man to show up on his six.

Pulling out his FBI ID, and concealing the pistol behind his right leg, he walked to the security suite door and rang the buzzer.

Someone appeared at the peephole and he held up the ID.

Cathy Kennedy opened the door. She held a pistol in her left hand, but pointed down and away.

"Do you know where Mr. McGarvey is?"

"Were you the man in the stairwell?" she demanded.

"I wasn't the only one. Someone was on his way down by the time I reached this floor."

She was skeptical.

"Goddamnit, we don't have time to fuck around here. You either know where McGarvey is or you don't."

"You came from upstairs, you must have seen him in the penthouse."

"He disappeared."

"No," she said. She started to raise her pistol.

Kamal was faster. He jammed the muzzle of his pistol into the woman's forehead just above the bridge of her nose. Beyond her he could see the two other security offices at their consoles.

"Anyone touches a telephone or hits any sort of a panic button or alarm, this woman will die, and then so will you."

Neither man moved a muscle.

"You're him," Kennedy said. "Nero."

Kamal was amused. "That name will do as well as any other," he said. "Now, where is Mr. McGarvey at this moment?"

"In the lobby waiting for you."

"Step back, lay your pistol on the floor, then call him up here."

"No."

"Holy shit," one of the security officers said excitedly.

"What?" Kennedy asked, not taking her eyes off Kamal's.

"The TMD is out of sync."

"What's it doing?"

"Oscillating, but I'm telling you that it's out of sync with the wind and load parameters on my board."

"Override it."

"The modem isn't showing up. It's almost as if it's been unplugged or something."

"It was you who brought down AtEighth," Kennedy said to Kamal.

"Get McGarvey here before it's too late."

"It's already too late, you son of a bitch," Kennedy said. "How long before we're off center by eight feet?" she asked the security officer.

"Christ, I don't know."

"Give me a guesstimate."

"We're only off by less than two inches. Ten, twelve minutes tops."

"Less," Kamal said.

Kennedy stepped back a couple of paces, bent down, and laid her pistol on the floor, then straightened up and went to the phone.

She looked away from Kamal for only a moment.

"It's me. Get McGarvey up here on the double. Nero is here, the building is—"

Kamal fired one shot, hitting her in the face just below her left eye. He shot both security officers, their bodies slumping forward.

He fired an insurance shot in the side of Kennedy's head, and then in the heads of the two security officers.

He picked up the phone where Kennedy had dropped it. "Mr. McGarvey?"

"He's on his way," a man responded.

Kamal hung up.

One of the red security key cards was laying on Kennedy's desk. He pocketed it, just in case he needed it later.

McGarvey was coming up in the service elevator. The

moment the doors opened Kamal would kill him, then take it to the service floor, one level beneath the lobby, and make his way out of the building through the delivery entrance.

He went out into the corridor just as the service elevator arrived. Immediately he stepped back far enough inside the room so that McGarvey wouldn't immediately spot him.

But it couldn't be McGarvey. There was no way the man could have made it up here this fast.

The doors opened and McGarvey's woman stepped out. She had a pistol in her hand.

Kamal fired two shots, one catching her somewhere below her neck, but the second smacking into the wall as she dropped and fired two shots.

He stepped back into the security suite as the elevator dinged, the doors closed, and it started down.

His stomach did a slow turn. A pencil on Kennedy's desk behind him rolled to the edge and fell to the floor.

He ducked around the corner to take a quick look. The woman was down and not moving.

But there was no time now for an insurance shot, and certainly no time to wait for McGarvey to reach this floor.

The Tower would come down very soon, and he wasn't about to go down with it.

He raced to the stairwell door, flung it open, and started down three steps at a time.

Sometime in the future he and McGarvey would come face-to-face again. And he was curious about how it would all turn out, but not concerned, merely interested.

For now he wanted to get out of the building, and out of the damage path, where he could watch at a distance as the place came crashing down on the UN.

SEVENTY-TWO

It seemed to take forever before the service elevator finally reached the lobby floor. McGarvey was on his cell phone to Pete, but she wasn't answering and a terrible black feeling rose up inside his breast.

He got aboard and using his security key card punched 50. As the car started up he called Otto, who answered on the first ring as usual.

"You're in the elevator."

"Pete doesn't answer her phone. Where is she?"

"Seven hundred eighty feet above street level," Otto said.

"Fiftieth floor?"

"Just a moment. Yeah, same as security."

"Christ. Call them."

"I'm getting no answer," Otto said after a brief pause. "But the building is moving out of true. Almost twelve inches now, and accelerating. It's swaying."

"Block nine-one-one and the cops and fire department, and pull up the mass damper panel."

"I'm on it."

The elevator passed the twentieth floor, and the car seemed to lurch just slightly. McGarvey didn't think it was his imagination.

"Come on, come on," he said, half under his breath.

"The panel's okay, but the modem is off-line. It's not communicating with the damper."

"Then why is the building swaying?"

"Wait," Otto said.

The car passed the thirtieth.

"The last instruction sent to the damper was to counteract one-hundred-mile-per-hour winds."

"Impossible."

"Coming from both directions."

"Stop it."

"I can't do it from here, Mac. The panel will accept my command to shut down, but it can't talk to the damper."

The car lurched again as it passed the fortieth.

"Can you hack the system from topsides?"

"No. And I don't even know if it can be stopped from there," Otto said. "Find Pete and get the hell out while you can."

"What about the people in the penthouse?"

"Jian's elevator is heading back up for its third trip. Most of them should get out in time."

The elevator stopped on fifty.

McGarvey, pistol in hand, turned in profile and stepped to one side to present less of a target, as the doors slid open. He reached up and hit the stop button.

Pete, lying facedown on the floor, wasn't moving. A fair amount of blood had pooled up on her left side just below her neck.

He swung his aim left to right. The door to security was open. Nothing moved, there were no sounds.

The building shifted to the left, seemed to hang there for a long time, then started back. It wouldn't be long now until the extreme movements out of true would defeat the building's engineering.

"Pete," he called softly.

Her left leg, which had been crossed over her right, moved.

She was alive.

Keeping low, McGarvey went to her, his pistol trained on the open door. He touched her on the shoulder with his free hand.

She groaned and turned her head to the side so that she could look up at him. She smiled. "I should have ducked faster," she said.

"I'll get you out of here."

"He was here, Kirk. He did it, and the building is going to come down."

"We're getting out of here."

"You have to stop it."

"I'm not leaving you, goddamnit."

"You're the only one who can do it now. You have to save these people. That's why we came."

He was torn in two. The same shit that had happened to him his entire adult life was happening again, and he didn't know if he could handle it. Or even if he should.

"Go," she said. "Do your thing. I'll live, I promise."

"Where's your phone?"

"Back pocket."

He got it and called Otto. "This is Pete's phone. I'm going topside. She's wounded. Talk to her."

"Hurry, Kemo Sabe."

McGarvey gave the phone to Pete and kissed her on the cheek. "I'll be back."

"I'll wait for you. Promise."

He gave her one last look as the elevator doors closed and the car started up to the machinery room topside.

The feeling of movement was far more intense in the huge cathedral of a space than it had been on the fiftieth. The mass damper moved several feet to one side, hesitated, then ponderously came back in the same direction the Tower was bending.

It was nearly impossible now for him to keep his footing. The place was electronically hardened to avoid hacking from the outside. Even Otto couldn't get in here.

Everything was too big. The mass damper itself was twenty feet tall, and just as wide at the base. It sat in a circular pool of oil nearly the diameter of the entire floor.

And the pile was moving far enough now that some of the oil slopped over the shallow sides of the pool.

Hydraulic pistons positioned at twelve points were attached to the mass of steel. Two of them moved in unison at opposite corners, and two more in the middle of the north and south faces moved in sync.

The building was swaying east and west of north and south. When it collapsed, it would either fall away from the East River up toward Fifty-first Street, or toward the river.

If the movements of the pistons were not symmetrical by some engineer's design, the Tower would fail as it moved toward the southeast. Toward the UN.

But there was no time.

McGarvey circled around the mass damper, finding the system's modem and other controls. Eight bundles of thick wires led from a distribution panel and disappeared into the concrete floor. The lights on the modem were all on and not blinking.

Nowhere could he find circuit breakers, or a panel of switches that would control the relays to send instructions, and electrical current, to the pistons.

He stared at the panels, totally at a loss what to do next.

The system was hardened against electronic hacking, but apparently also against physical sabotage.

Nothing he could do without military-grade explosives was going to stop the pistons.

A huge booming twang from somewhere far below was impossibly loud, and alien. Like some fantastical musician from hell was announcing the end of the world.

It couldn't be stopped. He was too late. He'd been wrong, everyone else right.

The pistons couldn't be stopped.

The Tower was coming down.

Another twang reverberated up the steel columns.

Motors. The pistons were moved by electric motors.

Behind each of the pistons was a mesh cage. Inside each cage was an electric motor about the size of a small desk. The cages were not locked.

McGarvey yanked open one of the cages as the motor came to life, moving its piston backward.

Pulling his pistol he fired one shot into one of the openings in the armature.

Sparks flew from the bottom of the motor, but the piston continued to move.

A third twang boomed, and the Tower's tilt was so extreme now that McGarvey could barely keep on his feet.

"Goddamnit!" he shouted at the top of his lungs.

He fired two more shots into the motor, and it ground to a halt, spewing more sparks and a lot of smoke.

Reloading with a fresh magazine, McGarvey went to the next two motors moving the pistons and fired into them. More sparks flew, and gradually the rest of the motors came to a halt.

Stepping back, he held his breath for a very long time.

The floor was tilted at least ten degrees off center, held in place only by the concrete-encased steel beams driven into the bedrock.

But the building was no longer moving.

Nero had not won. Not this time.

Holstering his pistol, McGarvey went back to the service elevator, but its controls were shut down. A safety precaution against the extreme tilt.

He went to the south stairwell and started down to fifty.

SEVENTY-THREE

Sitting on the floor beside Pete, McGarvey took off his shirt, balled it up, and stuffed it under her blouse to staunch the blood oozing from her shoulder wound.

"Everyone's on their way up," she said, her voice a little weak but not ragged. She was smiling tiredly.

She reached out a hand and he took it.

He had nothing left to give at the moment. Pete was alive, and for now it was all that mattered.

"Otto's waiting for you," she said.

McGarvey picked up the phone and put it on speaker. "I don't know what's stopping the building from falling over."

"Besides what you did?" Otto asked. "Good engineering, I expect. From where I sit it looks as if New York has its very own Leaning Tower of Pisa. For now anyway, until they can figure out how to fix it."

"Pete needs an ambulance."

"On the way. Gratto is standing by with a medical team. Soon as she's stabilized we'll fly her down to All Saints."

Furnished with the latest and best equipment to be found anywhere in the world, and staffed with the finest doctors and nurses, the hospital in Georgetown dealt only with intelligence officers severely wounded in the field. Both McGarvey and Pete had been treated there. More than once.

"How about the kids at the UN?"

"Most of them are already on the way out of the damage zone," Otto said. "But that was a damned close call."

"Tell me about it," McGarvey said. Relief was coming slowly. He felt as if he could lie down and sleep for three days.

"Hammond's actually on the phone with one of our people in public affairs, wants to know how he can get in touch with you."

"Is he still after the bitcoin deal?"

"Apparently he just wants to thank the Agency and you and Pete specifically. We're still trying to figure out how he knows who you are."

"What about Nero?"

"No sign of him. But there's a nationwide APB."

"No one will find him. He's too good."

"Until he comes back for you."

"I hope so," McGarvey said. "He had the help of a guy named Sa'ad al-Sakar, apparently an officer in the GIP. And I'd bet even money that he also has a source somewhere here. FBI, Homeland Security."

"I'm on it," Otto said. "What about you?"

McGarvey smiled. "Soon as Pete is up on her feet, she and I are taking the boat over to the Bahamas. No satphone, no SSB or marine radio."

"Not even smoke signals," she said.

"Vacation." McGarvey almost said "honeymoon."

A telephone number in Riyadh known only to a very few people rang at three in the morning. The GIP officer, sitting at the open sliding glass doors to his pool, let it ring several times.

"Sa'ad," his wife called from the bedroom. She was angry. "Who is it?"

"Go back to sleep," he called to her.

"Well, answer the fucking thing, so I can get back to sleep."

He picked it up. "Yes."

"I'm not finished," Kamal said, and the connection ended.

PART
SIX

Riyadh, Saudi Arabia

The morning was impossibly bright for a shackled Sa'ad as he was led outside into the courtyard after nine days in a windowless cell in solitary confinement.

"For crimes against the state," the tribunal judge had told him.

And against the Abdulaziz family, the worst of his crimes and the one never mentioned at his brief trial.

He'd been allowed no lawyer, nor had he even been able to speak in his own defense. His were the words, as one of the military judges said with distaste, "of the venom from a serpent's mouth."

ISIS had suffered a series of defeats in Syria and Iraq, and in the past two months there had been no further attacks against the Saudi border. The war was over for now.

This was the same safe house outside the city where Sa'ad had briefed Kamal what seemed like a lifetime ago. And in point of fact, he thought now as he was brought to the back wall of the courtyard, within the next few minutes it would indeed be a lifetime.

The two sergeants, not officers, who'd come to the cell for him turned him around so that his back was to the wall.

"Do you wish a blindfold, Major?" the older of the two asked, with some respect in his voice and his manner.

In his time here he'd been fed well, allowed to sleep normal hours, even given several newspapers, including *The New York Times,* to read.

But his life had unfolded in day-and-night pieces. Getting through the day, reading in the evening, then finally sleep, for the most part—surprisingly—without dreams, and then the next day.

He had not summed up his life until this very moment, avoiding thinking about anything except the days and nights, though he'd thought it should be something important. Maybe even important enough to leave a letter for his wife.

An image of Sarah—his first love at college in the U.S.—came back to him more clearly than it ever had since he'd returned to Saudi Arabia and started his career with the GIP.

"A blindfold, Major?" the sergeant asked again.

"No," Sa'ad told the man.

Five uniformed soldiers armed with U.S. military M16 assault rifles came from a door to the left, and lined up twenty feet away.

They were older men, like the sergeants. Veterans, not kids who might become squeamish.

"Do you have any last remarks, Major?" the sergeant asked.

Yes, a million of them, Sa'ad thought, but he shook his head. "Get it over with, please."

The sergeant stepped well out of the line of fire.

"Ready arms," he ordered.

The soldiers raised their weapons.

"Aim."

Sa'ad looked up at the fabulous blue sky. His desert sky. And he saw Sarah again.

"Fire," the sergeant ordered.

ᴀᴜᴛʜᴏʀ'ѕ ᴎᴏᴛᴇ

I always like hearing from my readers, even from the occasional disgruntled soul who wants to pick a bone with me, or point out a mistake I've made.

You may contact me, McGarvey, Pete, Otto, and Louise by sending a message to kirkcolloughmcgarvey@gmail.com. But please understand that because I'm extremely busy, quite often I won't be able to get back to you as soon as I'd like. But I will make every effort to answer your queries.

For a complete list of my books and reviews please visit Barnes & Noble, Amazon, or any of your favorite booksellers.

If you would like me to do a book signing at an event or a store, something I have absolutely no control over, or if you would like me to attend an event as a guest speaker or panelist, please contact:

Tor/Forge Publicity
175 Fifth Avenue
New York, N.Y. 10010
E-mail: torpublicity@tor.com

If you wish to discuss contracts, movie or reprint rights, or e-business concerning my writing, please contact my literary agent:

Susan Gleason Literary Agency
E-mail: sgleasonliteraryagent@gmail.com

Read on for a preview of

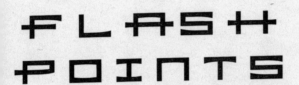

DAVID HAGBERG

Available now from
Tom Doherty Associates

ONE

It was early March but summer had already arrived in southern Florida, and except for a pleasant breeze off Sarasota Bay, the afternoon would have been overly hot for Kirk McGarvey and the eight philosophy students seated in front of him on the grass.

McGarvey, Mac to his friends, had been the youngest director ever of the Central Intelligence Agency—a job he had detested because he was no administrator. Since then he'd taken on a variety of freelance assignments for the Company, all of which had been too urgent or simply impossible for the government to handle on its own.

In between times he taught philosophy for one dollar per year at Sarasota's New College, a semi-private ultra-liberal and prestigious small college. His specialty was Voltaire, the eighteenth-century intellectual and wit, who'd maintained that common sense wasn't so common after all.

Slightly under six feet with the build of a rugby player and the grace of a ballet dancer, Mac was a man around fifty, with eyes that were sometimes green, or gray, like now, when he felt something or someone was gaining on him.

"How many of you know the name O. J. Simpson?" he asked.

One of the boys said, "He's the one who killed his girlfriend and some guy."

"His ex-wife and her lover," one of the other students said.

"He was acquitted," McGarvey said. His own philosophy had always been if you throw a stick into a pack of dogs, the one that barks got hit. His students over the past three years knew that they were being manipulated, but they loved it, because of the sometimes intense discussions that usually followed.

"Yes, but he did it."

"No doubt?"

One of the girls laughed. "You've been hoisted on your own petard, Mac," she said. "Voltaire, and I quote: 'It is better to risk saving a guilty person than to condemn an innocent one.'"

"Nice try, Darlene, but it's you who's been had, unless you don't believe in the basic premise of American jurisprudence."

Someone groaned. "Presumed innocent until proven guilty. But this is a course on Voltaire. Not fair."

McGarvey chuckled. A distant buzzer sounded, which marked the end of this period. "Five hundred words by Monday on what Voltaire would have thought about the trial. Arguments for why he would believe that O. J. was guilty and for why he would believe the man was innocent."

A forty-foot sloop out on the bay was heading south, probably for New Pass and the Gulf of Mexico. She was low on her lines, her dinghy was stowed and she had a wind vane for self-steering on the stern. A small, well-provisioned ship heading for happy places.

It was the last class on Friday, and his students, who often hung around to talk, took off. All across the small campus kids and instructors alike were heading out. Everyone here worked hard but played hard too.

His phone rang. It was Pete calling from his house on Casey Key, a barrier island a few miles south. She'd come down from Washington to spend a few days with him, as she'd been doing from time to time over the past year or so.

At one time she'd been an interrogator for the Company, but she'd fallen into helping McGarvey with an assignment that had started to go bad. And since then she'd been his unofficial partner, and a damned good operator in her own right. On top of all that she was in love with him, and he with her.

"How'd your day go?" she asked. She was nearly fifteen years younger than him, and in her interrogator days when she always worked with a male partner, the agency wags had labeled her and whoever her partner might be Beauty and the Beast. She was shorter than Mac, with the voluptuous figure of a movie star and a pretty oval face, and had become a crack shot with just about any variety of pistol.

"Good," he said automatically. But something had been nagging at him for the past week or so, and for some reason especially today. In his career, mostly as a shooter for the CIA, he'd had a chance to make a lot of enemies. From time to time one of them came gunning for him.

It had happened before, and he'd been getting the feeling that someone was nearby, watching him, tracking his routines, coming up on his six.

"I can drive up and meet you someplace for an early supper."

He wanted to say no. He wanted her out of the way, for the simple reason he was afraid for her safety. Every woman in his life—including his wife and daughter—had been assassinated because of who he was and what he did. And he was in love with her—against his will—and that frightened him even more.

"Marina Jack, outside," he said. The marina and restaurant on the bay just south of the Ringling Bridge was popular with the locals as well as tourists. It was almost always busy, and just now if Pete was going to be at his side, he wanted to be surrounded with people.

"Half hour," she said.

"See you there," McGarvey said, and as he headed back to his office he phoned his old friend Otto Rencke, who was the director of special projects for the CIA and the resident computer genius on campus there. He and Mac had a long history.

"You're done teaching for the day," Otto said without preamble. "You and Pete are meeting somewhere for a drink and something to eat."

"Right and right. Have your darlings been picking up on anything interesting lately?"

Otto's darlings were actually search engines a quantum leap even above Google, which sampled just about every known intelligence source on the entire planet, looking for threats to the U.S., especially to the CIA.

"Lotsa shit going down, but no nine/elevens just now. You getting premos?"

What Otto called "premos" were McGarvey's premonitions. He and just about everyone else on campus respected Mac's premos.

"Just around the edges."

"I'll call you back in a couple of minutes."

"Good enough," McGarvey said.

His tiny book-lined office was on the second floor of the philosophy department, already all but deserted for the weekend, one small window looking out across the campus toward the bay. The sailboat was approaching the buoy in the Intracoastal Waterway, which led out to the Gulf through New Pass.

He watched it for several moments, thinking about his wife, Katy. They had taken several trips from Casey Key on their Whitby 42 center cockpit ketch, twice out to the Abacos in the Bahamas. Good times, in sharp contrast to the sometimes almost impossibly bad times in his career and life. He'd been behind the limo in which his wife and their daughter were riding in when it exploded.

It was a memory permanently etched in his brain.

He took his Walther PPK in the 7.65mm version, his spare pistol, and an old friend, out of his desk and put it in his pocket. At that moment he thought it was important, though he couldn't say why.

Downstairs he nodded to a couple of instructors, but they didn't acknowledge him. He was wealthy by most standards, teaching for free, while they were scraping by on small salaries, and to hear them talk, busting their humps. In their view he was a dilettante, whose grades were always way too high on the curve.

Pete had sounded upbeat, looking forward to the weekend. She was leaving Sunday evening to return to Langley, where she was involved with training a half-dozen senior interrogators. The only complaints about her, so far as Otto had heard, came from the suits on the seventh floor who thought her methods had become overly aggressive in the past year or so. McGarvey had rubbed off on her.

Otto had sounded good too. Much happier now than in the old days because he was married to Louise, a woman nearly as smart as he was, and for whom he had an immense respect, and because of their adopted three-year-old daughter, Audie, who was Mac's daughter's only child.

The soft top on his '56 Porsche Speedster was down, the red-leather driver and passenger seat backs moved forward because of the sun. The car was one of his only indulgences—other than the Whitby. He had bought it totally restored two years ago for around fifty times the price when it had been new.

Maybe not a dilettante, he thought, getting in and starting the engine, and certainly not a billionaire like some he knew, but well off enough so that he could afford the toy, as Pete called it.

"You have the time in grade, and you deserve it," she'd said.

Something was wrong. Desperately wrong. A smell, a noise, something.

McGarvey looked for a shooter, for the glint of a gun scope lens on the rooftops across the street.

A car with tinted windows nearby.

Someone who obviously didn't belong on the school's campus walking away with a purpose.

A drone somewhere above.

Not bothering with the ignition key, he clambered over the door and got two feet away from the car when an impossibly bright flash enveloped him.

And then nothing.

TWO

The explosion echoed off the administration building across the street. Students within a hundred yards of what was left of the furiously burning Porsche hunkered down, bits of debris, rubber, plastic and leather raining from the clear blue sky.

One of the students, who went by the name of Antonio Gomez, stepped back, placing the cell phone he'd used to detonate the bomb in the pocket of his Bermuda shorts. He was a slightly built man with a dark complexion who could have been eighteen or nineteen, but in reality was twenty-nine. He'd come from Mexico City to study American government under Professor Frank Alcock. This was his first semester, and last, because he'd accomplished what he'd been paid to accomplish.

A girl who'd been standing a few feet away was on her knees, hands raised to the sky. "My God, my God, what's happening!" she screamed.

Within seconds other students who'd dropped to the ground were looking up, fear on their faces as if they knew that the bombing was just the first blow in a terrorist attack. More was coming and for the moment they were petrified.

Gomez wanted to pull out the Russian-made PSM pistol and put a couple of rounds into the silly girl's head to shut her up. He had two sisters, who like their mother were always whining about something, never satisfied with anything in their lives. Unlike him they were going nowhere.

Students started running in all directions, some across the street, others back through the campus toward the bay and still others to the north end of the parking lot and through the arch, to get away from the flames.

Gomez hunched up his backpack and followed a half-dozen students and several faculty to the south toward the Ringling Museum as the first of the campus cops from the nearby station came on the run. Already sirens were headed this way.

At one point he looked back, but the thick black smoke rising from the destroyed hulk of McGarvey's car obscured just about everything. The man had to have been killed instantly. The charred remains of his body could burn in hell forever.

Gomez's father, Arturo, had started out as a small-time attorney who specialized in defending Mexicans or those from Central and South America who'd illegally gotten into the U.S. and who were processed and sent by bus back across the border. He was paid to fast track their legal immigration, and to represent them in the U.S. court system, mostly in El Paso but sometimes in San Diego.

Money had been tight until someone from the Sinaloa drug cartel showed up in his office and hired him on a handsome retainer to defend mules—the runners who brought the product across the border into the U.S. He wasn't very successful, but he diverted the attention of the Mexican and U.S. drug enforcement people, making it easier for the real mules to operate.

His son, Antonio, had drifted for the next few years, playing drums in a rock band, working as a towel boy at a resort in Cancun, a waiter in Cabo San Lucas, and finally as a bartender at Puerto Vallarta. He was young and handsome, so he'd made decent money as a gigolo for older women coming down from the States for a little adventure.

All of it was more or less meaningless, until the same man, from the cartel who'd hired his father, hired him on a retainer to do odd jobs at the resorts in Puerto Vallarta, such as passing instructions and very often cash to start-up operators from the States. Three times over the past two years he'd been sent to the States, once to San Francisco and twice to Detroit, with messages that couldn't be trusted even to encrypted phones or computers or area managers.

Two months ago he'd been instructed to fly to Atlanta, where he was to meet with a man named Rupert Hollman at a room in the Holiday Inn near the airport. This time he carried no message. His only instruction was to do as Mr. Rupert instructed him to do, then return to Mexico City, where he would be paid one hundred thousand dollars U.S. It would be by far his largest payday ever.

"And this will be just the start," his cartel contact promised.

Rupert, wearing jeans and a long-sleeved polo shirt, had met him in a second-floor room. He was a tall man, with dirty-blond hair, blue eyes and an accent that Gomez couldn't quite place, except it sounded faintly French.

The meeting lasted less than ten minutes, during which Antonio was shown several photographs of a man Rupert identified as Kirk McGarvey.

"Do you know this man?"

"Never seen him before."

"He is a professor of philosophy at a college in Sarasota, Florida. Your job will be to leave for Sarasota this evening, where you will enroll in the school as a first-term student in American government. You have been accepted, your first year's tuition and room and board have been paid. You will be given a small stipend. Do you understand?"

"Yes."

Rupert handed him a manila envelope. "Everything is there, including your dorm assignment. You'll make friends, you'll study hard, maybe even fall in love with the right girl. You will fit in. Do you understand this as well?"

"Yes, sir; will I be meeting with a drug dealer on campus?"

"Nothing like that. Your main job, besides blending in, will be to study McGarvey. In fact you are enrolled in one of his classes. Watch his movements. Especially how he comes and goes from campus. Does he drive himself, or is he chauffeured by this woman?"

Rupert, whose real name was Kamal al-Daran, and who'd once worked as a freelancer for Saudi Arabian intelligence under the code name al Nassr, "the Eagle," handed Gomez several photographs of an attractive woman.

"Her name is not important, just finding out if she shows up will be enough."

"Yes, sir. Then what?"

"Once a week you will call a number. It will ring twice but no one will answer. You will enter a five-digit code, make your report and then hang up."

Gomez nodded uncertainly.

"Within two months, three at the most, a package will be delivered to you. Sweets and other presents from home. In fact, make sure to share the top layer with your roommate, a young man by the name of Dana Cyr."

"What else will be in the package? Drugs?"

"The instructions and the means for you to assassinate McGarvey and the woman if she happens to be with him."

Gomez sank into himself just a little. He'd known for the last year or so that his cartel contact would have other work for him someday. Real work. That of eliminating enemies of the Sinaloas. Six months ago he'd been taken to a remote private shooting range up north, where he'd spent

an entire week learning how to use a variety of weapons—
handguns and sniper rifles, mostly. He'd also been taught
how to use a number of poisons, and explosives—almost
exclusively Semtex, a substance for which he'd developed
a deep respect.

Gomez walked as far as the Ringling Museum and then
up to Tamiami Trail, just making the bus out to the airport.

Yesterday the package of sweets plus the one-kilo brick
of Semtex, the electronic detonator and the special phone
to send the signal, and the instructions to place the explosives under the driver's seat of McGarvey's Porsche and
send the signal as soon as the instructor got into his car,
had arrived by FedEx.

He was given the bus schedule and tickets to fly from
Sarasota to Atlanta and from there back to Mexico City.
His plane left one hour from now.

Sitting in the backseat of the bus for the short ride to
the airport, Gomez had time to examine his feelings now
that he had made what he figured was probably his first
kill. But he felt nothing, other than being successful, and
rich—with more to come. And with being his own man.

He was no longer a gigolo. He was an operator.